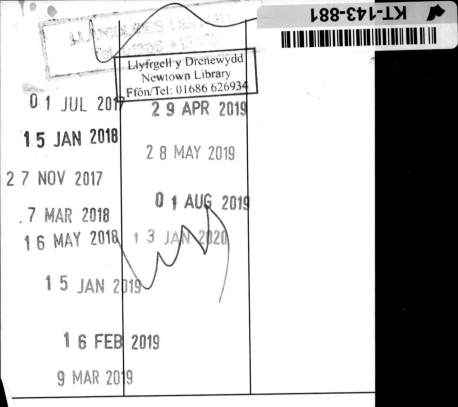

Watch Her Disappear

EVA DOLAN

Watch Her Disappear

Harvill *Secker*

LONDON

1 3 5 7 9 10 8 6 4 2

Harvill Secker, an imprint of Vintage,
20 Vauxhall Bridge Road,
London SW1V 2SA

Harvill Secker is part of the Penguin Random House group of companies
whose addresses can be found at global.penguinrandomhouse.com

Penguin
Random House
UK

First published by Harvill Secker in 2017

penguin.co.uk/vintage

A CIP catalogue record for this book is available from the British Library

ISBN   9781910701027 (hardback)
         9781473523142 (ebook)

Typeset in India by Thomson Digital Pvt Ltd, Noida, Delhi

Printed and bound in Great Britain by Clays Ltd, St Ives plc

Penguin Random House is committed to a sustainable future for our
business, our readers and our planet. This book is made from
Forest Stewardship Council® certified paper.

Watch Her Disappear

Prologue

Sixteen weeks on from the final surgery and still it surprised her to see a different face staring back from the mirror. A finer, prettier face, the one Corinne had wanted ever since she was little. She'd always known it was there, hiding under the skin, waiting to be brought out with some clever nicks of the knife and pricks of the needle: the real her.

The surgeon – that handsome boy with his floppy hair and costume drama accent – had warned her how disorientating the experience could be, how the face might not feel like her own for weeks or months, but even through the initial bruising and swelling she'd recognised this new and stunning woman.

She smiled, feeling silly, told herself not to be so bloody vain.

The face might be perfect now but the body needed its maintenance the same as it always had.

Corinne zipped up her top and, holding the buds from her iPod in place, pulled on a hot-pink beanie, tugged it down over her ears. She set the music playing as she left the house, Beyoncé hauling her out into the dawn light and the spring chill that made her nose sting.

Beauty is pain – isn't that what they said?

It was worth it, though. Every needle, every drawn-out recovery period, every one of these early-morning miles while Sam slept on in their bed, keeping it warm for when she got back home, sweating and buzzing, ready to slip between the sheets and work out the endorphins and adrenalin arousal that had to be satisfied before she could shower.

The thought almost turned her around but that heat was forty minutes away yet. Now all she felt was her cold muscles straining as she hit the main road and the air frost biting the skin across her cheekbones, sharp enough to raise tears in her eyes.

God, what she wouldn't give for some sun on her bones.

Feet pounding the path, breaths deep and even, icy into her lungs, she pictured a white sand beach and endless blue sea, her tan skin glistening and hot in a tiny bikini, eyes following her as she moved. Lust from the men, envy from the women.

That wasn't vanity.

People did notice her. Always had, but more so now.

Forty-something women were invisible – didn't they say that too? What did they know? Those women she saw everywhere who hit forty-five and gave up, embraced the greige, no time for make-up, some low-maintenance haircut that murmured, *oh, don't mind me*. If they were invisible they only had themselves to blame.

She sensed the attention as she ran along Oundle Road, commuter traffic already beginning to flow into the city centre, a prickle across her backside as they checked her out.

Ten minutes, right on the dot, the song changed, and she broke through the first wall of resistance, a fresh flood of energy singing in her veins.

She hummed along, kept pumping onwards, nodded good morning to an old guy with an Alsatian who she'd seen every day for the fifteen years she'd lived here. Nice old guy. His second dog and this one would outlive him, she guessed.

Without thinking she glanced at her former home, its reassuring bulk sitting behind high black metal gates which were closed to her now.

It tugged at her, the sight of the light on in her daughter's bedroom window. Knowing Lily was in there getting ready for school, teasing her hair into a fat bun on top of her head, painting the perfect cat-flick of eyeliner Corinne had practised with her . . . it was like a punch to the heart.

It would be easy to scale the gates and march up to the front door, kick it down if she had to do that to see her girl.

Don't give them the ammunition, she thought, hearing Sam's voice. Just stay calm, they can't drag this out forever.

All Corinne could do was call Lily during school hours and hope she kept answering her mobile. So far she had, despite the fact that they hadn't seen each other for almost two months, and she still seemed happy enough to talk, the same girl she always was, bright and chatty, even though Corinne's last visit had ended in a blazing row.

Corinne would be the first to admit she'd started it. That didn't mean she was wrong though.

She ran on, feet slamming down hard in her barefoot trainers, the impact shaking her spine as she turned into Ferry Meadows.

Ahead of her the parkland was wreathed in low mist, bare trees resolving through it. The acres of dull green were spiked with the brightly coloured coats of other early risers, following the narrow pathways snaking around the lakes. Runners and dog walkers. The usual crowd.

Her route took her down to the lock and over the River Nene, which was sitting high after the recent rain, churned up and muddy-looking, the smell of it catching in her nostrils as she crossed the metal bridge, damp and dirty and brown. They'd pulled a man out of there last month. Some drunk who'd fallen in as he relieved himself. Drowned with his dick out.

Such a stupid way to go. The same way her father died. The same river. Except he'd been further upstream, where the current was stronger. It took them months to find his body, snagged in the branches of a long-fallen tree, out towards the Wash. The coroner ruled it accidental but with the cancer eating him alive Corinne wondered if he hadn't decided to end it. A bellyful of whisky. A plunge into the water.

It was a kinder end than the old bastard deserved.

A pair of spaniels were playing on the path in front of her and she weaved around them, smiling at their owner, who mouthed an apology.

The path led her into shadow, narrowing to barely a body's width, tangled branches in need of trimming, hanging low. She ran on with a protective arm raised. Skirted piles of dog shit and a broken bottle. She winced as a piece of glass stuck in the thin sole of her trainer. Not sharp enough to cut but at every step it poked at her heel. After a few metres she stopped to dig it out, bracing her hand against the trunk of a big, old oak tree.

Bloody kids, using this place like a beer garden. No thought for anyone else, no respect for nature.

Corinne swore, trying to pick out the chunk of glass, her gloved fingers unable to gain a grip on it. It was in too deep, needed a point to lever it from the moulded sole.

Her pulse thudded in her ears, beating faster than the music coming from the buds.

Straightening away from the tree she looked at the ground around her feet, hoping to find something she could use to prise the glass out, but there were only twigs and dead leaves and small stones.

She was pulling her right glove off when a body crashed into her back.

Her hands shot out but not fast enough to save her face. She felt her nose breaking, her mouth bursting open, heard the crack of her fine new bones fracturing. Then the ground was moving, as he dragged her off the path and into the trees, her fingers desperately scrabbling through damp earth.

He pulled out her earphones and she tried to push herself up, ignore the pain, the blood in her mouth, the tears in her eyes which

4

she couldn't blink away. She planted her palms firmly in the mud and shoved away from it, but he had her pinned down, the full weight of him pressing on her spine. If she pushed any harder it might snap.

Then she was choking.

The music kept playing, a high voice singing tinnily as she gasped and clawed at the thin wire cutting into her throat, spots popping in front of her eyes, and she thought of Sam and Lily and her old face and her new face and the spots kept popping, red and black and getting bigger and overlapping, a rush like the blood in her ears, everything pressing in on her, the weight of the man crushing her, and it wasn't meant to be like this. She was meant to have a new life, be a new woman, the one she always wanted to be.

She saw her father, dripping wet and smiling, waiting for her in a blaze of white light. Heard his voice, that hateful, bitter voice of his, close to her ear, 'You asked for this.'

TUESDAY

I

'Is that you or me?' Ferreira asked, not enough energy to lift her head from the pillow and check the source of the ringing.

A warm hand curled around her middle and cupped her breast. 'I think it's you.'

'It sounds like mine.'

'It's on your side.'

'Must be then.' She reached out blindly and patted the table, brushing a condom wrapper onto the floor, finding her lip balm and a handful of change, and finally came up with the phone, swiped her thumb across the screen to answer. 'What?'

'Sir?'

She swore and rolled over, holding out Adams's phone, mouthed, 'Yours.'

He grinned at her, one eye stuck shut and his face sleep-creased, giving him a distinctly untrustworthy look. The stubble didn't help, or the yellow smear of a healing black eye he'd picked up last week when a suspect kicked off in an interview room.

'I'm not on today,' he said, holding her gaze as he listened to the voice on the other end of the phone, his thumb brushing circles around her nipple.

Abruptly his hand stopped and his mouth set into a hard line.

'Where was this?'

He kicked off the duvet and jumped out of bed, fully alert now, already straightening up into detective chief inspector mode as he paced in front of the window.

'Who found the body?'

Ferreira watched him move, saw the scratch marks she'd left on his buttocks, dug deep through his light tan. The sight of them made her twitch, remembering how he'd grunted as her hips bucked, his fingers in her hair, quickening breaths on her throat, and she wanted him back in bed, could have knocked him down and fucked him where he fell.

'Any witnesses?'

The corpse wasn't getting any deader. Maybe she could draw him back between the sheets. She didn't have to be in for another hour. All quiet in Hate Crimes, just a couple of low-level harassments rumbling on, minor assaults with no suspects, and an attempted murderer they were trying to track down with little expectation of flushing him out.

'Sounds like our man,' Adams said wearily, turning and catching her eye, giving a slight shrug of apology or regret. 'I'll be there in twenty.'

He tossed his phone down on the windowsill.

'You're lucky that wasn't Murray,' he said. 'She'd have recognised your voice for sure.'

'I said one word.'

'She'd have made you.'

'Be more careful where you leave your phone then,' Ferreira told him.

He leaned across the bed, the smile back in place, wide and hungry. 'If Riggott finds out about this you'll be for it.'

'You're the superior officer, I'll say you took advantage of me.'

'Nah, the old man knows you better than that.' He kissed her. 'I'll tell him you were using me to improve your chances of promotion.'

Ferreira flicked her eyebrow up at him. 'Climbing the greasy pole?'

He groaned. 'Let's find a better name for my boy than that.'

Adams went into the bathroom and switched the shower on, started whistling as he took a piss and Ferreira rolled her eyes. Such an old-man thing to do. There was twelve years between them but it was easy to forget when he made so much effort with his appearance, an almost laughable amount for a copper: the eye cream and the yoga and juicing. Balancing out all the long hours and vices that the job forced on you, the accretion of other people's suffering which left a mark more persistent than your own ones did.

The thought sent her calves itching and she slipped one leg out from under the duvet, looked at the scars which she'd discovered reacted to cold weather more than hot, irritated when she was tired or run-down or emotional, like they were psychic wounds rather than physical ones now.

Thirty-six individual puncture marks, stabbed into her legs as one of her former colleagues detonated a bomb vest packed with shrapnel, wanting a swift and glorious end to his racially motivated terror campaign.

She still thought about him, but not so often and not so brutally.

At least the scars were finally beginning to fade. Helped by some mossy-smelling oil she'd bought at the Chinese herbalist in Westgate arcade. She knew they'd never heal completely, though, and the prospect of showing her skin still filled her with dread.

Adams didn't mind. He had scars of his own and when they were together the backs of her legs were the last thing either of them considered.

It wasn't a good enough excuse to get her out of trouble if Riggott did find out about them. 'We're fucking because he's the only man I trust not to judge the state I'm in.' The DCS might feel a flicker of sympathy but rules were rules and like most people who broke them he wouldn't hesitate to punish anyone else who did the same.

Worry about it when it happens, she told herself, burrowing back down under the cover. They'd been careful, she didn't work directly under him, this was an easily containable situation as long as they kept it casual.

The shower went silent and a few minutes later he returned to the bedroom, snagged his jeans off the floor and stepped into them.

'You need to get a cleaner,' he said. 'There's so much limescale on that shower door it looks frosted.'

'I don't want someone going through my stuff.'

'Mel, if you don't get a cleaner in here soon it won't be safe for someone to touch your stuff. You'll need a fucking decontamination company.'

It wasn't like the place was actually dirty. A bit messy, maybe. She knew she could do with picking some of the clothes up, putting a wash in. But the floors were laminate and she was sure you didn't need to vacuum that or anything.

'I'll give you my cleaner's number.' He pulled on his shirt. 'You'll have to tidy up before she comes round though.'

'Might as well do it myself then.'

He sat down on the bed to put his shoes on. 'Or you could call your mum, I'm sure she'd love to keep tidying up after you. Give her a key, she can come round whenever she wants. She might even do your washing.'

'Shut up.' Ferreira aimed a lazy kick at his shoulder. 'What's the rush, anyway?'

'Dead jogger in Ferry Meadows,' he said, retrieving his phone. 'Strangled.'

'This your serial rapist?'

'It's his stamping ground.' A look of contempt twisted Adams's face. 'Early morning, lone woman with her earphones in . . . yeah, I reckon. Can't say we weren't expecting the bastard to escalate but I thought we had more time. Fuck, it's only been a couple of weeks since the last one.'

Ferreira frowned, seeing how edgy he was. 'They get sloppy when they escalate. Might be you find something this time.'

'Maybe.' He started out of the bedroom, stopped on the threshold. 'I'll call you later, okay?'

'Sure.'

The front door slammed and she lay back staring up at the ceiling. He was going to be raging tonight. They'd discussed the case already, spent hours talking it around, and part of her thought it was unhealthy how quickly they'd settled into a routine of venting at each other, something slightly sick that minutes after the sex was over their minds turned to crime. The other, less moral, part of her had already realised the sex was better when it came off the back of a bad day. All of that anger and frustration looking for an outlet.

Ferreira climbed out of bed and twisted her hair up into a pony-tail, kicking the dumped clothes into a rough pile she would deal with when she got home. There was a single pair of knickers in the drawer so she guessed the situation was approaching crisis point.

She stood under the shower for a long time, the heat lifting the smell of him out of her pores, idly wondering how much messier the flat could get before he refused to step foot in it. Much worse, she decided. All he really needed was a clear channel between the front door and the bed.

Once she was dried off and dressed she shoved a load of whites into the washing machine, thinking how much easier it had been living back at her parents' pub. There, clothes miraculously dis-appeared from her bedroom floor and returned neatly ironed and folded, a cleaner came in twice a week and there was never an empty coffee packet in the cupboard like the one she found now.

They couldn't understand why she'd wanted to move out. Between them her parents came up with endless arguments, mostly centred on the cost, which she could easily cover, and the isolation, which is what she wanted more than anything else.

Not isolation: privacy.

Quiet.

The first few nights in the flat she'd found herself missing the babble and thrum she'd grown used to. Music and voices coming through the floor, lulling her to sleep. But not any more, now she

13

luxuriated in the silence and the knowledge that when she closed the front door nobody would wander in unannounced.

Standing at the fake-wood counter in the kitchen she ate an almost black banana, looking down at the road three storeys beneath her, where a few people with briefcases and satchels were heading into the offices along Priestgate.

She'd need to go shopping after work. Put something in the cupboards besides that bag of pasta and the cereal she didn't have milk for. She kept meaning to set up a regular delivery but with work so unpredictable it was impossible to arrange a time she'd definitely be home.

All that could wait; right now she needed coffee.

There were five cafes within a minute's walk – one of the factors which swung the place for her – and she was in Caffè Nero paying for her triple shot Americano when her mobile rang.

'Mel, you up?'

'Can't you hear the jazz?' she asked, speaking loud enough to be heard above the music pumping out of the speakers overhead. 'Do you think I'd have that on at home?'

'I need you to get to Ferry Meadows.' Zigic's voice was strained, the sound of engine noise under it. 'We've got a body.'

She almost slipped, told him it was Adams's case, but caught herself in time.

'On my way.'

2

It was a morning for finding corpses, Zigic thought, as he walked towards the metal bridge that spanned the Nene. Clouds were gathering from the west, black and boulder-like, the charred and meaty smell of the crematorium in Marholm blowing in on the rising wind, strong enough to taint the sweetness of green shoots and damp grass.

A few onlookers were hanging around on the platform of the small Victorian railway station which served the decommissioned track running alongside the river. It was a tourist attraction now, saw only steam trains offering Agatha Christie afternoons or rides on Thomas the Tank Engine. They'd brought the boys last summer, Milan already too old to enjoy it, Stefan so hyper he'd been sick.

'Hey, hold up!'

He turned and saw Ferreira running towards him, bag slung across her body under her jacket, banging against her thigh. She tossed a cigarette butt away as she drew closer to him.

'You look knackered,' she said.

'Thanks.'

'Emily still keeping you up?'

Zigic started off across the bridge and she fell in step beside him. 'She's going to be a night owl, judging by her sleeping pattern.'

'Can't you give her something?'

He smiled. 'Whisky in her late feed?'

'I don't know, like baby Night Nurse or something?'

'They don't make Night Nurse for babies.'

'Oh.'

Despite the fact that she'd helped raise her own brothers, four of them all younger than her, she knew almost nothing about babies. Still, she was making an effort and it was funny watching her try to talk about something she clearly wasn't that interested in. Not as funny as the look on Anna's face when he took home the Che Guevara Babygro Ferreira had bought for Emily.

'Why are we here?' she asked.

'All Adams said was he thinks it's one of ours.'

'Have they got an ID already?'

'Not that he told me.'

They ducked under the tape and followed the path single file as it narrowed, Zigic pushing branches aside, noticing the broken glass and discarded condoms. Orton Mere was notorious for cruising but not this stretch, as far as he knew, and he wondered if there were witnesses who'd scarpered, scared of having to explain what they were doing there.

The tent was just ahead of them, a block of white erected in the sparsely planted copse to their right, eight or ten metres away from the path. Suited forensics officers were searching the ground around it, bagging and tagging, plucking things from the mess of last year's leaves, the mud and wind-blown rubbish.

Adams was waiting for them, suited up, hood pushed back to reveal a flushed face, dark hair plastered to his skull.

He held two more up, prepared for their arrival.

'You look like shit, Ziggy.'

'Noted.'

'He's not getting much sleep,' Ferreira said, pulling on her suit.

'Paying the daddy tax?'

'She's worth it.'

Zigic got dressed, tugged on the plastic foot covers which were never quite big enough and followed them into the tent. They stayed near the doorway, well clear of the body which showed signs of attention from forensics, hands in clear bags, areas of the ground

16

in small cordons, coloured tags flagging each of them for further examination.

'Who's on this?' he asked.

'O'Mara.'

'Where's Jenkins?'

'Skiing,' Adams said. 'I tried calling her back but you can imagine what kind of response that got.'

Zigic wanted to move closer but knew better.

The woman was flat on her front, damaged face turned towards them. Her nose had been broken, cheekbone too, Zigic thought, but he didn't need a pathologist's report to tell him the most likely cause of death was strangulation. He could see the white wire of a pair of earphones hanging at her throat and the marks it had left behind, the scratches she'd clawed into her skin there too, desperate and painful-looking.

'What makes you think this is one for us?' Zigic asked. 'Do you have an ID? Is she already on the system?'

'I don't recognise her,' Ferreira said.

'Not "her",' Adams said. '"Him".'

They turned as one. 'What?'

'Yeah, I didn't see it either until the doc told me. He comes down, takes a quick shufti at her, notices the size of her wrists – she was big-boned girl considering how skinny she looks – starts making that fucking whistling noise he does when he wants you to know he's on to something.'

'I hate that,' Ferreira said, inching towards the body, peering at the corpse. 'It's like, just tell us already.'

'So then he clocks the scars behind her ears, full facelift he reckons.' Adams shrugged. 'Then the old bastard squats down and peeks into her leggings . . . we've got a "him".'

Zigic stared at Adams for a few long seconds, waiting for him to crack a smile and admit it was a wind-up. He wouldn't put it past the DCI.

He wasn't smiling, though; he was watching Ferreira take another tentative step towards the body.

'I don't know . . . she *looks* like a woman.'

'Well, you're going to have to take my word for it.'

Zigic thought he detected a slight heaviness at the woman's brow, a coarseness to her hair which looked wrong somehow.

But it was nothing you'd pick up on from a distance.

'How did her attacker know she was actually a man?' he asked.

'Correct me if I'm wrong here,' Adams said. 'But you had a trans woman attacked last year, didn't you?'

Ferreira glanced back across her shoulder. 'Yeah, she was beaten up pretty bad.'

'And you're suggesting this is the same man?' Zigic asked. 'You've got a serial rapist attacking joggers – she's far more likely to be another of his victims.'

'Nope, she's too old,' Adams said. 'A good twenty years too old, I reckon.'

'He wouldn't know that until he got close to her.'

'For Christ's sake.' Ferreira straightened up. 'What, neither of you want to deal with this?'

'I want her dealt with right,' Adams said firmly, giving her a warning look she absorbed with only the barest blush. 'Now, my particular sadistic piece of shit uses a knife, okay? He wants compliance so the first thing he does – *always* – is nick the back of their necks so they know he's serious. We've not got that here.'

Zigic rubbed his face, already getting impatient.

Three hours' sleep last night, five the night before, and he was stuck listening to a man he basically loathed explain why he was going to hand over a challenging case which had no place in Hate Crimes.

He should have applied for extended paternity leave. He could be at home now, dozing on the sofa, Emily soundly asleep in her cot. Because of course she slept while he was at work.

'So, what do we see?' Adams asked. 'No disturbance of clothing. No cut. And a victim who's not only too old to be a target but she's also got the wrong hair colour. Our man always targets brunettes.' He pointed at Ferreira. 'Mel, no running along the river, yeah?'

She scowled at him.

'Maybe your guy only realised what he was dealing with after he'd knocked her down,' Ferreira said. 'Her hair's covered, he wouldn't have been able to see her face from behind. So, what does he see? A great pair of legs and good arse, which you don't often get on older women.'

Zigic cringed internally, wanted to remind her that Adams was technically their boss and needed to be afforded a degree of respect even if it was entirely fake.

She kept going though.

'He takes her down, she shouts at him, maybe she reverts to her male voice and he realises he's made a major fuck-up.' Ferreira's hands wheeled in front of her. 'Then what's he going to do? He's probably already aroused. He's got a hard-on for another man. He won't be able to deal with that head fuck, so he has to kill her. Maybe that's why he's escalated now.'

Adams sighed and Zigic prepared to weigh in in support of the theory, take some of the heat off Ferreira, but the sigh turned into a nod.

'You might have something there,' Adams said. 'Yeah, I don't hate that explanation at all.'

'So you'll keep it in CID, then?' Zigic asked.

'No.'

'What? That's a perfectly workable theory.' Zigic turned to Ferreira, who was walking around the body now. 'Mel, for God's sake don't stand on anything.'

'I'm being careful.'

He blinked away the grittiness under his eyelids, knowing that his fatigue was making the conversation feel so off-kilter, like the two of them were dancing around something he wasn't quite grasping.

Focus.

'Who found her?'

'Old girl out walking her dog,' Adams said. 'I've sent her in to give a statement but sounds like she didn't see anything.'

Ferreira had moved to the woman's feet, looking at her trainers.

'Did he drag her away from the path or was she running off-piste?'

'We've got drag marks.' Adams gestured somewhere away beyond the tent's walls 'Must have been strong, whoever did it.'

Zigic went back out of the tent, into the fresh air and the fine drizzle which had begun to fall, turned his face up into it as he shrugged out of the plastic coverall. He could hear Adams and Ferreira still talking inside and wondered why she thought she could change his mind. Wondered too why Adams put up with her being so blunt. He had a mixed reputation around the station, was one of those polarising inspectors who inspired loathing or blind adoration from his officers but nothing in between.

A minute later they were both out too, stripping off their suits.

'You get why this needs to be in Hate Crimes, right?' Adams said, slightly less aggressively now. 'A murdered transwoman, we can't have any mistakes. Someone makes a stupid slip of the tongue and we're going to be accused of prejudice against the LGBTQ community. How's that going to look?'

Zigic nodded agreement, thinking that yet again they were being used for PR purposes. He knew Adams was right but it didn't mean he had to like it.

'It's not going to look great if it turns out this was a CID case that got passed down to us in error, either.'

'That's why I'm sending Murray over to you. She's been leading on the serial rapes, so she's totally up to speed. We'll have her liaise, work it from that angle. That way nothing gets missed.'

'And Riggott's good with this?' Zigic asked.

'I'll square it with him,' Adams said confidently. And why not, he was Riggott's hand-picked successor according to the station rumour mill. 'You'll want to get a jump on the press with this, too.'

'I'll do that.' Zigic meant it to come out cold but all he heard was exhaustion in his voice.

A shout went up from the cordon and a couple of seconds later a PC came running towards them, one hand on his belt, the other at his radio, jogging along like he didn't do that as often as he needed to.

'Sir.' He looked to Adams. 'Woman here wants to speak to you, says she knows the victim.'

Adams stepped back, swept both hands towards Zigic.

'You're up, Ziggy.'

3

They had a name – Corinne Sawyer.

That was all they managed to get from her girlfriend before she crumpled to the ground at the edge of the cordon. She knew something was wrong, Corinne should have been home an hour earlier, was never late, always ran the same route, was always back by eight sharp. She kept repeating the words, *I knew, I knew it*.

Ferreira drove her home to a village a few minutes from Ferry Meadows, followed her mumbled directions past a small shop and onto a narrow lane with two churches facing each other down; they needed a lot of religion here apparently. The cottage they stopped at was built close onto the lane, a white-painted place with a thatched roof recently redone, a woven fox slinking along its apex.

A nice house, Ferreira thought as she got out of the car, eyeing the potted box plants either side of the low front door and the wooden shutters closed across the windows. The dead woman was a right fit for it.

The girlfriend . . . she wasn't so sure.

Sam Hyde hadn't moved from the passenger seat and Ferreira opened the door to coax her out.

She was much younger than Corinne, mid-twenties, but scruffy and plain, dressed in pyjamas with a raincoat thrown over the top. She had an unremarkable face overpowered by heavy black-framed glasses and red hair razed in a brutal undercut. Hardly the trophy girlfriend you'd expect an affluent older woman to have, and a cynical voice in Ferreira's head asked if that meant anything.

It was too early to make judgements but they seemed like a mismatched couple and that always pricked Ferreira's suspicions.

Sam Hyde unlocked the front door, jiggling the key with a practised movement and then shoving it open. That would be what they called period charm, Ferreira guessed.

Inside, the hallway was larger than she expected, big enough for a console table covered in photographs and a painted wooden pew piled with coats and bags, shoes kicked off underneath it. She followed Sam Hyde through a living room done out in ox blood and leather, curtains drawn, the debris of the night before still scattered about, into a surprisingly large and modern kitchen extension at the back of the house.

'Am I supposed to offer you tea?' Sam Hyde asked, voice dull and flat with the shock.

'I'll make it,' Ferreira said.

'I don't want one.' Sam put a hand to her throat. 'I don't think I can swallow.'

Ferreira led her over to a long oak table and made her sit down, told her it was a natural reaction, not to panic, it was just the shock.

'I don't understand how this happened. Corinne was strong.'

'There was probably very little she could have done to defend herself,' Ferreira said, not wanting to give away too much information.

'But she was a fighter.'

'Did she need to be a fighter?'

A grim smile tightened Sam's face. 'What do you think? You saw her. Do you think she's been living an easy life?'

'All I saw was a very well put together woman.'

'Shame more people don't think like that.'

Ferreira took a breath, aware of how delicate this was. 'Has there been any indication that Corinne might have been in danger?'

'From who?'

'You have someone in mind?'

Sam's gaze drifted away, towards the garden beyond the long glass wall, a wide expanse of empty lawn, nothing to see but a few birds and a tabby cat in hunting mode.

'There was a fight,' Sam said. 'Last night at the club.'

'What club?'

'The Meadham. They have a trans night once a month. Corinne always goes.'

Ferreira knew the place. An elegant old Georgian town house a minute's walk from her flat. It had been converted into a private members' club, not the kind of clientele for brawls, she thought.

'Were you there when this happened?'

'No, I usually go with Corinne but I wasn't feeling too hot so she went alone. It's always the same crowd, I wasn't missing anything.' Sam wiped at her face, the tears were still coming, but she was moving from the intense first flush of shock into the numbness stage.

'Corinne said it was something of nothing.' Sam frowned, fingers turning around the heavy silver ring she wore on her index finger. 'But . . . I just got the feeling she was lying.'

'Why would she lie?'

'Because I worry about her.'

'What did she tell you?'

Sam looked up to the vaulted ceiling. 'Some bloke was giving her verbals. Her and another woman. Corinne said she slapped him down.'

'Physically?'

'Verbally. She'd got a sharp mouth on her.' Sam smiled. 'I loved that about her.' The smile faded slowly. 'But I think she was lying. I noticed bruises on her arm when she was getting undressed. I think he went for her.'

She took off her glasses. Her eyes were smaller without them, not as puffy and red as they'd looked before.

'This man would be unlikely to have known Corinne's regular run,' Ferreira pointed out. 'Unless she knew him. Did she know him?'

24

'She told me he was just a drunk,' Sam said.

'We'll look into it,' Ferreira assured her. 'Who did know Corinne's routine?'

'Our neighbours, I suppose. Her family. She was a health freak, always had been. That's why she looked so amazing.'

The doorbell sounded, chiming through the house, and Ferreira went to let Zigic in. He stood with his hand braced against the frame, staring at the ground.

'What's wrong?'

He shook his head. 'Nothing, just tired.'

'I'll keep the lead, then. Alright?'

'Go for it.'

He trudged into the house and looked around the place with heavy eyes. He'd seemed okay at the scene but now she wasn't sure he was up to working the vital first day of the case. Maybe she could sneak into the evidence locker at the station, find him some uppers.

Sam Hyde was still sitting where Ferreira had left her and she gave Zigic the briefest glance as he sat down opposite her.

'This is Detective Inspector Zigic,' Ferreira said. 'He'll be leading the investigation into Corinne's murder.'

Sam Hyde nodded, seemingly unimpressed by the figure he was cutting in his crumpled jumper and rain-spattered parka.

'Have you had any trouble with your neighbours?' Ferreira asked.

Sam's face twisted briefly. 'Not trouble trouble.'

'But?'

'We're not a typical couple,' she said. 'Not around here. They're like, really vanilla, and we stand out, I guess. When we moved in last year one woman seemed really happy she'd got a pair of token lesbians to add to her social circle.'

'You're not though, are you? Corinne was still—'

'Yeah, she still had a cock,' Sam said, hardness coming into her voice. 'But she didn't get it out at social gatherings.'

Ferreira apologised quickly and Sam waved it off.

'No, I'm sorry. This is all . . .' She pressed her fingers to her mouth, squeezed her eyes shut. 'You need to ask. I get that. Corinne was transitioning. She was living as a woman full-time, she'd had most of the surgery, the cosmetic stuff, but she had to spend a year as a woman before she could have the gender reassignment done.'

'How was she doing with that?' Ferreira asked.

'Fine. Brilliantly.' Sam's face brightened. 'It's what she always wanted. Corinne *was* a woman, you have to understand that. She knew when she was four years old that she was a girl. She'd been living a lie ever since and now she was finally getting to be the woman she *knew* she was. It was like, I don't even know how to explain it, like she *existed* at last.'

'Why did she wait so long?' Zigic asked. 'For the surgery.'

The light went out of Sam's face. 'Her wife. Nina. That's why she waited, because that crazy bitch wouldn't even let her have control over her own body. That's who you should be talking to. She couldn't let her go. She wanted to break Corinne.'

4

Corinne Sawyer's photograph went at the top of the new murder board. It was the one they'd use for the press, showing her happy and attractive, unquestionably feminine, the kind of victim the public could warm to, whose killer they would want to see punished.

Zigic stood back while DC Bobby Wahlia plotted out the time she left the house and the rough time of death they'd established. The woman who'd found her body came along barely ten minutes later, describing in her statement the moment her little West Highland terrier started barking at Corinne's prone body, how she'd thought it was an accident until she saw the wire looped around her neck.

First thing tomorrow they would send a team down to the spot near the lock and speak to everyone who passed, catch the regulars who might have seen something out of the ordinary.

But for now all they had was a dead woman whose distraught girlfriend was blaming her ex.

As Sam had handed over Corinne's laptop and mobile phone she kept up a tirade against Nina Sawyer – who, it emerged, was still legally married to Corinne.

The laptop and mobile were with the techies now. More waiting.

Ferreira nudged him. 'Drink this.' She put a mug in one hand. 'And take these.'

He looked at the pills she dropped into his palm. 'What are they?'

'Speed.'

'You know what, I don't even care if they are.' He swallowed them with a mouthful of coffee, nodded towards the photograph. 'Would you have known she was a man?'

'She was a woman,' Ferreira said. 'You need to get used to saying that.'

'I don't need a lecture on gender sensitivity, thanks, Mel. But I'm asking if some random piece of shit – say, the type who'd target trans women for violence – would have thought she was.'

'Then, no. I don't think they would. Bobby?'

Wahlia stepped back from the board, capping a red marker pen. 'No way. She's got that Gillian Anderson vibe. Good bones, strong-looking but feminine.'

'So, we've established she was passing,' Ferreira said in a withering tone. 'Meaning you don't think she was murdered because she was trans.'

'Not if it was a random attack.'

'We know she had a highly predictable routine. What if her killer knew she was trans, hated her because of it, and targeted her where he knew he could find her?'

Zigic nodded. 'You'd better look back over the attack from last year. See if we've got any similarities, anybody they knew in common.'

'I was just about to pull the file,' Ferreira said, heading back to her desk. 'But from what I can remember that one was in town somewhere, looked like a random, pissed-up arsehole.'

'Let's be sure, though.'

On the other side of the office DS Colleen Murray was unpacking the material she'd brought up from CID, the serial rape case she was leading for Adams. The board had come with her and now sat behind her desk, four women's photographs watching over her, and Zigic saw why Adams had been so dismissive of Corinne Sawyer as another victim to join that line-up.

The women were all very young, round-faced and dark-haired. But the map on the board showed that the attacks had all been carried out along the stretch of river which ran from the city centre out westwards to Ferry Meadows. Corinne was murdered in this man's territory; it was a link they couldn't disregard.

28

The phone on his desk rang and he went to answer it – DCS Riggott.

'Let's me and you have a wee chat, Ziggy.'

Less than two hours after the body was found and he was already being summoned. Not a good sign.

Zigic went down to Riggott's office, found the door standing open, disarray spilling out through it. Inside, the DCS stood in his shirtsleeves, surveying the mess he'd created; desk pulled halfway across the room, chairs scattered, a new two-seater sofa pushed up tight against the filing cabinet.

'Don't just stand there gawping,' Riggott said, waving him towards the desk.

Grabbing the other end, Zigic followed his lead, setting it down a few feet from the far wall, in front of the framed mugshots which hung there, every serious criminal Riggott had put away during his career, enough to fill the space from floor to ceiling.

Zigic didn't think he'd want those men and women glowering at the back of his neck while he worked but it would be preferable to looking at them.

Riggott dropped his end of the desk with a crack. Zigic lowered his with a little more care.

'Is that what you wanted me for?'

'Sure, you're the biggest fella in the station, who else would I call?' Riggott shot him a thin smile and went for his chair, wheeled it around behind the desk. 'Get one yourself there.'

Zigic pulled a chair over.

'Right, your man down at Ferry Meadows,' Riggott said, taking an e-cigarette from his shirt pocket. 'What's the story?'

'It was a woman. Didn't Adams brief you already?'

Riggott rolled his eyes. 'I know how he was dressed and I realise you're a stickler for notions of political correctness but unless he was legally declared female – which I gather he'd not been – then you're dealing with a man who happened to be wearing ladies' clothing.'

29

'Corinne Sawyer was transitioning,' Zigic said firmly, knowing better than to give ground at this early stage. 'She was living as a woman full-time. Her friends and family knew her as a woman and her killer attacked her as a woman. I think that's more significant than the state of her genitalia.'

Another eye roll and Riggott propped his elbows on the desk. 'You're going to be a pain in my hole over this, aren't you?'

'If we want cooperation from the people closest to Corinne we need to respect the fact that she considered herself a woman.' He watched Riggott process the idea. 'And, of course, if this turns out to be a transphobic attack then we're going to be reliant on the trans community for help. Because it probably won't be an isolated incident. Not something this ferocious.'

Riggott leaned back, drawing deeply on his e-cig. 'You don't reckon it was targeted?'

'Way too early to say.'

'But your gut?'

'We've got a similar attack on file, it may be connected.'

A phone began to ring somewhere in the office. Riggott didn't move to unearth it. 'Adams has similar attacks too but you shouldn't go thinking you can rely on that paying off.'

'I don't think it will,' Zigic said, bristling at the condescension he detected in Riggott's tone.

'And don't let him derail your investigation because he's got a hard-on for this shite-stain Lee Walton.'

He'd seen the name on the board Murray had brought up to Hate Crimes with her, knew nothing about the man himself.

'I've got no intention of letting my case go,' Zigic said.

Riggott gave him a speculative look. 'Sure, you know what a terrier he can be.'

'Maybe he should be kept on a shorter leash.'

'How'd you know what fight a dog's got in him if you don't let him loose?'

Zigic was too tired for this, had no interest in verbal sparring or the stupid, trumped-up competition which lay behind it. Riggott was too much the careerist to understand that not all coppers saw their colleagues as fences to be hurdled in pursuit of advancement.

'If Walton's responsible I want him caught,' he said. 'But until Adams comes up with something more substantial connecting him to this, I'm going to follow the leads we have.'

'You have leads already?'

'There's acrimony within the family. Seems a good place to start.'

'Certain parties not happy about yon "woman" going for the chop?' Riggott asked. 'Must be a hell of a thing for a wife to deal with, that.'

'The wife's estranged. New girlfriend on the scene.'

'Girlfriend?' Riggott's eyebrows leapt for his hairline. 'Sounds like you've a good old-fashioned mess on your hands there.'

'We can hope.'

Riggott dismissed him with an order to keep him briefed and Zigic trudged back up to Hate Crimes. He went into his office, closed the door and looked at the paperwork spread across his desk, checked the emails stacking up in his inbox.

He could grab five minutes' rest while Wahlia and Ferreira gathered together whatever information they could. Despite the old saw that the first twenty-four hours of a murder case were the most important, policing didn't always work like that any more.

Previous generations had pumped the first day hard because they relied on door-knocking and street work, getting to witnesses before they forgot vital details or thought better of coming forward, running down informants. Now the first day was mostly waiting, for forensic reports and CCTV and financial records, the extraction of digital footprints from the devices where people lived the greater part of their lives.

The lack of CCTV around Ferry Meadows was going to be a problem for them. No cameras at the entrance on Oundle Road, even assuming that was their killer's route. None on the path Corinne had taken, obviously, and the park could be accessed from dozens of different points, all unmonitored.

Maybe this case would come down to old-school techniques after all, he thought, as he swung his feet onto the corner of his desk, feeling the tiredness in his bones fighting the pills he'd taken.

His body wanted to rest but his brain kept turning.

With a sigh he pulled his keyboard towards him and found the file on last year's attack, rubbed his eyes to bring it into focus. Ferreira had worked it and done as good a job as she could with the lack of forensic evidence and the victim's inability to give a description of his attacker, but they hadn't managed to find the person responsible.

Zigic remembered the man, had never seen him as a woman except in the photographs taken while he was unconscious in A&E by a doctor who was savvy enough to realise embarrassment might prevent the man from reporting his attack. It was arguably a cruel thing to do, calling the police in without the victim's knowledge, but Zigic saw from the statement given that if not for the doctor's actions they might never have known what lay behind this vicious beating.

The photographs showed a similar ferocity as they'd seen at today's crime scene. A woman severely beaten, eyes swollen shut, cheekbone fractured, nose ruptured so badly Zigic doubted that it could have mended well, and angry red marks around her hairline where a wig had been ripped from her head.

Simon Trent had come to the station patched up and humiliated, with his wife in tow. A small, plain woman with dark circles under her eyes and a lot of grey in her hair. He gave a statement because he had to but reading it through there was very little of use. He'd been out with friends for the night, split off to find a taxi but never made it to the rank on Cowgate. On Cross Street, a quiet road, cobbled and poorly lit, he'd been jumped from behind, his face repeatedly slammed into the pavement. A couple found him unconscious some time later and called an ambulance, stayed with him until it arrived.

They would need to speak to him again and this time his awkward silences couldn't be accepted. If there was a link to Corinne Sawyer's murder hiding between the lines of his bare-boned statement they needed to find it.

Attacks on trans women weren't that common in Peterborough and when Zigic searched the system he found no other unsolveds on record in recent years, the ones there were all closed, the usual drunks and cranks. But he knew it was a growing problem, that this particular form of violent intolerance was kept hidden far more than racism or homophobia because the victims were frequently living double lives which they didn't want to expose by going to the police. Simon Trent's wife was aware of his cross-dressing and she came over as broadly supportive, but what about their friends, their families and co-workers?

Did he come to in the hospital, with Ferreira waiting at his bedside, and feel like his whole world was about to come crashing down around his ears?

Zigic looked at the woman on his screen, beaten and unconscious, and wondered if she still existed. If Simone had been knocked out of Simon Trent on that summer night, or if she was hiding now, too scared to reveal herself again.

One thing he was fairly certain of, the Trents wouldn't be happy to have the police at their door again.

5

Zigic had driven past the Sawyer house a thousand times and always regarded it with a prickle of envy. It sat in half an acre of woodland, stern old oaks and yew trees looming over it, high hedgerows cocooning it from the traffic on Oundle Road. The hedge wouldn't keep out a determined intruder though, neither would the electric gates they were driving through, not with such a prize on the other side.

'Jesus,' Ferreira said. 'I thought Corinne's place was fancy. It looks like a hovel compared to this.'

'It's pretty spectacular,' Zigic agreed.

'How much do you think it's worth?' she asked, pulling up behind a sleek black sports car with an emblem Zigic didn't recognise. 'A mil? More?'

'A lot more,' Zigic said. 'I saw one on *Grand Designs* – the build for a Huf Haus like this was close to a million.'

She swore softly, then turned to him, grinning. 'I can't wait until I'm old enough to watch *Grand Designs*.'

They got out of the car and Zigic paused for a moment, taking in the bulk and sweep of the building. It was cold and sleek, aggressively modern, all black metal supports and toughened glass, sixty-foot wide and with a roof he could only think of in terms of wingspan, the way it seemed to unfold away from the central section where the main door was sited, the eaves overhanging to create long sections of deep shade.

Maybe it was the pills or the fatigue but he was sure he could feel thrumming under his feet. His eye drifted down to the paved area in front of the house, large white pebbles laid with exacting precision in drifting lines. A narrow grey path cut through them up to the door, slabs the size of tombstones.

'You good?' Ferreira asked.

He snapped out of it. 'Yeah, let's do this.'

She went to ring the doorbell. They'd been buzzed through the gates by Nina Sawyer but she hadn't come to meet them. Zigic pondered what that meant while they waited, looking at a gnarled olive tree sitting in a polished concrete pot nearby, silvery limbs contorted.

'They're not fussed about privacy, are they?' Ferreira said. 'I can see right through the house.'

'It's a statement, isn't it?'

'It's stupid. People see what you've got, they try to take it from you.' She tipped her head back, staring directly into a security camera mounted discreetly above the door. 'How do you get this rich and stay that naive?'

The door was opened by a tall, painfully thin woman swaddled in two layers of voluminous, nothing-coloured knitwear and a pair of khaki skinny jeans. She looked quickly between them, the tilt of her head reminding Zigic of a bird of prey, but she gave away nothing, her face all sharp angles, mouth set in a firm line.

'Please, come in.' No warmth in her voice.

She closed the door behind them and Zigic found his gaze drawn up towards the double-height ceiling. You could fit his entire house in the entrance hall, he thought, and have space to walk around it.

Behind him Ferreira was making the introductions and he turned to shake Nina Sawyer's offered hand.

'You have a beautiful home,' he said.

Her mouth smiled but the rest of her face held still. 'Thank you. It was a labour of love but worth the pain. Rather like actual labour.'

It sounded like something she'd said many times before, all the emotion long since lost from the words.

'I'm afraid we have bad news,' Zigic said. 'Maybe you should sit down.'

Nina Sawyer held her hand up. 'I already know. Sam was thoughtful enough to call me and let me know what happened to Corinne.' Her eyelids fluttered. 'I don't think it's quite sunk in yet.'

Zigic nodded. 'We'll try not to take up too much of your time.'

'Thank you, I am rather busy today.' She looked around herself, shoulders rising. 'Although none of that seems very important suddenly.'

'What do you do?' Ferreira asked.

'I manage our property portfolio.'

'Yours and Corinne's?'

She stiffened slightly. 'That's right. Although Corinne had taken a much more hands-off role in the last few years. She looked after the maintenance side of things and that became rather awkward.' She inclined her head towards Zigic. 'As I'm sure you can imagine. We subcontract the work now.'

So Corinne wouldn't be a loss to her professionally or personally, Zigic thought.

'I was about to make a coffee,' she said, forced brightness, playing the good host. 'Would you like one?'

They both accepted and she directed them away to another room. 'I'll only be a moment.'

Their footfalls cracked against the tiled floor, echoing high up to the ceiling, colliding with every hard surface they encountered, and Zigic wondered if you'd ever get used to that, the sense it created of being in a public space rather than a home.

Nina had pointed them towards a sitting room overlooking a terrace, nothing but shards of grey stone and white rendered walls out there, a set of garden furniture shrouded against the elements. The trees were closer than they looked from the driveway, casting jagged shadows across the floor as the sunlight broke through the thin, high cloud.

36

It felt like another public space, softened by thick wool rugs and brightened with large impasto abstracts, but as he sat down he realised it was an unused area. The modular sofa was uncomfortable, designed for perching not lounging, the suede armchairs too easily bruised for a family to use, and all of them set too far away from the perspex coffee table.

Ferreira quickly gave up on her perusal of the bookshelves and came over to the sofa, paused to open a chrome box on the table and closed it again before she sat down next to him.

'She doesn't exactly seem cut up about Corinne's death, does she?'

'She's had time to compose herself,' Zigic said. 'We missed the real reaction.'

'Why try to hide it?'

'Not everyone's a weeper, Mel.'

A minute later Nina Sawyer returned with a tray bearing their drinks, delicate white cups and saucers, a plate with a few biscotti. She set it down on the table and retreated to one of the camel suede armchairs, sat with her legs tightly crossed and one elbow propped on the arm.

'Please, help yourself.'

Zigic thanked her, standing to take his coffee. 'How much did Sam tell you?'

'Only that Corinne had been murdered. She said it happened at Ferry Meadows so I presumed Corinne was out for her morning run.' She pursed her lips. 'What on earth am I going to tell the children? They'll be devastated.'

'How old are your children, Mrs Sawyer?' Zigic asked.

'Lily's fourteen. Jessica and Harry are twenty-five and twenty-seven. They're hardly babies any more but with it happening like this . . .' Her eyes lost focus for a moment, as if she was already rehearsing the conversation, then she shook out of it. 'Corinne was always rather blasé about her safety. Well, you'd have to be to go running around there on your own. It just isn't safe for a woman. Even one like her.'

'You don't seem very upset,' Ferreira said.

Nina looked momentarily wounded. 'I lost my husband a long time ago, Sergeant. He left me the first time he dressed up as Corinne. I appreciate how heartless that must sound to you but it's the truth. I've shed all the tears I'm going to for Colin.'

'How long were you together?'

'Twelve years with him. Another fifteen with her.'

'How long ago did Corinne move out?' Ferreira asked.

'Almost two years ago. Once he decided on the transition that was it.' Nina's fingers twitched on the arm of the chair. 'I should have thrown him out the moment he told me about Corinne but we had a young family and I didn't want to upset the children. Colin was an excellent father.' Her eyes narrowed. 'Not so good on the husband front, though.'

'Must have been tough for you,' Ferreira said.

'It was.' Nina turned away towards a large canvas, its surface a mess of red peaks and troughs, scored through and raked away. 'But it's what we do, isn't it? We put aside our own needs for our men. Looking back I can't believe how naive I was.' She shook her head. 'I honestly thought it was just a phase I could help him through. Some childhood trauma resurfacing . . .'

'Did he have an unhappy childhood?' Zigic asked.

'His parents were horrible from what I heard. They both died before we were married.' She tucked a few strands of ash-blonde hair behind her ear. 'We can always find excuses for the people we love. His father ignored him, his mother hated him, he's depressed, whatever. I believed for a long time it was my fault.'

She cast a quick glance towards Ferreira, expecting her to understand, and Zigic saw the sympathy on Mel's face, thought it went deeper than her usual professional reflexes. A slight tightening of the skin under her eyes signalling genuine pain and he knew where it came from, hoped she could keep her own experience out of this, because there was no way he wanted to embarrass her by discussing it.

'Trans people are just born that way,' she said. 'There was nothing you could do.'

The clouds shifted and the room was plunged into gloom, dulling every shining surface.

'It took me a long time to realise that.' Nina sighed. 'It's amazing how completely you can delude yourself in that situation. I kept giving in to his demands, moving over for Corinne – they weren't the same person. As crazy as that must sound. She was the other woman in our marriage and she was . . . unpleasant. A bully.' Nina frowned. 'Of all the other women he had she was the one who finally ended our marriage.'

The sun asserted itself through the glass ceiling and the shadows of the trees formed shuddering patterns on the floor. Zigic could see the wind in the movement but the sound of it didn't penetrate the room. No traffic noise either in this hermetically sealed space, only an occasional pattering of small twigs hitting the roof.

'We need to ask you a few questions about Corinne,' he said, putting his cup down. 'Did she have any enemies?'

Nina laughed lightly and pressed her fingertips to her mouth. 'I'm sorry.'

'Why's that funny?' Ferreira asked. 'She has been murdered.'

Nina composed her face again, the angles sharpening. 'Well, it's ridiculous. Corinne wasn't the kind of person to make enemies. God, she barely *existed*.'

'And Colin?'

'He had a nasty streak, yes, but he kept that for me.' Nina's jaw clenched. 'I can't imagine anyone having reason to kill him. Unless you want to talk to every man whose girlfriend he screwed over the years.'

'Why didn't you leave him?'

'Colin could be very charming when he wanted to be. And, as I told you, we had a young family. I wasn't going to deprive the children of their father.' She seemed to soften at that, a little pink touching her eyes and the tip of her nose, and Zigic wondered why she thought she needed to play the unconcerned ex, especially at a time like this.

Nina caught him watching her, looked uncomfortable suddenly, as if aware that she'd accidentally revealed a sliver of vulnerability.

'Corinne was the problem. She didn't have any of Colin's redeeming features.'

Like they were two distinct people. Was that how Nina had coped with it? A huge feat of cognitive dissonance.

'Where were you between half past seven and eight o'clock this morning?' Ferreira asked.

'I was here.'

'Alone?'

'No, my daughter Lily was here and Brynn, my partner.' She drew herself upright in the chair, tightened her bony hands around her knee. 'I'd have thought Sam would be more useful to you than me. I've hardly spoken to Corinne since she moved out.'

'Can't you think of anyone who might have had an issue with her?' Zigic asked.

'I wish I could help you.'

'What about friends? Is there anyone she might have confided in?'

'There's a charity she was involved with,' Nina said. 'More of a support network really. For cross-dressers and their partners. Well, they say they're there for the partners too, but they're not. They just expect us to toe the line and play nice so the "girls" can do as they like.'

'And you were involved with them too?' Ferreira asked.

'I went to a few meetings in the early days,' Nina said. 'I wanted to support Colin. Show willing.'

'What's this charity called?' Zigic asked.

'Trans Sisters,' Nina said, rolling her eyes slightly. 'They have an office on Priestgate but they do most of their events at the Meadham.'

Zigic reached into his pocket and brought out a photograph of Simon Trent, virtually unrecognisable through his injuries but Nina nodded.

'*Simone*, yes. I spoke to his wife a couple of times. She wasn't quite as highly strung as the other women there.'

'Did you hear he'd been attacked?' Zigic asked.

'No, we were never friends.' She handed the photo back. 'But I'm sorry to hear it. His wife was actually rather a nice person.'

Zigic thanked Nina Sawyer for all her help, watching her for some hint of relief she refused to let slip. She took the card he offered and promised she would call if she thought of anything else, but, 'Really, we were strangers, Inspector.'

She saw them to the door and Zigic left the house wondering how Corinne had felt about no longer living there. Her family left behind, all of that sacrificed to be the woman she had always believed she was. Did her new life with Sam feel like a new start or merely compensation?

6

'No blood on the pavement,' Ferreira said, as she followed Zigic up the worn stone steps to the Meadham's main doors.

'Classy place like this, they'll wash it off.'

Inside, a young woman with a plastered-on smile sat behind a gilded reception desk with nothing on it but a large, leather-bound ledger. Her hands were folded over it protectively.

'Good afternoon, sir. Madam. Could I see your membership cards, please?'

Zigic showed her his ID. 'We're here about an altercation that happened last night. Were you on duty then?'

The smile disappeared and she glanced towards an ornate cast-iron staircase, which rose in a graceful curve above them, lit by a copper chandelier giving out a warm, burnished glow.

'Would you wait here, please? I'll fetch Mr Bentley.'

Ferreira was already gone, heading for the bar that opened off the main reception area, following the sound of low chatter and inevitable jazz. It was tasteful in a generic fashion. Dark wood floors and the walls half grey wainscoting and half painted in a noxious shade of yellow somewhere between bile and English mustard, with paintings that looked like eighteenth-century portraits until you examined them closer and saw the sitters wearing digital watches or Converse with their silk hose.

Zigic opened the ledger and flipped back to the evening before, saw a list of illegible signatures and printed names, the times they had arrived and left. He took a couple of quick photographs and slipped his phone away again, thinking how pretentious it was, the mere idea of a private members' club in Peterborough.

But this was the best road in the city, where the most expensive accountants and law firms plied their trade, companies which consulted on obscure financial practices and architects who wouldn't take on projects worth less than seven figures. It would appeal to people like that, he guessed, with its veneer of exclusivity and urban cool.

He tried to imagine Corinne Sawyer and Sam Hyde here, Nina before her, Simon Trent and his wife, wasn't sure if they were a better fit for the place than the suits he could see in the bar and the well-dressed woman coming down the stairs, shopping bags in hand.

Ferreira returned from the bar.

'Anything?'

'They have an impressive selection of rum,' she said. 'And I didn't have one, because I'm on duty and it would be wrong. But the barman was working last night, said it was all very chill, no trouble inside.'

'It doesn't seem like a trouble kind of place.'

'The Trans Sisters group were a private hire – it's a big party apparently, heavy drinking, good atmosphere. They're here the first Monday of the month and the management closes it down to anyone else.'

'So, it's unlikely the man we're looking for is a member.'

'Unless he came in with someone, yeah. Which isn't impossible. Just because you've got a group of people with something in common doesn't mean they all get on.' She peered at a pair of taxidermy weasels boxing inside a glass case.

'You should get one of those for your flat,' Zigic said.

'I've got a huge dead spider under a glass in my bathroom. Didn't cost a penny.'

The receptionist came back down the stairs, trailed by a guy in his late thirties; turn-ups, topknot, old-man sweater of the kind Zigic had last seen on his father sometime in the mid-eighties. It would probably be considered vintage now and cost ten times what C&A had originally charged for it.

They made their introductions, Bentley checking Ferreira out with a directness Zigic found immediately off-putting, before he clapped his hands together and suggested they talk somewhere a bit more private.

'The Smoking Room's always quiet this time of day.'

'You have a smoking room?' Ferreira asked hopefully.

'Nah, that's just what we call it but you can light up if you want. I'm hardly going to stop you.'

Bentley strode off through a high-ceilinged lounge where a few people were eating lunch, and a large group in the corner were having a meeting, tablets and laptops on the low table between them, surrounded by empty glasses. He moved through the place with a sense of proprietorial ease, said quick hellos as he passed regulars, told a waitress to find a man named Terry for him.

'Nice place,' Ferreira said. 'Not very Peterborough.'

He beamed at her. 'That was exactly the feel I was going for. I've been in enough gastropubs, know what I mean? People want a bit of luxury, bit of quirk. You can't just keep selling them the same old stripped floors and whitewash, can you?'

His accent sounded off to Zigic. Part public school, part cockney barrow boy. All irritating.

'We're in here.'

He took them into a snug, wood-panelled room, windowless and stuffy, with a small corner bar that sat unmanned and five tables surrounded by leather club chairs in jellybean colours.

'Can I get either of you a drink?' he asked, moving behind the bar.

They both declined, took their seats and waited for him to join them. He came back with a bottle of mineral water, sat down as he opened it.

'So, you're here about something that happened last night?'

'There was a fight outside your club,' Zigic said. 'The woman involved was found murdered this morning.'

'Shit.' He took a mouthful of water. 'Who was it?'

'Corinne Sawyer. Did you know her?' Zigic took out a copy of the photograph Sam Hyde had given them.

'Corinne, yeah. Blimey, that's insane. She was a great girl, total riot.' He looked at the photo, shook his head. 'I can't believe it. I was only talking to her last night.'

'What did you talk about?'

'Spurs. I'm a season-ticket holder, she was a fan. We're going pretty well this season.'

'Were you here all evening, Mr Bentley?'

'No, just early on. I like to be here when big parties arrive, make them welcome.' He placed the photograph on the table. 'But I've just opened a new place over on Westgate, a restaurant, and I'm trying to keep a close eye on it for a bit. Check everything's running smooth.'

'And was it?' Ferreira asked. 'Running smooth.'

'Yeah.' He smiled at her. 'I've got a good team in there. Great chef, tapped him up from a place in Cambridge. Pan-Asian cuisine – he does a banging *tom yum gai*. You should come and try us out.'

'So you can't tell us anything about the fight?'

'I don't know why Terry never mentioned it.' He teased at his beard with his fingertips. 'He doesn't miss much, not in that way. I mean, we don't exactly have them scrapping in the halls here but Terry's got a nose for troublemakers.'

'It was out on the street from what we've been told,' Zigic said. 'Is Terry here for security?'

'No, he's my manager. Good bloke, ex-boxer, knows how to keep everyone in line.'

This didn't seem like the kind of establishment to employ a thug as a manager but Zigic found himself wondering just how respectable their clientele were. He'd seen a lot of lunchtime drinking in evidence as they'd walked through the rooms and most employers didn't stand for that any more.

'How long have the Trans Sisters nights been held here, Mr Bentley?'

'Zac, please.' He crossed his legs, curled one hand around his ankle, flashing a watch with Osama bin Laden on its face. 'Since we opened. Nearly five years.'

'And have you had any trouble in that time?'

'No, they're a great bunch of girls. Love to party. Big drinkers. They've never met a cocktail they didn't like.' He grinned, shook his head. 'This is going to hit them hard. Do you know why Corinne was murdered? It wasn't because she was trans, was it?'

'It's far too early to say,' Zigic told him.

'Why did they end up here?' Ferreira asked. 'There are plenty of gay-friendly pubs in Peterborough.'

'They're not drag queens,' Bentley said coolly. 'And they're not gay. These are women who feel self-conscious when they go out, they want to be in a safe space, where they can let go without feeling judged. Honestly, and I don't mean to sound harsh, a lot of them don't look so great *en femme*. I've worked in gay bars, they'd get ripped to shreds.'

'So, you close the place down once a month out of a sense of altruism?'

Bentley's fingertips strayed to his beard again and he at least had the grace to look bashful when he answered.

'Wish I could say it's that, but I'm a businessman and they're big spenders, so I do whatever I need to do to make sure they're happy here.'

The door opened and a man stuck his head in. 'You wanted me, boss?'

'Come in, Terry. Close the door, please.'

He didn't look much like a boxer. Five eight, leanly built, his clean-shaven face unmarked. So either he'd not done it for long or he'd been good enough to stay clear of any heavy shots thrown his way.

'This about last night?' the man said, looking at Zigic, recognising him for the superior officer straight off.

'Did you see what happened, Mr . . .'

'Sutton, sir.' He nodded. 'Saw the end of it but I heard what happened to kick it off. Corinne and Jolene went out front for a smoke and this young lad came up to them after cadging a fag. They wouldn't give him one. Which sounded strange to me because Jolene's always free with her fags, especially when she's had a few drinks. I'd gone out myself to beg one.' He gave a weak shrug. 'Promised my girlfriend I'd quit but it's tough in this job.'

'Who's Jolene?' Ferreira asked.

'One of the regulars,' Sutton told her. 'Cracking girl. Her and Corinne are a proper double act.'

And yet Sam Hyde hadn't mentioned her.

Zigic gestured for Terry Sutton to continue.

'I only caught the tail end of it but they said the lad was getting aggressive, calling them slags, that kind of thing.' He looked to Ferreira. 'That's when I arrived. I was going to step in but Corinne had it under control, knocked him right onto his backside. He got up and went at her, so I got myself in between them, talked him down, made him leave.'

Zac Bentley was shaking his head at the story. 'Why didn't you call the police, Terry?'

Sutton spread his hands wide, shrugged helplessly. 'It was nothing. I didn't think I needed to. Bit of pushing and shoving, young mouth got put in his place. You wouldn't have thanked me for calling your lot out for something like that, would you?'

'It might not be related,' Zigic said. 'But we need to find this young man, so CCTV if you've got it, a description, anything you can think of, Mr Sutton.'

'I can do better than that.' He reached into his pocket. 'Dropped his wallet when he hit the deck, I only found it after he'd gone. Been keeping it behind reception in case he came back.'

Ferreira took it from him, checked it out while he waited, hands tucked behind his back, spine ramrod-straight. He looked tougher like that, broader across the chest, strong-shouldered and thick-armed in his dove-grey shirt.

'Jolene,' Zigic said. 'What's her surname?'

Sutton's eyes flicked up to the ceiling. 'Ah, I don't know. You don't really use surnames at dos like that. Though,' he smiled, 'the girls all call me Sutton – they like to make out like I'm their butler.'

'But your members have to sign in,' Ferreira said. 'You must know.'

'Not for group bookings. They show an e-invite and we let them in.'

Zigic thanked him for his help and Bentley dismissed him.

'Terry's a pussycat, don't let how he looks fool you.' He stood up and took his empty bottle around the back of the bar. 'Is there anything else I can do for you?'

Interview over, evidently.

'No, I think that's it for now.'

Bentley walked them back through the club. There was no sign of the lunch crowd thinning out as the afternoon drew on, in fact the bar sounded busier and a couple of women were signing in as they reached the reception area.

'Have you spoken to Evelyn Goddard yet?' Bentley asked. 'She runs Trans Sisters, she might be more useful re the whole "trouble" thing. She's about four doors down, other side of the street.'

'We'll talk to her,' Zigic said, taking a card out of his pocket. 'But if you do think of anything else . . .'

'Of course.'

Bentley put it away and brought out a card of his own, offered it to Ferreira with another one of those high-wattage smiles.

'If you ever want to drop in for a drink, just show them this. I'm usually here early evening.'

'Good to know,' she said, and even Zigic couldn't tell if she meant it as encouragement or threat.

Outside she zipped the card into the breast pocket of her leather jacket and Zigic grinned at her.

'What's the word I'm looking for . . . douchebag?'

'That's the one.' She slipped her sunglasses on. 'You want to try Ms Goddard while we're here?'

Zigic checked his phone; nothing in from forensics yet and nothing from Wahlia's trawling activities. An invitation from DCS Riggott to brief him at the end of shift and a query from the press officer regarding the most suitable pronoun for the statement he'd be making in a couple of hours. He fired a quick message back: 'her'. Anna had sent a short video clip of Emily giggling in her cot and he stopped mid-stride to watch it, her infectious laughter sending a smile across his face.

When he switched his phone off Ferreira was sheltering in the doorway of an estate agent's lighting a roll-up, a man on the other side of the plate-glass window shooting her a filthy look.

'So, the charity?' she asked.

'Right.'

7

'It was only a matter of time before something like this happened,' Evelyn Goddard said, inviting them to sit down with a flick of her wrist. 'The more visible we become, the greater the threat of attack, the more likely one of our number was to be murdered.'

Zigic took one of the chrome-and-leather chairs that sat low on the visitors' side of her expansive glass desk. 'There's currently no indication that Corinne was targeted because she was trans.'

Goddard smiled, broad and sharkish, the muscles of her face moving oddly. Was it Botox? Zigic wondered. Or just a side effect of the facelift which had sharpened her jawline and lifted her brows far above their natural position. She was a mantis of a woman, poised and alert in her high-backed chair, not a hair out of place in her sleek auburn bob or a crease in her immaculate white suit.

'Corinne,' she said. 'As if you knew her. As if you cared.'

'I can assure you we care deeply about what happened to her.'

'Yes, now you care. Now she's dead and you have the embarrassment of a murdered trans woman to deal with.' She cocked her head towards Ferreira. 'I bet he only brought you along for the feminine touch, show us the police are more than just a boys' club.'

'We're here because Zac Bentley told us you'd be willing to help,' Ferreira said frostily. 'Maybe he misjudged you.'

'Young lady, I have been helping trans people to deal with the prejudice and violence they face on a daily basis since before you were born.'

Now Zigic wondered how old she was under all that polish and surgical perfecting. He'd pegged her as early fifties but when he

50

studied the hand she held balled in a loose fist, he realised she was perhaps ten or fifteen years older than that, blessed with good genes and strong features and an expert eye towards cosmetics. The hands didn't lie though, something Anna had told him but he didn't know he'd absorbed. The hands and the neck, which Evelyn Goddard kept carefully hidden with a sculpted silk top that sat stiff across her throat.

For a moment he saw the wire cutting into Corinne Sawyer's windpipe and told himself they needed this woman's help even if she was going to make them pay for it.

'It's strange you coming here now,' she said, spreading her hands wide to encompass the stark white office, with its tasteful mono-chrome photographs of trans women artfully lit and shot to their best advantage, the soft seating area she hadn't invited them to use, and beyond it, the outer office where a staff of three had been busy at their computers while they'd waited for her to grant them admittance.

'I've seen you on the news, Inspector Zigic,' she said. 'I watched with great interest as the council and the local constabulary announced the creation of your Hate Crimes Unit. I saw you reach out to the Muslim community and the immigrant community and the gay community. Every embattled minority dutifully name-checked and assured that their concerns would be treated with the utmost diligence and sensitivity. And yet, no visit here. Why was that, I wonder?'

She answered her question before he could.

'Because we're a joke to you. Men who dress as women are just locker-room banter, aren't we? Freaks and perverts.'

'That could not be further from the truth,' Zigic said, fighting the urge to squirm away from the imperious chill of her gaze.

'Simone Trent,' she said. 'What about her?'

'She didn't want to pursue the case,' Ferreira said.

Evelyn Goddard gave her a disgusted look. 'Because she was terrified of the repercussions, yes. What do you do when a woman is too scared of her abusive husband to press charges? The law says you prosecute to protect her.' She laughed, humourlessly. 'That was a poor example, excuse me. You hardly have the best record of protecting abused women.'

'You're right,' Ferreira said, holding her hands up. 'Many of our fellow officers do a frankly abysmal job of protecting victims of abuse. And sexual violence. The rape conviction statistics – as a woman, they disgust me. But we are not those officers and our job is to get justice for the kind of victims quite a few of our comrades wouldn't give a damn about.'

Zigic prayed the conversation went no further than this office. No police officer could ever denigrate their peers in front of a civilian, that was the rule, set in stone, no matter how badly they behaved. He imagined a leaked recording hitting the press, Evelyn Goddard's revenge for their perceived slight against her.

'We should have come to you,' Ferreira said, contrition in her tone. 'I can't speak for Inspector Zigic but I was naive about the extent of transphobic hate crimes until Simone Trent was attacked last year. I genuinely had no idea what women like her have to face, because – I guess, naively again – I didn't think cross-dressing was something people could actually get angry about.'

Ferreira was at the edge of her seat now, one palm flat on the glass desk.

'But I can promise you we are going to find whoever killed Corinne. And we're going to find whoever attacked Simone too, and they are going to get locked up with the kind of big nasty men they only think they are.'

There was long moment of silence as Evelyn Goddard stared at Ferreira, the sound of a ringing phone bleeding in around the office door. As the seconds ticked past, Zigic became increasingly convinced she'd overstepped the mark. Just like she had at the crime scene this morning with Adams. Part of him saw it as a good thing, a sign that her recovery was continuing, the old Mel returning. Then he remembered what a nightmare the old Mel could be.

Finally Goddard turned to Zigic.

'Now I can see why you brought her with you.'

'Ms Goddard, if any of your people have attacks to report, even historical ones, I want you to know they can come to us.' He held her gaze now, felt it softening very slightly. He took out a card and slid it across her desk. 'They don't need to call the station, they can contact me direct and either I or, if they're more comfortable with a woman, DS Ferreira will help them. No other officers need to be involved.'

She took the card up, tapped it on her desk, wheels turning behind her eyes.

'Do you believe the man who attacked Simone might be responsible for Corinne's murder?'

'It's a strong possibility but at this stage we're keeping an open mind,' Zigic said. 'There's every chance Corinne was attacked simply because she was a woman.'

'The price of passing,' Goddard said under her breath.

'How well did you know Corinne?'

'She was a highly active member of the community, very involved with helping women who were just starting on their journey. She'd faced a lot of resistance from her family – which is hardly unusual of course – but she was kind and patient and the newer girls needed that.' She smiled faintly. 'Corinne was something of a den mother, I suppose you could say.'

'So, no enemies you can think of?'

A glint of anger in her eyes and she dropped Zigic's card onto the table. 'Not among our community, Inspector.'

'We have to ask.'

'Of course. Because people are usually killed by someone they're close to.' She steepled her long fingers in front of her. 'Except for trans women, who are generally murdered by men so toxically repressed that their attraction to another man inevitably results in violence.'

Adams's serial rapist. Escalating to murder because he'd fixed his sights on a woman who turned out to still, technically, be a man. The argument Ferreira had tossed out in the crime-scene tent being echoed now by Evelyn Goddard. It was the obvious assumption, the statistically likely one, perhaps, but he wasn't prepared to narrow the case down yet.

'The circumstances of Corinne's murder suggest somebody familiar with her routine.'

'So, you believe she may have been stalked before she was killed?' Goddard's eyebrows lifted slightly.

'It's another possibility.'

She leaned back in her chair, sagging a little at the core. 'You have lots of possibilities and very few certainties.'

'Which is why we need your help, Ms Goddard. We need to speak to as many of Corinne's friends as we can, find out if she confided in any of them. If she mentioned being scared of someone, feeling watched.'

'Surely her girlfriend would be the best person to ask.'

'People often hide their fears from their partners,' Zigic said. 'They don't want to burden them. But they'll tell their friends.'

Goddard drew herself upright again. 'This sounds suspiciously like a request for our membership list.'

'We'll treat it with absolute discretion.'

'You won't,' she said. 'Because you're not having it.'

'Ms Goddard, please. There is an extremely dangerous man out there, targeting trans women. In all likelihood he will strike again.' Zigic thought of Simone Trent's broken face, Corinne Sawyer's. 'I've seen what he's capable of and I can tell you now, a man that angry, he won't stop. Not until we stop him.'

Evelyn Goddard spun away from the desk, the ball of her thumb caught between her teeth. They didn't need the membership list to track down Corinne's friends and she must know that. Phone records and emails were far more reliable. The only reason to request the list was so they could check the members for criminal records.

And to find out if she would cooperate.

She pointed at Ferreira. 'I'm trusting you with this. You've talked a good game in here, I hope you meant it.'

'I appreciate that,' Ferreira said. 'It goes no further than me.'

Evelyn Goddard opened her laptop and asked for an email address, reminded them that many of the people whose details she was passing on were living double lives, some of them still hiding from their partners and families, that they had a lot to lose and one wrong word could irrevocably alter the balance of their existence.

As she tapped at her keyboard she rattled off the statistics for suicides among trans women – forty-four per cent attempted, twelve per cent succeeded – made sure they realised that fear of not being accepted was a major motivator.

Ferreira's phone pinged as the email hit her inbox. 'Thank you, Ms Goddard.'

'Please don't make me regret it.'

'There is one other thing,' Zigic said. 'You knew about Simone Trent's attack?'

She nodded.

'And presumably you would know if any other members of your group had been attacked?'

Another nod. 'There is someone I think you should talk to, but I need to speak to him first. It's a very delicate situation and I'm not entirely sure he'll be happy to discuss it with you.'

'Was he attacked?'

'Yes, but – let me speak to him.'

They could compel him to talk, Zigic thought. If she gave them the name they could pull him in, sit him in an interview room and work on him until he spilled. But Zigic didn't want to do it that way. If the man hadn't come forward when the attack occurred he had a good reason for it, and, as much as he hated to admit it, Evelyn Goddard was their best chance of extracting any useful information from him.

She looked uneasy, mobile already in her hand, thumb hovering over the screen, but her gaze was settled in middle distance, regretting cooperating already, he thought, wondering if she'd been right to trust them.

Lives would be ruined, he knew. Secrets were going to come out. This was not a case that could be investigated in the shadows.

8

It was gone four when they pulled into the car park at Thorpe Wood Station, the sky beginning to darken. Zigic was sick of coming to work before first light, returning after sunset, never seeing his home in daylight. Winter had seemed longer this year, damp and miserable without even the consolation of snow, but he realised it was likely the sleepless nights which had stretched the last couple of months out for him.

He didn't remember feeling so worn down when the boys were babies and couldn't believe he'd got *that* much older since Stefan was born.

Anna was sailing through it of course, buoyed up by happy hormones and the quiet hours she enjoyed while he was at work, Emily saving her crying for when Daddy got home.

He prayed she'd behave herself tonight while Anna was out.

'Your press awaits,' Ferreira said, as she switched off the engine.

There were three vans parked up in front of the station, print reporters chatting away, a few new faces among them, all very young.

Dead women brought out hacks like nothing else. A dead trans woman . . . he wasn't sure how that would play. Would it bring more publicity to bear on them or less? He suspected the tabloids might start sniffing around, work the story from the cheapest, most sensational angle. The real pressure would come from the broadsheets though. He'd read the recent articles in the *Guardian*, their coverage of transphobic murders in America, and he knew those reporters must be itching for a home-grown one to cover.

The press pack stirred as he and Ferreira moved quickly up the station steps but fired off no questions yet. They'd save that for the lights and the cameras, when he was under pressure not to misspeak, hope to shock him into voicing an unwise reaction.

Ferreira split away from him in the corridor, headed in the direction of the canteen.

Hate Crimes was almost empty when he went up, only Wahlia in his seat, files stacked up and spilling onto Ferreira's side of their shared desk.

It felt wrong, the office being so quiet when they had a murder on the board, but he tried to see the air of calm as a good thing, meant they had space to think, analyse.

'Sir, bad news.' Wahlia rose creakily from his chair, stretched the hours he'd sat there out of his neck, eliciting a sick crunch. 'Someone's already named Corinne Sawyer on Twitter.'

'Do we know who?'

'Local news account. They just aggregate anything that's hashtagged.' He brought it up on-screen and Zigic gave it a cursory glance. 'They've only got a few hundred followers so it didn't make much impact initially, but it got picked up by a couple of trans bloggers and it's started to spread during the last hour.'

Zigic shrugged out of his parka and dumped it on an empty desk. 'What's the response been? Anything useful?'

'The usual Twitter mourning bullshit for the most part. A few people who seem to have known her but it's hard to tell. This crowd like to feel involved in a tragedy.'

'Anything less supportive?'

'Oh, yeah, we've got a lot of that already,' Wahlia said. 'It's like seventy per cent abuse and trolling right now, arseholes piling in from all angles. There's stuff we could prosecute but I'm guessing that's not a priority.'

'Not unless it escalates offline, no. Can you keep an eye on it?' Zigic asked. 'This isn't a priority but we need to be aware of

58

anyone who might have known her. And any threats that look linked.'

'I've given Gilraye a heads-up,' Wahlia said. 'Some press officer she is, supposed to be monitoring social media and she didn't know a damn thing about it.'

'She'll be finessing the narrative as we speak, I'm sure.'

Wahlia smiled. 'Only narrative she finesses is the one that keeps her in a job.'

It wasn't entirely fair on Gilraye but not that far off the mark. She was good at handling the local press, kept them in line during routine investigations, giving just enough to make them feel informed and inclined to report developments in a positive light. When it came to major incidents she wasn't so sharp though, seemed prone to grandstanding and flattery, especially when the nationals were involved.

'She dropped off your statement,' Wahlia said, hooking his thumb towards Zigic's office. 'You want a coffee? Fresh pot.'

'Yeah, thanks.' He went to retrieve the statement, frowning immediately at what she'd written.

Despite the message he'd sent earlier she'd insisted on referring to Corinne Sawyer as Colin, used the male pronoun throughout and gave no indication at all that she'd been living as a woman at the time of her murder.

'This is useless.' He screwed it up and threw it at the bin, missed by half a metre in his anger. 'Christ Almighty, what decade is she living in?'

Ferreira came into the office, glanced at the balled-up paper and shoved a plastic-wrapped muffin into his hand.

'It's stale and disgusting but you obviously need the sugar.'

She retrieved the statement, smoothed it out flat on her desk and Zigic read it again across her shoulder, angrily shoving bits of the banana muffin into his mouth, wondering how Gilraye could really have believed this was suitable. Prejudice aside, it didn't even help their case because it in no way reflected the reality of what had happened this morning at Ferry Meadows. Nobody could have seen a male jogger get attacked and murdered. There would be no useful witnesses to that non-existent crime.

'Do you want me to fix this?' Ferreira said finally.

'We need to, don't we?'

'Unless you want Evelyn Goddard and Sam Hyde and everyone else who cared about Corinne to form a lynch mob and storm the station, yeah.'

Wahlia handed Zigic a coffee, brow furrowed, reluctance in his step as he moved back round to his seat.

'What, Bobby?'

'She'll have run it past Riggott,' he said. 'Are you sure you want to change something he's already okay'd?'

He was right. No way had something this sensitive not passed across the DCS's desk already. Then again, the fallout from going onto the steps and reading it as written was bound to be worse than the carpeting he'd take for changing it.

Ferreira was waiting, pen already uncapped and poised, a rebellious glint in her eye.

'Better to apologise afterwards than ask permission and be refused.'

'Do it,' he said quickly, before he had chance to think better of it.

While she worked he went to the board behind DS Colleen Murray's desk. No word from her during the day and no sign of her now. There were witness statements spread across her keyboard, old ones, nothing to do with Corinne Sawyer's murder, but when he nudged the mouse he found a CCTV image frozen on the screen. A stretch of road he couldn't immediately identify, trees a green smudge in the background, a silver car with an indistinct driver. The timestamp at the bottom showed 7.27 this morning.

'Bobby, where's Colleen?'

'Said she was chasing down a lead.'

'When was this?'

'About two hours ago.'

Zigic dialled Murray's number and she picked up on the third ring.

'I'm on my way in, sir.' There was an unmistakable thrill in her voice. 'I'll be a couple of minutes.'

It was a quarter to five. He needed to be on the steps, in front of the press, in fifteen minutes but he wanted to hear what Murray had uncovered.

'How's it coming, Mel?' He pulled off his jumper as he made for his office.

'Nearly done.'

Quickly he changed into the navy-blue suit he kept hanging from the filing cabinet. White shirt, black tie. The trousers felt tighter around the waist than they had the last time he put them on.

What was it? A month ago?

He needed to start running again. Had been saying that to himself since before Christmas, but there was always some distraction. He'd find the time, he decided. No way was he giving in to the dad-bod.

'Mel?'

'Typing as fast as I can.' She glanced up from her screen as he re-emerged from the office. 'That jacket's looking a bit snug. Sir.'

'It must have shrunk on the hanger.'

'Yeah, that'll be it.'

Zigic went to the window, saw Colleen Murray shove through the press pack like a cannonball in a trouser suit and sensible boots.

A minute later she entered the office, out of breath, her face flushed from tackling the stairs.

'You found something,' Zigic said.

She dropped gratefully into her seat. 'Yes, sir. There's a bloke we were looking at for the attacks. Real piece of work. Problem is his girlfriend keeps alibiing him.'

'What have you got on him?'

'History,' she said. 'He's got a record of violence against women going right back to his late teens, assault, rape, kidnap. Domestic violence off the scale but the women keep withdrawing their complaints, deciding they were to blame. You know the routine.'

'He threatens them?'

She nodded.

'Adams thinks that's enough to put him in the frame?'

'We have him working near the site of the first attack,' she said. 'Second victim was an ex-girlfriend of one of his cousins, she thought it might have been him but couldn't say for certain. Adams reckons if we can show her enough to guarantee a verdict she'll ID him.'

'You can never guarantee a rape verdict,' Ferreira said.

'And he was at Ferry Meadows this morning?' Zigic asked.

'Yes, sir. I've found him arriving just before seven, leaving half an hour later, just the right amount of time for him to murder Corinne Sawyer. She's not his type but I want to work on the link some more.'

'Lee Walton?' Zigic asked, remembering Riggott mentioning the name.

'Him.' Colleen nodded to his photo on the board.

It showed a bald, heavyset man with a square face too big for his features. Nothing remarkable about him, bland and ordinary, the kind of face you wouldn't notice in a crowd, wouldn't be able to describe in any detail later if you did. Perfect predator camouflage.

'I've been round his regular haunts,' she said. 'No sign of him. Girlfriend was at home but she wouldn't let me in. Best guess is he's put the fist to her again and she knows I'll try to get her down here to press charges.' She shook her head despairingly. 'Soft mare hasn't got the sense she was born with.'

Across the office the printer whirred into life, Zigic's statement done. He was already a minute late.

'Your bloke has a type,' Ferreira reminded her. 'We know Corinne isn't it.'

Murray shrugged one shoulder. 'Him murdering her doesn't fit either, but if Walton was within a mile of a woman who stubbed her toe I'd want to question him.'

Zigic took the statement out of the printer, scanned it quickly, happy with the rewrite. He folded the page so it felt more substantial.

'Alright, Colleen. Debrief Adams on this, he wants keeping up to speed.' She nodded curtly, no intention of doing anything but update Adams, he guessed. 'But tomorrow morning, first thing, I need you at Ferry Meadows with Mel. Best that you do it, just in case it is linked to your case. You'll know what faces to look for.'

'Yes, sir. Of course.'

'Right.' His fingers kept smoothing the sharp crease in the paper and he realised he was more nervous than he should be. Not because of the cameras or the questions, but because this was the first time in his career he'd disregarded an approved statement on a matter of principle.

He took a deep breath.

'It'll be fine,' Ferreira said.

On the way down, through the stairwell and past CID, he told himself once again that this was the right thing to do. Morally and tactically. He didn't want Sam Hyde to see her dead girlfriend referred to as a man, didn't want Evelyn Goddard to turn against them just as they were beginning to win her trust.

Out on the steps a fine raining was falling, like a shower of sparks as it passed through the intensity of the arc lights. Nicola Gilraye had done her best to keep the waiting press calm but there were low murmurs as he stepped out to face them and she shot him a hard look when she turned away, giving him the floor.

'Ladies and gentlemen, thank you for coming.' He made his voice strong and sure, stilled the nerves fluttering in his gut. 'At approximately seven fifty this morning the body of a woman was discovered at Ferry Meadows Country Park . . .'

9

Lily could hear the television playing in the kitchen, voices coming up through her bedroom floor. It made a change from the vacuum cleaner, which Nina had been chasing around the house for the last hour. Probably the second time she'd done it today, since she always started her top-to-bottom 'cleanse' as soon as she got up. Lily couldn't remember a single morning that she hadn't woken up to the smell of cleaning fluid.

Nina had been doing the kitchen floor when she got home from school. Red-faced from the exertion, ragged-looking, and Lily knew there was something wrong straight away. She'd put the steam cleaner down without turning it off and rushed across the gleaming floor, threw her arms around Lily's neck in a move so unexpected she froze, half choked.

'Corinne's dead.'

Nina whispered it in her ear as she hugged her and Lily didn't want to believe it but Nina kept talking, saying it was true, she was sorry, she knew how hard this was, she felt it too.

But she didn't feel it, Lily realised now, lying on her bed staring up at the ceiling. Nina was just acting out the role she thought she should. So she had held Lily upright and guided her to a seat, stroked her hair while she sat mutely shocked and shivering. Going through the motions.

Lily had seen the police cars this morning as she waited in the bus shelter for Jack's sister to drop him off, three or four of them heading into Ferry Meadows, and all she did was turn away from the road in case one of them saw that she was smoking and decided to pull over and be a fascist dick about it.

Now she knew why they had been there and she couldn't believe she hadn't felt it. Her mum, dead, so close to her. Dead badly. Violently. Murdered. And she'd felt nothing but relief that they'd kept driving.

Nina had known within hours but she let her stay at school, while the police walked around her mother's corpse, prodded it and poked it and photographed it, let her go on talking stupid shit with her friends while they loaded the murdered body of her mother into an ambulance or whatever they used and took it away. She'd eaten her lunch and gone to French and handed over a fake sick note to get out of games and all the time her mother was dead and Nina knew and she did nothing. Didn't call the school to send her home. Didn't come and collect her.

She had an excuse, of course.

'I didn't know how to tell you,' she'd said. 'It's the only thing I've thought about since Sam called this morning and I just couldn't find the right words.' Then she'd wiped her eyes even though Lily didn't see any tears. 'I thought I'd let you have a few more hours of normality, that seemed the kindest thing to do.'

As if she cared about kindnesses.

For a second Lily thought she was going to cry, felt her nose tingle, her eyes begin to sting. But the tears didn't come.

Why couldn't she cry?

She felt the loss right there in her chest, a heavy black lump too big for her ribcage to contain. Something pulsing and aching, weighing her down so completely that she couldn't move from her bed.

Distantly, a smarter, more in control part of her said she was in shock. And she guessed it was right. That voice usually had all the answers. On an intellectual level she knew her mother was gone, but her emotions hadn't caught up yet.

Only her anger was in play, shooting off in new directions, hitting Nina – for so many reasons – the police who would have joked over her mother's body and all the grief tourists who would come out to gawp, put flowers where she died and wait around for a camera crew who'd film them while they said how awful it was, how you don't expect something like that to happen somewhere like this.

She wasn't ready to think about the person who killed her yet. Was keeping that rage in a box for now. It was too massive to open. It was going to consume her.

Lily took her mobile out of her pocket, started going through the photographs she had of them together. The last lot had been taken at Christmas, and she thought that should hurt more, but it couldn't break through the fog.

Mum and her the last time they went shopping, photos they'd taken of each other in the changing room of Topshop in Cambridge, Lily in the suede jacket she didn't think suited her, Mum in a black leather pencil skirt, hands on her hips, looking like a Hollywood siren. They'd bought so much stuff it had taken four bags to hold it. Then on to Jamie's Italian for lunch, more photos they'd asked the waiter to take and he'd flirted with Mum but she'd said it was only to get a bigger tip. She'd been flattered though, Lily could see it in how she'd tried to stop her smile spreading too wide.

That thudding, black lump in her chest expanded a little more, pushing at her ribs, crushing her lungs, and she took a couple of shallow breaths which threatened to turn into sobs but didn't and still she couldn't cry.

Lily reached under her bed and pulled out the box where she hid her cigarettes. She wanted a joint but she couldn't get any weed. She went to the window where her drawing table sat, covered in half-finished sketches; stuff for art class and tattoo designs she was working on for her portfolio.

There was one she'd done for Mum, an elegant black swan encircled by a ring of dainty stars, perfect for the spot she'd chosen on the inside of her wrist.

She opened the window and leaned out of it to smoke, watching the traffic trundle by on Oundle Road. She'd spent hours at this window when she was little, waiting for her dad to come home, worrying when it got late, convinced he'd had an accident. Sometimes she'd work herself up into such a frenzy she'd cry and beg Nina to go out looking for him.

Then finally the electric gates would open and in he'd come. And some days Dad would get out of the truck and some days Mum but she didn't see the difference. Couldn't understand why it made Nina and Harry so angry.

It was the same person underneath. Who loved her and believed in her, who was happy for her to be whatever she wanted, because Mum understood that the worst thing you could do with your life was limit its scope and potential in some vain attempt to fit in.

A single tear ran down her face and Lily flicked her cigarette out of the window, braced herself for the floodgates.

But they didn't open. It was just the cold, making her eyes water.

Standing at her draught board she looked at the swan design and there it was, a little stab to her heart, a sliver of pain finding its way through the numbness. She wished Mum had had the tattoo, that no matter where she was now, what happened to her next, there would be some small evidence of how much Lily loved her stamped indelibly on her skin.

A light fist rapped on her door and Nina came in before she could tell her not to, a tray balanced on her spindly forearm.

'I thought you might be hungry.'

'I'm not,' Lily said, eyeing the rye bread toast she'd brought up with her, a couple of oat biscuits and a glass of juice.

Even if she was hungry she wouldn't want that. She wanted the kind of 'toxic crap' Nina wouldn't have in the house any more. Now it all had to be 'clean' food, no refined sugar, no simple carbohydrates, everything organic. Another way of exercising her control, and Lily wasn't sure if Nina even knew why she was doing it. If she'd noticed how this drive towards perfect health coincided with Mum leaving her.

It was as sad as it was infuriating and on some level Lily pitied her. She couldn't move on, not completely, not even now she was with Brynn. A part of her still wanted Dad but not enough to accept Corinne.

'You really should try and eat something.' Nina set the tray down on the dressing table, immediately started to tidy the surface around it.

'For God's sake, will you stop touching my stuff!'

Nina stopped, giving her a wounded look.

Lily dropped onto the stool in front of her draught board, sensing that this might be a long lecture, but Nina didn't seem to have the stomach for it tonight.

She went over to the bed, straightened out the covers before she sat down, knees pressed tight together, hands clasped. Had she actually been crying? The skin around her eyes was puffy and her nose was pink.

'I think we should talk about what happened,' she said. 'It isn't healthy for you staying up here brooding.'

'What do you suggest?' Lily asked. 'Maybe we should all sit down together and go through the family photographs? Talk about the good times you and Mum had.'

Nina pursed her lips; she hated it when Lily called her Mum. Thought that title should be reserved exclusively for her, whether she deserved it or not. The first time Lily called her Nina she looked like she'd been stabbed. Right through the heart.

Maybe she thought she could go back to being Mum again now.

'Your father and I had lots of good times,' she said. 'From the second I met Colin I knew he was the man I wanted to spend the rest of my life with.' Nina sniffed. 'And I wasn't a romantic, I thought all of that stuff was rubbish. But when I saw him in that shop . . .'

Lily had heard it all before, a meet-cute straight out of a cheesy romcom that the pair of them used to tell to anyone who'd listen. Dad in the glassware section of some long-gone department store looking for an anniversary gift for Brynn's parents. He'd picked up a piece of lead crystal and promptly dropped it. He'd had no intention of buying it, couldn't have afforded to, but he'd liked its lines, wanted to turn it into the light. Nina had been watching him across the low shelves, thinking how out of place he looked and how handsome he was too. She'd watched as a shop assistant ignored his apologies and insisted customers had to pay for breakages, saw him becoming more flustered until he took out his wallet and showed the woman just how little cash he had on him. She didn't usually approach strange men in shops, not even handsome ones, but something about his exasperation drew her along the aisle towards him. She tiptoed around the shattered pieces of the vase, fumbling for her purse, and offered to pay for the breakage if he would take her out for a drink.

Nina was smiling wistfully now.

'We were happy, Lily. It might not seem that way to you because by the time you were old enough to notice he'd already moved away from me. But it doesn't mean I don't care. And it doesn't mean I'm not just as devastated by his death as you are.'

'Her death,' Lily snapped. 'Why can't you say that?'

A flush crept up Nina's cheeks but she didn't react. That was her all over, completely repressed, contained. No wonder Mum needed to escape. How could you be with someone who guarded every reaction from you?

Except Lily knew she hadn't. She'd heard the arguments they had, heard Nina scream and rage in a voice too large for her body, like the fury bloated her and swelled until she had to release it.

They did the responsible thing. Never fought in front of the kids, but there was no hiding anything in this house and every whisper in the open-plan living room carried upstairs to the furthest corners.

'Have the police talked to you yet?' Lily asked.

Nina wrapped her arms around herself. 'They don't seem to know anything very much.'

Lily looked back across her shoulder at the room reflected in the broad window. The two of them looked closer together, foreshortened there in the glass, but they would never be that close in reality.

'It'll be random,' Nina said, eyes as blank as the wall she was staring at. 'Women get attacked at random all of the time.'

It was only later, when Nina had left, taking the tray with her, returning to whatever distraction she was going to use to get through the rest of the evening, that Lily realised how hopeful she'd sounded about the possibility of some stranger murdering Mum.

And she wondered what the police had told her, if maybe they'd questioned her, because out of all the people on this planet nobody hated Mum more than Nina.

10

The call came while Ferreira was stuck in traffic over the railway bridge; Evelyn Goddard with a name she admitted was fake and a location on the edge of the city which she was to head for straight away, the man already waiting for her.

'He won't go to the police station, so don't even ask him,' she said. 'And go alone. It's taken me the better part of two hours to convince him to talk to you. Just you, do you understand? He won't speak to a man about this.'

'How will I recognise him?' Ferreira asked, already eyeing the road ahead of her, trying to decide if she could get away with pulling a swift three-point turn.

'I'm sending you a phone number.'

Goddard rang off before Ferreira could thank her and a few seconds later the message came through. A fake name and a number which was likely untraceable; it should have concerned her. In any other context it would have made her suspicious of the man but in this case the air of secrecy felt like a guarantee of authenticity.

He was protecting himself because he was scared and if he was scared it was because he knew something important.

As she walked into the cavernous atrium Ferreira realised it would afford them greater privacy than some out-of-the-way pub or lay-by. A sprawling service station on the side of the A1, bustling at this time of evening with commuters and workers heading home; high churn, low-attention spans.

She made a slow circuit of the central seating area, passing half a dozen fast-food outlets, all packed with people queuing in

72

various states of agitation, the smell of fried chicken and toasted bread and salty, sour noodles making her stomach rumble. She'd somehow got through the day on nothing but coffee and chocolate bars from the vending machine and it took every ounce of willpower she had not to commandeer some chips from the man who crossed her path, hurrying towards a table with a family bucket hugged to his chest.

There were lots of lone men in there. Eating with joyless determination, closed off from the babble of voices and piped eighties pop playing too loud and tinny; a suicide soundtrack.

She scanned the tables but saw no one she thought might be her man. Then again, what was she looking for? Someone who'd look good as a woman, she realised. And it was a stupid assumption.

One bloke was staring at her and she held his gaze until he looked away, then took out her phone and dialled the number.

'Hello?'

'Where are you?'

'In Costa,' he said. 'I can see you.'

As she walked towards the cafe she turned on her phone's voice recorder – no promises made to Evelyn Goddard about that – and slipped it into her jacket pocket.

He sat cowed on the banquette along the back wall, trying to make himself invisible, but even sitting down she could see he was a lean, long-limbed guy, with thick black hair and a face which struck her immediately as beautiful. Not a word she'd often found use for when it came to men, but he was, and it made him conspicuous whether he wanted to be or not.

He'd hardly chosen the best seat for intrigue either. Eyes out, facing the queue for the counter and the plate-glass front which everyone who entered the building walked past. He wasn't made for informing.

'Aadesh?'

'Yes, please, sit down, people are looking at us.'

'Nobody's looking at us,' she said reassuringly, as she took the seat opposite him. 'They're all knackered and far too self-obsessed to even notice me and you.'

Behind her a woman was talking loudly on her mobile and it distracted Aadesh for a few seconds, the tight, high pitch of her voice as she laid into whoever was on the other end.

'I appreciate you agreeing to talk to me,' Ferreira said, leaning on the table as casually as she could, wanting to get close enough that he could whisper if he felt the need. 'Did Evelyn tell you what happened?'

He nodded.

'How well did you know Corinne?'

'Not very well at all. I'd met her a few times, but we weren't friends.'

Finally he lifted his eyes from the large cup of green tea he was holding on to like it was the only thing anchoring him and looked straight at her. He had pretty eyes, long-lashed and very dark, the skin around them perfectly smooth and unlined. He was younger than she'd thought, mid-twenties, but on the side of his face she noticed a spray of tiny dents dimpling his skin, too regular in size for acne scars.

Aadesh touched his fingers to them self-consciously and Ferreira apologised. He blinked slowly, dropped his hand.

'Did he do that to you?' she asked.

'Yes.'

Pavement grit, she thought, driven into his skin as he fell, and the thought of those tiny, hard pieces puncturing his skin made her calves sting. A sympathy reaction she pushed away quickly.

'You think the man who – you think he murdered Corinne?'

'There's a strong possibility. My job—' Ferreira stopped as a woman approached the next table to clear the cups left behind by its previous occupants. 'My job right now is to try and gather as much information as possible about any earlier attacks.'

74

'I'll tell you everything I can,' he said. 'But I didn't see him.'

She tried not to let her disappointment show. 'That's all I'm asking for, Aadesh. Whatever you remember.'

His shoulders straightened. 'I can't go to court. Did Evelyn tell you that? It's completely out of the question.'

'I won't ask you to do anything you're not comfortable with.'

He didn't looked comfortable, was becoming more agitated by the second. Ferreira could feel a clock ticking on this interview already and as she went to speak he reached into his pocket for his mobile, brought it out pulsing with an incoming call. His thumb hovered between call and reject, a young woman's smiling face on the screen.

'Your wife?' Ferreira asked.

'Not yet. We're getting married next year, when she's finished studying.' The phone kept vibrating in his hand but he couldn't reject her call and with each rumble she could see him becoming more agitated, maybe wondering how he would explain this absence, what excuse he would give for not picking up.

Finally it stopped but the silence did nothing to calm him.

She'd hoped to ease into the worst of it, take some time to build up a rapport with him, let him settle. But that wouldn't be happening.

'Can you tell me when the incident occurred?'

'Last December,' he said. 'No, sorry, the December before last. 2014. The 4th.'

'Okay. What time?'

'It was late.' He stared into his tea, a thin film forming on it. 'I'd been drinking . . . I, it was gone midnight. It was probably much later.'

Ferreira wondered if his vagueness was real or if it was an attempt to make his account seem too weak to stand up in court. He'd get ripped to shreds by any halfway competent defence barrister.

'You'd been out,' she said. 'Where?'

'The Meadham.'

Of course.

'I decided to walk home,' he said, shaking his head. 'It was stupid of me. I should have taken a taxi but I only lived ten minutes away.'

Going through the same process of accepting blame that every attacked woman Ferreira had ever spoken to experienced. I should have done this, I shouldn't have done that.

'It wasn't your fault,' she told him, trying and failing to catch his eye. 'None of this was your fault.'

'I took the underpass.' He spat the words out like a curse. 'I knew there was someone behind me but I kept walking. I didn't think. I'd taken that underpass dozens of times and nothing happened.'

'When you were—' What was term Zac Bentley had used? 'When you were *en femme*?'

'No.' He met her gaze then. 'That was the first time.'

Internally he'd still been male, Ferreira thought, he didn't make the calculations every woman made when she picked her route home. A man could walk through a badly lit underpass and expect to come out the other side perfectly safe. He'd done it before and wouldn't have expected it to be different just because he was dressed as a woman.

'When did you realise someone was following you?'

His brow furrowed. 'I can't remember very much of what happened. The doctor said that's not unusual with head trauma, the memory loss.'

'What can you remember?'

He let out a wobbly breath and hunched over the table. Ferreira caught the scent of sweat, acidic through the remnants of his aftershave; fear as he relived the disjointed moments.

'He was heavy,' Aadesh said, voice thickening. 'He was on top of me. He knocked me down from behind. I never saw his face but he was a big man. I can remember his teeth . . .'

He was back in the underpass, laid flat, helpless.

'I could feel his teeth on my ear.'

'Did he bite you?'

'No, he was talking, whispering in my ear. He called me a freak. He said I was disgusting.' Aadesh pressed his lips together, struggling to remain still, and Ferreira prepared herself to go after him if he bolted.

Unthinkingly she reached across the table to pat his hand, the way she would with another woman, and he snatched it away from her. His eyes were glistening under the soft lights, huge and haunted.

He started talking again, nervously, stumbling over his words and repeating himself, not giving her a chance to interrupt. He told her how he'd come to in a pool of his own blood, one eye swollen shut, teeth broken, his face throbbing from the impact with the ground. He remembered walking home across the railway bridge, shrinking every time a car's headlights washed over him, feeling exposed and vulnerable even though the worst thing that could happen already had.

When he got home he called Evelyn Goddard, then passed out in his hallway again for a time, overwhelmed by shock and pain. He didn't want to go to hospital but she made him. Wouldn't go there dressed as a woman.

Evelyn had cleaned the make-up from his face, very carefully, undressed him and put him in men's clothes again, drove him to the hospital and, at his insistence, dropped him at A&E. He wouldn't let her go in with him, knew she wouldn't support the lies he was going to tell the doctors there. He said it was a robbery. Claimed his phone and wallet had been stolen. They called the police who took a statement but it got swallowed up in the system, just as he'd hoped. Without a description they couldn't do anything.

He'd spoken for ten minutes and Ferreira heard nothing which would help her catch the man responsible, a lot which sounded like an attempt to overwhelm her with details so she would forgot the only question she needed an answer to.

'I'm sorry, Aadesh, but I have to ask this – was there any sexual element in your assault?'

He shook his head.

'Do you think he thought you were a woman?'

Aadesh smiled grimly. 'He knew I wasn't.'

'Why do you say that?'

'He ripped my wig off.'

The same as in Simone Trent's attack. The same man attacked both of them and maybe there were more victims out there yet, too scared to come forward. Ones who might have seen the man's face.

II

Zigic lay on the bed, Emily on his chest, playing with his beard. She'd become fascinated with it during the last few days, which had led to him losing several little fistfuls of bristles from under his chin. He was going to have to start wearing it shorter or risk going bald in patches as her inquisitiveness continued.

Across the room Anna was standing at the open wardrobe trying to choose an outfit. She had a pair of tights on already and knee-high boots, but the foot of the bed was scattered with garments she'd deemed 'wrong' in a number of unspecified ways.

'You'll look great whatever you put on,' he said.

Her answer stayed under her breath and he decided to talk to Emily instead.

'You're going to be a very good girl for Daddy, aren't you? Because Daddy has had a long and very tiring day and he needs to watch some rubbish television and maybe even have some sleep.'

'Don't make her feel guilty,' Anna said, pulling another wrap dress out of the wardrobe. 'She understands what you're saying.'

Zigic was pretty sure all Emily understood right now was the tone of his voice and the expression on his face but he knew better than to argue. For all her talk of finally having a much needed night out with the girls Anna didn't seem to be relishing the prospect.

'You can always cancel,' he said.

'I don't want to cancel.' She slipped the dress on and cinched it around her waist, turned one way and then the other in the mirrored door. Then she sagged suddenly and swore to herself. 'Everything looks shit.'

'Earmuffs!' Zigic wrapped his hands around Emily's ears quickly, trying to make a joke of it, but Anna wasn't playing.

He picked Emily up and put her in her cot.

Anna stared at herself in the mirror, hand clamped over her mouth, and he knew that pose, knew that next came the frustrated tears and the recriminations, complaints about the havoc Emily had wreaked on her body. The mad thing was he couldn't see it even when she insisted on giving him the full damage report. She felt just the same under his hands.

'Come on, you know you'll have a great time.' He slipped his arms around her, kissed the back of her neck. 'Drink some wine, flirt with some waiters—'

'Who's going to flirt with me? I'm a state.'

'You're beautiful.'

'You have to say that.'

'I will flirt you right out of that dress in a minute flat,' he said, lips grazing her warm, perfumed skin. 'But you have to keep the boots on.'

A car horn sounded outside the house. Anna forced a smile, meeting his eyes in the mirror, a sadness there which made his chest ache.

'It'll look fine with a jacket,' she said.

She threw her things into her handbag then went down into the living room where the boys were watching cartoons, kissed them both and told them to behave themselves while she was out.

Zigic grabbed her hand as she was leaving, pulled her back for a slow, deep kiss, provoking another long blast on the car horn and catcalls from her friends.

'Make sure you're filthy drunk when you get home.'

He fell back against the door, the crashing sound of cartoon violence filtering out into the hallway, as upstairs Emily started to cry, an operatic wail which made him briefly consider chasing down the car and begging Anna to come home.

'Emily's crying,' the boys shouted in unison.

Zigic rubbed his face, eyes dry and gritty.

Milan came into the hall. 'Dad. Emily. She's crying again.'

'Thanks, buddy. I've got it.'

'She's probably pooped.'

'There's a very good chance of it, yes.'

But when he checked he found her clean and dry. Of course it wouldn't be something as easy as a nappy change. She'd been fed already, winded, puked and cleaned up again, so she wasn't hungry. He took her to the window and showed her the moon rising above the back garden. She squirmed and bawled, tugged angrily at his beard again, like she couldn't believe this was the best idea he'd got to soothe her with.

Separation anxiety, he thought, although it seemed too early for that. He wondered if it was him. If he'd been working so many hours she hadn't formed the necessary attachment to him. Didn't she feel comforted by him? Wasn't his presence enough to make her feel safe?

He cradled her head and sang to her, self-consciously and out of tune, but slowly the bawling became a series of ever briefer cries, then grizzly mews and finally she stopped, red-faced but tired enough for him to put her down.

He crashed out on the bed, turned towards the cot to keep an eye on her, every muscle in his body giving up at once, but his brain kept buzzing. He thought of all the versions of Corinne they'd been given today and which if any were really her, how they could tease the truth of her from the conflicting stories; the bad husband turned worse wife, the den mother, the party animal, the woman finally finding herself with someone new.

The truth was in there, the slim thread of a motive too, and he turned those conversations around in his head, the words giving way to fleeting impressions which kept drifting away from him, the curl of an eyelash, a length of white cord, broken bones and suppressed tears and a knitted hat lying among dead leaves.

81

When he woke up again the house was silent and a sudden panic seized him. He stood so sharply his head spun.

Downstairs the living room was lit up, the television tuned to a dead channel. It was almost ten o'clock. Hours past the boys' bedtime.

Zigic ran back upstairs to their room, knowing they should be there, that logically nothing could have happened to them without him hearing it, but some small part of him, the copper who had sat with parents whose children were snatched or died because they 'only looked away for a minute', wouldn't believe it until he saw them safe and well.

He sighed with relief when he opened the bedroom door, found them both tucked up in bed, Stefan snoring, Milan hidden under a tented duvet, a torch burning as he read.

'I'm going to sleep,' Milan said, clicking off the torch.

Zigic took it from him, placed it on the side table along with his book.

'Have you brushed your teeth?'

'Yes. I made Stefan do his too. He's very difficult.' Sounding just like his mother.

'Good thing one of you's responsible,' Zigic said, smiling.

In the kitchen, rifling the fridge for something to eat, he considered the benefits of letting Milan do the parenting while Anna was out. He was sensible, mature for his age, managed to stay awake until 10 p.m. So far he was winning.

He made a sandwich and took it into the living room, switched on the news and immediately changed the channel, found a suitably soporific documentary on BBC4, some guy in chinos wandering around an art gallery, speaking in hushed tones. There was a lot of gilding, doe-eyed madonnas and mutilated saints.

Skinned, gouged, flayed – it was about humiliation as much as inflicting pain, he thought.

The images from Simon Trent's file came back to him. The red marks on his scalp where his attacker had ripped off his wig. So much damage done by that point. His face comprehensively beaten. Why that final act if not to humiliate him? A kind of unmasking.

This is what you really are – a man.

Zigic's mobile began to ring and he dug it out from between the sofa cushions; Ferreira on the display.

'What is it, Mel?'

'Evelyn Goddard's on *Newsnight*,' she said.

He switched over to BBC2, the presenter talking to a pair of grey-haired men, a war zone frozen on the screens surrounding them.

'That's not Evelyn Goddard,' he said.

'She's on later, they trailed it at the beginning. How the hell did she get this set up so fast?'

Zigic turned the sound down. 'She's an operator, obviously.'

'This is going to look bad on us. National press already.' Ferreira groaned. 'She's going to throw us to the dogs.'

He told her to calm down, wondering how much she'd had to drink. A slight slur to her words.

'Whatever Goddard says, we do our job. Catch the killer.'

'I thought your statement would buy us some goodwill,' Ferreira said. 'So much for that idea.'

He'd hoped the same and it surprised him how disappointed he felt. He'd done the right thing by Goddard and her people and yet it hadn't been enough. Defending himself to Riggott afterwards his main argument had been about winning the support of the trans community and the DCS accepted the logic of it, although he'd huffed and sworn for awhile, a performance demanded by his senior status. Riggott would wear it as long as the strategy worked. Now Zigic had to face the possibility that he'd misjudged the situation.

'What happened with the previous victim she put you on to?'

As he listened he saw a pattern emerging; the link with the Meadham and the charity, the attack that came from behind, no possibility of identification once again.

'Then he pulled his wig off.'

'Just like Simon Trent.'

'Got to be the same guy, hasn't it?'

'Goddard must have known that when she put us on to him,' Zigic said. 'She knew about Simon Trent, she knew the details of this attack because she was there straight afterwards.'

'We don't know how much Trent told her.' There was the sound of a lighter striking at the other end. 'No, she's got an axe to grind. If she knew this was a serial attacker when Trent was assaulted she'd have jumped on it back then.'

It made sense. Goddard was looking for a way to raise the profile of transphobic hate crimes and if she'd made the link back in December 2014 she would have used it, surely. Or maybe she didn't think those attacks were bad enough to stir up the anger she needed to harness. Only a murder could do that.

'Here she comes,' Ferreira said.

On-screen Evelyn Goddard sat demurely in another immaculate skirt suit, poised under the studio lights, as the interviewer spoke.

'*With the broadly positive public reaction to recent high-profile transitions, such as the former Olympic athlete Caitlyn Jenner and, in the UK, boxing promoter Kellie Maloney, you'd be forgiven for thinking that trans women were winning the battle against prejudice.*

'*But as police in Peterborough have today confirmed that the murder of a local trans woman is being treated as a hate crime, I'm joined by veteran activist and former Royal Navy commander Evelyn Goddard, to discuss the rising problem of transphobic violence.*'

'Navy,' Ferreira said. 'That explains a lot. She's got that alpha vibe.'

For five minutes Goddard held the floor, the interviewer doing no more than prompting her through a discussion of day-to-day transphobia, the micro-aggressions and verbal assaults, casual prejudice and shaming, and how those things could so easily build into violence. The steady rate of murders in America leading them back, finally, to Corinne Sawyer.

'Corinne's murder is not an isolated case,' Evelyn said.

She wasn't seriously going to flag the other assaults, Zigic thought, stomach lurching at the prospect.

'At Trans Sisters we receive hundreds of calls every week from women who have suffered violence related directly to their trans status. These women will not go to the authorities for a variety of reasons, sometimes because the perpetrator is a family member or partner, very often it's shame which stops them reporting it, but the defining factor is a distrust of the police. They simply don't believe they will be treated with care or respect.'

Ferreira swore down the phone, not the word Zigic would have used but the sentiment was the same.

'But the police are treating this as a hate crime,' the interviewer said.

'I've spoken to the investigating officers today and I believe in this case they will act properly, but this is one police force. The attitude of other forces around the country isn't so enlightened. And, as a result of their prejudice, trans people are being failed. They are being attacked and even murdered and in many cases the officers involved refuse to even acknowledge their chosen gender. Investigating their complaints within the framework of transphobia simply isn't considered.'

The interviewer thanked her, cutting her off as she took another breath, insisting that they were unfortunately out of time.

'Could have been worse,' Ferreira said. 'She seems to like us.'

'She's going to use us,' Zigic told her, feeling his mobile growing hot against his ear. 'She needs this to be a transphobic attack, that's why she brought up Simon Trent and that's why she talked Aadesh into meeting with you. She wants Corinne's murder to serve her agenda.'

Ferreira sighed. 'The link's there. This is a hate crime. Whatever she wants to get out of it it's irrelevant.'

'She gave us the link, Mel.'

'No, we had it.'

'We've got nothing,' he said, switching off the TV. 'Corinne's murder remains separate from the attacks until we have incontrovertible proof of a link.'

There was water running at her end, a cupboard door opening, and he pictured her in her new flat, wondered if she was alone or if whoever she'd been with tonight was already gone. If, maybe, she was waiting for Zac Bentley to finish up at the club. He'd hoped moving into her own place would settle her down but she seemed as erratic as ever.

'I want to talk to Simon Trent,' she said. 'If there's a link it lies with him.'

'He won't tell you anything. Not after all this time.'

'He'll tell me.' She slammed the door. 'Once I make him understand what's at stake.'

12

It was important to be kind to yourself, she thought, as she lit the candles which ringed the bathtub, two dozen tea lights in gold-foil holders and the special one she set between the taps, jasmine-scented and slow-burning. She closed her eyes and took a moment to inhale, thinking of delicate white flowers blooming at night when nobody would see them.

Instinctively she turned towards the space above the sink where the mirror used to be. It was just blank wall now, four screw holes marking the dimensions of her lost reflection. She had no need for that any more. No desire to see herself how other people had seen her.

She knew what she was.

And what she wasn't.

How cruel the world could be if you showed it your true face.

She pushed the thought away, focusing on the jasmine scent and the music coming out of the speakers in the bedroom, humming along to Melody Gardot, not quite managing to reach the high notes herself. Her own singing voice was lower and husky. She'd been told it was sexy, had character and depth, told there was a yearning quality to it.

She slipped off her cotton dressing gown and threw it onto the bed, avoided looking down at her naked body as she returned to the en suite where the air was steamy and sweet-smelling. The extractor fan had packed up weeks ago but she didn't want some plumber coming in here to fix it. This was her special place, her perfect little sanctuary.

With the lights off the room glowed, candle flames flickering, picking out the glimmers of gold in the tiled walls, and she closed her eyes as she lowered herself into the bath, bubbles breaking under her weight, re-forming over her as she sank back into the water, just the points of her knees showing.

The music played on and she tried to lose herself in it; Nina Simone now, a voice she could almost match, and she sang the words she didn't feel. She would have jumped to the next track but that meant getting out of the bath and she didn't want to have to look at herself again, so she kept singing, telling herself it was a performance like all the others she enacted.

That was her life. One lie after another. Speak like someone else, move like someone else, watch the tilt of her head and the angle of her wrists and the length of her stride, so many small pauses before she could answer the most basic question in case she gave herself away.

It was grinding her down but there was no other option.

The lie was necessary. It would keep her safe.

It hadn't kept Corinne safe, though, and she was living it more convincingly than any of them, with her girlish figure and unisex face. Not to mention all her money.

Nothing was too good for Corinne. She'd had it all, the great new tits and the electrolysis to smooth her skin, chemical peels and eye lifts, had her jaw slimmed and her nose completely rebuilt, the tracheal shave to remove that telltale bump.

Nina Simone gave way to Julie London and she knew this was the wrong playlist for the evening. More stinging words floating across the room. No combing of hair or fixing of make-up for her. Not after what happened.

Fucking Corinne. She didn't know how lucky she was.

The water was beginning to cool but she felt a terrible heat in her limbs, the anger at her core refusing to abate, violent enough that if she didn't smother it it would burn her alive.

88

For the first time in months she found herself replaying that night, remembering every stinging detail; the exact sound her heels made as they struck the pavement, moving faster, trying to get away, then the snap as her stiletto broke and the smell of piss rising from the cobbles as she went down.

A few tears rolled down her cheeks into the water, tainting it.

She climbed out and emptied the bath, towelled off briskly, rubbing her skin raw, disgusted by the sight of herself, all knuckles and knees and big, ugly feet. No wonder he went after her. Any idiot could see what she was.

Not in here though, she told herself, as she went into the bedroom. Here she was safe, she was as beautiful as she wanted to be. She took a bottle of rose otto body lotion from the dressing table, slathered it over her skin, appreciating the soft sheen it left across her shins, how it accentuated the shape of her thighs. This was the real her, even if nobody else saw it.

She pulled on a pair of small firm knickers, not looking down as she tucked everything away, smoothing her palm over the flesh-toned swell of her pudenda. A second pair went over the top, *café au lait* silk, edged with black.

The breast forms next, high and proud. A C cup, a little smaller than her figure could take but she'd tried larger and found she preferred these, a scant handful, model proportions.

So many girls went over the top, E cups, F cups, doing themselves up like the cheapest of whores and she knew what it was about. They were still men in their heads, couldn't shake that masculine urge for grotesque, porn-star bodies.

They were frauds and yet nobody else seemed to realise.

She'd seen it so often. Girls who'd been dressing up for ten or twenty years but still they carried themselves like men. Even the pretty ones sometimes. The ones who passed with ease, they remained men underneath, but because they looked right nobody questioned their commitment.

Corinne was a classic example of that.

The male entitlement was still there, the need to dictate and be deferred to.

She turned away from the thought, went to the shelf of wigs and took up a mid-length ombré one, platinum blonde at the top, darkening to a deep brown that matched her eyes. She chose a pair of cream silk pyjamas, the fabric catching slightly on her still tacky skin as she pulled them on.

Suddenly she wanted to look at herself but the mirrors were gone from here too, unscrewed from the doors of the fitted wardrobes, the lovely oak cheval she'd bought long removed, the triple-hinged mirror on the dressing table along with it. Smashed, but she wouldn't think about that now.

No, it was enough to enjoy the sensation.

It had to be.

She went to her dressing table and poured another glass of rosé as her laptop booted up. People were expecting things from her.

The Trans Sisters Facebook page was wallowing in grief for Corinne and she added her own message at the bottom of the post, doing enough to seem engaged, but she didn't feel a word of it.

She went to Twitter and made the same display of grief and outrage. Her mouth twisted when she saw the first hashtag – #JeSuisCorinne.

Like it was the same thing.

She clicked on it and saw tweets coming in from America and Canada, their sister groups getting involved, an RIP from Caitlyn Jenner favourited a thousand times already. A dark laugh rolled around her chest, this was too mad, it was surreal. The newly anointed high priestess of privileged trans women coming out in support of poor, dead Corinne.

The blogs had picked up on it now too, early evening in America and the news cycle was beginning its business of spinning the bare-boned police statement into revenue-boosting click bait, taking that one solid paragraph of information and padding it out with precis of other transphobic murders, quotes from eminent gender specialists and high-profile activists.

Evelyn Goddard had spoken of course – a recently posted article on Jezebel too long and boring for her to bother reading. She'd heard it all before and the speed Evelyn had churned this out made her suspect it was written months or years earlier, like those obituaries for ancient celebrities. Ninety per cent of it waiting on her hard drive for someone she knew to get murdered.

She walked away from the table, glass in hand, trying to shake out the irrational anger which stiffened her limbs.

How did this happen? Didn't Americans have their own problems to worry about? Wasn't there some mass shooting or offensive T-shirt Jezebel should be covering?

A string of curses rushed out of her mouth and she stopped at the sound of her voice, so deep and rage-filled, polluting this sanctuary. She washed the words away with another mouthful of wine and resolved to switch the computer off; there was no point torturing herself.

But she couldn't. It drew her back and she fell into the Twitter rabbit hole, masochistically scrolling down through her feed. They were a small community and they only had one topic of conversation right now.

#HerNameWasCorinne

#JusticeForCorinne

#TransLivesMatter

Corinne was dead and yes, that was terrible, but she wasn't the first woman to suffer and she wouldn't be the last.

The wine turned bitter on her tongue as she remembered the smell of the man's breath and weight of him pressing down on her, how the fabric of his gloves felt as his fingers dug into her thigh. And she knew she should have been more careful. Could see now why and how it happened and that it was her own stupid fault.

Her breaths came faster, chest constrained by her bra.

We're idiots, she thought. Naive and weak. Going out there into a harsh world, making ourselves conspicuous and vulnerable, and then when the worst happens we act like it's a surprise.

Did Corinne know what was coming?

She doubted it.

None of them ever did.

WEDNESDAY

13

They descended upon Ferry Meadows just before 7 a.m., with the sun climbing weakly in the cloudless sky and a sheering wind cutting across the open ground. Murray took one team down to the boating lake. It was the quieter side of the park at that time of morning, but she wanted to get a sighting of the man she and Adams had pegged as their potential rapist as much as she was interested in finding a witness to Corinne Sawyer's murder.

She was working her own angle in this case and Ferreira didn't like it. They needed a unified strategy and nothing she'd seen suggested the man was a serious suspect for either case. Murray was a waste of space on this investigation, placed in Hate Crimes for the sake of appearances only, her mind still buried in her own investigation. Now she was dragging manpower away to a position so distant from the murder as to be completely useless.

Ferreira had led her own team down the Orton Stanch road, following the route Corinne had taken twenty-four hours earlier, the one that led to her death. She stationed uniforms at every pathway around the murder site, stopping dog walkers and joggers, any random undesirables who were hanging about and might have seen the man who chased Corinne down and killed her.

It was busier than Ferreira expected and she was surprised how many women ran alongside the river at this time of morning. She'd always been more of a gym person, liked exercising in a controlled environment, and on the rare occasions she hit the road it was always around built-up areas. Even then she'd occasionally felt vulnerable, would run with one earphone pulled out, aware of every car that slowed, every man she passed, eyes always twenty metres ahead of her, watching for potential danger spots.

As she turned away from the wind, trying to get her cigarette lit, she thought of Aadesh, walking through that underpass, not realising how his choice to present as a woman changed all the rules of security and threat.

Had Corinne been the same? Did she know there was someone behind her but disregarded him because she'd spent fifty-two years as a boy then a man and the fear all women were taught from a young age had never been drilled into her?

Would Simone Trent have walked down Cross Street so confidently if she wasn't Simon underneath? Ferreira thought of the spot where he'd been jumped, his attacker coming from a gap between a vintage-clothing shop and an office block. Those were the points you were wary of, alleys and cuts, recessed doorways.

These were the things Evelyn Goddard needed to advise her fellow trans women on. More than presentation and prejudice, she needed to make them see how the landscape shifted when their gender did.

Ferreira inhaled deeply on her cigarette, watching the uniforms chatting to an old guy with an Alsatian, the dog getting frisky with PC Hale. But they obviously learned nothing from the man because soon he was walking on and when he passed her on the bridge, his dog's claws clicking against the metal footway, he nodded and wished her good morning.

The uniforms were already talking to another dog walker, a woman in a baby-blue fleece, with two excitable spaniels running free off their leads. Something about the woman's stance made Ferreira flick her cigarette into the river and start towards them.

PC Hale gave her a bare nod as she approached.

'Could you tell DS Ferreira what you've just told us please, madam?'

'I didn't really see anything,' she said, slightly anxious. 'I remember seeing that poor woman – the one who was murdered – I said good morning to her and apologised because Rollo and Bongo almost tripped her up.'

At the mention of their names the dogs came bounding over and started to investigate Ferreira's boots. She reached down and scratched one of them behind the ear, smiled at the woman.

'Whereabouts were you when you saw Ms Sawyer?'

'Just here,' the woman said. 'Right where we're standing now.'

'Was anyone else on the path?'

She nodded. 'But as I said, I didn't really see him. I was crouching down picking up some . . . well, you know. I always clean up after them, we have to keep this place nice, don't we?'

'Which way was this man going?'

'He was coming towards me. And he must have been running very quickly because one minute the path was empty the next I felt someone rush past, he only missed me by a few inches.'

Ferreira looked along the path. They were less than a hundred metres from where Corinne Sawyer was murdered, but the path curved and narrowed before that point and the man would have come up on the straight, easily visible assuming the woman was walking with her head up.

Unless he'd come through the bushes, waited, hidden, until he sighted Corinne, and then fallen in step behind her.

'How close behind Ms Sawyer was he?'

The woman squinted. 'Less than a minute, definitely.'

It had to be their man.

'Anything you can tell us about him?'

'I only saw his back.' She looked behind her, hand raised, dredging her memory. 'He was in black joggers, a hooded sweatshirt, white trainers, definitely.'

'Height?'

'About average, I suppose. Average build.' She shook her head. 'I didn't realise it was going to be important, I'm sorry.'

Ferreira told Hale to circulate the description to the rest of the team, ordered his partner to go after the old fella with the Alsatian. If this was his regular time and regular route there was a slim chance he'd seen the man's face. He took off at a sprint, one of the spaniels following at his heels until the woman called him back.

'Have you seen this man before?' Ferreira asked.

'No, this is the only the second time I've brought the dogs down here, we moved in last weekend and I'm still exploring the area.' The woman put her dogs back on their leads. 'We thought it was nice and quiet, safe.'

Ferreira assured her that it was, that incidents like this were rare. 'But there have been a spate of attacks along the river so you should be careful until we catch him.'

A few minutes after the woman walked away, PC Jones returned, shaking his head at Ferreira.

'Old bloke never saw a thing, ma'am.'

She sent them back to their post with the new information. They were past the time of Corinne Sawyer's death now, but it was possible someone had seen the man as he left the scene, running further into the parkland or coming back this way.

That was the thing with isolated spots, she thought, as she headed along the pathway towards the crime scene, you had to get to them and that was generally when killers were seen.

To the naked eye nothing remained to mark the spot where Corinne Sawyer was murdered, and without the distraction of the forensics tent she realised how exposed this place was, despite its sense of isolation.

The undergrowth was sparse but deep enough that within a few seconds he could have pulled her fully out of sight rather than stopping at the first shallow depression he came to, barely ten metres from the path. As she moved further into the copse Ferreira found the terrain increasingly uneven, plenty of dips and fallen trees which would have shielded the assault from any casual observer's sightline.

So why did he risk being seen?

It took time to choke someone to death. Much longer than people thought. Minutes of struggle and even once the victim was unconscious they were still hanging on, the parts of them which hadn't shut down yet conserving energy, ready to spring back when the wire was removed.

He should have been seen. Was ridiculously lucky not to be disturbed.

Unless someone did see the attack but wasn't brave enough to intervene, Ferreira thought grimly, making her way back to the path, feet kicking up dead leaves, uncovering a lost tennis ball gone grey from the weather and the bleached skull of some small rodent.

Half an hour later she recalled her team. A quick debrief revealed no new witnesses. She dispatched them back to their regular duties, called Murray and told her they were done. Nothing from her side either.

Back at the station Zigic was already in, looking much sharper than he had the previous morning, eyes actually open and she noticed he'd trimmed his beard which had been getting slightly vagrant-like recently.

'Anything?' he asked.

She told him about the sighting. 'So we know there was definitely a man there.'

'Worth the hour, then,' he said flatly.

'Had to be done, right?' She perched on the windowsill and started to roll a cigarette. 'I want to go and talk to Simon Trent this morning.'

Zigic dropped the used coffee filter into the bin, put a fresh one in its place. 'What, at work?'

'Best place.'

'No, Mel, worst place. Do you think he's going to open up to you there? You need him to feel safe, it was a traumatic incident, he probably won't want to talk to you at all.' Zigic spooned the weak Colombian arabica he insisted on buying into the machine. 'Speak to him this evening. Get him at home. Go in gentle.'

'I need him away from his wife,' Ferreira said. 'You remember what she was like, don't you? Watching him like a fucking hawk.'

'Then get around her.'

Ferreira shoved the window open and lit up. 'He's the key to this.'

'You've got more important things to get on with this morning.'

'Like what?'

'The list Evelyn Goddard gave you.'

'Bobby can do it.'

'Bobby can do what?' Wahlia asked, coming into the office carrying a limp so pronounced it looked put on for comedy effect. When he saw the pair of them grinning he shook his head. 'Bowling injury, wrecked my glute. I should have stretched first.'

'Who goes bowling?' Ferreira asked. 'You don't bowl.'

'It was my nephew's birthday. Little shit beat me too.' Wahlia gingerly lowered himself into his chair. 'Anyway, what job are you trying to put on me now?'

'She's doing her own work,' Zigic said, mock-stern, but Ferreira knew there was no point arguing about it. Best to let him have the small wins and save the fighting for things that actually mattered.

As democratically as he ran the unit it still paid to treat him like a boss sometimes.

Murray arrived a few minutes later, her earlier annoyance toned down to a mild expression of general disgruntlement. Her eyes were on the board behind her desk as she tugged off her mac. Ferreira had noticed how often Murray looked at it, how in any idle moment she found herself drawn to the photographs of the four women.

The case was weighing heavily on her. Adams would have made her the primary contact for the victims, knowing her maternal appearance would best suit the role, and she was struggling to keep a professional distance, Ferreira suspected.

Maybe she'd been too hard on her. She cared and that was a rare quality. Especially when it came to sex crimes where the general attitude from officers, male and female, was so often to somehow find a way to blame the victims.

'Okay, my small but perfectly formed team.' Zigic went to Corinne Sawyer's board, tapped it with his knuckles to be sure he had their attention. 'So, we have a sighting of the man who in all likelihood murdered Corinne but the witness couldn't give us a useful description, which means we have to do this the hard way.'

Ferreira half listened as Zigic doled out the day's tasks, only snapping to full attention when he stopped abruptly to take a call on his mobile, brows drawing together, his answers brief before he ended it with a promise that he was on his way.

'Colleen, I need you to take over on the guy Corinne had an altercation with at the Meadham on Monday night, okay?' He pointed to Wahlia. 'Bobby's got the details. Run him down first job, please.'

'Yes, sir.'

'Mel, you're with me.'

She flicked her cigarette butt out of the window. 'But I have a list.'

'It can wait,' he said, unamused. 'Corinne's daughter wants to talk to us.'

14

'Interesting,' Ferreira said, as Zigic pulled up outside the cottage Corinne had shared with Sam Hyde. 'Wouldn't you have expected her to go to her mother's?'

'They can't be close.'

'Kids have to pick sides, I guess.'

'They don't *have* to,' he said. 'And good parents wouldn't make them do it.'

'You think Corinne and Nina were good parents?'

Could you be, under those circumstances? he wondered. Once Mum and Dad started tearing chunks out of each other kids tended to suffer the fallout, even when the arguments went on behind closed doors, because kids always knew. They were like those ancient earthquake detectors, fine-tuned to every threatening vibration in their environment.

'Kids just want peace and security,' he said. 'They'll side against the person who shouts loudest even if they're in the right. Maybe that's what happened here.'

A young woman opened the front door to them. She had Nina's slim build, but was dressed in leggings and a shapeless brown jumper that reached almost to her knees. Travel clothes, Zigic thought, knowing that Jessica Sawyer had flown in from Dubai overnight, returning on the first available flight. The journey had left her rumpled and tired-looking and as they drew closer he saw the smudges of yesterday's make-up around her bloodshot eyes.

Before he could make the introductions she turned back into the house.

'She's throwing all Mum's things out,' Jessica said, heading for the stairs. 'I tried to stop her but she won't listen.'

A pile of bin bags, packed to bursting, sat next to the front door, giving off a faint hint of perfume.

They followed her up to a double bedroom converted into a boudoir-like dressing room, with purple silk curtains pooling on the carpet and walls papered in a gaudy flock, all except the longest which was taken up by mirror-fronted wardrobes, their contents exploded across the floor.

Throwing things out suggested method, organisation. This looked more like a raid.

Sam Hyde was on her knees, reaching into a drawer, pulling out slips of lingerie and shoving them into a black bin liner. She was wearing the same outfit as when they'd visited the house yesterday, looked like she hadn't slept since then, pale and drawn, lips cracked, lank hair sitting flat against her skull.

'I need to do this.'

'They're not yours to throw out,' Jessica said, her voice breaking.

Sam looked up at her, eyes widening, full of pain. 'I can't have them here.'

It was a grief response, Zigic thought. A knee-jerk desire to rid herself of anything which reminded her of Corinne, clothes which she remembered her wearing and which carried the smell of her still, as if it were the things causing her pain, not the loss of the woman who'd worn them.

Ferreira went over to her, squatted down. 'It's too soon to do this, Sam. You're hurting right now and you think this will make it go away, but it won't. If you clear Corinne out of the house you'll end up regretting it.'

'She's gone already. She isn't coming back.'

Jessica buried her face in her hands, shaking her head at the scene, and Zigic wondered if Sam had thought about her at all.

It was a profoundly selfish thing to do while Jessica was still processing the news.

'There's no point.' Sam slammed the drawer shut and opened the next one. 'She'll never wear these things again.'

'What about Lily?' Jessica asked. 'What if she wants some of Mum's things?'

Sam stopped abruptly, settled heavily back on her heels, and within seconds she was sobbing, shoulders shaking, tears flowing freely. Jessica went to her and pulled her upright, dragged her into a crushing hug.

'I'm sorry,' Sam said, voice muffled. 'I thought it would help.'

Zigic turned away, feeling like an intruder, and as he looked around the room he tried to picture Corinne in it, saw a very different aesthetic to that of the house where Nina still lived. Where that place was sleek and minimal this one was softly opulent. How long had Corinne wanted a room like this? Where she could make herself into the woman she'd always wanted to be.

Out the corner of his eye he saw Ferreira moving, thought she was withdrawing from their grief as she picked her way around the dropped clothes, but she'd seen something, was skirting around them to get at the drawer Sam Hyde had begun emptying.

She dipped into it and came up with a pink-cased mobile phone.

'What's that?' Sam stepped sharply away from Jessica.

'Isn't it yours?' Ferreira asked.

'No.'

'It must be Corinne's then.'

'I gave you Corinne's mobile.' The realisation was creeping across her face. 'No, no, she wouldn't have another phone. Why would she have two phones?'

The question only had one answer but none of them voiced it.

'We're going to have to take this with us,' Ferreira said.

Sam nodded, queasy-looking. 'I need to go and lie down.'

She rushed past Zigic and went into the bedroom across the landing. He caught the briefest glimpse of white walls and blue-striped bedding before the door closed. It occurred to Zigic that perhaps she'd been looking for something herself – not the phone necessarily, but something incriminating – and that was why the room was in such disarray.

Corinne had secrets even from Sam, then.

'I don't want to talk in here,' Jessica said.

There was a faint aroma of burning in the kitchen, two slices of charred bread sticking up in the toaster and the cover of the smoke alarm above it hanging loose.

'Do you want tea or something?' Jessica asked. 'Coffee?'

They both declined, took their seats at the long oak table and waited while she made herself a drink, brewing her tea strong, throwing two bags in a mug then loading it with sugar. She came over and took the chair at the head of the table, all the energy drained out of her.

'I really thought Mum was happy with Sam. But she must have been up to something, mustn't she? Why else would she have hidden that phone?'

'We don't know anything for certain yet,' Zigic said.

'Come on, you saw Sam's face. She wasn't even surprised.' Jessica frowned. 'Dad had affairs all the time. God, I hated him for that, he wasn't even subtle about it, always rubbing Mum's nose in it. But once I knew what he was going through I assumed the other women were a way of proving his manhood. Denial, you know?'

Zigic nodded, impressed by her capacity to rationalise what can't have been an easy thing for a daughter to accept. But it made him wonder why she was so unsympathetic towards Nina. Most daughters would take their mother's side after a lifetime of being cheated on, surely?

'I honestly thought Corinne was better than that.' Jessica's fingers went to the chunky wooden necklace she was wearing, tugging at it like she wanted to break the whole string apart, distress clear on her face before she gathered herself. 'Do you think that might be who killed her? If she was seeing someone?'

'Right now we're investigating a link between Corinne's murder and a series of attacks on trans women in the area.' Zigic tucked his fist into his palm, getting down to business. 'That's not to say this man couldn't have made contact with Corinne first – he was obviously familiar with her routine.'

'Had she ever mentioned being harassed?' Ferreira asked. 'Threatened?'

Jessica shook her head. 'We haven't talked much lately. I'm working away, it's tough . . . I did try to keep in touch but you just get tied up with stuff and you don't think—' She let out a gulping sob, pressed her hand to her mouth. 'You think your parents will always be there.'

Zigic waited while she fetched a piece of kitchen roll from the counter to dry her eyes, smearing the last of her faded liner across her cheek. When her mobile vibrated on the table she took a moment to realise what the noise was, glanced at the display and groaned.

'Work,' she said. 'My boss, checking if I need anything. God knows what she thinks she can do about this.'

Jessica flipped the phone's cover closed again.

'Have you spoken to Nina yet?' Zigic asked.

'I came straight here.' She must have caught his puzzlement. 'If you knew how she treated Corinne you'd understand why I don't want to deal with her yet.'

'She didn't cope well with the transition?'

Jessica laughed bitterly. 'She kept Corinne in the closet for years. She claims she did it to try and protect us but it was always about her.'

'The world can be a very intolerant place,' Ferreira said. 'Especially to kids whose parents are different. Are you sure she wasn't doing it for you?'

'It was an excuse. I don't think Nina even understands what it is to be transgender.'

The vehemence of her words sat Zigic back in his chair slightly and he found himself reassessing the conversation they'd had with Nina Sawyer, wondering if a hurt and abandoned wife could ever be honest about the break-up of her marriage. And whether Jessica was any more trustworthy. Both versions coloured by enmity, a history they didn't have access too. More contradictory versions of Corinne to add to all the others they'd been given.

He could see the logic of Nina's position though. Could imagine the kind of bullying the Sawyer children would have suffered in the playground once it came out that their father liked to wear dresses. In Nina's place he probably would have done the same thing.

'God, the fights they had.' Jessica rubbed her temple. 'I found out about Dad when I was ten, totally by accident. Mum had taken us to the cinema and my brother had an asthma attack on the way so we had to go back and get his inhaler. I ran in to get it and Corinne was in the kitchen doing the washing-up; dress, heels, full make-up and hair. The lot. I screamed because I thought we were being burgled.' She smiled. 'A burglar who does the washing-up. Then she turned round and I realised it was Dad under there.'

'That must have been a shock for you,' Zigic said.

'I was mortified. I mean, he looked ridiculous back then. I remember being painfully embarrassed for him because he seemed so proud of himself and so damn happy about standing there doing the dishes.' Her face hardened. 'Mum came running into the house – because I'd screamed – and she went ballistic. Harry's behind her having an asthma attack and she forgets all about him. Rushes over to Corinne, starts slapping her, screaming at her, pulls her wig off. It was horrific.'

Ferreira shot a fast glance at him across the table and he knew what she was thinking. *Pulled her wig off?*

But it meant nothing in the context of their case, he was sure. Nina Sawyer had reacted to seeing Corinne by removing the item which feminised her most, wanting her husband in front of her again.

Still, it was a more violent reaction than he would have expected from the cool and precise woman they'd spoken to yesterday, made him wonder what else she was hiding behind that indifferent facade.

'She'd known for years, of course,' Jessica said. 'She'd made Dad live this double life all because she didn't want her marriage to fail. And they were both miserable the whole time.' She reached for her tea, took a small sip. 'They were caught in this cycle of Dad trying to stop, letting Mum throw all of his Corinne clothes out so he wouldn't be "tempted", then he'd build up again in secret and she'd catch him and they'd fight. Endless binge and purge. All because neither of them was brave enough to just end it.'

'Maybe they stayed together because they wanted stability for you kids,' Zigic suggested.

Jessica snorted at the idea but didn't explain why it was such a preposterous notion. After her previous openness that struck Zigic as odd but when he pressed her on it all she would say was that her parents had always put themselves first.

'How did your brother take it?' Ferreira asked, scenting the same reluctance.

She didn't answer immediately, held on to her tea, brushing her thumb along the rim of the mug.

'It's harder for boys, everyone says so. They invest so much in their fathers. That whole template of masculinity thing. Harry didn't deal with it very well.'

'How old was Harry when Corinne came out?'

'Twelve. He didn't realise what was going on. But things got really tough once he was old enough to understand what Mum and Dad were fighting about. And by then Corinne was with us a lot more often at home. Harry grew up with her around.' Jessica sighed. 'It was tough for him.'

'Where does Harry live?' Ferreira asked.

'Castor,' she said. 'He wasn't going to move far from Mum.'

The next village to Zigic. He knew how easily you could access Ferry Meadows from there, had run down to the mere often enough himself. There were plenty of points where you could get onto the river and into the parkland, lanes which only a local would know. Escape routes, Zigic thought.

Jessica was watching them, fingers nervously working the beads on her necklace.

'You said whoever killed Corinne has attacked other people. Why does it matter where Harry lives?'

'We have to investigate all possibilities,' Ferreira told her.

'Look, Harry and Corinne didn't get on, yes, but there's no way on earth he would have killed her.'

Her voice echoed around the large, tile-floored kitchen, and she shrank slightly from the violence of her own words, turned away from them, then forced herself to look back to Zigic.

He explained the next part of the process, offered her a family liaison officer she didn't want and a number for a grief counsellor she declined. When she asked, haltingly, whether she'd be required to identify Corinne's body he told her it was already done but said she could see her if she wanted to.

'No. Thank you,' she said, relief washing over her face. 'I don't think I could cope with that.'

15

Wahlia was grinning at his computer when they got back to the station.

'What's so funny?' Zigic asked. 'Aren't you going through the list from Trans Sisters?'

'Yeah, nothing incriminating yet. This woman organised a disco flash mob to protest a boutique that threw her out of their changing rooms.' He rocked back in his chair. 'You've got to admit that's a pretty cool way of making your point, even if it did get her an ASBO.'

'Shame she had to do it,' Ferreira said, passing Wahlia a brown paper bag. 'Parma and mozza ciabatta. What was their problem anyway? Loads of places have unisex changing rooms now.'

Wahlia shrugged. 'Bigots, I guess.'

'Bigots with no business sense, judging by the size of Corinne Sawyer's wardrobe.' She took a bite of the roll she'd made Zigic drive out of his way for. Insisted they went to the Italian deli in Woodston where the queue was long but the food was excellent. 'Corinne was spending serious money on clothes.'

'Have we got her financials yet?' Zigic asked.

'On the way,' Wahlia told him. 'And the post-mortem report's in. Forensics too.'

'Just in time for lunch,' Ferreira said. 'As usual.'

'Like it's going to stop you eating.'

Zigic went into his office, put his own lunch aside for the time being. He'd never been queasy but he couldn't shake the feeling that it was disrespectful to the dead to stuff your face while you were picking over the most intimate details of their murders.

He set the emails to print, wanting everything on paper before he started to look at it, and went back out to Corinne Sawyer's murder board, wrote her son's name in the Persons of Interest column. Murray had added Lee Walton but he looked wrong, floating there, nothing to anchor him to Corinne, except for the sighting yesterday morning.

Behind him Wahlia was reading out another highlight from the Trans Sisters' criminal sorority and Ferreira laughed, the sound so rare in the office that it felt like a transgression. But he understood it, sometimes you need to step back from the darkness.

It was a shame the crimes currently on their boards weren't so puckish.

The power imbalance was painfully clear. Trans women lashing out against prejudice with humour and spectacle, because they didn't want to be punished yet again. The men who hated them, they lashed out in the usual way, with brute strength, knowing it generally achieved the result they wanted.

Almost without thinking he added Nina Sawyer to the suspects column. They knew she had the means to attack Corinne and the motive. Living so close to the murder site gave her ample opportunity. Togged up in sports gear she might pass for a man, with her flat, lean figure and height.

Assuming the man who'd been sighted running behind Corinne was actually her killer. There was every chance he'd sprinted past her within seconds of being seen, continuing his usual morning run, a missed witness rather than a suspect, but until he came forward and ruled himself out they wouldn't know for certain.

His description was on the board, a black silhouette of a man's head tacked up by Wahlia, giving them something to focus on.

'Harry Sawyer, you piece of shit,' Ferreira said.

Zigic turned away from the board. 'What's he done?'

'Homophobic attack on a man back in '09. He was given a suspended sentence and ordered to undertake anger management.'

'He got off light,' Wahlia said.

'Eighteen years old, no record. I guess he just got the right judge.'

Wahlia grunted. 'Another bigot.'

Ferreira tapped away at her keyboard. 'Oh, here we go. Mitigating circumstances, family problems, psychological issues owing to his father's decision to come out as a transsexual. I can't believe anyone bought that.'

'It's probably about right, though,' Zigic said. 'Jessica told us Harry was struggling with Corinne's emergence, it must have had a knock-on effect to his own sense of masculinity.' He held his hands up at the look she gave him. 'I know, it's no excuse, obviously.'

'You do know most men who cross-dress aren't actually gay,' she said.

He didn't. Hadn't even thought about it much until yesterday and he realised he was going to have to put some time in on the research front if they were going to progress with this case.

'It's a common misconception,' she went on. 'Most stay with their wives and girlfriends, the ones who are happy to put up with it. So Harry was way off base.'

'He won't have known that, though.'

'No, I guess not.'

Across the room the printer fell silent for a few seconds then started up again, slower now, bringing Harry Sawyer into the frame line by line, his mugshot emerging into the tray.

'So, we know he's got a capacity for violence,' Ferreira said, picking up her sandwich again. 'Murdering Corinne doesn't look like that much of a reach, does it? Especially now she's going for the final op. That's his dad gone forever. Maybe he starts questioning his own gender and sexuality. Like, is it genetic? Has he got "the gay gene" in him? That's why it's harder for boys, they worry they're going to go the same way.'

'Is this speculation or fact?' Zigic asked.

'I did some reading up last night after I talked to Aadesh. It's common for sons of trans women to break all contact, they don't deal with it anywhere near as well as daughters, because they see themselves in their fathers and they don't want to consider the possibility of being feminised. You know, because that's basically the worst thing a man can be.'

Zigic collected the post-mortem results and forensics report, bringing Harry Sawyer's mugshot with him. It showed a smooth-skinned young man, blue-eyed, dark hair worn close-cropped to his skull, a face not fully developed into manhood yet. He didn't look like he'd been in a scrap, which meant he'd targeted someone smaller than him probably, who couldn't or wouldn't fight back. Or jumped them in a such a way that it was over before they could get in any shots of their own.

'He's a bit effeminate, don't you think?' Ferreira said, as he pinned the photo to the board.

'Where are you getting that from?'

'Don't listen to her,' Wahlia said. 'She's got the worst gaydar.'

Ferreira turned back to her screen, jaw clenched tight, and Zigic expected her to snap at Wahlia but she didn't. Maybe it was a flippant comment. Maybe he didn't know how hard it would hit home. They were too close for him to be putting the knife in deliberately, Zigic thought.

'We'll talk to Harry Sawyer later, see what we can get.'

Zigic sat down at a free desk, thought, not for the first time, of how the promised funds for Hate Crimes had never materialised. A room kitted out for a staff of six, running with three permanent officers and whoever was spare during major cases. There was a whisper that Anti-Terrorism was due for expansion and this was the space being earmarked for them, but that rumour had been circulating for almost two years and they were still here.

It was only a matter of time though. Arrests of suspected terrorist sympathisers and recruiters were on the rise, fighters returning from Syria to their inconspicuous Midlands homes. Sooner or later they would find their way to Peterborough and this outpost would become a hub.

He put the thought aside, opened the post-mortem results.

Dr Irwin hadn't been allowed the same leeway Zigic took for his statement to the press and the paperwork was headed up as 'Colin Sawyer', in line with his birth certificate and the facts of his biology as Irwin saw them.

There were photographs of her face, the injuries not fully developed because she died so quickly after they were inflicted, but Zigic could see the breaks in her zygomatic bones, the mashing of her chin. Her nose was destroyed, her mouth split. As bad as it looked at the scene, this was worse, starkly lit and in high resolution, showing up every fine line on her skin, the surgical scars which she would have been at pains to keep hidden.

It was the photograph showing her hairline that stopped him.

'Mel, are you looking at this?' he asked. 'There's a clump of hair missing from the front of Corinne's head.'

'Hold on.' She swept through the images on her computer screen. 'What do you think that means? It's not where you'd grab someone to smash their face in, is it? You'd go for a handful at the back. Better purchase.'

'Did he think it was a wig?'

She spun in her chair. 'He was going to pull her wig off? Just like with Aadesh and Simone? Only Corinne's got her own hair so he ends up yanking a load out.'

'Makes sense.'

'But not if it's someone who knew Corinne well,' Ferreira said. 'They'd know she wasn't wearing a wig.'

'Depends how familiar with her beauty regime they were.' Zigic moved on to the next photograph, the ligature marks around her neck, checked back to the notes. 'Cause of death was definitely asphyxia.'

114

'No surprise there.'

He flipped through the rest of the report; substantial bruising on her back where she'd been pinned down, her assailant heavy enough to have displaced three vertebrae in her spine. Mention of the cosmetic surgeries she'd undergone, the evidence easily visible, an underlying issue with her kidneys, possibly brought on, Irwin suggested, by the hormones being used in her transition, but he'd know more when the toxicology was in. It had no bearing on her murder anyway, Zigic thought.

On to the forensics report, little more there.

'Fibres,' Ferreira said. 'Is that it? Nothing else, just fibres?'

'Unless we've both missed something, yes.'

'Christ.' She slapped the file down. 'All of that dragging and fighting and we don't even get a fleck of saliva or a bloody eyelash?'

Zigic tossed the report aside in frustration, turned to the board and let his eye range over it as the information settled in, seeing what fitted and what didn't. His gaze kept shifting away to the photograph of Harry Sawyer, his androgynous face staring back out of the mugshot, no shame, no fear, no guilt. Nothing in his eyes at all.

That was seven years ago.

Maybe the anger management had worked and he was now a model citizen, open-minded and accepting of all the wonderful permutations of human life. Or maybe a brush with the law had taught him to be more careful, pick his victims wisely, avoid CCTV cameras, make sure they never saw his face. All of this happening as Corinne's transition continued, confronting him day in and day out with a person who was and wasn't his father; the man he was supposed to emulate replaced by a woman who was wrecking his family.

People killed for far less.

16

It took a couple of phone calls to discover where Harry Sawyer was working. With a landscaping crew at a house at the edge of a village just off the A1, overlooking the rolling terrain of the Leicestershire Downs. There was a small private airfield behind it where a red microlight was dipping and rising on the air currents, body glinting in the afternoon sun.

Zigic pulled up on the untended verge outside the house, no space to park on the twelve-car driveway, which was stacked with large metal skips and vans, men coming and going, plaster-dusted and paint-spattered, in the process of gutting the place judging by all the activity. There were two forest-green vehicles from Moran Exteriors there, a twin-cab pickup truck and a heavier lorry with a flatbed, its ramps down while a mini-digger was loaded onto it, one man driving, another watching his progress, gesturing to keep him in line.

The entire front garden had been stripped back to bare earth and Zigic felt a visceral distaste at the sight of the ripped-up plants piled high, their bare roots to the sky. Large old shrubs and trees which looked ten or twenty years old, all perfectly healthy but surplus to the owners' requirements. Left there to dry out and die.

Ferreira went up to the man near the flatbed and asked where they could find Harry Sawyer. The man directed them round the back of the house.

'You know who that is, don't you?' Ferreira said, as they headed into the rear garden.

'Should I know?'

'It's Nina's new bloke, I saw his photo at the house.'

'So the son's working for the boyfriend.'

'Found himself a surrogate daddy, I guess.' She stepped over a trench running out the side of the house. 'A properly butch one too.'

The back garden was like a battlefield, lawn churned up with deeply rutted tyre tracks full of standing water, borders run over in places, the plants in them snapped and flattened. Zigic counted half a dozen tree stumps dotted about, five more gaping holes where others had been removed, and as they watched a JCB was straining to pull out another. It was stubbornly clinging on though, a metre wide and sturdy despite the earth around it having been dug away. On the far side of the garden the felled trees were being cut down into manageable sections by one man, while his mate fed branches into a chipping machine, the high, buzzing scream cutting across the site as it sprayed sawdust onto an already significant pile.

'Why would anyone do this?' he asked.

Ferreira shrugged. 'Suppose they want a change.'

'Doesn't it . . . offend you? They're ripping up perfectly good plants, destroying habitats.'

'There are worse crimes than remodelling a garden,' Ferreira said. 'I'm going to save my limited pool of rage for them.'

She was right, but it didn't improve his mood and when the tree stump finally came free of the earth with a painful cracking sound he felt he could have quite happily punched the JCB driver in the face.

'That's him,' Ferreira said, as the driver jumped down from the cab to inspect his handiwork, giving the stump a quick kick, as if checking it was really dead.

He saw them walking towards him over the uneven ground and let them come, reaching into his pocket for a leather tobacco pouch and starting on a roll-up.

The man-child in Harry Sawyer's mugshot was long gone. His shaved head had been replaced with a shock of dark brown hair, his boyish face half hidden by a bushy, ginger-tinged beard, and when he squinted against the sun the wrinkles around his eyes suggested the intervening years had been spent largely out of doors. He carried an air of capable physicality around him, a coiled-up energy in the corded ligaments of his neck and the flat, hard muscles discernible through his T-shirt.

Powerful enough to do damage. Quick enough to get away from it.

Zigic made the introductions and gave their condolences, speaking loud enough to be heard above the wood-chipping machine, the words met with a wince. Maybe because they didn't sound as sincere as when he'd said them to the rest of Corinne's family.

Harry nodded his acceptance, then stuck two fingers into his mouth and blew out a piercing whistle, catching the attention of the man feeding branches into the chipper. Harry made a cutting motion across his throat and the man turned the machine off. It wound down slowly, the background noises of the site taking over: a bass-heavy radio pounding inside the house, a generator chugging away, voices and hammering and birdsong.

Harry lit his cigarette before he spoke, and when he did his accent was more cultured than Zigic had expected, suggesting a more expensive education than his job required.

'Jessie called to say you'd want to speak to me.'

'Just a few questions,' Ferreira said. 'How did you get on with your dad?'

It obviously wasn't the start he was expecting but they'd decided not to dance around the subject.

'He wasn't my dad any more.'

'You didn't like Corinne?'

'We were all supposed to accept her like one of the family.' He leaned back against the JCB's mud-crusted tracks.

'But she was still your dad, too,' Ferreira said, doing a good job of sounding confused. 'How different could she really be?'

118

'You really have no idea, do you?' Harry shook his head. 'Imagine it, one day there's your dad, doing all the normal dad things, and the next he's in a dress and wig and heels, talking all like this.' His voice went high and breathy. 'Worrying about the state of his manicure, for God's sake, and whether his breasts should be bigger. Asking you which blouse looked better on him. Your *dad*. Are you telling me you wouldn't hate that?'

'Must have been tough.'

'Yeah, it took a certain amount of adjustment, I guess you'd say.' He inhaled deeply on his cigarette, exhaled through his nostrils.

A window opened in the house behind them and rock music poured out, a man singing along to it with a surprisingly good voice.

'Dad loved that song. He always used to have Zeppelin on in the truck.' Harry smiled slightly to himself. 'Zeppelin, Sabbath, Cream. We used to crank the sound up and let it blast out.'

'When was the last time you saw Colin?' Zigic asked.

The smile disappeared. 'Boxing Day.'

'Where was this?'

'Mum's house.'

'For Christmas dinner?'

'Something like that.'

He went for another hit of his cigarette, found it smoked down to the filter and flicked it away into a muddy puddle. He immediately started to roll another one and Zigic realised he needed something to do with his hands.

'What did you talk about?' Ferreira asked. 'The last time you saw her?'

Harry scowled at her and Zigic wondered if she'd slipped into the female pronoun by accident or if she'd done it deliberately to rattle him.

'*She* only had one topic of conversation,' he said. 'Herself.'

'Must have made for an awkward dinner.'

He sneered. 'We're all well accustomed to paying court to Corinne.'

'Why did you go, then?'

'Someone had to support Mum. She wouldn't have got through it on her own.' He flicked ash away. 'It takes her days to recover after she's seen him. Did Jessie tell you he drove Mum to a breakdown?'

When neither of them answered he nodded to himself.

'No, course not. Her and Lily love Corinne. They don't give a damn what he's put Mum through all these years.'

'Lily?' Ferreira asked.

'Our sister. Younger sister. She wanted to see him,' Harry said, disgusted by the idea. 'She whined about it all over Christmas so finally Mum gave in and invited him round for lunch. He turned up dressed like a—' He stopped himself but couldn't hide the contempt flaring his nostrils. 'He didn't stay long. Thankfully.'

'Why not?' Zigic asked, hearing a hint of triumph in Harry's voice.

'The usual. Him and Mum got into an argument.' Harry looked away, towards the airfield behind the house, nothing in the sky above it now. He just didn't want them to see whatever was in his eyes. 'You forget how toxic a bad relationship can be.'

'What was the fight about?' Ferreira asked.

He smiled sadly. 'They've got a lot of unresolved issues. They could argue over nothing.'

'Did he start it?' Ferreira shifted half a step towards Harry, into his eyeline.

'I can't remember.'

'Did you argue with your dad?'

'No. There was no point. He didn't care what I thought, he didn't care that he was upsetting Mum, nothing I said was going to calm things down.'

'Can you tell us where you were between seven and eight on Tuesday morning, please?' Zigic asked.

120

Harry blinked at him. 'I didn't kill Dad.'

'It's standard procedure. We have to ask.'

He looked troubled by the idea and Zigic couldn't believe it hadn't occurred to him that he might be a suspect. He knew his record even if they hadn't alluded to it yet.

'I was at home until half past seven,' he said. 'My girlfriend will be able to verify that if you need her to. Then I left for work. I have to be at the yard by eight o'clock. Uncle Brynn's very strict on timekeeping.'

The times didn't quite fit but it was close and a spouse's alibi wasn't worth much. They would check it out later.

'Uncle Brynn?' Ferreira asked, playing dumb. 'Colin's brother?'

'No, he's not really my uncle, we just call him that. Him and Dad have been friends since they were at school. They were more like brothers. He's with Mum now.'

'That's nice,' Ferreira said. 'That she's found someone.'

Harry nodded. 'He's good for her.'

They thanked him for his time, Zigic gave him a card he put away in the pocket of his combats and he climbed back up into the JCB without looking at them again.

Did he seem relieved? Zigic wondered, as they headed round to the front of the house. There was something he had almost caught as Harry Sawyer turned away, a hint of a smile, a slackening of a face, like he'd been holding a forced expression the whole time.

Out front the guy from the flatbed was closing the side door of a van, holding a chainsaw as he locked up, goggles hanging loose around his neck, protective gloves on, ready for more devastation.

Zigic tried to picture him in that sleek, aggressively modern house, alongside Nina, and found him an awkward fit. He looked the outdoorsy type, well built, with a broad weather-beaten face and wavy black hair threaded with grey. Rugged, Zigic supposed, because there was undeniably something attractive about him. The kind of look many women went for and maybe it was that quality which had drawn Nina to him after losing her husband to his own innate femininity.

'Everything alright there?' he asked.

Ferreira nodded. 'Yes, thank you, Mr Moran.'

'Listen, about Harry.' He shifted the chainsaw between his hands. 'He's playing the tough guy about his dad, pretending he doesn't care, but he's cut up like you wouldn't believe.'

'He seemed fine.'

'Harry's a deep lad,' Moran said. 'Always was, even when he was little. There's a sight more goes on in that head of his than anyone knows. And I'm telling you, he idolised Colin. Never mind all this that's happened with him deciding he wants to be a woman, or whatever, Harry loved his old man.'

'You two were pretty close as well,' Ferreira said.

Moran nodded. 'We were. Like brothers. His family weren't up to much and my mum and dad used to make sure he was fed and that.'

Ferreira braced her foot against the van's rear bumper. 'And how do you feel about it? The transition?'

'I felt like I was losing my best mate,' he said, face clouding over. 'It's so bloody stupid. He wasn't gone, he was still there, he just looked different. And now he really is gone, it's – shit, I don't know.' He shook his head. 'Shouldn't have come in today. None of us should. I thought it'd help Harry to be busy.'

Zigic wondered how Brynn Moran thought it would affect Nina and Lily, being left alone at home to tend their grief. Most families in this situation drew together, sat stunned and silent through the first few days when everything was raw and un-believable. They didn't get up and go to work like nothing had happened.

'Had you seen Colin recently?' Ferreira asked.

'No, not since Christmas.'

'What was the argument about?'

122

He looked bashful suddenly. 'It was Nina and him, the usual. He was having a dig at her because she's lost weight. Kept saying how she barely looked like a woman any more.'

'That's all it was?' Ferreira asked.

'You don't leave your wife then criticise how she looks. Of course Nina blew up at him.' Moran huffed, cheeks flushed. 'But, yeah, that was it. Typical family Christmas rubbish.'

Zigic asked where he was at the time of Corinne's murder and Moran was slightly more indignant than Harry Sawyer had been but gave the same answer; he left the house at half past seven to get into work by eight. Nina could vouch for him. Another alibi of dubious worth.

In the car Ferreira asked what he thought about Moran, but he was still trying to grasp what precisely about Harry Sawyer's behaviour was bothering him so much. Had there been a sly flick at the corner of his mouth as he turned away from them? Like he'd sold them a line and they'd bought it.

'Moran,' Ferreira said again.

'Reaping the rewards, isn't he?' Zigic said, pulling onto the road. 'He gets his mate's wife, his son, moves into his old house. I'd say he's done pretty well out of Corinne's transition.'

17

Nina had the contents of the fridge spread out across the island unit, so she could put everything back when she'd finished cleaning. She did this once a week, took out all the shelves and racks and washed them in some ecologically friendly gel, then went at every nook and cranny in the fridge with an electric toothbrush.

'I'm going to call those people from the TV,' Lily said, opening a bottle of mineral water. 'You know, the ones who do that programme about obsessive compulsive cleaners. I think they could help you.'

'Most daughters would be happy their mother was protecting them from getting food poisoning.' Nina dipped the brush in a bucket of diluted solution and moved on to the plastic channel inside the fridge door.

'Do you even know why you're doing it?'

Nina ignored her.

'Cleaning compulsion comes from a deep-seated psychological trauma.'

The brush kept whirring and Nina's shoulders squared, head tucking into her shoulder.

'You're trying to wash something away but it's not in the fridge. It's in you.'

Lily opened one of the glass jars near the coffee machine, took out a wholemeal biscuit studded with not enough cranberries. Home-made but there was no love baked into it.

'That's why nothing's ever clean enough, Nina. Because you're seeing dirt and germs and bacteria that aren't really there.'

The intercom buzzed and they both ignored it, Lily going for another dry biscuit as Nina resumed her epic battle with the microscopic manifestations of her disorder.

They'd been bombarded with callers this morning, neighbours and friends, journalists insisting that Nina needed to talk to them, that only they would give her a sympathetic hearing, a necessary counterbalance to whatever Sam was going to tell the journalists doorstepping her. As if they weren't the exact same people.

Lily had switched her own phone to silent, turned off the Wi-Fi, sick of the sound of messages pinging in every few minutes. Missed calls from whoever at school had the job of checking on students with murdered parents. Texts from her friends, but they all said the same thing because what was there to say apart from 'Are you okay?' and 'I'm so sorry.' And then the stuff from people she wasn't friends with, messages so toxic she knew she'd be getting into fights when she did go back to school because she couldn't let that kind of shit stand.

The intercom buzzed again and a few seconds later a message pinged through on Lily's mobile. Jessica – *let me in pls x*

Jessica had bolted the first chance she got. Off to university in Aberdeen, literally as far away from here as she could get on her grades, then a gap year to Australia and when she came back she moved straight down to London. She stayed there until a year ago, when she landed some stupid PR job in a Dubai shopping centre, taking blood money to whitewash the image of a country which would probably stone her mother to death if she went there to visit.

Which was the only way Mum would have seen her because she never came home unless it was an emergency. Hadn't even bothered for Christmas. She sent their presents over by DHL, Skyped an apology.

Lily buzzed her in and opened the front door. She looked like crap, washed out and knackered, but she didn't have any luggage with her, so she must have stopped off somewhere else already.

'Lillipop.' Jessica threw her arms around her and Lily collapsed into the hug, a few hot stinging tears running down her face. Jessica shushed her and stroked her hair and it was like it had always been, ever since Lily was small, running to Jessica for sympathy she didn't want from Nina.

Finally they broke apart and Jessica's cheeks were damp too. 'Sorry I didn't come yesterday. Sam called me in such a state, she doesn't have anyone else, and . . .' She looked up the stairs towards the door to her old bedroom. 'I wasn't ready. Coming back, it feels realer somehow. Do you know what I mean? She should be here.'

Lily understood exactly what she meant. Kept expecting the click of Mum's heels coming down the stairs and her bright, high voice calling out.

'I keep thinking she's coming back,' Lily said quietly.

'Me too.' Jessica reached out and dried her face with the cuff of her cardigan. 'The whole way home I was convinced I'd get here and find out it was a mistake. I was all worked up to shout at her for making me miss work.' Jessica shuddered. 'How's Mum doing?'

For a moment Lily didn't understand, then she realised Jessica meant Nina.

'Fine. Like, properly not giving a shit.'

'No, Lil, don't say that. She cares.'

Lily nodded. 'You'll see.'

They went into the kitchen where Nina was replacing the shelves she'd taken out of the fridge, giving them one final, very careful wipe-down. She stopped when she saw Jessica and hurried over to her, pulling her into a brief embrace.

'How was your flight, darling?'

'I didn't really notice.'

'No, of course. I'm sorry you had to find out over the phone but there really wasn't anything I could do. Not with you being so far away.' Nina squeezed her arms, a small gesture to erase the subtext. 'What time did you get in?'

Jessica hesitated. 'Yesterday morning.'

'Oh.' Nina smiled one of her acid smiles, didn't ask why but Lily knew she must have guessed and Lily could see it hurt her. The same prickle she'd felt herself when she realised. 'I'll make some tea, shall I?'

Nina asked Jessica about work, while she spooned green tea into a pot and took down cups, just the two, knowing Lily wouldn't drink the stuff. Jessica answered in a monotone, ever the dutiful daughter.

When Nina's phone rang she checked the display. 'Sorry, I have to take this. Would you finish the tea, Jess?'

She answered the phone as she left the room, using her cheerful but steely business voice, so Lily knew whoever was on the other end had something she wanted.

'See what I mean?' she said, climbing onto one of the high stools at the island unit. 'It's not normal.'

'What about our family has ever been normal?' Jessica leaned against the counter, arms wrapped around her middle. 'I've met someone. At work. Omar, he's a copywriter.'

'Great, good for you. So what?'

Jessica scowled at her but Lily didn't care. This wasn't about Jessica's love life and she couldn't believe she was bringing it up now.

'So,' she said, through gritted teeth. 'He wanted to come with me and I had to stop him because how was I going to explain that my dad – the dad I'd been telling him stuff about – was actually living as a woman?'

'Doesn't sound like much of a relationship if you're already lying to him about something that big,' Lily told her. 'All my friends knew about Mum. They didn't care that she was kind of different. And if they did I dropped them, because I don't hang around with small-minded freaks.'

'It's not the same.' Jessica rubbed her temple. 'This only seems normal to you because you've never known anything else. To everyone else it's really weird shit, Lil. Even I thought it was weird sometimes.'

'Well, I guess you won't have to work out how to tell him now, will you? Not now she's dead.'

Jessica didn't answer, just looked around the large, blisteringly white kitchen as if she'd never seen it before. Like it hadn't been her home too. Or maybe she was remembering the pancake breakfasts and the barbecues out on the deck, the birthday cakes and ice-cream floats, and Mum and Nina arguing late at night when they thought nobody was listening.

That was normal. No matter what Jessica thought, they'd been a family just like any other and the fact that Dad had become Mum didn't change anything.

'The police came to Sam's this morning,' Jessica said. 'They want to talk to Harry.'

'What?' Nina was standing a few feet away from them, had padded silently back into the kitchen. Her face was hard, blood-less. 'Why do they want to speak to him? He hasn't done anything wrong.'

'Maybe someone told them about Christmas,' Lily said.

'And who would have done that?' Nina turned towards Jessica.

'Don't look at me.'

'Yes, because you didn't come home for Christmas, did you?' Finally, a reaction. 'Oh, no, you were far too busy with work. And we all know how important Christmas is in Dubai.'

There was a sick pleasure in watching Nina lose it. She did it so infrequently that Lily couldn't help but nudge her on.

'Harry was pretty aggro with Mum.'

128

'It was nothing,' Nina snapped. 'And if you have a single shred of good sense in that head of yours you'll keep quiet about it. Do you realise how much trouble Harry could be in?'

Jessica was looking at her now, eyes wide, just as shocked by Nina's uncharacteristic outburst as Lily was thrilled by it.

'What did he do?'

'He threw Mum out,' she said.

'Why?'

But Lily didn't know. She'd heard the tail end of the argument as she came downstairs and she wasn't fully concentrating, had been up in her room smoking some of the weed Jack had brought in for her on the last day of school. It was stronger than she was used to and she was trying hard not to let the effects show, gripping the banister, watching her feet find the treads.

'You know what Corinne was like,' Nina said, fast regaining her usual poise, but Lily could see how much effort it was taking, in the tilt of her head and the stiff way she walked around the kitchen to finish the tea. 'Always a production.'

'What does that mean?' Jessica asked, still rattled.

Nina ignored the question, sipped her tea and pulled a face. 'This is stewed.'

'Mum, what happened?'

'It'll be nothing. The police always have to talk to members of the immediate family.'

'You know why they talk to the family?' Lily said. 'Because most people are killed by someone they know.'

'For Christ's sake, Lil, just shut up, will you?' Jessica was weary of them already, probably regretted coming home to this abnormal family. 'It's going to be someone she was seeing. The police found a phone in Corinne's wardrobe. There's only one reason anyone has a second phone.'

'It might have been an old one.' Lily realised how childish that sounded the moment she'd said it. But she couldn't believe Mum would cheat on Sam. She'd seen them together, seen the love there, nothing like how she'd been with Nina.

'Your father never could help himself where women were concerned.' Nina threw the rest of her tea in the sink. 'Why do you think he'd be any different just because he was wearing a dress?'

'She's right,' Jessica said. 'I don't even think Sam was shocked.'

'We always know.' Nina washed up her cup, a smile on her face when she turned round, grimly triumphant. 'Men think they're so good at hiding it but I always knew and I bet Sam did too. She was never right for him.'

'Like you were?' Lily asked.

Jessica told her to shut up again, quietly, that tone she'd used when they were younger. But she wasn't six any more, scared of her big sister's threats to decapitate her Barbie dolls.

'Just because you couldn't keep him happy it doesn't mean Corinne was going to cheat on Sam!'

Nina folded her arms across her chest, every inch the victor now. 'You'd prefer your brother to be a murderer than your father to be a whore?'

Jessica told Lily to apologise but Nina kept talking.

'Try to understand this, Lily, a man can be a whore every day of his life and nothing bad will come of it, but women live by different rules and if Corinne was sleeping around like she used to it was only a matter of time before she picked the wrong person.' Another filleting smile. 'Especially if she was looking for men.'

'She wasn't like that,' Lily snapped.

Nina gave her an indulgent look. 'You think you're so mature but you really have no idea what kind of person Corinne was.'

'She loved Sam.'

'She loved herself. Just like your father only ever really loved himself. With people like that there's never any room for anyone else. Not even their children.'

'Shut up!'

'He didn't come here at Christmas for you, sweetheart.' Nina walked over to her, braced her hands against the marble counter-top, spread wide like she was at a lectern. 'If he cared about you he wouldn't have behaved like such a bloody drama queen. He came here for me. To show off what he was turning into. And what an absolute mess of a woman he was.'

'Mum was beautiful.'

Nina shook her head. 'No, darling, no she wasn't. She was just an ugly person with a pretty face.'

Lily slid off the stool and stormed out of the kitchen, ran upstairs and slammed her bedroom door as hard as she could.

She wanted to hit something or smash something, go back down and slap Nina around her lying face.

She stopped.

Shit.

Boxing Day, coming out of her room, stoned . . . she remembered the lightness as she put one foot in front of the other, that sensation like her head wasn't quite connected to her neck. She was concentrating so hard on hiding how baked she was that she barely registered the shouting downstairs. Mum and Harry.

Mum laughing and Harry . . . what did he say?

Lily tried to get back there, remember what she'd heard, because it felt like it had weight to it and she would need to tell the police when they finally came here to talk to her. They'd talked to Jessica and now they were questioning Harry. Maybe he was at the police station already.

Concentrate.

She'd heard a slap.

Mum laughing and Harry talking, really quiet, and then a slap.

But Harry didn't hit Mum. She hit him.

18

Corinne's laptop and mobile phone were sitting on Ferreira's desk when they returned to Hate Crimes. The original mobile, not the one she'd found hidden in Corinne's wardrobe. That was still up in the tech department, waiting its turn. She felt sure that would be the one to yield the more interesting information, but for now she had plenty to go at.

She poured a coffee and sat on the windowsill smoking a cigarette while the machine booted up, listening to Murray debrief Zigic about the man who Corinne had got into a fight with at the Meadham on the night before her death.

'His alibi is cast iron,' Murray said. 'He works in the Amazon warehouse over Stanground, clocked in at seven, did a straight twelve-hour shift. No slacking.'

'Is it possible that someone else clocked him in?' Zigic asked.

'No way. They run a tight ship. He was there.'

Zigic sighed. 'Did you get anything out of him?'

'He was embarrassed,' Murray said, tapping a pen against her desk. She wanted to be done with this, Ferreira thought, get back to the women staring out of the board behind her.

'Embarrassed about what?'

'He said he was drunk, being stupid.' She shrugged. 'My gut says he's a decent enough sort, just acts like an idiot when he's had a skinful. Interesting thing was he had no idea Corinne and her mate were trans until I told him. He said he thought they were just a couple of rough old birds out on the pull. Think he fancied his chances, actually.'

Their first dead end, then.

Ferreira pitched the butt of her cigarette out of the window and returned to her desk.

She started with Corinne's browser history. This was the truest representation of a person you could get, she thought. Search histories and sites visited, the times and frequency. It told you things they'd never share with another human being, their deepest fears and darkest secrets, revealed obsessions and vices and kinks.

Corinne's greatest vice seemed to be shopping. She'd spent hours, late at night, on Net-A-Porter and Browns; her baskets showed totals into four figures, items destined never to be bought. She had Pinterest boards devoted to every article of clothing imaginable and her wardrobe at home suggested she'd denied herself nothing. Not when she was finally free to dress however she liked.

Binge and purge, Jessica had said. A cycle of extravagant spending while Corinne had been comfortable in her dual identity, then a forced catharsis when Nina found the clothes she'd been hoarding.

No wonder Jessica was so traumatised by the sight of Sam Hyde tearing apart her mother's wardrobe. She'd seen it before and she never expected to witness Sam enacting the same behaviour that Nina had.

She wouldn't find Corinne's murderer here though.

On to Facebook.

There was an In Memoriam post at the top of Corinne's page, set up by someone called Jolene – the friend who Terry Sutton had mentioned – and now Ferreira clicked on her photograph; a middle-aged woman with a strong brow and a nice smile, highlighted hair feathered around her face.

Hundreds of messages of condolence had stacked up already, the usual awkward clichés which people fell back on because the language of grief was the most elusive. A few were angry, though.

Whoever did this wants stringing up.

He'll get what's coming to him in prison.

133

I know what I'd like to do to this bastard.

Ferreira kept scrolling.

Most of her friends seemed to be trans or cross-dressers, although it was difficult to judge and Ferreira realised she probably shouldn't. But this looked like a closed world. Security settings at their highest, everybody very open, complaining about the pain from recent electrolysis sessions and requesting advice from her on everything from breast forms to books they could buy their kids to explain what they were going through.

Corinne was generous and helpful. A very different person to the one Nina Sawyer had described, but it was easy to be kind on social media, Ferreira supposed; less demands, less shared history, and unlike a marriage there was always the option of switching off.

Across the office a phone started to ring. Kept ringing, insistently. Murray's desk, but she was gone, and eventually Wahlia got up with a huff and answered it, took a message and stuck it to her computer screen.

'What are you doing?' Ferreira asked him.

'Checking out whether there have been any similar transphobic attacks nearby recently.' He stretched where he stood, reached around to dig his knuckles into his buttock. 'I really think I've done some damage here.'

'You've got office worker's arse, that's the problem.' She took a mouthful of coffee. 'You need to get out a bit more. Flex it.'

'I'm a finely honed machine,' Wahlia said, grinning. 'I could bench-press you, no bother.'

'Not in that state, you won't.'

Gingerly he lowered himself back into his chair. 'It wouldn't kill you to show some sympathy.'

'I'm not kissing it better, if that's what you're after.'

'Please.' He waved the suggestion away. 'I know where your mouth's been.'

134

She eyed him through the gap between their computers, trying to get a read on him, but his attention was back on his screen and she couldn't decide if it was his usual teasing humour or if he'd heard something about her and Adams.

Christ, were they the talk of the station already?

No, Bobby would tell her. If the gossip mill had her in its teeth she trusted him to give her a heads-up. He'd take the piss afterwards, of course, but that was only fair. She'd do the same to him.

'So, are there?' she asked.

'What?'

'Any neighbouring forces reporting transphobic crimes?'

'Nothing that matches what we're looking for,' he said. 'It's mostly random verbal attacks on strangers, pushing and shoving. I'll stay on it.'

Ferreira went back to scrolling through Corinne's Facebook page, stopping when she spotted an album of photographs taken in the Meadham.

Corinne in a white bodycon dress, holding her phone at arm's length to snap a selfie with Jolene. More photos of the crowd, the women done up in party wear, all glitz and gloss, a few wives and girlfriends among them, dowdy-looking in comparison and not quite so into the swing of things. Sam Hyde was in a couple of shots, cheek to cheek with Corinne, with Jolene.

Ferreira studied the faces in the background, saw Sutton, the manager, being hugged by a busty woman in a black wig and clearly loving it. Zac Bentley sitting at a table with Evelyn Goddard, heads bent close.

Some of the photographs were tagged with the names of the people in them but nobody she recognised. She went to the other albums, the older ones, knowing what she was looking for might not be strictly useful but feeling a tug towards it.

December 2014. There was Aadesh, his beautiful, fine-boned face perfectly painted and blowing a kiss to the camera. He wore a gold dress, cut low across the collarbone, glittery powder dusting his chest.

This was the night he'd been attacked. A few hours after Corinne snapped him he walked into the underpass at Bourges Boulevard and was knocked down, his face beaten, wig pulled off. And the man who did it had whispered in his ear – 'You're disgusting.'

He wasn't though. He was stunning.

Ferreira printed out the photograph.

A few minutes later she found one of Simone Trent and if it hadn't been tagged she wouldn't have recognised her. She'd only seen Simone as Simon, with his face swollen and bruised, stitches in his bottom lip, more across his cheekbone, both eyes blacked.

Simone had the same delicate features as Aadesh, a slim nose and narrow jaw, big eyes heavily made up. She printed that photograph too and when they were both done she stuck them to the board either side of Corinne Sawyer's.

Footsteps came up behind her and she knew it was Adams before he spoke, catching the rhythm of his step and a hint of his aftershave.

'More victims?' he asked, standing close to her.

'Old cases,' she said. 'But there's a link.'

Adams pointed to Aadesh. 'She's cute.'

'I've got her number if you want it.'

'Think I can do better on my own.' He smiled his bedroom smile at her and she was glad Wahlia couldn't see it. 'Where's the big man?'

'What's the problem?' Zigic asked, emerging from his office.

'Colleen's run down Lee Walton. Shitbag was hiding round his mum's, we dragged him out of the loft, said he was checking the insulation around her water tank.' Adams grinned but Zigic didn't seem to find it very funny. 'Thought it might be an idea if you sit in on the interview, see what he's got to say about Ms Sawyer.'

Zigic frowned. 'We haven't got anything on him.'

136

'He doesn't know that, and this guy rattles so fast we've been running a book on it. I'm telling you, if he's done something you'll see it. There's no filter with this arsehole.'

Adams started towards the door, expecting to be followed, and Ferreira saw the annoyance on Zigic's face as he collected together the scant paperwork he needed.

A minute later, back in her seat, focused on the screen, she felt Wahlia's eyes on her and when she looked up she was surprised by the seriousness of his expression.

'What?'

'Zigic is going to go ballistic if he finds out.'

'I don't know what you're talking about.'

'Sure you don't.'

'It's none of his business,' she said, voice angrier than she thought she was.

'You know how this works, Mel.' He shook his head, glanced away from her. 'If I can see it, Zigic is going to. Just, tone it down, alright? For your own sake.'

Wahlia returned to his work and she watched him for a few seconds, swallowing every denial and excuse that came into her head, knowing he was right.

This fucking job. It ruled your life, made any semblance of normal existence impossible, with the punishing hours and perception-skewing experiences, turned you into a curiosity or a fetish object for any man you might get involved with, because civilians never understood. Not really. They might enjoy the vicarious thrill but only for so long.

They couldn't handle the dark side.

She'd be more careful, but she wasn't going to stop.

19

'Shouldn't Murray be doing this?' Zigic asked, as they took the stairwell down to the interview rooms. 'She's done all the legwork.'

Adams slowed his step. 'Colleen's had one too many run-ins with Walton already. I can't have her in there again.'

'What did she do?'

'Went for him,' Adams said, a hint of admiration in his tone. 'She's wasted in the twenty-first century, our Col. She'd have made a banging seventies copper. Phonebook your ribs soon as look at you.'

'If you had anything on him maybe she wouldn't need to go in so hard,' Zigic suggested, stopping dead in the corridor. 'Why are you so fixated on Walton, anyway? I've heard what she's got. Your case is non-existent. He knew one of the victims, was working near another attack site.'

'He was at Ferry Meadows the morning Corinne Sawyer was murdered,' Adams said. 'Right place, right time.'

'And wrong victim, according to you.'

'That was before he showed up at the scene.'

'It's barely circumstantial.'

Adams drew himself up to his full five eleven. 'You reckon we should give up on those women just because he was careful enough not to leave any evidence behind?'

'I reckon you should find the evidence before you haul him in here,' Zigic said, gesturing along the narrow grey hallway, to the room where Walton was sitting waiting for them. 'What are you doing, other than letting him know how far away you are from pressing charges?'

'Walton's going to crack.'

There was instinct-driven fervour in Adams's eyes, a thin veil of it hiding the desperation he wouldn't admit to feeling. Zigic had seen it before, felt it himself, and he knew it was the wrong way to a pursue a repeat offender because Walton would see it too and he would take strength from it, emerge from the interview room buoyed up by the knowledge that Adams was more rattled than him.

'If you don't want to play I'll take Mel instead,' Adams said, waiting for him at the door. 'She's Walton's type. Good way to rile him up, putting her across the table.'

'She's busy.'

'Me and you then, Ziggy.'

Walton was smaller than he looked in his mugshot, broad and solid but compact, standing at the two-way glass panel picking something out of his teeth. Zigic caught his eye in the mirror, saw him smile, nose hitching contemptuously.

'Sit your arse down, Walton,' Adams barked, dragging out a chair and slamming it down on the suspect's side of the table.

Walton walked over, taking his time, still wearing that half-smile as he lowered himself into the seat. Nothing in his demeanour suggested fear or discomfort and Zigic wasn't surprised. It was just what he'd expect from a man who had been through the process several times already with no charges brought.

Adams took the wall seat and started to set up the tapes, leaving Zigic to sit directly opposite Walton, who looked him over with a speculative eye, trying to decide if he was going to be the good cop or the worse one.

Neither possibility appeared to trouble him.

Zigic thought of the women tacked to the board up in Hate Crimes, wondered if this was the man who'd attacked them. There was a predatory air around him, a sense that he took up more space than his physical presence actually filled. In his photograph he'd looked nondescript, inconspicuous, but the camera hadn't done him justice. He radiated a toxic air no still image would ever adequately capture.

That was why Adams and Murray liked him for it – pure gut instinct – and watching him across the table as he refused a solicitor, secure in his self-belief, Zigic found himself agreeing with his fellow officers.

'Right, Lee, we'll dispense with the bullshit,' Adams said. 'Tuesday morning, between seven and eight, where were you?'

Walton tipped his chin back. 'I went down Ferry Meadows.'

'Good.' Adams slapped the table. 'You're starting out honest for a change. What were you doing down there?'

'Fancied a walk.'

'And we're back to the lying.'

'Allowed to go for a walk, aren't I?' Walton looked amused, toying with them already. 'No law against it.'

'You a nature lover, Lee?'

'Bit of birdwatching, yeah. I love that.'

Zigic could feel the weight of all the previous interviews sitting heavy between the two men, every word loaded with significance.

Adams opened the file he'd brought in with him, took out a photograph of Corinne Sawyer. 'This bird?'

'I wouldn't use "bird" to refer to a woman,' Walton said smugly. 'It's not the 1970s, in case you hadn't noticed.' He turned to Zigic. 'And we all know that's not a woman.'

'Yeah? When'd you find that out?' Adams asked. 'Before or after you knocked her down?'

'Saw it on the news last night.' He nodded at Zigic. 'You look taller on the telly.'

'Perception's a funny thing,' Zigic said. 'I look taller on the telly, she looked like a woman from a distance. And from the back.'

140

'I never saw him.'

'I bet you didn't know until you'd knocked her down.' Adams got up out of his seat and walked around the table, stopped behind Walton, who stiffened very slightly but kept looking at Zigic. 'Did she keep it all neatly tucked away?'

Walton shook his head, smiling slightly but it appeared forced, and the amusement didn't reach his eyes.

'Did you touch it, Lee?'

'I told you, I never went anywhere near him.'

'Come on, we're all boys together.' Adams leaned down, mouth next to Walton's ear. 'One hole's as good as another, right? In fact, let's be honest, one hole's way better than the other.'

Zigic could see the discomfort coming through Walton's bravado now. He leaned very slightly away and Adams moved with him, left hand on his shoulder, the right on the table, almost an embrace.

'You've gone all bashful, Lee.' Adams's hand slipped across the table, fingertips at Walton's wrist. 'Why didn't you go through with it this time?'

'I never went anywhere near that . . . thing.' Walton threw his chin up towards Corinne's photograph.

'That's a powerful response to someone you never went near,' Zigic said, feeling himself being pulled into the gravity of their tussle. 'Does she disgust you?'

'*He.*'

'He, what?'

Walton straightened his expression out but it was too late, Zigic had seen the violence of his reaction, something deep and visceral and immediate. The kind of unthinking repulsion that might drive a face repeatedly into the ground, take a set of earphone cables and choke the life out of someone.

'Detective Inspector Zigic asked you a question.' Adams tapped his wrist and Walton drew his hand away. 'How do you feel about Corinne Sawyer?'

'I don't feel anything,' Walton said, turning into Adams's face, noses less than an inch apart. 'Except bored. With you and all this bollocks.'

'You've got bollocks on the brain.' Adams smiled. 'Was she the first cross-dresser you've found yourself attracted to?'

'Fuck off.'

'No, hold on, correct me if I'm wrong here, Lee. The last time we arrested you, after you raped Jenny Moir, weren't you about to fly off to Thailand? Stag do, wasn't it?'

'I flew out after you had to release me,' Walton said, confidence back. He didn't even deny the charge. 'Still got five days in.'

'Five days of screwing lady boys or raping children?'

Walton's jaw clenched for a second. 'I'm no fucking paedo.'

'So, you went for the lady boys then,' Adams said. 'Glad we cleared that up.'

'I don't have to sit here and listen to this.'

But he didn't move, beyond folding his arms over his chest and inclining his body away from Adams slightly. Zigic wondered if he was actually enjoying this, winding Adams up and watching him go, while Adams believed he was doing the exact same thing to Walton.

They were feeding his ego.

Weakening their own position.

He needed to do something, get something out of this interview.

Zigic brought a sheet of paper out of the folder and passed it across the tabletop. 'This is a map of Ferry Meadows Country Park. And this –' he tapped a point with his pen – 'is where you left your car. Where did you go from there?'

Walton gave him a sceptical look. 'Around the lake.'

'Mark it up for us, please.' Zigic handed him the pen and watched as he squinted over the black lines which tracked around the areas of blue lake and the green of the golf course and the open spaces, the patches of woodland. He drew a wavering trail which looped around and returned him to the car park at the edge of Gunwale Lake.

Behind him Adams appeared distinctly unimpressed with the turn his interview was taking but he was watching too and as Walton lifted the pen from the paper he leaned across his shoulder.

'That's not much of a walk,' he said. 'You drove twenty minutes across town to take a ten-minute walk?'

'I'm not in very good shape.'

'CCTV footage shows you spent almost forty minutes there,' Zigic said. 'What were you doing?'

Walton tapped the pen against the desk a couple of times before Adams snatched it out of his hand.

'Looking at the lake. It's very soothing, water.'

'Forty minutes would take you from your car to the point where Corinne Sawyer was murdered and back again,' Adams said, coming round the table to his seat. 'Thirty minutes would do it, actually. Giving you plenty of time to knock her down, realise you'd made a slight miscalculation about the contents of her leggings and then kill her.'

'I didn't go anywhere near her.'

'How do you know?' Adams snapped. 'You don't know where she was killed, do you, Lee?'

Walton glanced at the map.

'How would you know that?' Zigic asked.

'I know I didn't see her so I can't have been near there.'

Adams drew a circle at the murder site. 'You didn't go here?'

'No.'

'You went nowhere near that spot?'

'I just said, didn't I? No.'

'So why do we have an eyewitness description of a man, who bears a striking resemblance to you, running along behind Corinne a few seconds before she was killed?'

'Eyewitness?' Walton said, voice thick with derision. 'You know how reliable they are.'

Next to him Zigic felt Adams tense and knew from the way Walton looked at him that this was not the first sighting which had come to nothing. Another woman, another attack; an old skirmish Adams had lost being thrown up in his face.

'This is different,' Adams said darkly. 'You murdered this one, Lee. You lost it, didn't you?'

Walton started to protest, the same denial he'd been repeating since they started the interview, but Adams cut him off.

'And you weren't careful this time. You were too angry with her to protect yourself, all you could think about was that cock between her legs and how much you'd wanted to fuck her and what that made you.'

'I didn't touch her.'

'*Him*,' Adams said, drawing it out, relishing the effect it was having on Walton. 'You touched *him*, didn't you? You killed *him*.'

Walton brought his palms down hard on the tabletop, signet ring chiming against the scratched surface. 'Tell you what, you search my house, search my fucking car, you'll find nothing because I've done nothing.'

'We'll do that, Lee. Thank you for your cooperation.'

Fifteen minutes later they were in DCS Riggott's office and Zigic was the only one without a glass of Jameson's in his hand, the only one who didn't perceive a breakthrough in Walton's petulant outburst at the end of the interview. Riggott had been watching the live feed, the now empty room still showing on his computer screen.

'First chink in the armour.' He raised his glass to them in toast.

Zigic decided not to point out that Walton had only agreed because he was confident they'd find nothing beyond traces of cleaning fluid on the no doubt very recently valeted interior.

'I thought we were punting on him,' Adams said, swirling the whiskey around in his glass. 'I only got him in to rattle his cage a bit, but the way he reacted . . . we should have this back in CID now.'

'On what basis?' Zigic demanded. 'You've got no witness, no motive and no evidence against him. Walton has a type and Corinne doesn't fit. You said that yourself. It makes no sense for him to kill her.'

144

'And you've got a better idea?' Adams asked. 'Didn't look like that from what I saw upstairs. Your attacker has a type and she doesn't fit that either.'

'Come on now, lads.' Riggott made a smoothing gesture with his hand, smiled. 'You don't need to fight for Daddy's approval.'

On cue Adams laughed and Zigic remembered how it had been back in CID, the two of them detective sergeants under Riggott at the same time, Zigic with a few months' seniority but that made no difference. Adams had modelled himself on Riggott, favoured the same good suits and neat hair, same management style; that mix of violent admonishments and post-work intimacies in the pub, drawing a team around him more assiduously than Zigic had.

When the next DI post came free Adams took it, stepped up like it was his God-given right, and at the time Zigic wondered how much Riggott had cleared his star pupil's path. The previous incumbent retired suddenly, citing stress, but who wasn't stressed in this job? Rumour was Riggott pushed him, some scandal that the man's pension wouldn't have survived.

It burned for a few months but then the Hate Crimes department was mooted and his own promotion came and Zigic barely gave the situation another moment's thought.

But now, sitting in Riggott's office, looked over by the stuffed pheasants on top of his filing cabinet, the smell of three worn-out bodies mingling with the sharpness of the whiskey, it all came back to him. The frustration of banging heads with Adams, knowing every move in their power struggle was being observed and weighed and measured by Riggott. They had fought for his approval and Adams won.

Before long they'd be back there, Zigic knew. Or, at least, suspected. Felt an unease he kept pushing away, but with every new whisper about budget cuts and rationalisation and changing political priorities it stirred again. They were under the axe. The whole station, the entirety of Cambridgeshire Constabulary, everyone waiting to see if the long-rumoured merging of local forces would go ahead and whose position would be for the chop.

Hate Crimes was expendable. Always had been. A trial programme which hadn't been fully rolled out across the country so could be called a failure and quietly wound up, its caseload absorbed into CID – how many times had Riggott said that? – and as it was absorbed it would be marginalised. Even though the reported cases were increasing year on year and the world didn't seem to be getting any more tolerant.

Riggott and Adams were laughing now, some joke he'd missed while he was lost in thought, and even the pitch of their laughter was the same.

The bottle was out again, Riggott pouring two more large measures.

'Sure you won't, Ziggy?'

'I've got a press conference in half an hour.'

Riggott gestured towards the door. 'You'd best be off then, don't want to keep the family waiting.'

Dismissed, just like that.

As he closed the door behind him he heard Adams speak and another rough bark came out of Riggott's mouth; Daddy's favourite keeping him entertained.

20

It was dark by the time Ferreira reached Simon Trent's house, a red-brick terrace on a sparsely lit street with a disused church almost opposite, its crumbling bulk a smudge of darker black against the gloom. The site was boarded off for redevelopment, one- and two-bed apartments, high-spec, gated, a residents' gym. Ferreira had been eyeing them since the architect's scheme went up.

The place she was renting was fine, for now. Not as new and sleek as she would have preferred, none of those luxury touches, and it had been freezing over winter, with the boiler not working properly, but climbing out of the car into driving wind and a light, stinging drizzle, her imperfect flat seemed suddenly very tempting.

A hot shower, a large drink. Slip into her pyjamas and watch a film. Or call Adams. Let him entertain her instead.

All she had to do was turn round and leave Simon Trent with his secrets.

The wind whipped her hair across her face and she hunched her shoulders against it, feeling the cold cut into the exposed gap between the waistband of her jeans and the hem of her leather jacket. She started moving before she could change her mind.

This wasn't how she wanted to do it. She wanted him alone, vulnerable to her questioning tactics but also free from the judgemental presence his wife had proved herself to be in the hospital. She should have ignored Zigic's advice.

Not advice, she reminded herself. His *order* not to approach Simon Trent at work.

Drawing closer to the house she heard a door open and slowed her pace, straining to make out the woman's features as she stepped into the porch light.

Donna Trent. Slimmer and with newly blonde hair, but it was definitely her, getting in her car and driving away. Hopefully for a long evening's distraction.

It was as good an opportunity as she was going to get.

Simon Trent answered the door wearing a white towelling dressing gown and an expression of impatience which quickly gave way to discomfort.

'I suppose you want to come in,' he said, making it clear how welcome the prospect was.

Ferreira thanked him and stepped into a cheerfully decorated hallway, bright runners on the tiled floor, abstract prints on the white walls. She found herself wondering whose taste it was, couldn't picture the dowdy wife she'd met picking out these things. But even a brief glance under a weak light had told her Donna was no longer the same woman she'd met a year ago.

Simon was different too.

She'd spent the last few hours looking at photos of him as Simone, had begun to think of him almost exclusively as her, a high-maintenance, incredibly glamorous 'her', and she'd half expected to find him presenting as Simone when the door opened, all spray-tan and glossy hair and pout.

But there was no trace of her on the small, nervous man who stood in front of Ferreira now, his pale-skinned face bearing the after-effects of his attack; an unevenness to the sweep of his right cheekbone, a kink at the bridge of his nose where it had been imperfectly reset.

Given the damage done to him it could have been much worse, but Ferreira knew from personal experience how even the faintest scars grew grotesque if you looked at them for long enough.

Simon's were far from faint and she imagined the internal ones were even more ragged and ugly, slower to heal, prone to festering. Those were the scars that poisoned your blood.

'I'm not really dressed for visitors,' he said, tightening the cord of his towelling robe.

'Why don't you go and get changed?' Ferreira suggested. 'I'll wait.'

He nodded and took off up the stairs.

She went through into the living room, where there were more bright colours and white walls, an L-shaped red leather sofa hooked around a glass coffee table. It should have been homely but there was something hollow about the room and she wondered how much time Simon and Donna spent in here.

She couldn't picture them snuggled up on the sofa together, chatting about their respective days at work, bitching about colleagues and worrying over deadlines.

They'd been through something terrible. How did you act, as a couple, on the other side of such a violent attack? Events like that could break the strongest partnerships. Not enough sympathy shown, a suspicion of blame being laid on the victim, impatience or insensitivity or just the sheer grind of having to keep picking the other party up when it all came flooding back and knocked them down hard.

Ferreira was surprised they were still together. Guessed they were a stronger couple than she'd thought.

'Can I get you a drink?' Simon asked, standing in the doorway, dressed in yoga pants and a T-shirt. 'Coffee or something?'

'I'm fine, thanks.' She went to the sofa and sat down. 'You've heard what's happened to Corinne?'

Simon took the seat furthest from her, perched on the edge of the cushion with his hands tucked between his thighs.

'Only what I've seen on the news.'

It was a lie, she'd checked out his Twitter and Facebook accounts before she left the office. Not his, she supposed, but Simone's. Was he embarrassed or so accustomed to lying about Simone that it came as second nature now?

'Did you go to counselling after the attack?' she asked.

'No.' Simon closed his eyes. 'I'd had enough of doctors.'

'I can put you in touch with someone now. It's never too late for you to get help.'

'I'm fine. I can deal with this on my own.'

'You don't have to.'

'I don't need any help.'

Ferreira thought of the interview they'd conducted last year. Simon sitting very stiffly in a hard plastic chair, his hands between his thighs under the table. It was the same closed-off, defensive posture he was aiming at her now, answering every question with as few words as possible, those catching in his throat, but he never cracked.

He'd been bottling it all up since that day, she thought. Pushing it down. But so much suffering couldn't be contained and she feared for him.

'Where's Donna?'

'Pilates,' he said. 'She'll be a couple of hours.'

'How are you two doing?'

Simon shot her a hard look. 'We're fine.'

'What about Simone?'

His gaze dropped to the floor and he ground his hands together. 'I told you, I don't do that any more.'

Ferreira didn't want to press him, could see the toll it was going to take, but she had no option. So much of this job was about weighing the damage you would do against the damage you could prevent.

She didn't want another dead trans woman joining Corinne Sawyer on the murder board and Simon was going to have to pay the price.

'I need to ask you some questions about that night.'

150

'I've already told you what happened.'

'We've reason to believe the man who attacked you might be responsible for Corinne's death.'

Simon hunched over tighter, like he'd been punched in the stomach. Like she'd done that to him.

'I've spoken to another woman he attacked,' Ferreira said. 'Before you, this woman was followed into an underpass and severely beaten. Her wig was stolen. The same as he did to you.'

'Then ask her to help you.'

'I have and she's given us as much as she could but I need you to think very carefully about this man.'

He shook his head, biting his lower lip. A hint of Simone coming through in that oddly feminine gesture. She was still in there. Bottled up with all the rest of it.

'Is there anything you didn't mention in your original statement?'

Her words hung in the air and eventually she realised he wasn't going to give her the answers she wanted. Not that easily. He'd been evasive in his initial interview because he wanted to protect himself and nothing that had happened to him in the intervening year had changed that.

'Simon, please, you are the only person who can help us now. Think of Corinne's family, her children.' The words sounded weak; it was the wrong approach. 'Simon, this man is escalating. Okay? If he's killed Corinne there's no telling what he's capable of or who he'll target next.'

He stood sharply and walked across the room to the bookshelves. They were cluttered with framed photographs of Donna and him, their wedding, their holidays, all smiles and sunshine, scenes very distant from this one and none of them showing the other side of his personality. He wasn't looking at them though, his eyes were closed, head resting against the edge of a shelf, despair etched in the line of his jaw.

She wondered if Donna realised how much pain Simon was in.

151

'You ruined my life,' he said at last, turning towards Ferreira. 'Why did you tell her?'

'Who?'

'Donna,' he snapped. 'Why couldn't you just say I'd been mugged?'

Ferreira blinked. 'But Donna knew you were cross-dressing. We didn't grass you up. She went to the Meadham with you. She was supportive of your choice.'

A cold laugh broke out of him. 'She was never supportive. She went there to keep an eye on me. She didn't trust me. She thought if I went on my own I'd meet a man and leave her.'

'And is that what you wanted?' Ferreira asked. 'A man?'

'No.' Simon slammed his palm against the edge of the shelving unit so hard that a small photo frame fell flat on its face. 'I'm not gay. It was never about sex.'

It was a strong reaction, the kind she'd usually associate with a lie, but she found she believed him, knew what a touchy subject sexual attraction was for cross-dressing men.

'How would lying to your wife about the attack have changed anything?' she asked.

'Because she realised I wasn't safe,' he said, desperation in his voice. 'Anyone can get mugged, she would have accepted that. But she—' He gulped down the emotion, went on quieter. 'I could have died. She didn't want to lose me, so she gave me a choice. Keep putting myself at risk and be on my own or stop and be safe.'

'And keep her?'

He nodded. 'You did that.'

'No, Simon. The man who attacked you did it.' Her words were harder than she meant them to be but there was no taking them back.

Simon brushed past her, went to sit down again, curled up into a tight ball at the far end of the sofa. Another glimpse of Simone in his posture, scared and defensive.

'I made my statement. I can't tell you anything else.'

'Look, you don't have to go on record. You won't have to give evidence.' The same lie she'd told Aadesh and she hated herself for it once again. 'But maybe there's something you've remembered since the last time we talked?'

She tried to catch Simon's eye and failed.

'Please, did he say anything to you?'

Simon's jaw clenched firm and he was back there. On Cross Street. Walking drunk along the uneven pavement, thinking of the party he'd just left and the taxi he needed to find.

'I'm not going to do this,' he said, turning away to face the curtained window. 'Please, get out of my house.'

21

Some days took more effort to wash off than others.

Today had left a layer of filth on her so thick she was sure she could see the grain of it ground into her skin, a greasy sheen which would take hours to soak and scrub off in her sanctuary.

It was the looks that did it, every sly side-eye or outright stare heavy with disgust, all those dirty thoughts they carried and laid on her, making her a repository for their hates and lusts and all the complicated, dangerous states in between.

You needed to purge yourself of other people.

While their thoughts lingered you would always only be partly yourself and partly what they decided you were. A freak, a creep, a pervert. If enough of them believed it, could it make you so?

No. She wouldn't give in to that kind of thinking.

She had to remain vigilant.

Mindful.

She'd been reading a book about it. She needed to live in the moment, be thankful for what the universe had bestowed upon her. This safe haven, it was her happy place, the one she returned to when the looks and the insinuations got too much to bear, but sometimes being here in the flesh was less soothing than escaping to it in her mind.

Here, there was nowhere else to hide. No further escape from herself. Her sanctuary was taking on the dimensions of a prison cell. Worse, an isolation unit. Like she was infected with something so damaging she couldn't be exposed to other people.

No, they were the contagious ones.

This was where they couldn't touch her.

Be in the moment, she told herself. Retreat from that negativity. You were supposed to reframe it as a weak voice, one easily shouted down with the positives in your life.

What were they, though? What did she really have to feel thankful for?

She was still alive, but that gave her scant comfort. She had a future which held no promise and a present that existed only here and no matter how she tried to find some positives nothing worked to drown out that voice that taunted her.

Sunshine, flowers, the smell of freshly brewed coffee – was that enough to live for? She was supposed to take pleasure in the small things like that, be kind to herself, but the one kindness she could grant herself had been snatched away and it was the only thing she truly cared about.

Those mindfulness books were not written for people like her.

The tools they gave you weren't designed for problems of this magnitude, were like trying to kill cancer with camomile tea.

Evelyn had brought this on.

She'd been fine. Coping, at least, until Evelyn called. *Just checking in. Wanted to see if you needed to talk.*

How many calls like that had she made today?

She fed off other people's suffering. A psychic vampire.

It was obvious what she really wanted. Some problem to deal with, some drama to burrow into. Had she tried Corinne's family and been refused entrance? Now she was looking for another victim.

Evelyn didn't care who suffered, they were all just so much collateral damage in the war she was fighting – recognition not all of them wanted and equality most knew they could never achieve. She was no better than Corinne, just another rich bitch who'd sailed through her transition and come out the other side a powerful woman, carrying all the privileges of her masculinity into a feminine existence.

She started this.

Her and Corinne.

Getting murdered like that, drawing attention to herself, blowing the whole sorry problem wide open just as the wounds were finally healing. Corinne had brought the police back to her, with their questions and suspicions. They thought she held the key to finding Corinne's killer and they wouldn't respect her silence forever.

Could they compel her to talk?

If the policewoman came to where she worked that would be it. All the whispers and gossip verified at last, everyone would know what she was. Friends, family, everyone. Even if she refused to tell the police what they wanted to know their interest would be enough to give her away and no lie she could think of would save her.

If they looked closely, properly, like they hadn't done when she was first attacked, they might find enough to make her talk. Because she knew once they had her she would break.

She wasn't strong enough to go through that again.

Time had passed and the wounds had healed but she felt weaker than ever, so much effort invested in keeping going that there was nothing else left in her to fight them with.

She closed her eyes and tried to find a moment of calm but instead she found herself back there, with his breath against the back of her neck and the cobbles hard against her cheek, feeling the points of her broken teeth, tasting the blood in her mouth, and his hand, twisting in her hair before he drove her face down into the ground one last time.

There was nothing useful she could tell them.

Even if she wanted to.

She hadn't seen his face. Didn't know who he was, although she looked for him every time she left the house, sure she would somehow sense him and he would feel it too. Like fated lovers their eyes would meet and they would both just *know*.

156

They wouldn't believe her, though. They would show her the faces of men just like him, books full of them, hundreds of violent, sadistic men and ask her was he among them.

He probably would be. She wasn't his first, she guessed, and she won't have been the last. Men like that, they did what they wanted, knowing women like her would be too scared to stop them.

She looked down at her body, seeing what she was and hating it. That was who she would always be, that was who would have to go to the police station and appear in court, admit the lies, the terrible shame she carried while people sniggered and pitied.

Sergeant Ferreira said she wouldn't have to give evidence but she was a poor liar too, desperate and scared in her own way, driven by her own failures.

Only one of them could get what they needed out of this situation.

She tried to lose herself in the music, appreciate the beautiful melody and the sweetness of Karen Elson's voice, but she had picked the wrong track again and it felt like the song had been written about her, too many painful points of similarity to bear.

She needed to go through and delete every stinging song, for the sake of her sanity, but they were all sad. Too many bad men and broken hearts and women suffering every indignity the world could throw at them. Who was this aimed at? – people so secure that they regarded another person's pain as entertainment? Or was it women like her? Was she supposed to hear those words and know she wasn't alone in her darkest moments, that others had been through bad times and survived, if not stronger then at least wiser?

Nobody survived, not really. She hadn't. A shell remained and the shell could read books on mindfulness and do the stupid little exercises in it, enjoy the scent of the jasmine candles and the light they threw across the gold-flecked tiles, but underneath, deep down, she was broken, smashed as violently and completely as the mirror which no longer hung above the sink.

Half of her had died that night on the cobblestones.

And she'd known that for a long time, had been running from it, making excuses to herself and other people, none of them convincing. The facade she'd built was crumbling, undermined by forces outside her control, chipped at and eroded.

She was a person without reflection.

Half alive. Half real.

She was nothing.

THURSDAY

22

Emily woke them at 2 a.m., then again at half three, five and a few minutes before six. Brief cries which they took turns answering, Zigic checking her nappy, changing her once, trying and failing to feed her, his bare shoulder covered in regurgitated milk. He was so tired he almost left it there and climbed back into bed, but thought better of it, knowing he'd regret the decision.

Next to him Anna appeared to be dozing quite contentedly and not for the first time he envied her ability to switch off so instantly and completely. She'd get up to Emily and be asleep again within seconds of her head hitting the pillow.

Once he was awake that was it, no turning off his brain again.

He kept thinking about the interview with Lee Walton yesterday afternoon, remembering the arrogance coming off him in waves as Adams pressed. There was no question in Zigic's mind now that Adams had the right man for his rape case but he couldn't see how Corinne Sawyer's murder fitted with Walton's MO.

Adams was going to keep pushing for the case to be reassigned, though, and Riggott seemed well disposed towards the idea.

Part of Zigic could see the logic. He was increasingly unconvinced that Corinne's murder was linked to the attacks on Simon Trent and Aadesh. They seemed almost opportunistic. An attacker looking for a trans woman, knowing he would find one coming out of the Meadham on the first Monday of the month.

The circumstances of Corinne's murder were different. A daylight attack, out in the open, miles away from the club. Right from the beginning it had suggested somebody familiar with her routine, which made it personal rather than transphobic.

Or, perhaps, a combination of the two.

This was the problem with hate crimes, you didn't know you were dealing with one until the person responsible showed themselves, revealing what had driven them to act. They had been here so many times before, assigned cases because of the ethnicity or sexuality or faith of the victim, running down lines of inquiry predicated on prejudice, only to find out that the guilty party's motivation was completely different to the one they assumed.

Corinne was a trans woman, but she wasn't only that, and there could be a dozen people with reason to want her dead. A dozen different motives entirely unrelated to her trans status. Her murderer might not even have realised what she was until the news got out.

The idea brought him back to Walton, attacking what he thought was a 'real' woman. Disturbed before he could rape her. Running from a witness who hadn't yet come forward. Was that why he was so rattled by Adams's baiting over his sexual proclivities? Because he was wrangling with them himself?

Fine to be a rapist, but was an attraction to someone with male genitalia too much for him to bear?

Zigic sighed into the dimly lit room. The things he had to think about while his wife slept on next to him and his baby daughter lay babbling softly in her cot.

He was dreading the boys getting old enough to understand what he did for a living. All those awkward questions he would have to find tactful answers to once they became aware of the news as something more than an annoyance preventing them from watching cartoons. Milan already knew Daddy was on television sometimes, but he took it in his stride, didn't quite realise yet that his friends' parents weren't. It was still just boring noise, even to a child as clever as him.

Stefan hadn't noticed yet and Zigic suspected he'd ask the toughest questions, not out of intellectual curiosity, but because he'd always been the one to say the wrong thing at the wrong moment. Always that child who'd ask why the man behind the counter in the shop was so fat or if the over-made-up lady passing them in the street was a clown.

On the bedside table the clocked ticked round to six forty-five and he realised he might as well accept that his night's sleep was over.

He took his clothes into the bathroom and showered quickly. Downstairs he put a pot of espresso on and stuck a bowl of porridge in the microwave, only remembering last night's decision to go for a run as the timer pinged out. He couldn't keep putting it off, but the sky was almost completely dark out still and he told himself it wasn't safe running along icy country roads in those conditions. He'd get back to it in a few weeks when the clocks changed, sure Emily could be relied upon to wake him nice and early.

The local news was replaying yesterday evening's press conference, a truncated version but he remembered every trembling word Sam Hyde had forced out, how Jessica had taken over, her voice clear and strong as she made a passionate appeal for witnesses, anyone who could help identify the person who killed her mother.

Zigic hoped it would yield a witness, some new information, but his gut told him to expect the usual clutch of armchair psychologists pointing the finger at Sam or Jessica, interspersed with an occasional psychic, several false confessions and a heavier than average payload of vitriol.

Half an hour later he pulled into the car park at Thorpe Wood Station, found Murray's battered Corsa already tucked into a space, but when he went up to Hate Crimes he found her desk empty, no sign of her coat or bag.

She'd be in CID, Zigic imagined, getting her real morning briefing from Adams before she attended his.

He went over to the board where Corinne's murder was plotted out.

No witnesses, no physical evidence, a murder weapon which told them nothing, except that her killer had felt powerful enough to attack her empty-handed. You could argue it showed a lack of premeditation, strangling her with the cord from her earphones, but Zigic didn't believe that. He thought it suggested somebody physically powerful and arrogant. They didn't expect her to put up a fight. Or at least not enough of one to necessitate bringing a knife or a hammer.

A purely random attack might have played out with no weapon, but would it have escalated into a throttling so quickly?

They were looking at a short window of opportunity, a sudden, violent clinch.

Something which had been building up long enough to block out any moment of self-doubt or fear. He examined the photograph of her body, lying face down among the dead leaves. There were some signs of struggle there to be read on the ground, but it had been brief and fruitless.

Ferreira arrived carrying a large coffee and the fresh-faced look of someone who had got an unbroken eight hours' sleep.

'Rough night again?' she asked, slinging her bag under her desk.

'You're giving me a complex here,' Zigic said.

She smiled. 'It's nothing a high dose of vitamin C and some concealer won't fix.'

'Or a medically induced coma?'

'Weekend soon,' she said, dropping into her chair. 'You'll survive till then, right?'

'Emily doesn't know what weekends are.'

'Teething?'

'No, we've still got that to look forward to.' He swivelled to face her. 'So, did you get anything out of Simon Trent?'

Ferreira gave him the story as she rolled a cigarette. It was about what he expected; evasion, ambiguity, reluctance bordering on obstruction. If the man didn't want his attacker caught during the first, painful days after he came round, when everything was still raw, there was no reason to think a year of recovery would change his position.

'He knows more than he's admitting,' Ferreira said, tapping her unlit cigarette against the desk. 'I wouldn't be surprised if he knows exactly who attacked him. Or, at the very least, he could give us a decent description.'

'But he said he never saw the man's face.'

'Yeah, he said that, but he'd had plenty of time to consider his story before we questioned him properly.'

'Why lie?'

'To make it all go away – why else?' She went and opened a window, lit up. 'If he gave us a description we'd have stood a better chance of catching the bloke and charging him. Then it goes to court and Simon has to stand up in front of the world and tell the whole story. He's outed. No going back from that.'

Zigic rubbed his face, still not used to the shorter beard, which felt spiky under his palm. 'Another dead end, then.'

'Maybe.'

'We can't keep pushing him, you know that, Mel.'

She flicked ash out of the window. 'So you want to let it go?'

'I don't see what else we can do. He won't talk to us. Aadesh won't talk to us.'

'He knows more than he's saying, too. I'd put money on it.'

'Without a solid, and willing, witness, we've got nothing.' Zigic's eyes drifted away from her, towards the photographs of Aadesh and Simone, tacked up on a separate board now, a virtually empty one. 'We don't even know if this is linked to Corinne's murder.'

'No, but we're pretty damn certain their attacks are linked and motivated by transphobia.' She stabbed a finger at the board. 'They are hate crimes. We're a hate crimes department. Aren't we supposed to investigate?'

'The case stays open,' Zigic said. 'We investigate it. But for now we're going to concentrate on the fresh body.'

He went into his office to prepare his briefing notes, aware of Ferreira stalking between the empty desks, and when he looked up he saw her smiling at her mobile. Definitely not work, but none of his business. She slipped her phone away quickly when Wahlia came into the office. He was moving better today, but there was still a tentativeness to his step and he braced himself as he sat down, swearing while Ferreira jokingly fussed over him.

She was in a suspiciously good mood, now that Zigic thought about it. Had been for a few weeks. He'd put it down to the move out of her parents' place, assumed she'd been making the most of her freedom. Hoped some of it was her continuing recovery. Her confidence had returned at work but he imagined the personal side of things would take longer.

Murray arrived a few minutes later and Zigic went out onto the floor to begin his briefing.

'Right, today we're going to start a deep dig into Corinne Sawyer's life,' he said, standing in front of her board. 'Not Corinne as a trans woman, just Corinne as a person. Because nothing we've found so far suggests that she was attacked specifically because of her gender.'

Murray raised her hand. 'Shouldn't this be going down to CID in that case?'

'We'll continue to liaise,' Zigic said coldly. 'But for the time being, at least, this is our murder to solve. So, Bobby, I want you to get hold of everything you can on Corinne's business. See if there's anything in there which might suggest a motive.'

'Yes, sir.'

'Colleen, I want you to confirm or break – preferably break – Harry Sawyer's and Brynn Moran's alibis. Which means you talk to Harry's girlfriend and Nina Sawyer.'

'They're hardly going to grass their fellas up,' she said, with a slight roll of her eyes.

166

'No, but I want their statements on record.' He looked at the photograph of Harry Sawyer on the board. 'We know Harry has a capacity for violence. He's worth a closer look.'

'What about Lee Walton?' Murray asked, not raising her hand this time. 'He's given his consent for a search, hasn't he?'

'He has,' Zigic said. 'And, as I'm sure you're already aware, DCI Adams will be handling that side of the investigation and briefing us should it yield any results.' Colleen had the good grace to drop her gaze momentarily, rumbled. 'Walton is long odds on this one.'

'But he was at Ferry Meadows,' she said, looking directly at him again. 'That has to mean something.'

'Adams is handling it.' Zigic stared back at her for a few seconds, long enough to be sure the message had got through. 'Mel, we need to talk to this "Jolene" everyone keeps telling us about. If she was Corinne's best mate she's well overdue a visit.'

'I'll get her details.'

Zigic could feel Murray's discontent swelling across the room, and he knew exactly where it came from. She cared. Too much maybe. About those women who watched her from the board; but this was his department and his case and she was going to have to learn to deal with that.

'Right, crack on then, folks.'

23

Zigic managed to catch twenty minutes' sleep while Ferreira drove, only coming round as she drew onto the driveway of Jolene's austere Victorian semi. It was a nice house in a nice village. Commuter belt, affluent, not what Zigic was expecting, but then again, why did he think Jolene wouldn't live somewhere like this?

It was the name, he realised. American and slightly trashy, inextricably linked in his mind with the Dolly Parton song. He wondered if that was why Corinne's friend had picked it. If she liked the idea of being that kind of woman, irresistible and intimidating.

Ferreira went ahead of him to the glossy red front door, dropping a heavy cast-iron knocker which was answered a few seconds later by a tall, slim man with a deep fake tan and carefully styled brown hair, dressed in skinny white jeans and a black shirt open three buttons down. He had the look of a stage psychic or a celebrity nutritionist.

'Jolene?' Ferreira asked.

'Not today,' he said, with a wan smile. 'Joe Sherman.'

Ferreira made the introductions and they followed him into a high-ceilinged hallway which gave away the house's real purpose. They knew from her Facebook account that Jolene and her wife ran a discreet, appointment-only beauty salon for cross-dressers and trans people. The space was decorated with rather less discretion, dominated by a huge, heavily foxed mirror and gold console table, bearing a vase of faintly rotten-smelling lilies. Opposite that, a glass cabinet displayed hair and beauty products.

'Do you not—' Ferreira paused. 'Are you not Jolene all the time?'

'I'm not trans,' he said, adopting a patient tone, like a teacher might use with a pupil who'd already failed to grasp their lesson several times before. 'I'm a cross-dresser. So sometimes I wake up and I'm Jolene and sometimes I'm Joe. Today's a Joe day.'

Ferreira apologised and he touched a quick hand to her arm, smiling again, warmer this time, showing perfect, bleached teeth.

'Don't be silly, you're allowed to ask.'

'We're very sorry about Corinne.'

He nodded. 'Thank you. The whole group's been devastated by the news. How are her family coping?'

'Haven't you spoken to them?' Zigic asked.

'I called Nina, but she didn't pick up.' He cast a sad glance towards the cabinet. 'She blamed me for getting Corinne into all of this. A lot of the wives do. They'll put up with their men messing around in dresses at home, but we make them beautiful enough to show themselves in public.'

'How about Sam?'

'We're going round later,' he said. 'She won't be looking after herself properly. Von'll cook something.' He gestured for them to go through into another room before shouting up the stairs – 'Von, police are here, can you come down, love?'

It would have been a sitting room originally, well proportioned and quite grand in its day, Zigic imagined. Now it was like any other hairdresser's, two chairs in front of lit mirrors, all the usual accoutrements placed ready for use. Another small station for manicures and, in front of the fireplace, a grey velvet sofa and two armchairs arranged around a low table littered with magazines.

'How long had you known Corinne?' Zigic asked, taking one of the chairs.

Joe tidied the magazines into a pile before he sat down. 'Oh, years. Fifteen, sixteen. We met at an awful bloody gay bar in

Cambridge.' He put a hand out. 'Not that Corinne was gay. Or me. But your options were a bit more limited back then. No Internet to speak of, no forums or support groups. The young ones don't know how lucky they are now.'

He was a talker, that was good.

'You two were close then?'

'We were.'

'Did Corinne ever mention being threatened by someone?' Zigic asked.

'No, she was very popular.'

'In the community?' A quick nod. 'What about outside it?'

'As far as I know.' He recrossed his legs. 'Look, Evelyn Goddard said you'd told her Corinne's murder might be linked to some other attacks.'

'It's a theory we're looking into,' Zigic said. 'But right now we're more interested in any elements of Corinne's life which might have put her in danger.'

Joe looked away as his wife came into the room and Zigic thought he detected a slight stiffening in the man's posture. Was she the weak link here?

'This is Von,' he said.

She was short and barrel-shaped in black leggings and a matching tunic, long dark hair chopped into a blunt fringe which poked at her heavily kohled eyes.

'Have you told them?' she asked, sitting down next to her husband.

He shifted uncomfortably on the sofa. Said nothing.

'You're not going to do Corinne any harm now, Joe.' She had a smoker's voice, low and husky. 'They need to know.'

Ferreira inched forward in her chair, concentrating on Von. 'We need to catch the man who did this. Believe me, people like this, with this capacity for violence, they don't stop.'

Von sighed. 'Corinne was on the trawl.'

170

'For what?'

'A bloke.'

Ferreira glanced at Zigic, eyebrows raised, and it would have seemed unprofessional if he didn't share her absolute bemusement.

'But she's with Sam,' he said. 'She left her wife for Sam. Why would she want to start dating men all of a sudden?'

'The hormones,' Von said, like it was the most obvious thing in the world. 'She was transitioning, pumped full of oestrogen. It's way more common than any of that lot want to admit.'

Next to her Joe was looking at his hand, curled into a fist on his thigh.

'It's like us,' she said, talking to Ferreira now. 'Our oestrogen levels change within our cycle, right? So when we're ovulating we want big, butch men who'll give us strong babies, and when we're menstruating we're attracted to more androgynous, girly men. Same with Corinne, she was straight as a die when she was Colin and when she was just cross-dressing. But the minute she started having the injections her hormone balance changed, she became more female, a straight female, okay? So she wanted a man.'

Von sounded very certain but the science seemed overly simplistic to Zigic. Was that really how it worked? Pump a man with a certain hormone and you change his sexual orientation?

'It wasn't like that,' Joe said wearily. 'Corinne was testing herself.'

'How?' Ferreira asked.

'She needed to know that she passed as a "real" woman. That's a huge thing for people at her stage of transition. A lot don't – I'm not being bitchy but surgery can only do so much and some will never pass as natal women. Corinne wanted men to believe in her as a woman.'

Von snorted softly. 'She wanted a man, Joe. There's no shame in it.'

171

'Did she find one?'

'Don't see why she wouldn't have.' Von shrugged. 'She was a good-looking woman. Elegant, poised – I made sure of that.'

'Von teaches comportment,' Joe said. 'She used to be an actress, didn't you?'

'An extra.'

'You were better than that.' He reached out and squeezed her hand. 'Von's in very high demand with the girls. She teaches them how to sit like ladies and walk like ladies. It takes a lot of conditioning – a *lot* – to knock the old habits out.'

'Corinne had it down though,' Von said, with a hint of pride. 'The moves, the voice. She was an excellent pupil.'

'You realise that if Corinne was dating men who didn't know she was pre-op, then she was putting herself in a seriously dangerous situation,' Ferreira said.

Joe gave her a withering look. 'Asking for it, was she?'

'That is not what I said.'

Von told him to calm down. 'She's right. How do you think some bloke was going to react if he found out?'

'How would he?' Joe said. 'She wasn't going to sleep with anyone.'

'What did she tell you about these men?' Ferreira asked.

Joe glanced at Von. 'It was nothing heavy. She went out on a couple of dates. Different men. She wouldn't see any of them twice in case things started to get serious.'

'It doesn't take two dates for things to get serious,' Ferreira said.

Von laughed. 'My kind of girl.'

Zigic could see the pair of them getting on. Found he liked Von's bluntness himself too. She was the only person they'd spoken to so far who didn't treat the subject with reverence or delicacy and wasn't politicising it either.

'Where did Corinne meet these men?' he asked. 'Online?'

'No, she'd just go into a bar and pick someone up,' Joe said. 'Seems archaic, doesn't it? But she preferred going old-school. Honestly, I think she liked the challenge.'

'Was Sam aware what Corinne was doing?'

'Are you joking?' Von asked. 'Why would she tell her?'

'Maybe she worked it out.'

'Corinne was careful,' Joe said. 'She . . . well, we were her alibi, so to speak. Or I was. You have to understand Corinne wasn't doing anything wrong. She wasn't actually cheating on Sam. I wouldn't have covered for her if I thought she was.'

Zigic didn't believe that. People covered up their friends' infidelities all the time and what was a two-year relationship with Sam compared to a fifteen-year friendship with Corinne?

'What do you think of Sam?' Ferreira asked.

Von gave a showy sigh and raked her fingertips through her hair. 'Honestly, I've always thought they were a weird couple. You'll have talked to Nina already? I couldn't understood why Corinne would go from someone like that to, you know, a butch.'

'They were in love,' Joe said. 'And Sam was good for Corinne. She's given her unconditional support, which is more than you can say for most women in her situation.'

Was that bitter edge aimed at Von? Zigic wondered. Was she holding him back from taking the next step? Not that it mattered to them or the case, but he knew how it might colour the couple's perception of Corinne and Sam's relationship.

He glanced at Ferreira, gave her the nod.

'Okay, well, I think that's all for now,' she said, rising from her seat and fishing out a card. 'If you think of anything else that might be useful, you can reach me on this number.'

Joe nodded, Von smiled, taking the card, and offered to see them out.

When they were at the front step, Zigic already heading for the car, Ferreira stopped and turned back.

'Do you know Simon Trent?'

'Simone, yes. We haven't seen her for, oh, it must be over a year now. Lovely girl, great bones.'

'Were you aware that she was attacked last year?'

'I heard about it.' Von pulled the door up behind her, moving out into the porch. 'Do you think whoever attacked her killed Corinne? Because – oh, I shouldn't say . . .' But she was going to, would have insisted even if they tried to stop her, Zigic guessed. 'Look, I saw her out a couple of times with men. Just having coffee, nothing salacious, but they were obviously dates.'

Ferreira cocked her head. 'How do you know they were dates?'

'Lovey, I know sexual tension when I see it.'

Von flinched as Joe shouted her name from inside the house and quickly reached into the hallway to press a button that started the electric gate opening.

'Drive safely,' she said and closed the door on them.

Back in the car, pulling onto the narrow country lane, Zigic took out his mobile and rang Wahlia, told him to chase up the tech department over Corinne's second mobile phone. He wanted it done by the time they returned to the office. Beers on him if they succeeded. It was a cheap trick but he'd known it work before.

'I told you Simon was hiding something,' Ferreira said, toeing the accelerator to overtake a tractor. 'Simone's dating men, Corinne's dating men, I bet Aadesh was too, not that we'll get him to admit it. This is our link.'

'Maybe.'

'Please, maybe.' She grinned at him. 'You can feel it too. Don't deny it.'

She was right.

The adrenalin was pumping, the sleepless nights forgotten. This could be the breakthrough they'd been pushing towards. Corinne was dating. Men who thought she was available and willing and, crucially, physically as well as visually female.

It only took one man not to respect her boundaries.

A couple of drinks too many, a straying hand . . .

24

The promise of beer money had done its job and Zigic went up to pay off his bribe to the techies while Ferreira got to work on the information they'd pulled off Corinne's second phone.

Across the desk Wahlia was waiting on hold with an instrumental cover version of Coldplay's 'Yellow' piping out of his phone. Ferreira didn't think it was possible to get more middle of the road than the original but there it was, played on piano with whining strings in the background, pure aural anaesthetic.

'Have you got in touch with Corinne's bank yet?'

'On hold with them now. Some genius doesn't believe the protocols, wants to check with his supervisor.' Wahlia glanced at his phone as the music stopped, then grunted with annoyance as another song began. 'Wankers, think I've got nothing better to do with my time than listen to this shit.'

'Maroon 5, gross.'

'You recognised it. That's embarrassing.'

'My brother was a fan.'

'Sure he was.' Wahlia nodded. 'I bet you had all their albums. Posters on your bedroom wall. Which one did you fancy? Not Levine?'

She scowled at him. 'We don't have to be friends, you know.'

On-screen she scrolled through the emails they'd lifted from Corinne's second mobile phone, taking it one user at a time. There were two dating site apps, and this was where they would find the serious candidates, at the point where brief messages weren't enough and the communications became longer and more involved, moving out of that closed bubble and into a place halfway between fantasy and real life.

There were a dozen contacts marked as VIP and the first few she went through were non-starters. Flirtations which didn't take off, an obvious lack of click, even though Corinne appeared to be trying her damnedest to give those men what they wanted.

She was tailoring her behaviour to each of them. Demure with this one, filthy with that, and Ferreira wondered if it was a response to the men or whether she was trying on personas like she'd try on different outfits, figuring out which suited her best.

According to the dates on the emails Corinne had been doing this for close on a year, soon after she'd begun to live as a woman full-time.

She thought of what Von Sherman said about the hormone therapy. Corinne starting her treatment, the oestrogen working its way into her system, building up there, smoothing her skin and thickening her hair, making her feel . . . different, new sensations, new emotions, or at least ones she perceived differently.

Was Von right, did transition change who Corinne was attracted to? Was that why she suddenly started to show an interest in men after a lifetime of marriage and affairs with women?

Or was it simpler than that? Corinne feeling free to act on impulses which Colin had to repress and deny with a string of infidelities, overcompensating in a manner which now looked almost like a cry for help.

Ferreira knew how much you could hide of yourself within a relationship and how fiercely you could commit to a lie when the truth was unpalatable to everyone, including yourself. She knew just how far some men would go, how cruel and creative they could be when a convincing facade needed building around them.

She bit down on her tongue, focused on the words on her screen, pushing away the ones she'd spent the last two days ignoring as they swam up at her from the deep, dark place she'd buried them.

Focus on the job, she told herself, finger tapping the keyboard, eyes fixed unblinking on an elaborate fantasy Corinne had spun out for some man who'd made it clear he only liked submissive women; beautiful, silent receptacles.

But within a couple of lines her brain stopped absorbing the words, still snagged on the man's initial message – *'Tell me what you want me to do to you.'*

She saw an arched back, tattooed along the spine, fists clenched around rucked white cotton, the fall of her hair as she moved and the smell of oiled skin.

'Found Corinne's boyfriend yet?' Zigic was standing at the side of her desk, amused-looking. 'Or are you just reading that for pleasure?'

'It's kind of vanilla for me,' she said.

'Think there's anything in it, though? Domination fantasies—'

'Don't automatically translate into violent tendencies.'

He shrugged. 'Yeah, you'll never convince me that's true.'

There it was, the Zigic puritanical streak. He was probably the only copper living or dead who'd never used his handcuffs for recreational purposes.

'I think we're wasting our time here,' Ferreira said. 'If Joe was right about Corinne picking up guys in bars she might not have met any of these ones. There's no sign of dates being arranged so far. Just a load of wank-fodder.'

'Were any of the men pushing for face-to-face meetings?'

'One guy raised the issue but Corinne cut off contact as soon as he started to press her on it. The rest didn't seem very fussed about moving it into real life.'

'Maybe he didn't like that,' Zigic suggested, hopefulness in his tone.

They'd been here before, last year, a murder which appeared to hinge on the victim's use of hook-up sites and Ferreira supposed it was only natural that Zigic believed this one might too. He didn't understand how the culture functioned, how casual it was, the sheer disposability of the people involved.

'Okay.' She met his expectant gaze. 'This all reads like Corinne is experimenting. And it happens, you know, loads of people use dating sites as ego trips or cheap entertainment. They're not looking to meet "the one", half of them aren't even interested in hooking up, they just get off on knowing the possibilities are there if they ever wanted to act on them. These men she's talking to, if they wanted sex they wouldn't be hanging around chatting, they'd call her a cock-tease and move onto the next profile. They're play-acting just as much as she is.'

Zigic frowned. 'Are you sure about that? Maybe they're enjoying the seduction. Building up anticipation before they finally meet.'

'No.' Ferreira smiled at how earnest he was. 'They're really not. And that's not something Corinne was interested in either, judging by how she was handling them.'

His shoulders dropped. 'She might have been arranging meetings by phone, we've got no record of that, have we?'

'I'm checking the texts and call logs next.'

Zigic went into his office and Ferreira returned to the long stream of messages, more of the same all blurring into one, the superficial differences disappearing within a predictable framework. She switched over to the call logs, found four numbers with heavy usage, always in the daytime, and she guessed it was easier to hide them from Sam than it would have been in the evening.

Out at work, in her car, alone. Sam wouldn't know what Corinne was doing or who she was talking to.

Something had piqued her suspicion though, Ferreira realised. Something had sent her riffling through Corinne's wardrobe, and what would she have done if she found this phone before they did?

Was it possible she knew about it already? Was she looking for it purely to dispose of it and obliterate the motive against her buried behind its locked screen?

They hadn't considered her a suspect but thinking about it now, wasn't it strange Sam came looking for Corinne so quickly? That she knew exactly where to find her among the thousands of acres of Ferry Meadows, the multiple entrances and exits?

It was the most common, tediously predictable of motives. Woman has affair, partner murders them. One of the biggest killers of women in the world: jealousy.

Ferreira rolled a cigarette and went to smoke it on the windowsill, damp, cold air seeping through her clothes and into her bones as she sat there, thinking about Simon Trent again, whether access to his phone and laptop would show them similar behaviour.

From what Von had said his behaviour sounded similar to Corinne's routine of picking men up in bars. Did he think Simone was a good enough mask to throw off any workmates or friends of his wife? Simon and Simone were two different people, it wasn't a crazy assumption, but still, it showed a wilful disregard for his security. Smacked of a desire to be caught.

And yet he'd buckled to his wife's ultimatum: Simone or me.

Ferreira didn't believe he'd stopped cross-dressing. Knew enough about the psychology to realise that would be torture. Simone was still in him, she couldn't be erased or denied, not forever. She was the person Ferreira needed to speak to, the one who'd been attacked, who would want revenge, but how to get to her when Simon was so firm in his denial of her continued existence?

She took a deep drag on her cigarette, trying to imagine the willpower involved in suppressing part of yourself like that. The pressure it would exert on you hour by hour, day by day, and how long you could go on before you cracked.

Simon was cracking. The anger he displayed when she suggested he was interested in men. She'd put it down to knee-jerk heterosexual defiance, but now she knew better. She'd got too close to the truth.

180

'Mel, with me.' Zigic was already heading for the door, one arm in his parka. 'Nina Sawyer has just called to report her daughter missing.'

'Jessica?'

'The other one, Lily.'

25

They found Nina red-eyed and furious when they reached the house, not the reaction Zigic expected from a mother whose teen-aged daughter was missing. When they tried to get her to sit down she only scowled and resumed stalking the length of the entrance hall, ballet pumps tapping against the tiles.

'How long's Lily been gone?' Ferreira asked.

'Her bed hasn't been slept in.' Nina shook her head, fist pressed to her mouth. 'She must have crept out yesterday evening sometime.'

Not twenty-four hours missing but she was young and grieving and Zigic knew they couldn't leave her out there on her own.

'Has Lily ever done anything like this before?'

Nina turned sharply on her heel. 'No, of course she hasn't.'

'You've tried her mobile?'

'She left it here.'

'Okay, have you called Lily's friends to see if she's staying with any of them?'

'I don't have their numbers. Not her new friends.' The disapproval was clear in her voice. 'Lily was excluded from school last year. I don't know any of the crowd she hangs around with now. She never brings them home.'

'Can you give us any of their names?'

'She doesn't talk to me about school,' Nina said, and the first hint of sadness rippled around her chin. 'She hardly talks to me at all any more.'

Ordinary teenage rebellion, Zigic wondered, or something deeper?

'Could she have gone to someone Corinne knew?' he asked. 'Her family, maybe?'

'Corinne's parents are both dead and he was an only child. There isn't any family for her to go.'

'And your parents?'

'They live in France over the winter.' Nina hugged her arms around herself. 'There's only us left now.'

'What about Brynn's family?' Zigic asked. 'They were close, weren't they? Have they stayed in touch?'

'Bob and Maura, yes they did. Maura always wanted a daughter, so . . .' She trailed off, making Zigic wonder how well she'd fulfilled the role since becoming involved with Brynn. 'But I tried them already, Lily isn't there.'

'You've called Sam?' Ferreira asked.

'Why would she go there?'

'It was Corinne's home.'

Nina didn't reply, only dipped her chin and looked away from them both, eyes fixed on a large black canvas hanging like an abyss opposite the front door.

'Have you called Sam to check?' Zigic asked.

She shook her head and Ferreira immediately took out her phone, paced away from them into the furthest corner of the entrance hall, her low conversation over in seconds. She nodded at Zigic; Lily found safe and well.

'Mrs Sawyer, you do realise it's an offence to waste police time,' he said.

'I believed she was missing,' Nina said fiercely, her voice dropping an octave. 'Her bed hadn't been slept in, what else was I going to think? I suppose you'd have preferred not to be bothered.'

'You thought she was missing but you didn't think to call the person she was most likely to be with?'

Nina crossed her arms, high over her chest, more defence than defiance. 'Well . . . why didn't she call me to let me know Lily was there? She must have known I'd be frantic. I am not the one in the wrong here.'

They left her to her denial, Zigic feeling a rising sense of annoyance at her for bringing them out here when they had better things to do.

'Fucking woman,' Ferreira said, as the front door closed behind them. 'There's no way she couldn't have guessed Lily might go to Sam's. To not even call and check . . .'

Zigic waited until they were pulling out of the driveway before he spoke. 'We should go and fetch the daughter.'

'Let her go home when she's ready. Christ, would you want to deal with Nina right now if you were her kid? I'd have run off, too.'

'The girl's taken off for a reason, we should talk to her while she's away from her mother.'

They drove to Corinne and Sam's house in the next village and Sam Hyde let them in with an apology.

'If I'd known had Lily snuck out I'd have told Nina she was here. She said Nina knew she was coming round. I didn't think she'd lie about it.' She cast a quick glance towards the staircase, where a black parka was thrown over the banister. 'She can stay here as long as she wants. I think she needs some space.'

'It's best we take her home.'

'You sure that's what's best for her?'

'She's legally a child,' Zigic reminded her. 'Nina's her legal guardian and we have to respect what she wants.'

Ferreira started up the stairs and Sam looked after her, frowning.

'Did Corinne keep a copy of her will at home?' Zigic asked.

Sam turned back to him, a quick snap of the head. 'Yes – why?'

'We need to see it.'

She led him through into the kitchen and went to an alcove where a few shelves had been placed to create a workstation, a laptop sitting there, phone and notepads. She pulled out a box file stuffed with paperwork. Not a very secure place to keep a will but not everyone bothered with security and he was glad Corinne hadn't.

Footsteps raced down the stairs and the front door slammed closed as Sam placed a large manila envelope on the table in front of him. Lots of paper in it, suggesting complicated arrangements.

'Looks like you're staying for a bit then,' she said. 'Coffee?'

'Tea would be good, thanks.'

'You must spend half your life in other people's kitchens drinking bad tea,' she said, smiling across her shoulder.

'It's not always bad.'

She switched the kettle on and Zigic asked about Brynn's parents as she made their tea.

'Have you met them?'

'A few times, yes,' she said. 'They're really lovely people. I mean, Corinne had a shit time with her own parents. Not because of how she was, they were just horrible, mean-spirited people. Bob and Maura were more like her mum and dad.'

'Are they local?'

She gave him an address and he made a note of it, thinking that the Morans might be able to give him a window onto the Sawyer family, that perhaps Corinne had confided in them the way she hadn't to anyone else. In the absence of her birth parents these surrogate ones were the next best thing.

Sam brought over their drinks, placed a biscuit tin in front of him, the same Emma Bridgewater one they had at home, printed with red hearts. He started to reach for a chocolate digestive then thought better of it; no running, no biscuits.

'I know I shouldn't ask but it's all I've been able to think about,' Sam said, gaze directed into the steaming mug she held between her palms. 'Was Corinne having an affair?'

Zigic thought of everything they had found on Corinne's phone, wasn't sure 'an affair' was the right description but it was definitely a kind of infidelity.

185

'She'd been in contact with men,' Zigic said, prompting a strangled gasp from Sam.

'Men?' Her eyes widened and she bared her small, back-slanting teeth in a grimace. 'But she wasn't – she didn't – oh my God, I can't believe she did that to me.'

'We don't think she was sleeping with any of them. We're not even sure if she met any of them right now.'

'Well, I guess that's something,' she said, her tone caught between sarcasm and bewilderment. 'I knew something was wrong. Corinne wasn't as physical with me as she used to be. We were – God, I can't believe I'm telling you this – we had a good sex life. We were . . . creative. I thought I was all she needed.' Sam shook her head. 'But, men? I thought she'd met another woman. I don't even know why this seems worse.'

Zigic felt a prickle of sympathy towards her, thinking of the unconditional support she'd given Corinne, the acceptance and love, and now she was hearing that none of that was enough to keep her from exploring other options.

'I've seen it happen before,' she said sadly. 'I was working at the Meadham when we first met, I'd been there for a couple of years, I knew a lot of the girls. I watched them taking their first steps into that world, bringing their wives and girlfriends along. But some of them, the partners fell away, and then they started bringing men in. Chasers – that's what we call them. It's a fetish for some guys. Everyone knows that but they don't care because they want men and they can't get normal guys so they put up with those freaks.'

'Are these men regulars on the scene?' Zigic asked.

'A couple of them have done the rounds.' She picked a biscuit out of the tin and dropped it straight back in. 'They're playing a game, just the same as the girls are. It's not something most men are going to boast about. They're users. Scum.'

'Did any of these chasers go for Corinne?'

'Just Sutton.'

186

'Sutton – the manager?'

She nodded.

Zigic remembered his broad shoulders and thick arms, the way he spoke about the women, joking but familiar. He'd made no secret of liking them as a group, seemed to enjoy their company and attention.

'How did Sutton behave around Corinne?'

'He's a flirt,' she said. 'But he understood that we were together. He tends to go for the new girls. They're more vulnerable, you know, desperate for approval. Corinne didn't need that from him, she had me.' Sam frowned, readjusting her perceptions. 'I don't know what to think any more. Maybe she was totally different around him when I wasn't there.'

'Like on Monday night?'

'I should have gone with her.'

'It wouldn't have changed anything,' Zigic said. 'We don't even know if the Meadham is part of this.'

She bit her lip. 'I've seen Sutton coming out of the office up there.'

'With a woman?'

'Yeah, that's where he takes them. He doesn't want to go out with them. He just wants his dick sucked by someone who knows how to do the job.' She smiled grimly. 'Who better than a cross-dresser for that, right?'

Zigic didn't know how to answer, so he took a mouthful of his tea and let the words dissipate before he spoke again, aware of the birdsong beyond the long glass wall and the low hum of the washing machine boxed away behind one of the cupboard doors. Life went on, washing still needed doing, the mundane tasks didn't stop because you were dying inside.

'What's Sutton's reputation like within the community?' he asked.

She considered it for a moment. 'Harmless lech.'

'Can you be a harmless lech?'

'He knows where the line is,' she said. 'If a girl's not interested he generally backs off.'

'Generally?'

'I heard he got a bit obsessed with one girl, but I don't know the details.' Sam shrugged. 'They're such a bunch of gossips it might not even be true.'

Or it might be, Zigic thought, picturing Simone Trent and Aadesh, wondering if they were the kind of vulnerable girls Sutton went for. Stunning but not yet sure of themselves in their new guises. If Sutton had seen encouragement which wasn't there, failed to spot that he'd crossed the line or charged across it focused on getting what he wanted from them. At any cost.

26

'Is this it?' Lily asked.

She turned a circle, biker boots squelching in the wet earth, looking for some evidence that Ferreira had brought her to the right place, something incontrovertible to prove that this was the spot where Corinne had died.

But there was nothing. No dried blood. No scrape marks. No gaping hole in the ground big enough to echo the scale of her grief.

It was just a small clearing between the budding trees, a slight depression which had hidden Corinne and her killer from the eyes of anyone passing on the nearby path.

Lily had insisted on seeing it for herself and Ferreira thought the girl deserved that much. In her position she would want the same thing, would need to test the atmosphere of the place and try to get some sense of her mother's soul lingering in air. She wasn't a religious person but under those circumstances even she would need to be sure.

'It's so close to the path,' Lily said. 'Why didn't someone stop him?'

Ferreira didn't have a good answer for her so she said nothing. The area was quiet at that time of morning but deep down she didn't quite believe the attack had gone unwitnessed. She'd dealt with enough cases where street fights were watched by crowds who never stepped in, murders which took place in houses separated by the thinnest of walls and yet nobody called the police until long after the screaming had stopped once and for all.

People didn't step in. They didn't want to get involved. Told themselves it was none of their business or they'd only get hurt if they tried to intervene. Anything to absolve them.

Lily squatted down and touched the earth. She seemed a strange kind of girl, completely unlike the rest of her family, with her grungy goth vibe, the long dyed black hair and stacked silver rings, dressed in grey leopard-print jeans and black jumper with an elaborate Mexican skull on the front.

Maybe she saw herself as an outsider and that made her more sympathetic to Corinne's situation.

'Why didn't she fight back?' Lily asked and she sounded like a child right then.

'It's not easy to fight back when someone comes at you from behind. You're off guard. Even if you're stronger than them you can't do much to defend yourself.'

'Mum was strong.'

'We think it happened very quickly,' Ferreira said, hoping she'd take some comfort from that.

Lily straightened up, her gaze sweeping across Ferreira, to the pathway and back again. 'But Mum was running on the path. So he must have dragged her over here. She had a chance to fight back.'

The girl was smart and that made this job harder. She wanted the truth but Ferreira couldn't give her it.

'Did she know him?' Lily asked. 'Is that why she just let him hurt her?'

Ferreira shoved her hands into her pockets, skin stinging with cold. 'I can't go into details with you, I'm very sorry, Lily, I'm afraid it's procedure.'

Lily squinted at her. 'It's usually a family member, isn't it? Or a lover? Statistically.'

A gust of wind battered Ferreira's back and she spread her feet to brace against it, now wishing she'd refused Lily's request to come here. If only she'd been a copper about it and driven her home to her mother, instead of letting sympathy overrule her better judgement. She'd seen something of herself in Lily, that was the problem. Recognised the watchfulness and the firmness which had come through in her request, an adolescent overconfidence which she suspected didn't run very deep. She played the same trick at that age, too much make-up and mouth, cultivated a look which said 'don't fuck with me' because it was safer than appearing approachable, opening yourself up to people who might hurt you.

'Jessica said Mum was having an affair.'

'We're looking into it.'

Lily let out a small growl of frustration. 'Why won't anyone tell me what's going on? My mum is dead!'

'I know how tough this is and—'

'Really?' Lily snapped. 'Has your mum been murdered?'

She should have taken her home. The girl was fragile and angry and it was her family's job to hold her hand through this, but evidently they weren't helping and it made Ferreira wonder what the atmosphere inside the house was like.

'I'm sorry,' she said. 'You're right, I don't know what you're going through but I can see that you're in a lot of pain and I just want to help.'

Lily apologised, a mumble almost lost on the rising wind.

'I can't deal with this.'

'There are people you can talk to,' Ferreira said. 'I can put you in touch with a counsellor if you'd like.'

'It won't help.'

'No, maybe not,' she admitted. 'Can't you talk to Nina about this? I'm sure she's struggling too.'

'You don't know what she's like.' Lily wandered away a few steps to touch the cracked and mottled trunk of a dead tree. 'She was so vile to Mum at Christmas. Making all these snide little comments and bitching about her appearance.'

'Is that what the fight was about?'

191

Lily nodded but didn't elaborate and Ferreira could see her reluctance. Harry and Brynn Moran had both minimised what had happened, had tried to pass it off as the usual seasonal sniping that had taken place at every dinner table as the holiday brought families together to air their petty grievances. She'd thought there was more to it at the time and now, watching Lily circle the tree, she was convinced the argument was anything but standard.

'Do you want a hot chocolate?' she asked.

They walked back to the car park near the lake and Ferreira ordered two chocolates from the small silver wagon stationed on the tarmac. In the car she started the engine to get the heater running, wriggled her toes inside her boots.

'It must have been hard for your mum,' she said. 'Walking back into her own home for Christmas. Is that the first year she'd gone back for it?'

'Yeah. Nina wouldn't have her there the year before. She wouldn't let me go to Mum's either.'

'But this year she was okay with it?'

'I basically had to beg her to invite Mum.' Lily took a mouthful of chocolate, as if washing away the taste of those remembered words. 'She only agreed because she wanted to show off.'

'Show off what?'

'That she was "moving on".'

'With your uncle Brynn?'

'Yeah.'

'What's he like?'

She shrugged. 'He's nice. He was always around when we were kids so it's not that different. I reckon he could do better. She talks to him like crap most of the time but he doesn't seem to mind. I think he's kind of a sub.'

A submissive. It was an odd term for a fourteen-year-old girl to use. Ferreira didn't think she'd have even been aware of it at that age, but times changed.

192

'Him and Corinne were close, right?'

'Before, yeah. They'd been best friends since primary school.'

'And after?'

'Until Brynn moved in with us, yeah. He doesn't give a shit about Mum transitioning. He knows she's still the same person whatever she looks like. But Nina wasn't going to put up with them still being friends, was she?' Another sip. 'That'd be like her losing.'

'That's sad,' Ferreira said. 'If they've been friends all this time. Didn't they see each other at all any more?'

'No. I think Nina was jealous of them being so tight. She's got Brynn now, she didn't want to share him with Mum. Even though they were friends first.' Lily's face hardened. 'That has to be more important than anything, doesn't it? You shouldn't let someone tell you who to be friends with just because you're sleeping with them.'

'Lots of people lose their friends when they get into a relationship,' Ferreira said, feeling like the wise old head and not liking the sensation. 'How were they at Christmas?'

'Brynn tried to keep Nina in check. She was making all these digs and he tried to calm things down. He gave up in the end and went to hide in the kitchen.' She frowned into her drink. 'It was always going to blow up.'

Ferreira turned to fully face her. 'What happened?'

'I don't know. I'd gone upstairs to check my phone and when I came down I heard Mum and Harry arguing in the hallway. Harry had hold of her under the arm. I mean he was *dragging* her out of the house. Her own fucking house.' Lily scowled and Ferreira could see how fresh the anger still was in her. 'I don't know what Harry said to Mum but it sounded serious. Mum slapped him.'

Ferreira let the words settle for a moment, thinking of Harry Sawyer and his history of violence. How would he respond to being hit?

'He must have upset her,' she said. 'How had they got on up till then?'

'Harry was backing Nina. Every little dig, every nasty joke.'

'Did any of them mention it after Harry threw her out?'

Lily looked down at the cardboard cup in her hands, thumbnail flicking at the ridges. 'You don't know my family. We don't talk.'

'Did you ask?'

'Of course I asked. They all ignored me.'

'What about Corinne?' Ferreira tried to keep her tone as neutral as possible. She could see Lily squirming where she sat, knew she was already regretting what she'd said. 'Surely your mum told you why she slapped Harry?'

Lily scrunched down in her seat, hiding half her face behind the fur trim of her parka. 'She said he was being a little shit. It was probably nothing. He'd had a few beers, he was mouthy. He always is but it doesn't mean anything.'

'Had Corinne ever hit any of you before?'

'No. Never. She wasn't like that.'

'So, it must have been something pretty bad for her to react like that,' Ferreira said gently, hoping to draw her out. But she could see Lily shutting down. Too much said and now she was wondering if she'd damned her brother. 'Lily, listen to me, I want you to think very carefully about what you heard.'

'I didn't hear anything,' she snapped. 'They were arguing. Everyone argues. It doesn't mean Harry killed Mum. He'd never do that.'

She reached for the door handle and Ferreira elbowed the locks.

'What are you doing? You can't keep me in here.' Lily looked scared, eyes wide and tearing up. 'I don't know anything.'

Shit, she'd spooked the kid.

'I'm going to take you home, okay?' she said, using her softest voice. 'I have to deliver you back to Nina.'

They drove the rest of the way in silence, back to the Sawyer house where Brynn was waiting at the front door for them, hands on his hips.

'These are my numbers,' Ferreira said, giving Lily her card. 'If you change your mind about the counselling or you think of anything else you want to tell me, just call.'

Lily got out of the car and almost ran to the house she'd slipped out of last night, as if it was the last safe place she had.

Ferreira turned round on the wide driveway and drove back to Sam Hyde's house, found Zigic sitting on the low stone wall in front of the church opposite, phone in his hand, looking unbothered by the wait.

'Sorry,' she said, as he got in. 'Lily had a bit more to say than I expected.'

She told him the story as they headed along Oundle Road and it didn't sound as damning somehow without the fear she'd seen on Lily's face and the girl's sudden back-pedalling.

'Murray called me a few minutes ago,' he said. 'Harry's girlfriend has verified his alibi.'

'So what? She was never going to do anything else.' Ferreira accelerated onto the parkway. 'What about Brynn?'

'Same. Nina was adamant he was at home until half past seven. But we've got a window of opportunity for both of them even with the alibis.' Zigic shifted in his seat, taking out a large manila envelope and putting it on the dashboard. 'Sam told me something interesting though. Turns out the manager from the Meadham has a fetish for cross-dressers. He's been with a few of them she says.'

'Corinne?'

'Sam says not. But he was flirting with her.'

Ferreira's hands tightened around the wheel. 'I knew it was going to come back to that place. We should talk to him.'

'Let him defend himself?'

'Or hang himself.'

27

Zac Bentley was in reception glad-handing a couple of suits when they arrived at the Meadham and Ferreira saw his professional composure slip, just a few degrees, the megawatt smile dim and drop from his eyes. He looked less together in general. His topknot not quite as neat as last time she'd seen him and did that Sleaford Mods T-shirt really go with the hacking jacket and the red trousers? It all seemed a bit desperate.

They walked straight past him, into the bar where the lunch-hour trade had slowed to a couple of small groups. Sutton was restocking one of the fridges and he straightened up sharply as if he'd felt their eyes on him.

'Afternoon.' Looking between them, smiling. 'What can I get you?'

'A chat,' Zigic said. 'Somewhere more private.'

That killed the smile.

'Smoking Room's empty.'

'That'll do.'

They followed him out through reception and Zac Bentley called after them. 'Is there a problem?'

'No problem,' Zigic said, eyes dead ahead.

They went into the same wood-panelled room as the last time they'd been here. Ferreira wondered if it was actually open to the public because there were no signs of use and the heating was off.

Sutton went to the bar. 'Are you sure you don't want something?'

'We're on duty,' Zigic said, taking a seat. 'But go ahead if you need one.'

'Force of habit.' Sutton joined them at the table, sat down, stood again, shoving his chair a foot back, giving himself leg room his stature didn't require. 'What's this about?'

'Corinne,' Ferreira said.

'I thought it might be.'

'You and Corinne.'

He scratched his neck. Not quite a tug at his collar but the same impulse and he was right to feel uncomfortable. Zigic had called Von Sherman on the way into the city centre and didn't get any joy from her but a couple of minutes later her husband called back and Zigic stuck the phone on speaker. Joe was hesitant at first but obviously Von had pushed him to speak to them and what he said caused Ferreira to put her foot down, wanting to get Sutton's side of the story as soon as possible.

'We have a witness', Zigic said, 'who saw you coming out of an office here with Corinne last summer. The office you use during the Trans Sisters events when you need privacy.'

Sutton smiled nervously. 'There's no law against it.'

'There is if you were coercing her,' Ferreira said.

'I didn't coerce anyone. She knew what she wanted.' His eyes brightened at the memory, like he was sharing with friends rather than police officers.

'Did you have sex with her?'

'Just a blow job.'

'How often did this happen?' Zigic asked.

'Only the once.'

'That must have been disappointing for you,' Ferreira said. 'Why didn't she want a repeat?'

Sutton shrugged, looked genuinely unconcerned. 'It was a pissed-up fumble, not the beginning of a bloody relationship. You don't know what that lot are like when they've had a few, totally out of control most of them. They can't let loose anywhere else.'

'Handy for them having you around to play with.'

'All consenting adults.' Sutton smoothed his palm along the thigh of his black wool trousers. 'They're a good group of girls. Bloody stunning most of them. I'm not made of stone.'

'And the fact that most of them are still technically men doesn't bother you?'

Sutton shot Zigic a furious look. 'No, it doesn't.'

'And the fact that Corinne was in a relationship?'

'That was her business.'

Ferreira thought she saw something stirring behind his eyes as he tried to hold himself still in the leather chair.

'What about Simone Trent?' she asked. 'Another consenting adult?'

He nodded. 'Beautiful girl. She's been missed.'

'Do you know why she hasn't been coming to the Trans nights?'

'I heard she got beat up.'

Ferreira held out her phone, showing Sutton a photo of Aadesh, glammed up in that striking gold dress. 'Do you know her?'

'Jasmine, yes. But she was out of my league,' Sutton said, tongue darting out quickly to wet his lips. 'I don't think she liked men, anyway.'

'How do you know that?'

'Just a vibe I got.'

'Did you try it on with her?'

'No. Like I said, she was out of my league.'

'She was beaten up as well – did you hear about that?'

'No.' Another slow scratch of the skin behind his ear and Ferreira thought of Aadesh telling her about his attack, the man's teeth grazing his earlobe, wondered if it was the teeth she was looking at now. 'I wondered why she'd stopped coming. I dunno, I thought maybe her family had got wind of it or something. Not very tolerant of the whole gender-bending in her community, are they?'

'What did she tell you about her family?' Ferreira asked.

'Nothing,' he said quickly. 'I just assumed she was Muslim.'

'Because she was brown-skinned?'

He put his hands up. 'Look, I'm not prejudiced, it just seemed likely.'

Zigic took over and Ferreira watched as Sutton answered the rest of his questions, the basics now, address details, where he was at the time of Corinne's murder. She studied the set of his shoulders and the way his foot rotated in the air, knew that this was often an indication of dishonesty but not a good enough one to take to the CPS.

He'd known all three victims. Had admitted to having a sexual relationship with two of them, a sexual interest in the third and, even if the cases weren't linked, it was a route worth pursuing.

Sutton provided an address on Rivergate, but no alibi; he lived alone. No one to question his movements. No one to corroborate them either and he admitted that it looked bad without any prompting.

Zigic thanked him for his cooperation and they left Sutton in the chilly wood-panelled room, not quite ready to get to his feet again, it seemed. As they walked out of the club Ferreira eyed the grand staircase, picturing Corinne coming down it, and wondered if their 'pissed-up fumble' had been more significant than he suggested. It was natural to lie now, minimise what had gone on between them. He was younger than Corinne by a good fifteen years, not the worst-looking bloke in the world, easy to believe she'd have been attracted to him. Enough to make it regular.

'I need to eat,' Ferreira said, as they hit Priestgate.

Zigic looked along the road. 'Am I finally going to get to see your new flat?'

'Only if you want dry cereal and tap water.'

'Caff, then?'

'Caff.'

They ended up in a new place on Cathedral Square. It was almost empty when they walked in and she went to a table in the window, back to the wall. It was always a race which one of them would sit eyes-out, just the way it was with coppers.

'My shout,' Zigic said, checking out the menu.

She picked and he went up to order.

Through the window she watched the street without taking any of it in, thinking of the route between Sutton's riverside apartment and the place where Corinne was murdered. He could have easily taken the towpath into Ferry Meadows without being seen. No CCTV cameras along there.

Zigic came back with their drinks, sat and took the manila envelope Sam Hyde had given him out of a deep pocket inside his parka.

'I don't like Sutton,' she said.

'No, I didn't think you would.'

'He's got better access than anyone.' She emptied two sachets of brown sugar into her coffee. 'And he knew all three women.'

'We've got no reason to believe the attacks are linked,' Zigic said.

'You don't think he's a linking factor?'

'Only if he did it.'

'He's not right.' Ferreira stirred her coffee. 'He's got a fetishist's mentality.'

'That doesn't make him dangerous.'

'It makes him highly focused.'

'I think you're confusing a fetish with an obsession.'

'There's barely a fag paper between the two,' she said. 'A fetish is just a repository for someone to pour all of their own . . . issues into. With cross-dressers, he's not interested in the person, he's interested in the presentation, right? They're not autonomous beings to him.'

Zigic raised an eyebrow at her. 'Joe Sherman said Corinne was happy enough with the state of affairs there. She was a grown woman, she knew what she was doing. We've got no evidence Sutton stepped out of line with her.'

'At the time, no. But what about afterwards?'

'We don't know about afterwards,' Zigic said. 'And I doubt he's going to tell us unless we can find some way of compelling him.'

'There's probably security cameras at his apartment block.'

'We'll get the footage.'

Ferreira propped her chin on her fist, watching Zigic open the envelope he'd brought with him, taking out a copy of Corinne Sawyer's will. It was six pages long and Ferreira didn't know if that was standard or complex. Lying in hospital, during her long recovery, she'd resolved to have a will drawn up, determined to leave things in order if she wasn't so lucky next time. But once she was released she decided against it, because really, what did she own to worry about? A car that wasn't paid for, a rental agreement on a flat, and six bin bags' worth of clothes.

The prospect of laying that out in front of a solicitor, admitting that that was what her twenty-nine years on the planet boiled down to, was one she couldn't face.

After a couple of minutes she asked, 'Who benefits, then?'

'Most of the estate goes into trust for Lily,' Zigic said. 'It matures when she's eighteen. It's structured to pay her way through university, then another release when she's twenty-one.'

'What about Sam?'

'There's a life insurance policy payable to her.'

'How much?'

'Five hundred thousand.'

Ferreira let out a low whistle. 'That's a pretty good motive for murder.'

'Isn't it. But there's no guarantee she knows about it.'

'Come on, she gave you the thing. It was right there in the house, she could have looked at it whenever she wanted to.' Ferreira sipped her coffee; it was acidic, cold-pressed. 'When was the will written up?'

'March last year.'

'Six months into their relationship, then. Doesn't that seem a bit soon to be making someone a major beneficiary in your will?'

Zigic nodded, didn't look up. 'Corinne must have thought they were serious.'

'Does Nina get anything?'

'No. Neither does Harry. There's a payment for Jessica in the form of shares in the business. She'll be holding a ten per cent stake.'

'That's not much.'

'Her stake's estimated at three hundred thousand. At March 2015 prices.'

'Did you think they were that rich?' Ferreira asked.

Zigic slipped the will back into the folder. 'I thought they were well off, I didn't think it would be on this scale. But, three million in a rental portfolio isn't crazy. If they bought back in the nineties they probably only paid a small percentage of what the properties are worth now.'

The waiter brought over their food, a chicken wrap for Ferreira, salad for Zigic.

'What are you eating salad for?' she asked. 'Is this because I made that crack about your jacket looking a bit tight?'

'No.'

'Men can carry a bit of heft, you know.'

'"Heft"?'

'I'm just saying.' She took a bite out of her wrap, chilli hitting her tongue, not as much as she'd use at home but enough to make her eyes water. 'That kind of money, any one of them could have killed Corinne over it.'

'We need to get hold of the divorce application,' Zigic said. 'Corinne and Nina are still married, remember? There's serious money at stake and now Corinne's dead Nina can probably challenge the will and keep hold of everything.'

'Is that how it works?'

'Yeah.' He speared a crisp piece of lettuce. 'And I bet Nina knows it, too.'

28

'Your mum's been frantic,' Brynn said, closing the door behind her. He was red in the face, more agitated than she expected and Lily guessed he'd been forced to listen to some rambling speech from Nina about what an ungrateful little bitch she was. He was wearing his smart work clothes today, cords and a jumper, so he'd been with clients rather than on-site and Nina had dragged him home, wanting an audience for her maternal concern.

He'd bought it. He always did.

'She called the police. Why didn't you stop her?'

'She was worried about you. What else was she going to do?'

Lily didn't believe that for a second.

She shrugged off her coat and threw it over the banister. Brynn immediately retrieved it and took it to the hidden space under the stairs, slid the door shut, the wall appearing seamless again. That was this house all over, everything secreted behind flawless facades.

'She should have known where I was,' Lily said, kicking off her boots. 'Why didn't she phone Sam?'

'Come on now, you know that wasn't going to happen.' Brynn frowned at the muddy footprints she'd brought in with her. 'All you had to do was text her so she knew you were okay.'

She started off towards the stairs and Brynn caught hold of her arm.

'Your mum's in a state, Lil. Just cut her some slack, will you?'

'She doesn't fucking care.'

He gave her a warning look. Brynn didn't like her swearing and usually she minimised it in front of him but right now it didn't seem important.

'She might not show it around you but she's really not coping with this.' He was speaking almost in a whisper, knowing how voices carried through the house. 'Whatever happened between her and Colin in the last few years, they were together a long time and she still cared about him. She might not have liked Corinne much, but she loved your dad. Try to remember that.'

Lily wanted to snap at him. Remind him Colin had been gone for years and Nina was the one who drove him away. But he looked totally deflated, so tired and sad that she couldn't bring herself to correct him.

'Did you miss him?' she asked. 'Dad. You were friends for so long. How could you just give up on him?'

'I didn't give up on him, Lil.'

'You let Nina get between you. He always said you were like family. He said he loved you like a brother.'

Brynn sat down on the staircase, covered his mouth with his hand as he began to cry, almost as if he was ashamed of the tears. Lily squeezed onto the step next to him and put her arm around his shoulder, whispered that she was sorry, she didn't mean to upset him. But secretly she was glad because now it meant she wasn't alone in her grief any more.

They'd been best friends since they were five years old. Dad had told the story often enough, the first day of school and Brynn peed his pants in the playground, stood crying while a crowd of kids laughed around him. Dad elbowed through them, stood at his side while the taunts flew. The biggest kid there stepped forward, whipping the rest up. Dad rushed the older boy and slammed him to the ground, punched him in the face until a teacher came and pulled him away, still kicking out. But nobody was laughing any more. And nobody bullied Brynn again, knowing what they'd get if they tried it.

Lily could see that nervous little boy in him now, as he wiped his eyes on the cuff of his jumper and tried to be a man again, and she felt his pain in her own chest.

'Sorry,' he said awkwardly. 'It keeps sneaking up on me.'

'Me too.' Lily tried to smile, but couldn't. There was no softening this feeling. 'I keep thinking about all the time I didn't see her in the last couple of years. All that time we should have had together.'

'You never know when people are going to leave you,' Brynn said, his chin dimpling again. 'That's why you have to be kind to them. Your mum too. Even her.'

Lily drew away from him and stood up. Why did he have to bring her into this?

'I'm going for a nap.'

She trudged upstairs, hearing the hiss of the steam cleaner from the kitchen as Nina tried to purge more non-existent dirt from all her shiny surfaces.

In her room she flopped down on the bed, turned her mobile phone on. There were messages stacked up on the screen, one from Brynn, six from Nina. Jack texting yesterday, asking if she was alright, saying people were worried about her. The battery was almost dead and she decided to let it bleed dry. Didn't want to talk to anyone. Not even him.

She shouldn't have insisted on going to where it happened. That was in her head now and it was worse than she ever could have imagined.

Mum dragged off the path, through the mud. She would have been so scared. Did she shout for help that never came? Did she see someone run past without stopping?

Shit. Did she see them see her and still keep running?

Lily wanted to believe she fought back. Punched and kicked and scratched at the man who killed her. But the way Sergeant Ferreira described it, the things she didn't say, Lily knew it hadn't been like that.

Mum had died face down in the dirt, breathed her last breath into it.

Her beautiful new face . . .

Lily curled up under the duvet, blocking out the last of the afternoon light, remembering how wet the earth was, the rotten smell of it, the mulch of black leaves and dead things all gone to sludge.

Every time she walked through fallen leaves, saw a cracked and mottled tree trunk, caught a hint of wet grass on the air – *every time* – she was going to think of Mum's last moments. She would be back there, squatting within sight of a deserted pathway, knowing how easily she could have been saved.

Exhaustion overcame her and she dozed for awhile, a mercifully dreamless sleep broken by the sound of a tentative fist tapping at her bedroom door.

Harry came in without waiting for an invitation. 'Lil, are you awake?'

She threw her duvet off. 'What do you want?'

'Brynn said you were upset.'

'I'm fine.'

'Do you want to talk about it?'

'Not to you.'

Harry came over and sat on the foot of her bed. He smelled of grass and leaves, and for a moment she was back there, fingers in the dirt where Mum died.

She pushed the thought aside, tried to remember the last time Harry had been in her bedroom, couldn't. She was ten years old when he moved into his own place, still young enough to idolise him. It was a long time since she'd felt that way.

'Carly and the boys are here. Aren't you going to come down and say hello?' he asked.

'I don't feel well. I'm staying up here.'

He sighed, rubbed his palms on the knees of his jeans. He seemed nervous but she wasn't sure why. Was it because the police had spoken to him? Had they already started to act on what she'd told them?

No, he wouldn't be here if they had.

She looked at his hands, the size of them, and knew there was enough strength there to have choked the life out of Mum. But she couldn't believe he'd done it.

'We're all upset, you know,' he said. 'You're not the only person who's lost their . . . parent. Do you think I don't feel like crap right now? I loved Dad.'

'This isn't about Dad.'

'Yes, it is. Because he's never coming back now,' Harry said, his voice thickening, and Lily realised he actually believed there was a chance Mum would have changed her mind, decided being a woman was a phase or a mistake and gone back to how Harry wanted her to be. 'We'll never see him again.'

'Her,' Lily said firmly. 'He was gone years ago.'

'You don't get it.' A pain looked crossed Harry's face and for a moment Lily saw Mum there, remembered the pictures of them together, how everyone said Harry was the image of Dad. Mum's cosmetic procedures had wiped the likeness away but seeing that glimpse of her when he frowned made her heart ache.

'How you feel now,' he said. 'That's how the rest of us felt when he decided to transition. We've been bereaved for months, Lil. Don't you understand that?'

The sympathy she was beginning to feel drained away.

'It's not the same thing.' She kicked out at the bunched-up duvet. 'You didn't lose Dad, you just wouldn't accept what he wanted to do. If you loved him you'd have loved Mum, too.'

'It's not that simple.' He twisted on the bed, facing her properly. He was heavy-eyed, skin slack under his beard. 'He changed so

208

much. You didn't know him before Corinne. You don't realise how bad he got when he was her.'

'That's rubbish.' Lily shifted onto her knees, propelled into defence. 'They were the same person inside. If anything Mum was nicer.'

'To you maybe.'

'You started it,' Lily told him. 'You hated her because Nina wanted you to.'

'I hated how she was treating Mum, that's all. You were too young to realise what was going on most of the time. Corinne made Mum's life totally unbearable.'

'And Nina didn't do anything wrong, I suppose?'

'You think all that wasn't hard on her as well?' he said, anger bubbling up in his voice. 'It wasn't just Dad putting a dress on now and again, you know. Why don't you try looking at this from Mum's point of view for once? How do you think she felt about it?'

'I don't care.'

Harry stood up, moved away to her desk.

Nina had sent him up here, using him like she always did, wanting someone else to do her dirty work. As if he could talk her round. After how he'd behaved at Christmas and all of the times before that, ridiculing Mum, belittling her. Even when he was trying to play the good guy he was just as bad, saying she was suffering from a mental disorder, a form of body dysmorphia. God knows where he'd picked up that term but it was the same old insult dressed up in scientific language: she was a freak.

'Why did Mum hit you?' Lily asked.

He turned round slowly, but didn't answer her, his eyes flicking towards the door.

'At Christmas. I saw it, Harry. What did you say to her?'

'She was unhinged, I didn't need to say anything to her.' He shoved his hands into the back pockets of his jeans. 'It was probably the hormones scrambling her brain.'

Lily smiled scornfully at him. 'Is that the best you can come up with? I think the police are going to want a better explanation.'

'You told the fucking plod?' He stormed towards her and Lily scrambled off the bed away from him. 'Why the hell did you do that? They're going to think I killed Corinne!'

'Did you?'

Harry winced, gripped the back of his neck, an expression of absolute horror on his face. 'For Christ's sake, Lil. No, I didn't. I can't believe you asked me that.'

Lily almost apologised but he walked out of the room before she could speak.

She swore to herself.

Of course he wasn't responsible.

You couldn't murder your own blood and hide it.

But a small voice in the back of her mind piped up – people did it all of the time. Murdered their husbands, or more often their wives, killed their children and hid the bodies and made tearful displays of grief, played innocent until the police could prove otherwise. Kept lying long past the point of doubt.

29

Back to Corinne's secret fantasy life, and in light of the afternoon's conversations Ferreira felt even less convinced they would uncover the murderer there.

Sutton knew all three women and had had sexual contact with Corinne, which bumped up the likelihood of him being responsible, simply because prior intimates were statistically the greatest danger to women. Far more so than random attackers who jumped out of the shadows.

She didn't like how flippant he was, how pragmatically he appraised Jasmine as out of his league, suggesting he considered Corinne fair game, expecting gratitude for his attention.

There was more to him, she thought.

But no potential lead could be left unexplored, so she sent over the emails to the tech department and asked them to trace the IP addresses, see who, if any, was local, then set Bobby to work on the mobile phone numbers, let him work his charms on the providers or the dating site firms, whoever was most susceptible.

There was no sign of meetings being arranged via text message. It was just more of the same with a few dick pics thrown in, the calibre of them suggesting Corinne was aiming down in age, attracting young men drawn by the idea of an experienced older woman. The photographs she'd sent back were all of her chest and Ferreira had to admit the boob job she'd had done was very good, a sentiment shared by the intended recipients judging by their responses.

The only odd note was in Corinne's correspondence with a man who'd picked the username 'HungDaddy' – Ferreira checked; he deserved it. They'd engaged in the usual sex talk and his taste was pretty standard. But around a third of their conversation was about football, both of them Spurs fans and once he got over the initial shock of her interest they went on at length about tactics and transfers and injuries, seemed to be messaging each other as they watched games.

It was the only instance of friendly, vaguely bantering discussion in all of what she'd read and Ferreira began to wonder how much Corinne missed that kind of thing.

Would Brynn be who she usually dissected each match with? Her almost-brother, her oldest friend, the man her children called uncle and had accepted so smoothly into their family because he'd been a regular presence ever since they could remember.

How could you drop a friendship like that? Brynn still seemed attached to Colin's memory and Colin was still in there. There was no reason for them to break contact. Except that Nina would hate it if they didn't.

She tried to decide what she'd do in that position. Being told by your lover that you couldn't see a particular friend was a massive red flag. Indicated controlling behaviour, the cutting away of a support network. At the very best it was an unreasonable demand to be at the centre of your attention.

She didn't think she'd put up with it, but had never been placed in that position.

If you thought you were in love and the issue was framed correctly, maybe it would be easier to let a friend slip away than keep being accused of privileging them above all else.

Zigic came back into the office, returning from a debriefing in CID.

'What happened with Adams?' she asked.

'Walton's car came up clean. He is not happy about that.'

'Like it was going to be anything else. Walton's not that stupid.'

212

'We had to check,' Murray said, turning away from her desk, a defensive edge in her voice. 'You might want to take a look at this, sir.'

Zigic went over to her desk and Ferreira was at his elbow a few seconds later, both of them focusing on the image from a CCTV camera. It showed a car park, bordered by a black tarmac pathway, and beyond that a grey sheet of water, mottled and shadowed by clouds. One of the lakes at Ferry Meadows, the one near the boat-house, Ferreira realised, the place Lee Walton had been on the morning of Corinne's murder.

The date stamp at the bottom of the screen was over two weeks old though.

'Why are you checking this far back?' Zigic asked.

'I wanted to get a feel for Walton's routine,' Murray said, her shoulders squaring. 'And it turns out he's got a very interesting one. He's been to Ferry Meadows nine times in the two weeks leading up to Corinne's murder.'

Ferreira leaned over Murray's shoulder. 'Is that his car, the silver one?'

'Yep, that's him.' Murray unpaused the footage and the driver-side door opened, Lee Walton climbing out, hopping over the barrier and onto the pathway before disappearing out of shot. 'He's going there at different times of the morning, between sunrise and eight thirty.'

'He needs it to be light enough to see who's about,' Ferreira said.

'Exactly.'

Zigic folded his arms, clearly unimpressed with what Murray was showing him. 'Corinne's routine was far more stable than that. She'd have been home by the time he arrived.'

'He's scouting for a victim,' Ferreira said. 'Isn't that the obvious answer here? He's going at different times because he's looking for the right type?'

Zigic nodded. 'Which isn't Corinne.'

Murray changed to a different section of film. Ten days previous, 7.56 a.m. Sunlight glinting on the car's windscreen, shimmering over the gently wavering surface of the lake. A man ran past, a scruffy white dog following on a long lead. Then Walton got out of his car and stepped over the barrier again, straight into the path of a woman in neon-pink leggings and a matching beanie, who swerved around him, before sprinting on.

'And there she is,' Murray said.

'Play it again.'

The same few seconds and this time Ferreira was watching for Walton's reaction to Corinne, saw nothing as she ran past him. He had his eyes down, was concentrating on zipping up his coat.

'He didn't even notice her.'

'He noticed her,' Murray said firmly.

Again she took the footage back and whatever interplay she was witnessing Ferreira didn't see it. Corinne was moving fast, past Walton in a second.

'I don't think he did,' Zigic said. 'He's not looking in her direction as he goes over the barrier, he doesn't look after her once she's gone and his attention is elsewhere when she passes him.'

He stepped away from her desk and Ferreira could see the uncharacteristic anger stiffening his shoulders and arms. Knew he was coming to the end of his patience with Murray. He was a good boss and he expected that to count for something with the officers under him. Respect given, respect returned. But Murray was fixated on Walton, wasn't prepared to pursue any other lines of inquiry. She'd done everything he asked her to, but grudgingly, making the minimum effort so she could return to this as quickly as possible.

Maybe she thought Zigic was a pushover after working under Adams for so long, someone she could steamroller despite being a lower rank.

214

On the desktop Murray's hand made a quick fist and opened again. 'Walton is there on the morning she's murdered and now we've got him stalking her in the weeks leading up to her death.'

'This doesn't even meet the loosest criteria for stalking,' Zigic said, glancing at Ferreira as if for support. 'It's coincidental.'

'In fairness he's obviously up to no good,' she said. 'But we've been through this, Corinne isn't his type.'

Murray stood up, looking between the two of them with an expression of barely checked fury. 'She might not fit the typology for the victims we know about but Walton is filth. He's a fucking animal. Who knows how many other women he's attacked who haven't come forward yet. He's got a record going back to his teens. You know how this works. Men like him escalate, they want fresh challenges. Their victim type evolves. It broadens out.'

'You've got nothing to tie Walton to Corinne.' Zigic walked away, went to pour himself a coffee.

'And you've got nothing to suggest this is a Hate Crime,' Murray snapped. 'What are we looking at here? Some bloke she was dicking about killing her? Her son getting pissed off and going for her? If this isn't a Hate Crime it should be in CID.'

Zigic slammed his cup down, coffee sloshing over his hand. 'If you can't work as part of this team you should be in CID.'

'I'm liaising,' Murray said.

'You're obsessed.'

'That piece of shit has been building up to this for years,' Murray said, stabbing her finger towards the screen. 'If you can't see that . . .'

'Yes, DS Murray?' He waited, giving her a hard stare. 'If I can't see that, what?'

She looked away from him, mumbled an apology.

Zigic jerked his head towards the door. 'Go home, Colleen.'

'But—'

'Go home and make sure you've got your head straight by tomorrow morning.'

Murray snatched her bag from under her desk and strode out of the office with her chin in the air, footfalls ringing out hard all the way to the stairwell door.

'You know she's taking this straight down to Adams, don't you?' Ferreira said.

'I don't give a shit what she does.'

Ferreira backed away with her hands up, went to the windowsill to roll a cigarette. He was under more strain than she'd realised, or wasn't coping with it as well as he usually did. The sleepless nights, perhaps, piling up now. They all knew Riggott wanted the case moving from them, that he could whip it away at any moment. This footage might be enough for Adams to sway him and they had no counter-argument.

Zigic was staring at the board and Ferreira eyed it too, knowing what he was thinking – *this* is all we have to show for three days' work.

Nina Sawyer, Harry Sawyer, Brynn Moran, Sam Hyde. Up there because they were family and families could always find a reason to kill one another.

Walton – sexual sadist, recidivist, in the area.

Sutton – 'chaser'. Maybe worse.

'Is there a link we're missing?' Zigic asked.

'Where?'

'Between Walton and Corinne.'

Ferreira looked at the paperwork piled up on Murray's desk. 'If there was one she'd have shoved your face in it.'

Zigic checked his watch. 'Let's look at this afresh in the morning. Maybe the tech department will come back with something from Corinne's phone.'

'Ever the optimist.' Ferreira slammed the window shut.

'Morning briefing at half eight,' he said. 'Any bright ideas welcome.'

216

30

If it hadn't been on his way home Zigic probably wouldn't have stopped in on the Morans after he left the station, but their bungalow was a few minutes away and this seemed like a good time to catch them in.

As he pulled up outside he realised he'd been mistaken. There was no car on the cracked concrete driveway and the front windows were in darkness. But as he switched the engine off he heard music playing, a dull bass thud coming from somewhere in the back garden.

The peeling gates at the side of the house swung open under his hand and he followed the crazy-paved path towards an outbuilding which was too big for the suburban garden. What was left of it had been divided up with railway sleepers into planting beds, narrow walkways between them, all immaculate in comparison to the overgrown tangle at the front of the house.

Machine noise buzzed out of the workshop, temporarily drowning out the music; a high, sharp whine which drilled into the roots of his teeth as he approached.

Through a long window he saw a man bent over in concentration, dust flying up towards his craggy, grey-bearded face. Singing and nodding his head as he worked, no goggles to shield his eyes, no ear protectors. He was of a generation who didn't believe in health and safety, which was probably why he needed his music on so loud, Zigic thought.

The workshop door was open, revealing a cobbled-together run of counters all cluttered with what Zigic took to be motorbike parts, maybe from Harley-Davidsons if the collection of old advertising panels clustered on the far wall were anything to go by. There were two bikes under dust sheets, one stripped down to its bare bones, in a poor state of repair, but the place seemed well enough equipped to rebuild it three times over.

Zigic waited until the man switched off the grinding wheel he was using to blast the corrosion off a chrome part, leaving only Planet Rock to raise his voice over.

'Mr Moran?'

He turned the sound down on the radio, squinted at Zigic momentarily. There was reddish dust in the lines on his face, gingering his beard.

'Saw you on the telly, didn't I?' he asked. 'You're after that bastard who killed our Colin.'

'That's right.'

'Poor bugger,' Bob Moran said. 'He never deserved that. All this time he's been living a lie and he finally gets what he wants and some bastard goes and does that.'

He walked over to a fridge tucked under a steel table, took out a bottle of beer and snapped the top off by banging it against the edge of the countertop.

'You havin' one?'

It was a good beer and he was off duty. 'I will, thanks.'

Bob Moran handed him a bottle, unopened, watched as he levered the top off with the metal fob of his car keys. A faint smile tweaked one corner of the older man's mouth; test passed.

'You must think we're a rum lot.' Bob leaned against the worktop. 'Colin leaves Nina to go live as a woman, then she goes and shacks up with his best mate.'

'That's not so unusual when a relationship breaks down,' Zigic said.

'He's always fancied her. Never did owt about it, not until Colin moved out. Brynn wouldn't have done that. He's not the sort. And not with his best mate's missus.'

218

'Even though Colin was cheating on Nina the whole time they were married?' Zigic asked, surprised they'd got here so fast. He would have taken things gently but Bob Moran was obviously a man who didn't stand on ceremony.

'Colin were a bugger with the women. Always had a bloody harem hanging off his arse, since he were a kid.' Bob nodded to himself, eyes sparkling at the memory. 'Mind, he were a good-looking lad.'

'They were close, Brynn and Colin?'

'Like brothers,' Bob said. 'His mum and dad lived a few doors up from us. They were no good, them two. You only had to take one look at that old bastard to see what he was made of. Pure shithouse, drunk half the time and even nastier when he was sober. She weren't no better. Mouth on that woman.' He shook his head sadly. 'She was the one who used to belt Colin. We should've said summat, but everyone smacked their kids back then – who was going to listen to us?'

Zigic could see how much it pained him still, ancient history now but his bewilderment still fresh and sharp. He thought about what Lily had told Ferreira, Corinne slapping Harry, and wondered if it was a common occurrence within the family. Whether Corinne was just repeating the cycle.

How many kids took the beatings for as long as they had to, waiting to grow big enough and strong enough to finally raise their own fists in retaliation? Was that slap the last time Harry Sawyer would take it?

'How long have Corinne's parents been gone?' Zigic asked.

'His mum went nigh on twenty years ago, his dad a couple of years after that. But he hadn't had owt to do with 'em in a fair bit before that. Colin moved out when he was sixteen, went down to London to work labouring on Docklands. We never thought he'd come back but then one morning, three, four years later, right out the blue, we found him out the front of the house asleep in his car.'

Corinne's early life seemed impossibly remote from how she'd ended up, in that sprawling, modernist house, with her three-million-pound property portfolio and the educated, middle-class wife she'd left behind. Again, Zigic found himself struggling to reconcile this new element with the many versions of Corinne they'd been given by the people who knew her. She seemed to be a chameleon, reinventing herself, editing herself, showing different sides to the different people in her life.

'When was the last time you saw Corinne?' he asked.

'Few weeks back, she come round to bring Maura some seeds.'

'How did she seem?'

'Same as usual. She was happy.' Bob shifted his weight from one foot to the other, wincing slightly. 'Bloody sciatica, feels like I'm being stabbed.'

He moved back to the opposite counter and lowered himself onto the stool.

'Was anything bothering her?'

'Not that she mentioned to me.'

'What about your wife? Might Corinne have confided in her?'

'Maybe. But she didn't say anything to me about it.'

'Are they close?' Zigic asked.

Bob nodded. 'Always were. Now Corinne's . . . how she is, Maura loves that. She always wanted a daughter. It's the best of both worlds for her.'

Nina Sawyer had said the same thing and Zigic thought he'd detected a hint of reproach in her tone at the time. Maybe even envy.

'She's got Nina now. A daughter-in-law. Isn't that the same thing?'

Bob put his beer bottle down, the glass chiming against a piece of metal. 'It's not the same as with Corinne. Maura was a sight better mum than Colin had at home, there's no substitute for that history.'

'It must have been awkward for you two,' Zigic said. 'Corinne on one side, Brynn and Nina on the other . . .'

'Not really.'

Zigic drained his own beer, held on to the empty bottle. 'What about Brynn? Nina didn't like them being friends still, I imagine.'

'She'd have got over it.'

'But she hadn't yet?'

The radio was playing, turned down low, a Green Day track Zigic recognised but didn't like filling the silence.

'You still see the lads you were mates with before you got married?' he asked finally. 'You put your woman first if you're any sort of a man. Brynn were in a tough spot but he weren't going to upset Nina by taking Corinne's side in all of this.'

'All of what?'

'This. The divorce. The change. All of it.'

'Is she really that demanding?'

'You must have talked to her already. You need me to tell you the sort of woman she is?'

'She's under a great deal of stress. I'd like to know how she is when that's not the case.'

Bob Moran sucked in his cheeks. 'Honestly? I never much liked her when she was with Colin and don't much like her now.' He put up his hand in defence. 'I'm not saying she didn't have a hard time of it with Colin – God knows he never treated her right, with all the other women and that, but if anyone could drive a good man to go looking elsewhere it's her.'

'Aren't you worried what she'll drive Brynn to?' Zigic asked.

He meant murder but Bob Moran either didn't understand or chose not to.

'Brynn's as loyal as a dog. He won't go on like Colin did. Soft bugger worships the ground she walks on. Loves those kids like they're his own.' Absently he began to sweep the reddish dust on the counter into a pile with the side of his hand. 'He's always been that way. With Colin, with his other girlfriends. He'd walk through fire for the people he cares about.'

On the radio the hour sounded and Zigic thought of his family at home starting another evening without him.

'I'd like to talk to your wife at some point,' he said.

'She's over the home visiting her mum. I couldn't tell you what time she'd be back. Once they get chanking . . .'

'I'll stop by another time, then.'

Bob Moran nodded. 'Plenty more beers in the fridge.'

31

Ferreira spent forty minutes on the treadmill, trying to find the 'bright idea' Zigic wanted. Stepping off with nothing but a twinge in her calf, she showered quickly, thinking about the drink she'd earned and the new series of *Scandal* she'd left downloading while she was at work.

The streets were already busy with people out rehearsing for the weekend as she drove through the centre of the city. She wasn't in the mood for it, though. By the time she pulled into the car park under her building her legs were beginning to ache and for once she ignored the stairwell and took the lift up to the fourth floor.

She slipped the key in the lock, threw her bag down and only distantly registered that the radio was playing in the kitchen.

Had she left it on this morning?

Something cracked and she heard a muffled curse.

Instinctively she looked around herself for a weapon, couldn't find one. She had a baton but it was in the car. The knives were all on the other side of whoever was in there. For half a second she debated giving them fair warning and decided against it. Drop them first; ask questions later.

As she headed for the door, clenched fist held poised to strike, Adams came out, a glass in his hand, tea towel over his shoulder, looking for all the world as if he belonged there.

'What the fuck are you doing?'

'Welcome home, yourself,' he said, the smile he'd been wearing straightening into a wounded line. 'Thought you might fancy dinner. I bought steak.'

'How did you get in?'

He held the glass out like a peace offering but she didn't take it.

'Come on, Mel, don't be like that.'

'You broke in.'

'I was trying to do something nice for you.' Again he pushed the glass on her and she took it, needing the alcohol to calm her down. 'And I didn't break in. Your neighbour saw me waiting in the hall and took pity on me.'

Adams went back into the kitchen, where a chopping board sat on the worktop, red peppers and onions finely sliced, a row of spices lined up nearby. Reflected in the darkened window it looked like an ordinary scene, him cooking, her sipping a drink, but it didn't feel right.

'Which neighbour?'

'The woman next door,' he said, slamming the flat of the knife blade down on a clove of garlic. 'She had a key. The tenant before you gave her it so she could look after his plants.'

Ferreira noticed the small silver key lying on top of the day's mail, pocketed it. 'Why did she think it was okay to give you a key to my flat?'

He flashed her a pointed smile. 'You know how persuasive I can be.'

'That's not an answer.'

'I told her I'd lost mine. She seemed to think I lived here.' He went for his wine. 'You're acting like I've done something weird.'

'How would you've felt if you came home to find I'd conned my way into your place?'

'If I came home and found you standing in my kitchen in a little pinny . . .' He took a step towards her, his hand running around her waist, and despite herself she felt her body mould automatically to his, head rolling away as his lips brushed her ear. 'I'd eat whatever you put in front of me.'

She pushed him off her. 'Don't do this again.'

He wasn't forgiven and she wouldn't forget, but he was in the flat now and she was hungry and there was no point sending him away before she had what she wanted.

This wasn't how it was supposed to go, though. They weren't a couple, they didn't go in for thoughtful gestures. They just fucked.

Ferreira peeled off her jeans and threw her jumper onto the chair in the corner of the bedroom. What did he want from her? Some cosy night in in front of the TV, some semblance of domesticity? Adams wasn't the kind of man who craved that.

Adams – Christ, she couldn't even use his first name in her head. That was how emotionally intimate their 'relationship' was. Some men would only ever be their surnames, the ones you had to keep at a distance, the ones whose depths you weren't interested in fathoming. Even in bed, even when she was breathless and half blind, every muscle in her body clamped around him, he would never be Billy.

She pulled on a pair of wash-faded pyjama bottoms and a vest, then dragged her hair into a high, unflattering ponytail. No make-up, not even the bare minimum swipe of lipstick. If he wanted to play at domesticity she could do that.

In the kitchen she found her glass refilled and the look he gave her when she walked in suggested her choice of outfit wasn't entirely successful. Shouldn't have gone with the white vest, she thought, as she took a long mouthful of dark rum.

'Is that quinoa?'

He sparked the gas under the pan. 'It is.'

'I don't eat that.'

'Have you tried it?'

'It's wanker food.' Ferreira took a tin of tobacco out of a drawer. 'Can't you do rice?'

'Let's just agree that I'm actually a slightly better cook than you, yeah?' He started measuring out spices and stirring them into the quinoa.

225

'You don't know what kind of cook I am.'

'So, next time you can make dinner.'

Already assuming this was going to become a regular thing. She sealed her cigarette and moved the pan aside to light up, wondering if she'd been stupid not to see it coming.

While he cooked they talked about work, discussed the challenges of the case and the situation within the Sawyer family, getting through more drinks and more cigarettes, the smell of spices filling the kitchen and then the hiss and sear of the steak, which smoked so much as it hit the heat that she had to open the window. She switched off the lights and watched the cloud of fumes billowing into the night air.

Along the street she saw a taxi pull up outside the Meadham and thought about Aadesh and Simone for the first time in what felt like days. She still hoped one of them might feel stirred by Corinne's murder into coming forward with information she was sure they had, but held out little hope. They both had far too much to lose.

'Close up,' Adams said. 'Dinner's ready.'

They took their food into the living room, ate sitting on the floor at the coffee table, and for awhile the meal distracted them. He did most of the talking, his favourite chefs and which supermarket had the best butchers, a restaurant in town she really should try. Adams was way more of a foodie than she'd realised and, she had to admit, he was a pretty decent cook too. The steak perfectly done, the quinoa nicely spiced. Even the wine he picked was okay.

'How was the wanker food?' he asked when she'd cleared her plate. 'Better than rice?'

'It was fine.'

'I'll convert you, give it time.'

He topped up her wine and she leaned back against the sofa. Maybe this was better than the evening she'd planned after all.

226

He was talking about Walton again and she tried to focus, but the words washed over her, all she caught was the defeat in his voice. He wanted to nail Walton so badly but even he could see the prospect slipping away.

Suddenly he shook out of it. 'Dessert?'

'I'll get it.' Ferreira struggled to her feet, swaying a little. 'Coffee?'

'No, let's finish the wine.'

She found a chocolate torte in the fridge, cut two thick wedges and went back into the living room. Music playing soft and low, a Dirty Three album she hadn't listened to in years, too many memories snagged in its plaintive strings and the feverish build of the tempo. A tangle of sheets and fingers twisted in hair, one last performance before the fighting started.

I Remember a Time When Once You Used to Love Me.

He couldn't have picked a worse song if he was inside her head watching the scene play out, the break-up sex she didn't know she was having soundtracked by it. Of all the things she hated Liam for that was what stung the worst, taking her to bed knowing what he was going to say before he'd even regained his breath.

'This is a bit morose,' she said, flicking on to another artist and composing her face before she turned back to him.

She curled up at the end of the sofa and he moved next to her.

'You know what I don't get,' he said. 'Why was Corinne interested in blokes all of sudden? Do you think he was a closet job?'

Ferreira licked chocolate off the back of her fork, letting the tines scratch her tongue. 'You realise gender and sexual orientation are two different things?'

'I've heard that, yes. But seems to me nobody spontaneously turns at that age. You're either born like it or you're not.'

The music was still running in her head, a few bars of raw violin on repeat, mixed up with the conversation she'd been having the last time she heard it. The same thing they were talking about now but with more heat and desperation. Even the setting was uncomfortably similar, another rented flat that didn't feel like home yet.

'Doesn't really matter, does it?' she said, putting her plate on the table and draining her wine glass. 'Sexuality isn't binary, it's on a spectrum. Colin was probably bi when he was a man and then he's Corinne and he could explore it easier.'

'Matters if it got her killed.' Adams slipped his hand inside the leg of her PJs, no insinuation in his touch. 'Her girlfriend can't be very happy.'

'I don't think Sam killed her. She's upset, understandably. She loved and accepted every version of Corinne. I guess she thought that was enough to keep her.'

'Not if Corinne wanted cock.'

'You can buy all the cock you want in Ann Summers.'

'But it's not like the real thing,' he said. 'You can joke about it but if she wanted a man she wanted the full package. Being bi was just a stepping stone.'

Ferreira stretched out on the sofa. 'Why do men always think a bi-guy is secretly gay and a bi-woman is secretly straight? You all think your cocks are so special.'

'You seem to enjoy it.' He lay down next to her and she wriggled away to accommodate him on the sofa, his arm under her neck, knee slipping between her legs. 'Mel, I know what happened.'

She gave him a warning look. 'No, you don't.'

'I heard—'

'You heard what? Station gossip. That's all you know.' The alcohol had dulled her anger but it was making her maudlin and she wished she hadn't mixed her drinks. Wished she'd thrown him out the second she saw him standing in the kitchen doorway. She ignored her instincts far too often.

She'd done it with Liam. Seen the signs, but she wasn't prepared to let him go without a fight, even if it cost her her dignity.

228

'We all make bad judgements,' Adams said, stroking her arm. 'We think we're above it because of the job we do, but the truth is we lose all reason once we've clocked off. Especially when it comes to relationships.'

'I knew what he was,' she said. 'He never lied about it.'

Adams waited and she didn't mean to say it, but the drink and the day and that heart-punch of a song conspired to loosen her tongue, and she was talking, uninterrupted, the first time she'd told anyone.

They'd met in a gay bar in the city centre, Ferreira with her brother Paolo and some of his friends, Liam there with another group, and during the night they merged, the two of them the only smokers and the trips outside got more frequent, the conversation more flirty, until they decided that his flat was the right place to finish it. In the taxi she joked about him going to gay bars to trawl women, knowing he'd have his pick, but he insisted it wasn't like that. She didn't believe he was bi, not in the taxi and not in the one she took home the next morning.

She didn't believe it when they went on their second date, or the fourth or the tenth. Not when she saw the gay porn in his bedroom or when he asked her to use a vibrator on him.

Twenty-three years old. A good Catholic girl, by upbringing if not belief, well into rebellion. She found it funny when he fancied the same men as her, a turn-on when they watched porn together. She played the man for him when he asked her to, connecting with some new part of her sexual make-up she hadn't known about before.

They made plans for the future, talked marriage and kids. Maybe he wasn't as serious about it as she was. At the time it felt like an equal conversation but memory was a slippery, sly thing and now, looking back, she knew she'd deluded herself, or else how could he have dropped such a massive, obliterating bombshell on her, six months after she moved in with him?

229

'Turns out he'd been seeing this guy for months,' she said. 'It was "the real thing". I was just . . . shit, I don't know, a test.'

Adams was giving her that soul-boring look of his. 'You didn't turn him, Mel.'

'I couldn't keep him though.'

'And you think you just weren't enough woman for him?'

'Obviously I wasn't.'

She felt raw and exposed and half of her wanted Adams to leave, let her work this shit out on her own, but the other half needed the distraction of the platitudes and compliments he was whispering in her ear, the pressure and rhythm of his fingers between her legs.

Some things just had to be fucked out of your system.

32

Tonight she would be her full and proper self. It was the only way to do this, fearlessly, boldly and as beautiful as she could be.

The decision had come like an epiphany. Standing behind the counter at work, dealing with some young guy who was giving her the usual look. He saw what she was, even through her daytime disguise, and maybe he liked what he saw.

Some of them did, but not many, and she knew the ones like him were a threat. Full of their own dangerous complications; want and repulsion, lust and regret. Yes, she'd met plenty of men like him and she knew what they were capable of.

If it wasn't for that last, appraising glance he shot back across his shoulder when he left, the touch of his tongue to the point of his incisor, which accompanied it, she might have continued with this sad compromise forever. Always hidden, always guilty, trying and failing to gather up the spilled pieces of herself which scattered across the cobblestones the night she thought she'd died.

Some of her had, but enough survived. A piece too big to hide but too small to sustain any real kind of life. She'd tended it and indulged it, brought it up to this sanctuary and patiently rekindled it like the embers of a faded fire. There was a long way to go but she would have got there.

Now all of that care was for nothing, because of Corinne and Evelyn and her own naivety.

Evelyn was pursuing her. She'd called once yesterday and twice today, a couple of text messages for good measure, because that was her style. She ground you down, kept going until you agreed that she was wise and all-knowing and you caved to her demands.

'You need to come clean to the police.'

She'd put the phone down straight away but Evelyn called back and gave the rest of her speech to voicemail.

'This isn't just about you any more. I know you're scared and I know you feel you have too much at stake, but I promise I will see you through this. This is the right thing to do. For them and for you. We need to give them everything we can to help them catch this bastard.' A sigh and the sound of cut-glass chinking. 'You must want to see him punished for what he did to you. Please, just talk to me if you're not ready to talk to them yet.'

Yet.

Meaning it was inevitable that they would come for her again and that Evelyn was on their side. No huge surprise but still it hurt to be manipulated by her like that. The woman she trusted, who had seen her through so much, preparing to throw her to the wolves.

So, they were coming.

She didn't know much about police investigations but she watched enough television to realise they would be under pressure to find Corinne's killer, even if they hadn't pursued her own attacker. An assault was just another point on the crime statistics. A murder was news.

And as the days kept passing with no arrest they would start to become desperate, pursue anyone they thought was holding out on them.

Evelyn must have spoken to them already, maybe told them more than she had herself. She didn't know everything but what she did know would expose contradictions – outright lies – and that would be enough to pique their interest.

Sergeant Ferreira saw right through her anyway. She'd backed off eventually but there was a hardness hiding behind her own daytime disguise that suggested an arrest would always outweigh the safety of any given individual standing in the way of it.

They would want statements. They would want her to appear in court. Expose herself to her attacker and the judge and the jury, open herself up to the ridicule of the public. They didn't care what happened to her after that, the damage it would do, how it would rip apart her life and those of the people she cared about.

Her mobile rang on the dressing table and she checked the display, no intention of answering but she needed to know who it was just in case Evelyn was on her way, bringing the police with her, about to storm her sanctuary.

But it wasn't. It was the other 'her' in her life – the screen showing a selfie she'd taken with her eyes squeezed shut and her lips puckering towards the camera. It felt like so long ago now. She still smiled and laughed but not with such sincerity or spontaneity, was watchful and calculating in a way she hadn't been a year ago, suspected she'd been lied to about the attack but wasn't quite brave enough to vocalise the nature of her suspicions.

The ringing stopped and a few seconds later a message came through – *About to take off. Call you when I can. xx*

She sent back three kisses and an exploding heart, tears welling in her eyes, then switched off her phone.

A bottle of rosé sat on the table next to it. A very good bottle, the most expensive she could find, flecked with pieces of real gold that shimmered and twinkled as she raised her glass to the light. She thought of the glimmering specks already in her system, imagined them suspended in her blood, gilding the walls of her heart and lungs.

In the bathroom she felt a split second of surprise on seeing her reflection, still not used to the mirror being back in place. It was a painful sight but she steeled herself for it, knew it would be her only company for the rest of the evening.

She picked up the bone-handled straight razor she'd bought when she first started to shave. It was just like the one her father

233

and grandfather owned, a real man's implement, and she'd always felt a fraud when she used it. Like she was playing out a version of masculinity they'd drilled into her, their ideas fortified by films and adverts.

Now she would subvert that.

Carefully she lathered up her face and shaved every last bristle, feeling a swell of contempt as she rinsed the blade, seeing the hateful black hairs dirtying the water. It was a tricky job, one she'd long since given over to an electric razor, but tonight it was the right tool, and by the time she was finished her skin was smooth and glistening.

Except the spots where—

No, she wouldn't let him in here again. She refused to see the damage he'd done to her. Not now. Not tonight. He would love to know she was thinking of him, that he could still touch her, across the city, after all of this time.

She closed her eyes for a moment, pushing away the memory of the icy cobbles under her cheek, the pressure on her back and the smell of his breath as he told her what she really was. She focused on the music. The right choice tonight, only happy songs, ones for women as fierce as she needed to be.

Without looking at herself she reached for a pot of face cream and worked it into her skin, the rose scent calming her a little more. While it sank in she went back to her desk, poured another glass of wine and switched on her laptop.

The words were waiting for her. They'd come so swiftly and easily that she realised they had been inside her for years, ready to be written down when she needed them. She had them memorised now and she ran through them under her breath as she stood in front of the mirror once again, looking at herself properly.

You couldn't feel your way through this part of the process. You had to be rigorously honest about yourself and your flaws, or else how could you paint them out?

She took up a jar and brush and started to cover the scars, two thin layers of cosmetic filler in each one, that was how you made them disappear, then she switched to a palette and painted contouring lines to narrow her brow and jaw, make her slightly too big chin recede. She lifted her cheekbones and slimmed her temples, leaving her nose until last. She'd had a good nose before but now it was kinked and no amount of clever tricks could disguise that.

Let it stand, then. It would be testimony to the act that brought her here, a symbol of hatred and prejudice marring what was otherwise perfection.

The rest was easy and even though she hadn't made herself up since it happened she could have done it without a mirror, her hands holding the memory, conditioned by thousands of applications, countless hours of transformation. She watched herself come in to being once again, this face emerging from the other one, lashes batting, lips pouting, just as beautiful as she had always been.

In the bedroom she laid out the clothes she would wear, a decision which had taken the better part of two hours, but she knew the outfit would be analysed and picked over, that she would be judged more harshly on that than her words if she got it wrong.

She'd settled on a chic, slate-grey bodycon dress with a faint plaid running through the fabric. A Roland Mouret copy. Not exactly cutting edge but this wasn't a fashion statement she was making. Understated, almost sombre; it signalled her intent.

On went the tight, flesh-toned knickers, and for a moment she just stood there with her hand cupping the curve of her pudenda, saddened by how right it felt and how completely impossible it was to ever truly have. She took a deep breath and pulled a black silk pair over the top, then the matching bra, and finally stepped into her dress, finding it slipped on just as easily as the last time she wore it, on a shopping trip to London, back in the days when she was brave enough to go out like this, walk down busy streets and into clothes stores; perfectly credible, enviably attractive.

235

Those days felt as if they were part of another person's life. More like witnessed events than memories.

Another mouthful of wine and she climbed into her high black suede heels, feeling her whole body straighten, like someone had pulled on an invisible string running down from the top of her skull and through her spine. Her shoulders went back, her hips jutted forwards, all poise and defiance as she strutted into the bathroom to raise a silent toast, then drank down the last of the gold-spiked rosé.

This was it.

No more hiding, no more lies, no more fear.

33

'Do you want me to see to her?' Anna asked, mumbling into Zigic's shoulder as Emily released another wild, howling cry. 'Dushan, are you awake?'

He blinked at the clock on the side table; half past one. Forty minutes since Anna changed her nappy, two hours since he finally got Emily to sleep in the first place. Technically it was his turn.

'I'll go.'

'She probably just wants another feed.'

Emily calmed a little as he lifted her out of the cot, wrapping a blanket around her. Her hand made a grab for his beard but couldn't find purchase on its newly pruned form; small victories, he thought as he carried her down into the kitchen.

While the bottle warmed up he walked round the table, sure he'd nod off again if he made the mistake of sitting down. He switched on the radio, tuned it to 3, a soft lilting piece of music filling the room. Sometimes it helped but not tonight, when she seemed to interpret the music as a challenge, something to be drowned out with more crying.

Milan appeared in the doorway, his sleep-creased face a picture of very grown-up exasperation.

'I can't sleep with all this noise,' he said.

'She'll calm down in a minute. Go back to bed, buddy.'

Milan huffed. 'I have school in the morning, you know.'

'I am aware of that.' Zigic gestured towards the stairs. 'Now go and get back into bed, please.'

The timer on the bottle-warmer pinged and Zigic waved Milan out of the room, heard his feet slowly mounting the stairs, a hard-done-by trudge that made the flight sound twice as high as it was. It was a difficult life he had, Zigic thought, with a slight smile, as he sat down and fed Emily.

Her hands closed around the bottle, just in case he didn't know what he was doing and within a minute she was already falling asleep, still sucking as she started to doze. When he took it away she murmured but didn't stir any more and he sat there for awhile, cradling her against his chest, half convinced that the second he moved she would wake up and treat them to another one of her piercing arias.

If only there was a way to sleep sitting up, with his eyes open, holding on to her safely.

Carefully he carried her back upstairs and laid her down like she was made of glass, holding his breath the whole time. Moving with a cat burglar's stealth he made his way round to his side of the bed and just as he was pulling back the cover his phone rang.

Emily cried, Anna swore into her pillow and he apologised to both of them as he snatched his mobile up from the table where it had been charging – on silent, he thought – and left the room.

'Mel, for Christ's sake, what are you ringing me at this time of night for?'

Three minutes later he was in the car, pulling out onto the ice-speckled road. She'd called for uniform already and he caught them up on Thorpe Road, blue lights blazing ahead of him as he tailed them through the sparsely peopled city centre. Only taxis and pizza deliveries on the road for company, past the courts and the cathedral, which glowed an anaemic pink against the night sky, heading for Park Road.

The house was in darkness, a stately Edwardian villa, semi-detached, well maintained under the street lights. Ferreira's car was at the kerb, a silver Mercedes on the driveway, and she was standing next to it with Evelyn Goddard, who tore her gaze away from the house as Zigic parked up and went over to them.

238

'What do we know?' he asked.

'She posted the video just after midnight,' Evelyn said, shivering inside her shearling coat. 'I started getting calls about ten or fifteen minutes later, nobody knew what to make of it but when I saw it I knew exactly what she was planning to do.'

'It was a suicide note,' Ferreira said. 'I tried to get in but the place is locked up tight.'

Zigic called over the uniforms, who already had the ram out of the back of the patrol car, waiting for the go-ahead. It took four hefty swings to break down the front door and then they were moving through the house, switching on lights, Evelyn calling for Jasmine, Ferreira shouting for Aadesh, until Evelyn corrected her gently – 'Ryan, his real name's Ryan.'

Zigic scanned the place as he followed, taking in the bland decor, finding everything tidied away and immaculate, but devoid of personality.

Upstairs there were three bedrooms, only the largest furnished and no sign of the occupant.

Evelyn stopped at the bottom of a second flight of stairs, a narrow channel running up them towards a closed door.

He told her to wait, called a uniform in to make sure she would, and led Ferreira up into an attic room more elaborately decorated than the rest of the house. It was lit by recessed spotlights set low on a dimmer and fitted out with mirrored wardrobes and gold damask wallpaper, a large armchair under a skylight, a dressing table against a wall with a closed laptop sitting on it next to an empty bottle of pink champagne.

Another door stood ajar to his right, music playing beyond.

Ferreira was hanging back and he saw something akin to fear as she brushed her hand over her hair.

He went in.

The bathwater was red, its surface still, but the flickering light of two dozen candles danced across it and the face of the woman lying there, conjuring an appearance of life so convincing that Zigic held his fingers to her neck much longer than he needed to, waiting for a pulse to come fluttering under them, looking at the cuts she'd made along her arms, long and deep, from wrist to elbow.

This was more than a gesture. She meant to die.

'Is he alive?' Ferreira asked. 'It takes ages, you know. It can take like an hour. More.'

Zigic stepped back from the bath, avoiding the pearl-handled straight razor near his feet and the spots of blood which had flicked off its blade as it fell.

'He's dead.'

'Are you sure?'

She started towards the bath but he grabbed her shoulders and backed her away into the corner of the small en suite. 'Mel, he's dead. There's nothing we can do now.'

Ferreira squeezed her eyes shut, shaking her head. 'I did this. He didn't want to talk about it and I made him.'

'You don't know what was going on in his head.' He kept one hand on her shoulder, trying to get her to look at him, but she was staring at the body. 'Nobody kills themselves because of one conversation, okay? He could have been fighting with depression for years, this isn't on you.'

'Bullshit. I talked to him two days ago and now he's done this.' Her hand shot out. 'Look at this fucking scene – it's a statement. It's totally staged. This is a message.'

'Yes, it probably is,' Zigic said, as softly as he could. 'But not for you.'

'You haven't seen the video.'

He felt the floor lurch under him at the chill in her voice. 'Did he mention you?'

She slipped away from him and sat down on the lid of the toilet. 'Not by name.'

'But he mentioned the investigation?'

240

She shook her head, a bitter smile cutting her face. 'He made it crystal clear he felt like he was being harassed by us.'

'I need to see it.'

Evelyn Goddard's voice was going off downstairs, arguing with the uniform, demanding to be let up in that imperious tone she'd learned in Her Majesty's Navy. The PC patiently explained that she was to stay where she was, but Zigic could hear that he was wavering, too used to obeying whoever ordered him about with the greatest degree of authority.

'How was I supposed to know he'd do this?' Ferreira said, speaking from behind her hands, eyes wide above them.

'You were just doing your job. How would we get anywhere if we couldn't talk to victims of crimes?' He squatted down in front of her. 'We'll discuss this tomorrow, okay? Go home, get some sleep—'

She glared at him. 'I'm not going to sleep.'

'Mel, I will deal with this,' he said, straightening up, encouraging her to her feet. 'Don't talk to Evelyn, just walk out and go home.'

'This is my mess.'

He closed the en suite door. 'This is a mess, I'm not going to deny that. But right now we are in a house with a suicide and a very vocal, very well-connected, transgender rights activist. Do you see where I'm going with this?' She wasn't even looking at him, staring instead into the bloody bathtub. 'Evelyn has seen the video, she knows exactly what was said and she's going to be looking for any reaction you give that will support her feeling – her highly probable conviction – that we're responsible for this.'

'Then I should stay,' Ferreira said. 'It'll look weird if I'm the first responder and I just walk out. She called me specifically. She knew what she was doing.'

Zigic took a deep breath, inhaling the meaty tang of blood and the mingled scent of jasmine and rose. She was right. Evelyn Goddard hadn't called 999, she'd contacted Ferreira after seeing the video. Was it cynical to assume she had an agenda beyond her concern for a friend's safety?

'Okay.' He rubbed his forehead, still trying to formulate a plan, but the flickering light of the candles was making the scene so grotesque that he couldn't fully concentrate. 'Okay, go and call for an ambulance. I'll speak to Evelyn.'

He started to open the door and she lunged to close it again.

'I think you should see the video first. You need to know what we're dealing with.' She took her mobile out and handed it over to him with the screen paused. 'Give me yours – I'll deal with Evelyn and make the call.'

Zigic hesitated but handed his phone over. 'Be careful what you say to her and don't let her up here.'

Ferreira went back out through the dressing room and as soon as her foot hit the top step Evelyn Goddard started firing questions at her, some of the authority gone from her voice.

'Where is he? Is he alright? Why haven't you called an ambulance, for God's sake?'

'It's too late for that,' Ferreira said. 'I'm so sorry.'

Zigic closed the door again, trusting her to calm the situation as well as she could, and tapped the screen.

The woman's photograph was stuck to a board in the office and he'd seen it dozens of times during the last couple of days, but she didn't look like that on-screen, no more party girl, drunk and smiling. Didn't look like the dead version of herself in the bath either. This 'her' was somewhere between the two; she sat tall and straight as she stared into the camera, sombre in her black dress.

Before she even spoke her intention to be taken seriously was clear.

'I'm not going to hide any more,' she said. 'I'm not going to be scared any more and I've had enough of lying about who I am. This is me. I'm Jasmine.' Her eyes dipped and she pressed her lips together, visibly steeling herself. 'Last year I was attacked by

242

a man who beat me up because of who I am. Because of what I am. What we all are. I've been hiding ever since and it shouldn't be that way. We shouldn't let men like him control us and make us feel ashamed or scared to go out in the world. They call us freaks and weirdos and perverts, but they're the ones who are sick. Not just the violent abusers, but the people who act like they're better than us because they fit into a neat little box that society terms "normal". They use that word to oppress us and we let them.'

She blinked, her eyes shining large.

'Because we're afraid of letting the world see who we really are. I wish I was brave enough to be me properly, but I'm not. That man is still out there and maybe some of you have been hurt by him too and if you have then I'm deeply, truly sorry that I didn't do more when he attacked me. I wanted to help the police but I can't. I didn't see his face, I didn't know him. But they won't leave me alone because they think I'm lying to protect myself from exposure. I promise you all – my sisters – that isn't the case. Whatever is said about me in the coming days, please know that this is the truth.'

She paused for a long moment and Zigic looked at her, lying there in the bath, growing colder, the faint trace of life he'd seen when he walked in now completely gone.

'I hope you all find the courage to live better lives than I did.'

The video ended and for a moment he stared at the frozen screen, still processing her words.

No wonder Ferreira felt so guilt-stricken. Her interview was unquestionably a contributory factor and they would need to deal with the consequences of that.

Zigic switched the light on and went to blow out the candles around the bath, wary of the fire hazard. It felt like an intrusion on the careful scene Jasmine had created but now reality had to take precedence and the banal work of removing her body would soon begin, the ambulance on its way.

He found Ferreira and Evelyn Goddard in the spartan living room at the front of the house. Ferreira sat on the arm of the sofa, Evelyn perched on the edge of a tub chair, her heavy shearling coat wrapped tight around her.

She stood as Zigic entered the room. 'Well, I hope you're both very proud of yourselves. You started the week with one dead trans woman and now you have two.'

'Ms Goddard, I'm going to have to ask you to leave, please.' Zigic gestured towards the door. 'Until we have confirmation of cause of death, this is a crime scene.'

She drew herself upright and walked over to him. 'Oh, it is a crime scene, alright. We all know Jasmine committed suicide because you people drove her to it with your harassment tactics. You have caused her death just as surely as if you'd held her down and cut her wrists yourselves.'

Before either of them could speak she swept out of the house, barging aside the PC stationed at the front door, climbed into her car and pulled out of the driveway in a furious spray of gravel. Somehow he doubted that parting shot would be the last they heard from her on the subject.

FRIDAY

34

Adams was still in the flat when Ferreira got home and she left him to the bed, curled up on the sofa and tried to get some sleep, knowing she would need to be sharp when she went into work in a few hours' time.

Sleep wasn't coming though. She spent the darkest hours of the night thinking back over the interview with Aadesh in the service station on the side of the A1.

Not Aadesh, she reminded herself once again.

Ryan. Ryan Bhakta.

He'd died as Jasmine though, making that final statement to the world he felt unable to continue living in.

Around six she gave up on sleep altogether, put on her running gear and hit the pre-dawn streets, ran a circuit out towards Ryan's house, which was in darkness, the business of removing his body and securing the broken front door all done with. Ran on along Lincoln Road, past her parents' pub, open already and doing a brisk trade for breakfast. For a moment she thought about going in, but sprinted past without stopping, not up to the barrage of questions and recriminations which her visits always seemed to entail. They kept expecting her to cave in to the loneliness of single living and return to her old bedroom above the bar. Right then it was too tempting to risk crossing the threshold.

She ploughed on, concentrated on the rhythm of her breathing, the sound of her feet on the pavement and tried to block out everything else, but she kept thinking of that interview, the elusiveness of Ryan Bhakta's gaze, the spill and tumble of his words and how little information they held.

Had she pushed him too hard? She remembered how nervous he'd been, avoiding her eyes as he described the attack which had driven him deep into the closet, up into that beautiful bathroom in the attic of his characterless home. He'd been hiding for years, she supposed, from his family and friends, and what about the woman he was going to marry?

Did she know about his double life?

Ferreira doubted it. Dreaded breaking the news to her.

She wondered how devout Ryan's family were, whether they would be able to cope with the truth when it inevitably came out. Because they could, perhaps, spare them the details of his suicide, but the video he'd made would eventually break out of the Trans Sisters private group and into the public domain and then there would be no more hiding the fact that their son, brother, cousin, wasn't the man they thought he was.

Before long she was back in the city centre, running past the train station and ducking into the underpass beneath the Queensgate roundabout, the one where Ryan was attacked. A lone man was coming the other way, suited and carrying a Costa coffee, a leather messenger bag slung across his chest. He moved aside slightly to let her pass, didn't make eye contact. One of those men who was sensitive enough to appreciate how uncomfortable he could make a lone woman in an isolated spot.

It wasn't until she was in the shower, wine-sour sweat sluicing off her body, that she realised Ryan Bhakta had lied to her.

If he'd been walking home from the Meadham the night he was attacked then he wouldn't have taken the underpass. It was in completely the opposite direction to his house. So, why tell her it happened there?

Either he wasn't going home or it happened somewhere else entirely. It seemed a stupid lie to tell, but her gut said it must mean something.

She dried off and got dressed, went into the kitchen where Adams was standing at the counter in his boxers eating a slice of toast.

'You know it's customary to leave while your casual fuck is in the shower?'

'Think that's only one-night stands,' he said. 'Coffee?'

'No.'

If Ryan had been attacked somewhere else in the city centre it was too late to do anything about it. No way to gather viable forensic evidence after such a long delay and so much contamination. Any CCTV they might have recovered would have been recorded over or wiped long ago. Had he simply lied about the location to muddy the waters? Hoping to make her job more difficult, hoping she would give up on him and look for another potential witness?

'What happened with your suicide then?' Adams asked.

'What usually happens with them. He was dead when we got there.' She told him everything, knowing it would be round the station within minutes of the day shift starting anyway. He listened with a serious expression on his face, DCI mode, and when she finished he shook his head.

'You need to call your union rep, right now.'

'It won't come to that.'

'This is a highly sensitive case, Mel. And you've got a woman on the warpath, of course it's going to come to that.'

'Goddard was the person who put me on to Ryan.'

'Yeah and that means she needs to shift the blame on to someone. You think she isn't feeling guilty right now?' he said. 'Either it's your fault or it's hers. Which way do you think she's going to jump on that one?'

Ferreira swore under her breath. She knew he was right, but speaking to her rep made it official. An admission of guilt before she'd even been accused of anything. Could she really be held responsible? One meeting. Was that really enough to constitute harassment? She knew it wasn't, not legally speaking, but if Evelyn Goddard shouted loud enough Riggott might decide the bad publicity outweighed the truth. The people above him definitely might.

'I'll think about it,' she said. 'Let yourself out, yeah?'

Ten minutes later, up in Hate Crimes, she switched the lights on and started a pot of coffee, got her breakfast from the machine in the hallway while her computer booted up. She should have eaten at home but Adams was crowding her with his I-know-best attitude, just when she didn't need to be lectured.

Seven twenty.

Zigic would arrive within the hour, likely with his own ideas on how best to handle the situation and she wanted a firm hold on it before he did.

She stopped in front of the board; Simone and Jasmine, their photos tacked up next to each other, both women gone now, one more completely than the other. She wondered whether Simon Trent had heard the news yet and how he would react to it. If Evelyn Goddard contacted him now he could tell a good story about the pressure she'd put him under, going to his house, bullying him into talking when he had nothing to say.

Ferreira shook herself out of it.

Work the case. Get the result. Riggott and his bosses might overlook her supposed transgression if she found their man.

Now she had Aadesh's real name she could see the initial report on his attack and that was where she started. On 18 December at three thirty-five in the morning two officers had spoken to him in the triage area at City Hospital, called by a nurse who – the report noted – suspected his attack was racially motivated.

Ryan Bhakta disabused the responding officers of that notion, made it clear that the man who attacked him was simply a thief, after his wallet and the mobile phone he claimed he was using as he walked, so distracted by it that he didn't realise he was being followed until he hit the deck.

PCs Hale and Bright.

She would speak to them later but from the state of their report she doubted they could tell her anything more. Late in their shift, in the run-up to Christmas, they would have been dealing with one punch-up after another, cautioning the aggressive drunks, guiding the more vulnerable ones safely home. The trip to A&E to deal with Ryan had probably been a welcome respite. Easy paperwork. Give him a crime number for his insurance company and bank. Take a statement and forget about it.

Ryan's version of events was thin on detail. He was jumped from behind. Never saw the man's face. Didn't remember anything after the first punch to the back of his head knocked him out cold.

Hale detailed the extent of his injuries: broken nose, fractured cheekbone, two broken fingers on his right hand. They sounded bad on paper but the photographs looked even worse, his face and neck a mess of small cuts and blossoming bruises. He'd turned away as they were taken, as if worried what else the camera might capture.

How long had it taken to recover from such bad wounds? she wondered. It was little more than a year between the attack and his suicide. Easy to imagine him still depressed, anxious, possibly suffering PTSD . . .

She caught herself.

She wasn't supposed to be working on her defence.

Back to the file and she noted the location Ryan had given them for the assault. The cathedral precincts. An isolated spot at that time of night, one most people, men or women, would avoid entering alone. Narrow back lanes, running between high stone walls, poorly lit, deeply shadowed. A magnet for predators.

It was on Ryan's way home but not the most obvious route.

Maybe he thought he was safer walking through there than running the gauntlet of nightclubs and pubs on Long Causeway. Fewer people crossing his path meant less likelihood of meeting the wrong one.

Her desk phone rang and she answered it.

Riggott – 'Mel, a word in my office.'

She'd been expecting it but not so soon and she felt the previous twenty-four hours dragging at her as she made her way down to CID. The dregs of the night shift were still there, finishing reports, the earliest arrivals for the day shift already in, looking about as perky as she felt.

She knocked and Riggott called her in, told her to take a seat.

He still had his overcoat on, must have decided this bollocking was urgent, but she saw no signs of anger on his face and the DCS wasn't a man to hide it when he was annoyed with you.

'Turned into a proper shite storm, this case,' he said, shrugging out of his coat.

'Sir, in my defence—'

'None of that, now. Save it for the investigation.' He sat down, looked across the desk at her with an expression verging on pity. 'I don't need to tell you how badly this is going to play for us, do I?'

'No, sir.'

'Your woman Goddard has a sight more pull than I reckoned on.' Riggott took an e-cigarette out of his pocket. 'But, for what it's worth, I'd have said you're in the clear. Some poor conflicted soul goes and tops himself . . . going to take a clairvoyant to prove what was going through his head.'

'He left a video,' Ferreira said. 'He basically accused us – me – of harassing him to his death.'

Riggott nodded. 'Aye, I've seen it. Best you give me a look at the report.'

'I've got a recording of our interview.'

252

The busy cafe, the hushed conversation, the look in Ryan's eye like he could bolt at any moment.

Riggott's eyebrow flicked up at her. 'You're too honest for your own good, Mel.'

'I haven't done anything wrong,' she said, forcing herself to hold his penetrating gaze. 'The tape shows that.'

'Is it on record?'

'He'd only speak to me off the record. I made it for my own use.'

'Then wipe the thing.'

'I can't do that.'

Riggott hunched over the desk, the light casting deep pools under his eyes. 'Darlin', however clean you think you'll come out of this, I guarantee you'll regret turning it in. Don't go gifting them a rope. Not unless you fancy swinging from it.'

He was right and this was so far beyond wrong that it made her feel sick, watching him watching her, waiting to see which way she'd go.

Was this a test of her integrity?

Riggott had always had a reputation for loyalty towards his junior officers, was known to fight for them like a mama bear defending her cubs, and it was generally accepted that he'd bent the truth himself plenty of times too. More than a man who'd made DCS should have rightly got away with.

'Whatever happens, it'll likely not be career ending,' he said, leaning back. 'But it's a blot you don't want on your record. Believe me, Mel, stink like this doesn't fade quick.' He tapped the desk. 'Think what's best for you now. There's no helping that dead lad.'

She sighed, feeling like she'd failed his test, but unsure how.

'Is that all, sir?'

He nodded. 'Send me the report and the tape, then take yourself on home.'

'We're in the middle of a murder investigation.' The words came out louder than she intended. 'Sir, you can't suspend me, please.'

253

'I'm not suspending you,' he said. 'I'm telling you to take the day off sick so we can see how the dust settles.'

'But—'

'No, not "but",' he snapped.

'We're undermanned as it is.'

Riggott threw his hands up. 'Did you see the fuckin' sign on my door? Any more lip and I will suspend you.'

She apologised, hauled herself up, surprised by how weak her knees were. When she went for the door handle she saw that her fingers were trembling and she walked out through CID feeling like a marked woman. Out of the corner of her eye she saw Adams but kept moving, looking dead ahead, went up to Hate Crimes and sent her report of the interview over to Riggott. Still shaking, she grabbed her bag and her keys and left the station.

35

Morning briefing was quieter than usual and as he outlined the plan for the day Zigic's eyes kept straying towards Ferreira's desk, the chair sitting spun out from her computer, a half-eaten chocolate bar next to the mouse, a cup of coffee gone cold nearby.

He should have got in earlier, talked to Riggott. Maybe he could have explained the situation, smoothed things over. If nothing else he would have pointed out that they needed every officer they could muster if they were going to catch Corinne Sawyer's murderer, and since Ferreira had been so heavily involved with speaking to the Sawyer family, she was the last person they could afford to lose at that moment.

As it was he arrived to a fait accompli.

A message from Riggott and another from Ferreira, apologising for fucking things up. When he called her her phone diverted straight to voicemail.

It was only one day, but tomorrow was Saturday and with no overtime budgeted for the case they would lose the weekend too, no chance of her being back in the office before Monday, and by then the pressure would have increased. If they couldn't make significant headway today there was every chance Corinne Sawyer's murder would be moved to CID as next week began.

Wahlia and Murray were watching him, waiting for their orders.

She'd arrived early, apologised for her outburst at the end of yesterday's shift, but he'd been where she was, showed contrition he didn't feel to senior officers, and he knew nothing had really changed in her attitude. He needed to work with what he had, though.

'Alright,' he said, eyeing the board. 'So, today we're going to speak to the main players in the Sawyer family. I'm not expecting anyone to break down and confess, but we've got limited lines of inquiry, as things stand, and my feeling is they are the right place to focus our attention.'

Murray frowned, stayed silent.

Zigic gestured at Wahlia. 'Bobby, I need you to pick up where Mel left off yesterday. Chase up the rest of the information on Corinne's phone, see if there are any other men we should be looking into.'

'Yes, sir.'

'Also, I want us to have a very firm handle on the particulars of Corinne and Nina's divorce negotiations before we talk to her. There was a lot of money at stake and I think we can safely say that's a valid motive.'

Murray piped up. 'But Nina was in line to come out with a big pay-off, wasn't she?'

'One point five mil,' Wahlia said. 'Straight fifty/fifty split.'

'Not like she was going to be destitute then.' Murray reached for her tea. 'Why kill Corinne and risk losing all that?'

It was a fair question but Murray's tone grated on Zigic. He forced himself to ignore that and said, 'Because it's never just about money. Say you were Nina, and you felt like you'd wasted the best years of your life on a man, been integral in building up a business, maybe even done the bulk of the work. Then he walks out on you. Hands it all over to another woman – how would you feel?'

She hid her mouth behind her mug; he knew just how she felt about it. Her own divorce had been acrimonious and saw her move from a large, detached house in a good village to a two-and-a-half-bed semi in a rough suburb, while her husband started afresh with a new woman fifteen years younger than her.

'No, this isn't just about the money,' he said. 'It's about what it represents.'

Murray sighed. 'Are we seriously considering Nina Sawyer a suspect, then?'

'Why not?' Zigic shrugged. 'She knew Corinne's routine. And since we don't have a concrete sighting, there's no telling whether it was a man or a woman who killed her.'

'We've got a footprint of a size 10 shoe at the scene,' Murray reminded him.

'And it's a site that sees heavy footfall.'

Murray leaned forward in her chair, elbows on her knees. 'So, we're saying the girlfriend's a potential suspect, too?'

'If she suspected Corinne was cheating on her, yes. It's the oldest reason in the world.'

'But did she know that?'

'We have to assume she suspected,' Zigic said, remembering their conversation. 'Sam Hyde is an outside bet, though. Right now I want us to concentrate on what happened at the Christmas dinner. Everyone's admitted there was an argument but nobody has given us an explanation.'

He stood up and went over to the board, rapped his knuckle against Harry Sawyer's face. 'The daughter told us Corinne slapped Harry. He physically threw her out of the house and she slapped him. We need to nail down why that happened and if it represents a motive.'

'They'll close ranks,' Murray said. 'I've talked to Nina, and Harry's girlfriend, remember. They're holding firm.'

Zigic folded his arms. Ten past eight and he was already sick of her negativity. If he had any other option he'd send her back up to CID right now.

'We don't need them to give anyone up. We do this the old-fashioned way, alright, Colleen? We get them talking, we make them go over what happened as many times as we have to until one of them slips up and tells us what we need to know.' He opened his hands up wide. 'Is that how I want to do this? No. But we don't have a ton of other options, do we?'

Zigic made the calls and within an hour the Sawyer family started trickling into the station. They presented no resistance, but really, how could they? The family of a murder victim, not accused of anything yet, none of their houses searched, it would be madness to do anything but cooperate fully when a detective inspector requested they come in for a chat.

Innocent and you came to genuinely help. Guilty, you couldn't afford to draw attention to yourself by delaying.

Despite Murray's grumbles she proved to be an asset in the interview room. She looked like a woman who'd seen everything, suffered more than her fair share, and that made people feel comfortable around her. Jessica was the first to arrive and having proven very open previously, Zigic wasn't surprised when she spilled the same old story to them, only with more emotion this time.

She'd held it together through the press conference but her grief seemed to be on a time delay and now it was catching up with her. Her voice cracked when she said Corinne's name, she stumbled over her words and repeated herself, questioned herself, didn't appear to be functioning on the same level mentally as she had before. Grief had removed all the old certainties.

The problem was Jessica had been away at Christmas and only knew what she'd heard second hand; too much drink flowing at the table, Nina sniping, Corinne giving as good as she got, and then Harry throwing her out of the house.

'Why did he lose his temper with her?' Murray asked.

'He was drunk.'

'Did Corinne provoke him?'

Jessica held her hands on the table, fingers knitted tightly together, visibly debating with herself. 'Harry and Corinne always had a . . . fraught relationship.'

258

'Fraught how?'

'Harry loved Dad, he idolised him. We've been through this already, I don't understand why I need to tell you it all over again.'

'Because Corinne hit him,' Zigic said. 'Was she always like that?'

'No.' Jessica drew herself up in her chair.

'I understand that you want to protect Corinne's memory but we know she slapped Harry and these things rarely happen in isolation.'

'She was a very loving mother.'

'And what kind of father was she before that?'

'The same,' Jessica said. 'She didn't suddenly change personality.'

'Obviously she did, if that's the first time she hit one of you.'

Jessica didn't reply but he could see she was flustered.

'Harry must have done something to antagonise her,' Zigic said. 'Something very serious.'

'Corinne wasn't that kind of person. She didn't believe in people hitting their children. She said it was what bad parents did.'

Like her own, Zigic thought, remembering what Bob Moran had told him, the beatings meted out by Corinne's mother.

'So she was a bad parent?'

'No!' Jessica looked exasperated.

'If bad parents hit their kids and Corinne hit Harry, then what did that make her?'

'You're twisting my words,' she snapped. 'Corinne was patient with us, even when we were being complete terrors. She didn't even react when . . .'

'When what?'

She pressed her lips together, dropped her gaze. 'It was nothing. It was years ago. Why does this matter? Harry didn't kill her.'

'Harry has a history of violence,' Zigic said shortly, slipping into the unfamiliar bad-guy role. He opened up the file he'd brought in with him and took out a photograph of the man Harry Sawyer had attacked when he was eighteen. He was a slightly built, middle-aged guy, bald and pale, with a badly broken nose and black eye. 'Did he ever talk about why he did this?'

Jessica stared at the photo, frowning deeply. 'I – he said it was self-defence.'

'It wasn't. Harry pleaded guilty.' Zigic watched her sag slightly, no more hiding from the kind of man Harry was. 'He attacked this man because he was gay. No other reason but that.'

'He was only eighteen.'

'Yes, it was years ago,' Zigic said, throwing her words back at her. 'Is that what Corinne didn't hit Harry over?'

Jessica stayed silent, looking at the man's battered face.

'How do you imagine she felt, knowing her son did this to someone just because of their sexuality?' Still she didn't reply. 'Corinne must have wondered if Harry wanted to do that to her, don't you think? Harry attacked this man but really he wanted to hurt Corinne?'

Jessica looked away from them both, visibly struggling to hold herself together.

Zigic took another photo out of the file and slid it over the table. He should have warned her and he should have apologised for showing her an image of Corinne, dead, barely recognisable, but he needed to shock her now.

'Jessica.'

He tapped the photo and she looked at it automatically, just a split second before she recoiled, gasping, her hand over her mouth, eyes squeezing shut.

Zigic put the photograph away again. 'Do you see? It's not so different, is it?'

'I'm leaving.' She pushed away from the table and hesitated for a second, looking between the two of them, as if seeking permission.

Zigic gestured towards the door. 'You're free to go.'

Part of her didn't want to, he could see it in how she hitched her handbag onto her shoulder and the slowness of her step as she headed for the door. She knew something but she wasn't quite ready to tell them yet. The shock had done the trick; now they would have to wait until she'd wrestled with her conscience, her love for Corinne versus her loyalty to her brother.

36

Ferreira didn't know the exact spot within the cathedral precincts where Ryan Bhakta had been attacked. But walking slowly along the narrow alleyways, feeling the dip in temperature, even in full sun, hearing her own footsteps echoing, she could see this as the perfect place for bad things to happen.

As she crossed the cathedral green and headed out towards Bishopsgate she'd encountered a handful of people, shoppers who'd opted for the cheaper parking near the river, a couple of solicitors she knew going from their city-centre offices to the Crown court. All walked with purpose, as if they knew this wasn't a good place to linger.

After dark the precincts had a reputation for sexual assaults and robberies and most people avoided them. A combination of poor lighting and blind corners and scant passers-by made this isolated, uncameraed warren an ideal hunting ground. There would be no witnesses to hear you scream for help here, little chance of a Good Samaritan intervening.

It wasn't even an efficient shortcut for Ryan Bhakta and, once again, pausing to look up at the dark, spreading branches of a yew tree in the neighbouring cemetery, she wondered why he had come this way.

She tried to imagine making the decision he had made that night. All dressed up in a short dress and very high heels, would she have walked down here?

Absolutely not. She'd thought he was foolish when he'd told her about taking the underpass – that odd lie – but this was outright madness.

Ferreira slowed as she passed a tiny, studded oak door set into the wall. It was barely five feet high, cut to suit the demands of a previous millennium. She didn't know. She remembered being brought here on a school trip, trudging around the cathedral at the back of the group, wondering how anyone felt the hand of God in such a sterile, soulless place. She'd committed herself to atheism by then and was determined to feel nothing.

But now she was older she could feel something emanating from the place and it was as if the soft, worn stone had absorbed a thousand years of quiet suffering and fire-and-brimstone sermons, all the pain and guilt, the forced and false piety it had witnessed. It seemed to ooze out and gather in the claustrophobic precincts, making the air heavier, attracting more bad energy to the place.

She huffed out a fast breath and pushed the idea away.

Ridiculous, she told herself, as she turned on her heel and strode back towards the green. The precincts felt eerie because she was confused and pissed off and, yes, scared about what was going to happen to her now. She'd never made a cock-up of this magnitude before, not a solo one anyway. When you were part of team the burden was spread, not equally perhaps, but you didn't have to bear it alone. She'd gone to speak to Ryan Bhakta, off the record, on her own, made promises she couldn't keep trying to get information he didn't have.

And now he was dead and she was to blame in everyone's eyes, including her own.

Walking across Cathedral Square she turned her phone around in her jacket pocket, thinking about taking Riggott's advice and wiping the conversation. The more she thought about it the less she believed it was a test. He was telling her how to save herself further trouble and if anyone knew how to do that it was Riggott.

She went into a cafe, ordered a coffee and a bacon roll, took the seat in the window as a pair of women got up to leave.

Messages were piled up on her phone, Zigic and Adams, one from Evelyn Goddard warning her off talking to Simon Trent.

I think you've done enough damage already, don't you?

The woman had some fucking nerve. This was her doing as much as anyone's. She knew Ryan Bhakta well enough to judge his mental state, should have realised what reliving the attack might do to him.

Looking at the text Ferreira felt a near-irresistible desire to speak to Simon Trent again.

A waitress brought over her coffee, told her the food would be a few minutes. The cafe was busy, conversations humming along behind her, and she tuned them all out, went online to check the social media reaction to Ryan Bhakta's death. The usual players were discussing it on Twitter and the video he'd made popped up in a few dozen tweets, a couple of blog posts had already begun the work of dissecting it, apportioning blame, directing action. The trolls were playing their usual game too, targeting the messages of sympathy, harassing the grieving, judging and mocking and delighting in worsening the suffering of strangers.

As she scrolled, a new tweet appeared, the *Independent* running the first newspaper article, a rehash of other people's words – the involvement of the Hate Crimes department was there, no statement yet from Nicola Gilraye and nothing new to add but it meant the rest of the circus would soon follow.

For a moment she debated getting in touch with Gilraye to check what the press officer was doing to stem the flow, but it would have been a naive move. Gilraye had no real influence over the Fourth Estate, let alone this lawless Fifth one which was already gearing up to demand the head of whoever they deemed responsible.

It was only a matter of time before this got too big for Riggott's bosses to ignore.

A different waitress arrived with her bacon roll and Ferreira put her phone down for a few minutes while she ate, taking no pleasure in it. She just needed enough fuel to propel her through the coming hours.

When she was finished she called Bobby.

'Is Zigic there? Can you talk?'

'He's out of the office,' Wahlia said. 'What the fuck's going on?'

'Like it isn't all over the station.'

'It's not your fault though, is it? Riggott shouldn't have suspended you over that.'

Ferreira pressed her fingertips to her temple. 'I'm not suspended, Bobby. He just needs some breathing space.'

'Have you been online?'

'Yeah, it's escalating.'

'Mel, the press are all over this. They're saying we pushed someone to kill themselves. This is serious, you know that, right?'

'I am fucking aware, thank you.' The man at the next table shot her an icy look above his newspaper and she aimed one right back at him. 'I need you to do me a favour.'

'You could try asking nicely,' he said.

'Bobby, please, not today.'

'What do you need?'

She lowered her voice. 'I need Ryan Bhakta's medical records, the report into his injuries from the attack. Everything you can get your hands on.'

Wahlia made a clicking sound with his tongue.

'I wouldn't ask if it wasn't important,' she said. 'Nobody else is looking into this and I'm pretty sure we've missed something. He lied to me, right? He lied about the whole thing. There has to be a reason for that.'

'We know the reason,' Wahlia said. 'He wanted to throw us off the scent so it wouldn't go any further.'

'But the location . . . why lie about that?'

'I don't know. But it's not going to be in his medical records, is it?' Wahlia was on his feet, she could hear him pacing the office. 'Look, you should keep your head down. Getting any more involved is only going to make it worse.'

She stared out of the window at the people passing by, not really seeing them, trying to find a reason good enough for him to help her.

'You don't want dragging into this,' she said. 'I get it. I'm tainted.'

'Mate, it isn't that and you know it.' He sighed. 'Shit. Alright, I'll see what I can do. Bear with me, okay?'

'Thanks, Bobby.'

'You owe me.'

'Anything you want.'

She drank her coffee and ordered a second when the waitress came to clear her plate, asked for a slice of cheesecake to go with it. She wanted a cigarette but the cafe was heaving now and she knew that if she moved she'd lose her table, so she waited, scanning through the Google results for Ryan Bhakta.

She ignored the newer ones, knew what they were saying, and concentrated on the pre-suicide information, looking for some clues about the man he really was.

LinkedIn gave her a four-year-old profile, showed him in a white shirt and gold tie. He looked the same as when she'd seen him, barring the slight kink at his broken nose and the scars on his face. He'd been doing something in IT back then but the page hadn't been updated for awhile and showed his last employers as one of the city's larger light manufacturing firms, which had been bought out and asset-stripped to destruction about eighteen months ago.

He had a Facebook profile but that was all and it was set to private, giving her nothing. It seemed odd for a man in his mid-twenties to have such a small social media footprint but she supposed he'd been living through Jasmine so completely that he had little need for a parallel life as Ryan.

The cafe continued to churn around her as she waited for Wahlia to get in touch again, women with kids in pushchairs coming in,

266

toting shopping bags and complicated allergies. Outside a weird-looking guy, fifty at least but dressed twenty years younger, sat smoking a cigar and nursing an espresso as he watched the street with a degree of interest that sparked her copper's instincts. Nothing to be done about it but he put her back up.

Why didn't everyone's instincts work that way? she wondered.

Was she a copper because she could see what people really were or could she see through them because her experience as a copper had taught her how to?

She thought of last night's conversation with Adams and groaned quietly into her fist. First dinner and now drunken heart-to-hearts. She could have distracted him, but some sad part of her had wanted to talk about Liam again. She'd hardly thought about him in years but this case had brought it all back; Corinne rejecting Nina and then Sam, neither of them enough to keep her happy, not when her body started screaming out for a man. No amount of love or sexual ingenuity or, shit, loyalty, had been able to override that desire in Corinne.

Ferreira knew how they felt, like they'd lost a battle on behalf of all womankind, and she wondered if they would cope with it better than she had.

Her phone pinged and she snatched it up – a fresh message from Adams asking if she was alright. She didn't want to talk to him but she knew she might need all the allies she could get very soon, so she fired off a quick reply, said she was fine, had gone home to catch up on her sleep.

Another coffee and a slice of lemon cheesecake later Wahlia finally managed to get Ryan Bhakta's medical records over to her, along with a brusque email – 'as requested' – which she imagined was less for her benefit than anyone who would read it later as part of an ensuing investigation. She called him and thanked him, hanging up when Zigic's voice sounded in the background.

She went outside to smoke while she read the file. The parts pertaining to his attack were as she expected, just more detail to add to the version PCs Bright and Hale had recorded, but then she stopped, feeling her heart pumping faster. She reread the short section, trying to think of another explanation, but there was only one. And it was worse than she feared.

37

Nina Sawyer proved a tougher prospect than her daughter. Didn't want to be there, didn't want to go over old ground again, couldn't see why they were so interested in her and her family when Corinne had *obviously* been murdered by some random 'thug' out on the prowl around Ferry Meadows.

'I am absolutely not blaming Corinne, women should be safe to walk down the street naked if they choose to, but we all know better than that, don't we?' she said, looking at Murray, because she was the woman in the room and she would understand.

Murray nodded slightly and Zigic knew she was thinking the same thing as Nina. Except the 'thug' Murray had in mind wasn't quite so random.

Nina shook her head. 'It's a shame you don't take assaults on women more seriously, then you might actually manage to lock these animals up before they graduate to murder.'

'So you'd like to see tougher sentences?' Zigic asked.

'Of course I would,' she said, bristling slightly. 'You might not be able to rehabilitate them but at least the rest of us are safe while they're in prison.'

'Is that how you felt when Harry got a suspended sentence?' The skin around her eyes tightened, but she didn't reply. 'That was a brutal attack. Should he have been locked up to protect the rest of society?'

Nina shifted her gaze back to Murray, maybe assuming another woman would understand. 'He acted in self-defence. Harry was barely old enough to shave, let alone extricate himself from unwanted sexual advances from a man old enough to be his father. He was scared.'

'You can tell yourself that,' Zigic said. 'But we all know it was an unprovoked attack. Your son is a bully and a thug.'

A faint blush glowed through her foundation; she'd come into the station decked out in full warpaint, hair done, dressed in black tailored trousers and a silk jumper, looking every inch the poised and polished businesswoman. Seen like this her wealth was obvious, the confidence which it inevitably spawned in a person. Zigic was surprised she hadn't arrived with an expensive solicitor in tow, but she seemed certain of her ability to handle this solo.

'Harry may have had his problems when he was younger but he hasn't been in any trouble, of any kind, since Corinne moved out. She was the agitating factor there, even the judge understood that. Frankly, I think it's a great credit to Harry how well he's turned out. Given the kind of example his father set him.'

Zigic was aware of the clock ticking behind her. Harry Sawyer was on his way into the station, Brynn Moran waiting to be spoken to next; he'd driven Nina, asked how long he could expect to be there, he had an appointment with a prospective new client in the afternoon.

They'd left Lily, the younger daughter, at home, and Zigic wondered if it had been an oversight or defensive action. Once he'd realised he dispatched a patrol car to collect her, wishing Ferreira had been in the office to do the job. The girl had met her already, spoken to her at length, it would have made the whole thing much easier.

Time to change tack.

'Mrs Sawyer,' he said, 'we've been looking into your and Corinne's divorce proceedings and it seems to us that you're stalling—'

'I am challenging inconsistencies in the accounting,' Nina said. 'That takes time, yes, but I won't be fobbed off with a smaller settlement than I'm due.'

270

'But you have that and more.' Zigic took out a photocopied document, turned to the page Wahlia had marked with a little pink tab. 'As of November the 25th last year, you have a fifty per cent share of the business, plus the house you're currently living in and a villa in the Algarve.'

She glanced at the paperwork, shrugged. 'And your point is?'

'Why haven't you signed?' Zigic asked. 'It seems a fair settlement.'

'To you, maybe.'

'You weren't holding out because you wanted him back, then?'

'Oh, now you're just talking nonsense.' She examined her fingernails, looking bored. 'What you won't find in the paperwork you have are the details of how our business started. It was my money that funded the first properties in the portfolio, and my parents who supported us financially during the last recession, when we almost lost everything. I am entitled to far more than fifty per cent of that business.'

Zigic watched her sitting there haughtily, much more comfortable now their discussion had moved away from her son and on to the less treacherous subject of money. It told him everything he needed to know about her own suspicions.

'How did Corinne feel about you delaying the completion of your divorce?' he asked.

'She wasn't happy, but she made me unhappy for long enough.' Nina tossed her head, ash-blonde hair swishing over her shoulder. 'If she wanted to speed things up all she had to do was agree to my requests.'

'Did she mention it at your Christmas get-together?'

'We have a family rule, no business or politics at the dinner table.'

'Must have been awkward, though. Having that hanging over the festivities.'

Nina shrugged again, shoulders sharp through her jumper. 'She should have thought about that before she insisted on coming.'

'Her and Harry had a set-to – what was that about?'

'I don't know what you mean.'

'I think you do,' Zigic said. 'Things got heated. Corinne slapped him.'

For a moment he seriously considered whether she knew anything about it, she looked genuinely perplexed, as if she thought he was trying to catch her out.

'That doesn't sound like something she'd do,' Nina said. 'She was always quite volatile but I'd never known her to be violent. Or Colin, for that matter.'

'Maybe she was upset because Harry threw her out,' Zigic suggested and got nothing but another slight shrug. 'Why did he do that?'

'I don't remember that happening.' She glanced away again, towards the blank wall at her right. 'One minute she was at the table and the next she'd left. I thought it was rather rude of her not to thank us for lunch, but it wasn't entirely out of character.'

Zigic made Nina go through the meal in detail. The questioning quickly annoyed her but he wanted her distracted by the minutiae, knew it was the small errors in a timeline which could reveal their lies. But she kept answering his prompts, what they ate, what they drank, who was cooking and whether she was in the kitchen.

'Brynn's a far better cook than me,' she said. 'I left him to it.'

'While you and Corinne and Harry stayed at the table?' She nodded. 'At what point did Harry throw her out?'

'I – I think it was after dessert.'

'But you're not sure?'

'We'd all had rather a lot to drink,' she said defensively. 'God, it was weeks ago, how can you seriously expect me to remember?'

'Fights tend to be memorable.'

'There was no fight.'

272

'Harry threw Corinne out and Corinne slapped him. That's a fight by anyone's definition of the word,' Zigic said. 'Now, the more you deny it, the more we have to think it was about something significant.'

Nina folded her arms, the fine gold bracelets she wore clinking together. 'Who told you about this? How do you even know it's true? I didn't see anything. Nobody else saw it.'

'It happened and if you genuinely weren't told about it then, again, we have to think it was a serious fight or else why wouldn't Harry tell you?'

She pondered it for a moment, eyes searching the tabletop for an answer, and Zigic found he believed her dismay. Lily knew, because she'd told Ferreira. Harry knew, because he'd done the deed and felt Corinne's wrath stinging on his cheek. But maybe neither had told her about it.

'We were in the living room,' she said slowly. 'Brynn was making coffee and Corinne was upstairs with Lily. I don't remember her coming back down.'

'"We" being you and Harry?'

'Yes. So he can't have thrown her out because he was with me,' Nina said triumphantly, daring him to contradict her. 'Corinne must have finally realised she'd outstayed her welcome and left.'

'Except we know they had an argument in the hallway,' Zigic said. 'And we know Corinne struck Harry. So your recollection of events is clearly flawed. And I'll ask you again – have you ever witnessed violence between them before?'

She glared at him. 'Of course not.'

'But Harry clearly has a temper.'

'He does not have a temper.'

'How would you explain this act of violence then?'

'A fabrication,' Nina said.

Zigic sighed, took back the document from the table in front of her and placed it in the file. 'Thank you, Mrs Sawyer, that will be all for now.'

'What an absolute bloody waste of my time,' she said, standing smartly, collecting her leather tote bag and tucking it into the crook her arm.

'DS Murray will see you out.'

Colleen stopped the recording and Nina let herself be escorted from the interview room.

Wahlia was waiting for him in the corridor.

'Thought you'd want to know before you spoke to Brynn Moran,' he said, holding out a sheet of call logs. 'Conversations between Corinne and Brynn Moran in the fortnight after Christmas. Found them on Corinne's second phone, which seems a bit off.'

Zigic checked them over, three calls, all during the day, durations of less than a minute for the first two. Moran called Corinne, she called back the next day, then another return call from him. That one was longer, four minutes plus.

'This could be anything, Bobby. They were friends from way back, and Lily Sawyer told Mel he was acting as a peacekeeper between Corinne and Nina. It's not unexpected that they're talking.'

'Maybe not, but if he's peacekeeping after Christmas doesn't it suggest he might know what the almighty bust-up was about?'

38

The doctor Ferreira needed to speak to was with a patient when she arrived at City Hospital's A&E department and she tried to see it as a win that she'd caught the woman, but after an hour waiting among the walking wounded, her nicotine craving got the better of her and she nipped outside for a quick smoke, came back to find her window of opportunity snapped shut.

The nurse behind the desk apologised. 'We thought you'd left, sorry. She won't be long, please take a seat.'

Fifteen minutes later Dr Linley came through the swing doors with her own cigarettes clutched in her hand and invited Ferreira to follow her out to a little area beyond A&E where the staff went to smoke, protected from the judgement of their patients and charges of not practising what they preached.

'Yes, I remember him,' she said, when Ferreira showed her the photograph of Ryan Bhakta. 'But that was ages ago. Why are you talking to me now?'

'New information has come to light recently and my department has taken over the case.'

Dr Linley nodded slightly, flicked ash off her cigarette into a steel bin. 'I thought there was more to that one, but the officers who came didn't seem very interested. Long night, I suppose. I'd been on two days straight myself.'

'What made you think there was more to it?' Ferreira asked.

'In my experience people who have been robbed are angrier. He was shaken up, certainly, and with his injuries no one could blame him for being rather dazed. But usually there's a bit of rage in evidence too.' She took a thoughtful drag, staring across the square of cracked concrete towards a picnic bench where a couple of nurses were sitting eating their lunch. 'And there wasn't enough blood on his clothes. There was some on his jumper but he was very . . . neat, for someone who'd been knocked down and beaten. No scuffs on his trousers, no rips.'

'That's because he went home and cleaned up first.'

She pursed her lips. 'Unusual. Especially given the state he was in. But – I'm sorry, what department are you from, Sergeant?'

'Hate Crimes.'

'Oh. Ah, you see, I thought perhaps it was an incidence of domestic violence.'

'Why?'

'The way he was cleaned up. I assumed it must have happened at home.'

'Did you press him on it?'

'I did, but he was adamant it was a robbery and once somebody's decided on their story they very rarely change it.' The doctor frowned, looking down at the toes of her white clogs, a few spots of dried blood there. 'We can give them all the assurances we like but when they're scared, well, what can anyone say?'

Ferreira murmured her agreement, wishing the doctor had pressed harder, that Bright and Hale had been more insistent. But in truth none of them could have done any more. Ryan Bhakta knew how he wanted to play the situation from the moment he called Evelyn Goddard to his home. Ferreira wondered if she knew the truth, would have liked to ask her to her face.

Dr Linley dropped the butt of her cigarette into the bin and shoved her hands into her pockets. 'So, if you're Hate Crimes, I take it this was a racially motivated attack?'

'No, Mr Bhakta was a cross-dresser.'

'Was?'

Shit, she wasn't going to reveal that. Too much coffee, not enough sleep.

'I'm afraid he killed himself,' Ferreira said, pausing to get her own story straight. The doctor didn't need the entire truth, just the most suitable selection. 'He was dressed as a woman when he was attacked. We've only recently learned this and we believe he was targeted by a man who's been responsible for other attacks on trans women in the city—'

'The woman at Ferry Meadows?'

'Possibly, yes.'

Dr Linley fished her cigarettes from her pocket and lit up a second one. 'How can I help you, then?'

'When you examined Ryan, did you see any evidence that he'd been sexually assaulted?'

Mid-drag and her eyes widened at the question. 'No, none. But I wasn't looking for it and he didn't mention anything so I just dealt with the damage I could see. Why do you think he might have been?'

'A week after he was admitted here, Ryan went to a walk-in clinic where he was treated for an infected anal fissure.'

'There are lots of reasons for having an anal fissure. Consensual anal sex being one of the most likely.'

'But it was only a week after the attack and he didn't go to his GP with it, he went to a walk-in, where no one would know him.'

'Have you tried asking them?'

'The doctor who saw him was a locum, he's currently in Croatia as part of a group treating Syrian migrants.'

'Noble work.'

'And off-grid, right now,' Ferreira said. 'As far as we know Ryan Bhakta was heterosexual, which means he probably wasn't having anal sex consensually. In your opinion, given the timing, is it likely that he sustained that injury around the time he was attacked?'

Linley's mouth twisted. 'In a theoretical case, I'd say it was quite likely. But without knowing his sexual history, or having examined the injury myself, that's as far as I'm prepared to go.' She shook her head. 'I suppose it explains his demeanour though. He didn't look me in the eye once.'

Ferreira thanked her for her time and backtracked through A&E, calling Bobby as she walked. The phone kept ringing until it finally went through to voicemail as she climbed into her car. She dialled the station and got put through to his desk. No answer there either.

She tried Adams.

'I need a favour.'

'Straight to the point, then?' he said. 'Since you're supposed to be at home I'm guessing you've kicked the duvet off and you can't be arsed to retrieve it yourself?'

'I'm not at home.'

She could hear his smile down the phone. 'I'm such a great detective.'

'Yes, you are,' she said, snapping her seat belt into place. 'You're the very best in the station and that's why I'm asking you to chase up some forensics for me.'

'And get castrated by Riggott? I'm not risking that, you know how much I love my balls.'

'How's he going to know?'

The babble of CID noise in the background cut off as he went into his office, blinds rattling against the glass when the door closed. 'What are you doing?'

'Following up a lead.'

'Riggott suspended you.'

'Technically, I'm off sick,' she said. 'Which means you *can* help me and I have a very strong lead, which means you *should* help me.'

'On the Sawyer murder?'

'Kind of.'

278

Behind her a red-faced man in a people carrier was furiously revving his engine, wanting her out of the space. There were plenty more but apparently he wanted this one.

'Kind of, how? Who is it?'

'Ryan Bhakta.'

'The suicide?' he asked. 'Are you fucking insane?'

'He was raped,' Ferreira said. 'I've seen his medical records and I've just talked to his doctor—'

'You've gone rogue now – this gets even better.'

'Yeah, I'm slamming a guy's head in a car door as we speak,' she said, eyeing the driver still waiting for her to vacate the space. 'Look, if Ryan was attacked by the same person who murdered Corinne then we might have a DNA sample from the swabs taken from him when he was in A&E. He was badly beaten up, there's going to be samples, right?'

Adams let out a long sigh. 'That actually is quite a good idea.'

'Yeah, I'm not a bad detective either.'

'Why haven't you taken it to Ziggy?'

Ferreira closed her hand around the steering wheel. 'Because I don't want to get him in any deeper grief than I already have.'

'Great, but you'll drop me in it?'

'Everyone knows you're Riggott's golden boy. Worst he'll do is have a big rant at you then pour you a drink and all's forgiven. Zigic can't afford the flak right now.' He didn't deny it, didn't agree either. 'Just, please, check for me, on the quiet, and if I'm right then I'll pass it on to Zigic.'

'So I don't even get the glory?' Adams asked.

'You know what you'll get,' Ferreira said, and ended the call.

39

'Sorry for keeping you waiting, Mr Moran.' Zigic closed the door, went to sit down next to Murray, who was already setting up the tapes. 'We'll try not to take up any more of your time than necessary.'

Brynn Moran unfolded his burly arms and laid them on the tabletop, an ancient but expensive watch hitting the scarred melamine with a crack. It had the look of a family heirloom, the kind given out at retirement when jobs were still for life. His entire appearance was that of a man unconcerned with how he looked, but Zigic saw through the facade. His jumper was moth-holed, but cashmere, his jeans too well cut to be anything but a designer brand. The effect was somewhere between gentleman farmer and green-energy entrepreneur, which Zigic supposed was exactly right for the owner of a landscape gardening company which catered to the wealthy locals.

Once again he wondered at the kind of couple Brynn and Nina made. She was so neat and precise, chilly in temperament and demeanour.

Was Brynn her bit of rough? Different enough from the man Colin had been that she felt secure in her ability to keep him?

Or maybe he was being unfair to Nina. Murder rarely brought out the best in people and he suspected those who put up the highest, most formidable defences were the most vulnerable underneath.

Murray went through the basics, asking again about Brynn's alibi, information he'd already supplied, about his friendship with Corinne and how and when he and Nina got together. Simple questions, designed to put him at ease. He answered shortly, stayed in neutral.

Unlike Nina and Jessica he didn't try to fill the quiet when Murray let a sentence hang.

Zigic hated dealing with suspects like this. He wanted a spewer. Then again, with the reticent ones you at least had the advantage of knowing anything they did say would be carefully weighed and meaningful, if not always in the way they intended.

It was odd though, considering how talkative he'd been when they'd spoken to him a few days ago. He'd been more than happy to spill back then. It made Zigic wonder what he might have learned in the meantime. If he was watching his words because he knew he was bad at keeping secrets.

Murray wasn't softening him up, they were just wasting time.

Cut to the chase, Zigic thought.

'Mr Moran, had you been in contact with Corinne recently?'

'How recently?' he asked. 'I saw her at Christmas, we had her over for dinner. Boxing Day.'

'What about since then?'

'I didn't see her in person, but we talked on the phone a couple of times.'

Zigic held his hand still on the blue cardboard file he'd brought with him, no need to put the evidence in front of Moran since he'd been good enough to admit it. He was slightly disappointed. Would have liked him to lie, giving them the opportunity to unfoot him.

'Who called who?'

'I called her, she called me back.' He scratched his eyebrow with a green-rimmed thumbnail. 'I might've rung her again. Or she rang me. One or the other.'

The truth, again. Given up so easily it took on the cast of a lie.

'What did you talk about?'

Moran heaved a deep breath. 'Lily, mostly. Corinne wanted to see her and Nina wouldn't let her go round there.'

'She's a teenage girl,' Zigic said. 'Surely she'd do whatever she wanted.'

'Yeah, but Nina would have kicked up merry hell as soon as she noticed she was gone. Corinne wanted her organised visits back.'

Zigic tried to remember what he'd read in the notes from their divorce proceedings, didn't recall anything about custody wranglings.

'Why had the organised visits stopped?' Zigic asked.

'They hadn't, not officially.' Moran shifted his weight in the chair, hunched over, weary-looking. 'After all that at Christmas, Nina put her foot down, told Corinne she wasn't welcome any more and not to come and get Lily at the weekend.'

'Why didn't Corinne take it up with the court?' Murray asked, and Zigic could hear her own history bleeding through in her voice, the angry edge. 'If they'd made legal arrangements Nina couldn't stop her seeing her daughter.'

'That's what I was calling Corinne about. I thought if she apologised for how she'd gone on when she was round ours, Nina might calm down about the whole thing.' He showed them his open hands, rough red palms, heavily calloused. 'I just reckoned it was better for everyone if we sorted it out among ourselves.'

'And did Corinne apologise?' Zigic asked, opening the file to check the dates.

Moran grimaced. 'No. Like a couple of cats in a bag, them two.'

'The last time you called Corinne – Thursday 28th of January – that was almost a month after the argument. They still hadn't made peace?'

'No.'

'Corinne must have seriously offended Nina then. What did she say?'

Another wriggle of discomfort in his seat. 'She was harping on about Nina's appearance. Saying she was anorexic. Telling her men liked something to grab hold of. It was a load of rubbish. Nina's got a fantastic figure and she works hard for it.'

'What about Harry?' Zigic asked.

'How d'you mean?'

'Harry and Corinne had a falling-out, right?'

'He was only defending his mum.' Moran cupped one big fist inside his palm, rubbed his thumb over his knuckles. He looked to Murray. 'You know how boys are with their mums. And Harry's been the man of that house for a lot of years.'

'Until you came along,' Murray said.

'Harry and me get on fine. Bloody hell, he's been working with me since he left school. He's like my own son.'

'Do you have children?' Murray asked.

He shook his head. 'Never met the right woman.'

Had he been waiting in the wings for Nina all this time, knowing what Corinne was putting her through, just waiting for the inevitable split to happen so he could move in on that ready-made family?

'Harry and you are close, then?'

A wary nod.

'He confides in you?'

'We're men,' Moran said, with a rueful smile. 'We don't go in for confiding much.'

'Did he tell you Corinne slapped him?'

'Yeah.' Moran pressed his balled fists to his chin. 'Shocked me, that. She'd never been the type for it. Colin was a scrapper when we were kids but that was his mum's doing. Old cow used to knock seven bells out of him. Way she went on Colin swore he'd never lay a hand on his own kids, no matter what they did.'

'Not even when Harry got in trouble with the law?'

Brynn frowned. 'He wasn't happy about that, but he blamed himself. He knew what it was about. Harry thought Colin was gay; he goes after some gay fella. Doesn't take a genius, does it?'

'Sounds like you and Colin confided in each other,' Zigic said.

'We were like brothers, it's different.'

He was still grieving, the sadness hanging over him, there in the tone of his voice and the droop of his eyes whenever he said Colin's name. Not Corinne – she was a different person, an agitant to be appeased, an unwelcome guest at his new family's table. Days into the inquiry and it still surprised Zigic how the people around her struggled to reconcile the two versions of Corinne, how polarised their feelings were.

'Harry threw Corinne out of the house,' Zigic said. 'What did she say to provoke him?'

'From what I can make out it was Harry doing the provoking. He said—' Brynn braced against the edge of the table as he gathered himself. 'Harry told her it didn't matter what she did, or how much money she spent on herself, she'd always just be a freak in a dress.'

'Did you witness this directly?'

'No. Harry told me afterwards. I think he was a bit ashamed of himself.'

'That didn't come from nowhere,' Zigic said.

'She'd been winding Nina up. Harry'd just had enough.' Brynn drew his hands off the table. 'He feels terrible about it, of course. The last thing he said to his dad and it was that. No taking it back now. Not for any of them.'

Fifteen minutes later, with Moran dispatched back to reception, Zigic stood in front of the murder board, looking at the photograph of Harry Sawyer. He imagined him in Corinne's face, spitting the words at her, a precisely calibrated insult guaranteed to pay her back for an afternoon sniping at his beloved mother. Corinne shouldn't have lashed out, but it was an understandable response.

How much further had that argument gone, though?

Could either of them let it lie?

284

If Harry didn't see Corinne as a woman then maybe he'd consider it a fair fight. The father he hated, who he'd long since rejected. He'd already sought a proxy victim in the man he'd beaten up when he was still a teenager.

Seven years on – seven years of insults and provocations – did he need to hit back at the real person now?

40

It was turning into a day for unanswered phones and Ferreira was getting sick of being ignored. She was outside the museum on Priestgate, the sound of a school trip somehow making it through the glass doors, children shouting, obviously having more fun than she was. The phone kept ringing in her ear until she swore and gave up.

Watching the upper window of the accountants' office across the road she tried a different number, went through to reception and asked the woman there for Simon Trent. She gave a fake name and said she wasn't an existing client, no, just interested in a quote, please.

'Mrs Pope, how can I help you this afternoon?'

'Simon, you can come downstairs and talk to me or I'll come up there, it's your choice.'

His voice caught in his throat and he rattled off what she imagined was his usual sales pitch, paused, then assured her that, yes, it would be no problem to speak face-to-face, just let him check his diary.

Ferreira rolled a cigarette and waited for him to come down. She'd give him ten minutes to extricate himself, didn't want to embarrass him, despite her threat. This was a delicate business and assuming he was still in touch with the community he would know what had happened to Ryan Bhakta, meaning he was probably spooked enough already.

But there was only so much room for delicate manoeuvring now.

Adams had called while she was driving back into the city centre – forensics had come back as a no-go on the swabs taken from

Ryan Bhakta after his assault. The samples had been checked at the time but filed as contaminated. She supposed that was no great surprise given that Evelyn Goddard had cleaned off his make-up before driving him to A&E, washing away any trace of evidence along with it.

Good work, Evelyn.

A couple of minutes later Simon Trent emerged from the building opposite, the collar of his grey pea coat turned up to shield his face.

'We can't talk here,' he said.

'The Meadham then,' Ferreira suggested. 'It's private.'

'But they know me there.'

'They know Simone, not you.'

They walked to the top of the road and up the worn stone steps, Simon lagging behind her. When the receptionist saw Ferreira her face dropped and she hesitated for a brief moment before she regained her composure.

'Would you care to speak to Mr Bentley?'

'Not today.' Ferreira smiled. 'We're just here for the ambience.'

She led Simon into the panelled bar at the front of the club, the one where he'd partied as Simone. It wasn't so boisterous this afternoon but busy enough that the music and the background chatter would mask their conversation. While she went to the bar he slunk away to a table in the corner, sat down under a print of Margaret Thatcher with a pink mohican.

Sutton was working behind the bar and he told the young guy with him he'd serve the lady.

'Any news?' he asked.

'We're getting there.' Ferreira gestured at the pumps. 'Keeping your hand in?'

'One of the girls called in sick. A "twenty-four-hour" virus,' he said with a grin, as if their previous conversation had never happened. 'Kids today think they invented bunking off with a hangover.'

'While the pros work through them?'

He winked at her. 'What you having?'

She ordered, paid Sutton and pocketed her change, took the drinks over to where Simon was sitting, trying to make himself invisible against the slate-grey panelling. His fingertips worried at the arm of the velvet tub chair, where countless other fingers had already rubbed the fabric bald.

When you started looking the place wasn't half as fancy as it thought it was.

Nice enough though. She could imagine coming in here of an evening, sampling that extensive rum selection. The food on the surrounding tables looked decent too. And it was only a short stumble home. For a split second she saw herself in there with Adams and wiped the thought away; they were not a couple, they did not go on dates.

'What do you want?' Simon asked, when she sat down.

'I just need to talk to you for a few minutes.'

'Like you talked to Jasmine.'

'I thought you weren't in touch with the group any more,' Ferreira said.

He dropped his gaze. 'Word gets out. Everyone knows you were harassing her, just like you're harassing me. How can you live with yourself?'

Ferreira felt the words like a slap. Told herself to let it go.

'I'm trying to catch this bastard, Simon.'

'And you don't care who you trample on to get to him. Do you have any idea what you've done?'

'Do you know what was going on in Jasmine's head?'

'She was scared. She knew you were going to expose her.'

'So she exposed herself?'

Spots of colour rose on his pale cheeks, the tiny scars there heating up. 'It was the only way she could be herself. She got minutes – that's all – four minutes of being herself and then she had to kill herself, because the price of continuing was too high.'

288

'Society sets the price,' Ferreira said. 'Not me. Whatever else you think, you have to know I'm on your side.'

He laughed, a dry huff of a sound, not loud enough to draw attention from the tables around them. 'Evelyn Goddard is going to have your job.'

His certainty sent a chill through her. Like it was a done deal.

Simon was nodding, buoyed up now by his belief in Evelyn Goddard. 'She's a powerful woman, you know.'

Ferreira had done nothing but try and help him and yet she was the bad guy. Not the man who'd attacked him and shoved him back in the closet. He wasn't brave enough to face that enemy, but her, yeah, he could throw his attitude at her.

'You know what Evelyn is?' she asked, leaning across the table. 'She's the reason you got attacked. If she hadn't covered for Jasmine we'd have got the bastard back then and he wouldn't have been walking the streets six months later to hurt you.'

A glass smashed behind the bar and Simon flinched at the sound.

'Evelyn wiped away every trace of DNA we might have used to identify that man.' Ferreira stabbed at the table with her finger. 'That's the kind of woman she is.'

'She was just trying to protect Jasmine,' Simon said, but all confidence was gone from his voice now. 'If you found the man—'

'What? What's the worst that would have happened? Jasmine would have gone to court and given evidence and people would've known she was a man who liked dressing up as a woman sometimes? So fucking what? She'd have got her revenge. She could have lived her life openly. She wouldn't have had to hide any more.' Ferreira threw Jasmine's own words at him and she saw them hit home. 'She didn't kill herself because I talked to her, she killed herself because she was sick of having to live a lie, Simon.'

He cast a nervous glance towards the next table but they weren't interested.

'I know what you're trying to do.' There were tears in Simon's eyes and when he reached up to wipe at them with the pad of his middle finger Ferreira saw Simone in the movement.

'Have you seen the sympathy that's out there?' she asked. 'Nobody hates Jasmine. Nobody thinks Corinne was a freak. You don't need to keep hiding.'

'You just want me to help you,' Simon snapped, back in control. 'You don't care what happens afterwards.'

'I'll tell you what'll happen afterwards – nothing.'

'What about Donna?'

Ferreira thought of his wife, the woman who'd forced him to choose – Simone or his marriage – the woman who'd blossomed since he went back in the closet.

'Anyone who tries to force you to change who you are is not worth being with.'

Simon stood suddenly, knees banging the table so hard that his bottle toppled and Ferreira grabbed it before it fell but lost him in the process. She called to his retreating back, drawing a few looks, not his though.

If she went after him what would she say? How could she possibly raise the issue of whether he'd been raped now?

Ferreira mouthed a silent but vehement 'fuck' into the air.

'Making friends?' Sutton asked, coming over to wipe down the spilt Coke on the table.

'Did you recognise him?'

'No – should I have?' Sutton frowned. 'Is he one of our Monday-night regulars?'

'Not lately, but yeah.'

'I never recognise them when they're not dressed up.'

'He sucked your cock,' Ferreira said.

Sutton's face darkened and he walked swiftly out of the room. She felt a momentary satisfaction in unnerving him, but realised it had been a cheap, pointless shot, driven by temper.

She thought about Simone and whether she'd get on better talking to her. If such a thing was even possible. She knew, deep in her gut, that Simon had more information than he was sharing, had felt it right from the moment he came around in his hospital bed and averted his eyes from her. Until this morning she'd assumed he'd seen the man's face, maybe could identify him; now she was sure the secret he was keeping was about the nature of the attack itself and that was something he might never feel ready to reveal.

41

Harry Sawyer wouldn't talk to them without a solicitor present, despite Murray's assurances that it was only an informal chat. He wasn't buying that. He'd been here before and realised he was in trouble.

'Good sign,' Murray said, shaking her crisp packet at Zigic across the canteen table.

He declined, was supposed to be avoiding junk food, although he wasn't convinced the cheese sandwich he'd bought was much healthier. They had an hour to kill before Harry's solicitor arrived and coming down here for a late lunch was as good a use of the time as he could think of.

The alternative was returning to his office to write up the report Riggott had requested on Ferreira's handling of Ryan Bhakta. The DCS had given him until Monday, almost as if he was allowing them a chance to get their story straight. Zigic was sure Bhakta's suicide stemmed from a lifetime of personal struggles and the fallout from a particularly brutal attack rather than the short conversation Ferreira had had with him earlier in the week, but he knew it looked bad on her and him and their department in general. And he was well aware that the sword which had been hanging over their collective necks ever since Hate Crimes had been founded had dropped almost within touching distance.

He wasn't going to lay this all on Ferreira, though.

In her position he would have done the same thing, any good detective would, and he already knew he was going to make that absolutely clear. How he did that was what troubled him.

Murray crumpled up the empty crisp packet. 'Going for a fag.'

Zigic took out his mobile and called Ferreira's number. She picked up after two rings and he could hear music in the background, chattering voices.

'Where are you?'

'Having lunch,' she said. 'Thought I'd enjoy my day off.'

'Well, don't get too used to being a lady of leisure.'

'You've spoken to Riggott?' she asked, a bright note coming into her voice. 'What did he say?'

'I haven't spoken to him yet. He wants a report by Monday.'

'Oh.' Glasses clinked together at her end and she thanked somebody. 'I'll just have to wait and see what happens, won't I? Not like I'm completely unemployable. There's always private security.'

She was slurring slightly and Zigic pinched the bridge of his nose, picturing her getting hammered in some bar, trying to drown the guilt and the worry he knew he'd be feeling in her position.

'We need to talk,' he said. 'After work, okay?'

'I'm not going anywhere.'

'I'll call you later.'

'Yes, sir.'

She rang off and Zigic looked at his lunch for a second before throwing the paper napkin over the remnants of his sandwich. He should have tried to reassure her but he didn't want to lie and he'd never been much good at pep talks.

As he was heading back up to Hate Crimes again his phone rang, an unfamiliar number on the screen. He paused in the stairwell to answer.

'There's something I need to tell you.'

'Jessica?'

'I should have said this ages ago, but I didn't want to cause any trouble.' She sounded distressed. 'I owe it to Mum.'

Above him the stairwell door banged and Murray called his name from the top of the next flight. He held a finger up.

293

'What is it, Jessica?'

Zigic listened while the story spilled out of her, punctuated by sniffs, her voice getting thicker and more choked until the final words, when she dissolved into tears. He thanked her but she was already gone.

'Solicitor's here,' Murray said. 'What was that all about?'

He updated her as they went down to the interview rooms. Murray didn't seem very pleased with the development, questioning the importance of what Jessica had told him and when he insisted it mattered, questioned her reliability.

Murray wanted it to be Walton so much she'd probably refuse to believe a signed confession from any other suspect.

Harry Sawyer sat with his knees spread wide, leaning back from the table, but he snapped to attention when they walked in, pushed his jumper up to his elbows, straightened his watch on his wrist, getting himself ready. Next to him the solicitor had the same expression of bored implacability they all wore in this situation. Just another client on another regulation case.

Murray ran through the usual spiel, explained that Harry was free to leave whenever he liked, and he nodded, eyes cutting quickly towards the door as if he might test the theory at any moment.

He was nervous. Had good reason to be, Zigic thought.

Or maybe it was only experience making his knees shake under the table and his tongue dart out to wet his chapped lips. There was a bottle of water on the table in front of him, half drunk, the label shredded.

Murray got the initial questions out of the way, as with Brynn Moran, and then Zigic took over, getting down to their real business.

'On the 26th of December last year, you had an altercation with Corinne,' he said. 'Tell us what that was about.'

'She was mouthing off at Mum.'

'And you decided to stop her?'

'Somebody had to.'

'Is your mother not capable of defending herself?' Zigic asked.

Harry shifted his feet under the table, trainers squeaking on the linoleum floor. 'Corinne bullied her for years. Mum's the victim here.'

'Corinne's the one who was murdered.' Zigic studied him, saw only the barest flicker of panic around his eyes. 'You physically removed Corinne from the house – is that right?'

'I escorted her out.'

'And as you were "escorting" her, she hit you.'

'She didn't.'

Zigic sighed. 'We know she did, Harry. We've had it confirmed by two sources. Why did she hit you?'

Harry Sawyer wet his lips. 'She hit me because I told her she was a joke.'

'Not a freak?'

He shrugged. 'A joke, a freak, what's the difference? I can't remember exactly what I said. I was offensive, but she'd been offensive to Mum. I don't have to apologise for that.'

'You said "it didn't matter what she did, or how much money she spent, she'd always just be a freak in a dress".'

A hint of embarrassment coloured his cheeks. 'There's no law against being rude to someone.'

'It depends how far it goes.'

'It didn't go any further. She left.'

'What about after she left?'

'I didn't speak to her again.'

'Before she died?'

Harry Sawyer shook his head. 'No. I had nothing else to say to her. I wouldn't have been there for dinner except Mum needed someone to watch her back.'

Interesting choice of words, Zigic thought. He was making it sound even more combative than the others had, and it made him wonder if that was how Harry Sawyer saw the dynamic within his

295

family. A fight, a war, a situation where backs actually had to be watched. Or if he was just the kind of idiot whose dialogue was peppered with the hyper-masculine language of violence.

'Did you hit her back?'

'No.'

'Why not?'

'Because I was raised not to hit women.'

'But you don't see her as a woman,' Zigic said. 'She was just a "freak in a dress". A man. And we know you've got no problem hitting other men.'

Sawyer's jaw clenched, cords rising in his neck. 'I was a kid.'

'And how old were you when you beat your dad up?'

'I told you, I didn't hit her back.' Sawyer was trying to stare him down but Zigic had seen much worse from much tougher men. All he saw when Sawyer put the hard eye on him was fear gilded with bravado.

'Not her,' Zigic said. 'Not Corinne. I want to know how old you were when you beat your *dad* up. Colin.'

There was the fear, its covering stripped away, and Sawyer retreated behind his hands, curled them up like he was cold and held them over his mouth. The classic pose of someone who was about to lie.

'I didn't do that.'

'You broke two of Colin's ribs, you knocked out three of his teeth and perforated his eardrum.' Zigic's turn with the hard stare now. 'That was a hell of a beating, Harry. What were you, fifteen, sixteen?'

'Who told you?'

'Why? Are you going to beat them up too?'

'Jessica,' he said, shaking his head. 'She wasn't even there.'

'No, but she saw the results of your anger-management issues,' Zigic said. 'And I guess she's not the only member of your family wondering if you're a murderer about now.'

296

Sawyer planted his palms flat on the table and for a moment Zigic thought he was going to kick off, welcomed the prospect and the advantage it would give them, but he didn't. He just flexed his sinewy hands, the muscles in his forearms tensing, and then caught himself, withdrew slightly.

Easy to imagine those thick fingers with her earphone cables looped around them for purchase as he choked the last breaths out of her.

'I didn't kill Corinne.'

'You despised her,' Zigic said. 'She disgusted you.'

'I didn't kill her. I've got an alibi. Take my DNA, take my fingerprints, see if I did it.'

He slammed his arm down on the table, slapped his inner elbow, as if Zigic might produce a needle then and there. Zigic raised an eyebrow at him.

'You know the process better than that, Harry. You've been here before.'

'Then you know I didn't do it, because I'm already on your system.'

Sawyer was breathing hard, a vein throbbing at his temple. Maybe he thought he'd been more careful and they had nothing to test against. They didn't have much, but there was a size 10 shoe print at the scene and fibres on Corinne's clothes and very soon a search team would be at his house looking for items to match them.

'I'm leaving.'

'No, Harry,' Zigic said. 'You're not.'

42

The key found the lock on the second attempt and Ferreira slammed the door behind her, the sound ringing through her head, feeling like she'd been punched. She didn't think she'd had that much to drink and the food should have soaked it up but she felt toxic already.

In the kitchen she drank two full glasses of water and that didn't help. It just sloshed around, giving her a colder kind of nausea. She put the kettle on and went into the bathroom to throw up. She needed to be sober when she talked to Zigic. Her whole career could be riding on that conversation and she needed him to see how seriously she was taking this situation.

Almost three o'clock.

She knew she should get some sleep, meet Zigic fully rested and alert, but her mind kept turning, running down the same lines she'd been exploring since the early hours of the morning. There was something she was missing about Ryan Bhakta's assault, something frustratingly out of reach. The doctor in A&E had known he was lying, she just didn't know why or about what. Bright and Hale might remember something more useful but she wasn't going to risk making contact with them. She'd done enough today, with little to show for it, beyond a belief that Ryan had been raped.

How would Zigic react when she told him that? She'd almost done it over the phone but decided it was a conversation best had face-to-face. He wasn't going to be happy about her independent investigation. He never did approve of that, too much the team player.

298

It was the least of her worries now, she realised.

In the kitchen she brewed a pot of strong coffee, made a couple of slices of toast she ate dry, every mouthful an effort, and chased them with an ibuprofen.

She took her coffee into the living room and curled up on the sofa with her laptop. This was going to be an act of self-immolation, but she needed to see what was being said.

The vitriol level had risen steadily since the last time she looked and the tone was darker in the wake of Ryan's suicide, as if this kind of death attracted a different breed of troll to murder. Less condemnation of lifestyle more sick humour, a few dozen persistent offenders competing to hit the bottom of the barrel.

That wasn't Ferreira's concern though. As much as she'd love to press charges on every one of the bastards.

The Peterborough Constabulary Twitter account was being bombarded with calls for an official inquiry, accusations of prejudice and bullying, hundreds of different accounts saying they'd hounded Jasmine to her death – nobody used Ryan Bhakta's name. As she watched, somebody posted a link to a petition calling for the sacking of the officer responsible. They didn't know who that was yet but they wanted a head to roll. The retweets started instantly and she closed the tab, went over to the Trans Sisters Facebook group.

More of the same there, just coming from fewer people. They were furious, talking about legal action and contacting their MPs, the IPCC, taking it to the European Court of Human Rights if necessary.

She took her coffee into the kitchen and poured a slug of rum into it. No point worrying about the clear head now. Gilraye would be monitoring the social media accounts, she'd pass the details on to Riggott and he'd pass them up from there.

When the mug was empty she poured another shot into it and smoked a cigarette standing staring out of the window. Simon Trent's office, the Meadham, the Trans Sisters HQ; all of the main players in this case were within a hundred metres of her. She imagined Evelyn Goddard sitting smugly at her big glass desk, watching Ferreira's career implode in a social media witch-hunt. It was what she'd wanted from the moment they first met her; a scalp.

How much of this was she engineering? Was it fanciful to think she could do that?

Ferreira took another drag, realised she was being ridiculous. Nobody needed to orchestrate proceedings. Once Jasmine posted that video it was inevitable that the community would start looking for somebody to hold accountable and then the roaming band of opportunistic agitators would come along for the ride. They'd spend a few days on this before they found another cause to fill their lunch breaks and their empty evenings, but by then her career could be over.

Evelyn Goddard was the only person she could get to right now and part of her knew it was a bad idea but she was beyond caring.

Within five minutes she was being buzzed into the office, met at the door by a doughy man wearing shorts and Crocs, despite the weather, who told her she wasn't welcome there.

'You let me in,' Ferreira said, already moving. 'Where's Ms Goddard? Through here, yeah?'

She went into Evelyn's office without knocking, walking in on an unexpected scene, Evelyn pink-eyed, with a bottle of her own uncapped on the desk, a generous measure poured into a tumbler.

'Thought you'd be celebrating,' Ferreira said, closing the door on the receptionist's protests. 'You've got what you wanted. We're being pilloried.'

'I didn't want that.' Evelyn drew herself together quickly, retrieving her jacket from the back of her chair and pulling it on over her dress, taking the opportunity to wipe her eyes while she was turned away. 'I only wanted you to take our concerns seriously.'

The fight deserted Ferreira as she watched Evelyn settle herself into her chair again. She looked her age today, older and frailer

300

than the woman they'd dealt with previously, and Ferreira realised she didn't have the stomach to argue with a grieving pensioner.

'For what it's worth, I really am truly sorry about Ryan,' she said. 'All I ever wanted was to find the man who attacked him and make sure he couldn't hurt anyone else.'

Evelyn picked up her glass. 'I was out of order – what I said to you at the house. It was the shock. I knew Ryan was depressed, but I had no idea he was so close to the edge. He never really recovered.'

'Most people don't recover from something like that. Not without help.' Ferreira sat down, debated her next words for a moment, knowing they were make or break. 'Did you know he'd been raped?'

The eruption she feared didn't come. Instead Evelyn buried her face in her hand and muttered quietly to herself.

'I suspected as much,' she said finally. 'Ryan's manner was so strange when I arrived at his house. He seemed . . . ashamed. I couldn't understand it at the time, but the more I pressed him about what had happened the quieter he became. I've known plenty of girls get beaten up for how they were dressed – God, I've had men try it with me. Normally we don't feel ashamed in that situation, we're scared or we're angry or both, but never ashamed.'

'Did you ask him directly?'

'I didn't need to.' Evelyn drained her glass in one swift draught. 'I undressed him, remember. I saw the blood. And the semen.'

Ferreira sighed. There it was, all the evidence they needed, gone.

'We could have got him,' she said, trying to keep the accusation out of her voice. 'If only Ryan had come forward.'

'I hoped he might be strong enough to do that one day.' Evelyn reached for the bottle of Laphroaig and poured another stiff measure in; the whisky didn't seem to be touching her. 'I hoped, eventually, I'd be able to convince him to think of the greater good.'

'That's why you asked him to talk to me?'

She nodded, the muscles in her face tightening briefly, and she looked down into her glass before she spoke. 'And . . . it's why I kept the clothes.'

Ferreira shot up in her seat. 'What?'

'I'm sorry, I know I should have come forward sooner,' Evelyn said, almost babbling. 'But how could I do that without Ryan's consent and cooperation? I could hardly just march into the police station and say, "Examine these, they're covered in a rapist's DNA." She pressed her fingertips to her lips. 'Poor Simone, she could have been spared.'

Ferreira was on her feet. 'Evelyn, where are the clothes now?'

43

They'd agreed to meet in the pub near Zigic's house, a quaint place with a fire roaring up the inglenook and a pool table in need of refelting.

These village pubs attracted a weird clientele but Zigic had suggested it and she wasn't going to argue. Any closer to the station and they would have run into familiar faces. Here there were only a handful of dusty builders around the bar, an ancient guy in a three-piece tweed suit who probably manned that stool from midday to closing, and a couple of women with big handbags and lanyards picking over their meal in an otherwise deserted dining section.

Somebody had left a copy of the local paper on the bar but she didn't bother to pick it up. They were hours behind the curve, the front page given over to redevelopment plans at the marina project on the side of the River Nene.

Ferreira ordered a Coke and took it outside, sat near the patio heater and checked her phone while she waited. Messages from Adams and Bobby, one from Zigic five minutes ago saying he was on his way.

There was more activity on the force's Twitter feed, but no answers from Gilraye. It made her wonder what the press officer had been doing with her time. Ferreira wasn't naive enough to think it would be anything for her benefit. It looked bad though, downright unprofessional, and she questioned whether Gilraye understood the dynamics of social media at all. If you let a vacuum develop other people would fill it and your continuing silence would come to be regarded as a tacit admission of guilt.

When she googled Ryan Bhakta she saw that the *Guardian* had a short article on his suicide, headed up by the video he'd posted as Jasmine. The piece mentioned that police were investigating a serious assault he'd suffered in 2014 but stopped short of implying a link between the two facts.

Someone, somewhere, had provided the paper with information about the attack. Maybe from within the Trans Sisters group, assuming anybody knew Ryan well enough to put his real name to the video of Jasmine, but even then details of the assault would have had to come from a limited pool: the doctor in A&E, Evelyn Goddard, a leak inside Thorpe Wood Station.

Given Evelyn's recent change of attitude Ferreira thought the last option was the most likely. Whether it was a controlled leak or some PC looking for a backhander, she wasn't sure. If it had come direct from Gilraye then they were circling the wagons and she was on the wrong side of them.

She should have talked to Riggott again. Monday was an eternity away and the weekend stretched ahead of her, waiting to be filled with more doubts and fears and whatever opinion pieces the weekend editions would run. Now the *Guardian* had broken the story the rest would soon follow suit. The coverage of Corinne's death had been extensive and this fresh angle was a godsend for hacks with deadlines. A quick rehash, a video clip; easy filing.

Ferreira rolled a cigarette, shivering in her leather jacket.

They could stop this, she told herself.

Evelyn had given them the means. It wasn't too late to turn the story. Catch the man who'd attacked Ryan and Simon and maybe killed Corinne too. Save her reputation.

Zigic came out of the pub's back door, carrying a large glass of red wine.

'Been that kind of day for you too?' Ferreira asked.

'Back-to-back interviews,' he said, straddling the other side of the picnic table. 'My throat needs wine.'

'You up to talking a bit more?'

He took a mouthful, nodded as he swallowed. 'It's already helping.'

'I know where to find the clothes Ryan was wearing the night he was attacked.'

Zigic's eyes widened, the patio heater casting a stark light on the side of his face, rendering his shock almost cartoon-like.

'You were supposed to be taking the day off.'

'My career is on the line, in case you've forgotten,' Ferreira said, sharper than she meant to. 'I wasn't going to sit around on the sofa watching fucking daytime TV, was I?'

He placed his wine on the table. 'Mel, I really don't think it's going to come to that.'

'Have you been online?' She shook her head. 'Of course you haven't. Look, we're getting pummelled. The press have caught on to the video, the pressure groups are in attack mode – hasn't Gilraye updated you on any of this?'

'No.'

Ferreira took another drag on her cigarette and told him what she'd done, seeing his initial annoyance quickly give way to curiosity, and a hungry glint came into his eye when he realised just how far they'd progressed since this morning.

'Evelyn was raging though,' he said. 'Are you sure we can trust her?'

'We don't need to trust her, do we?' Ferreira stubbed out her rollie. 'We search Ryan's house as a matter of course – the video has opened up a new line of inquiry on a previously dormant assault – it's only natural we go and look for information there.'

'I can't believe she kept the clothes,' he said.

'She thought she'd convince him to tell us the whole story eventually. Evelyn isn't an idiot. She knew we'd be able to retrieve DNA long after the fact. It was just a matter of waiting for Ryan to be ready.'

Zigic considered it for a moment, looking at the fingerprints he'd left on his wine glass, turning it around in the light. 'You know there's no guarantee Ryan didn't find them and throw them out. He wouldn't have wanted them in his house.'

'He might have, yeah. But we need to at least check.' She sipped her Coke. 'I think we should go tonight.'

He sighed. 'Not tonight, Mel.'

'Tomorrow then,' she said. 'First thing. We can get the clothes over to forensics, fast-track them, we'll have a result by Monday, Tuesday at the latest.'

'We don't have the budget for that.'

She threw her hands up. 'This could be Corinne's murderer we're talking about. One search and we clear that *and* two serious assaults.'

'You know as well as I do this isn't currently linked to Corinne's murder.'

The door opened and one of the women from the dining section came out with a cigarette already hanging from her lip. She smiled at Zigic as she walked past, didn't go more than three metres away before she lit up, and they looked at each other, the conversation on hold temporarily.

'What are you doing this weekend?' Zigic asked, his tone achingly relaxed.

'I'm away with the choir on Saturday, we're singing in Lincoln Cathedral.' He grinned behind his glass. 'What about you? Anything fun?'

'I thought I'd take the boys to the cinema. If I tie them to the seats I can get some sleep while they're distracted.'

They kept chatting as the woman smoked her cigarette and Ferreira decided that if she lit another one she'd snatch it out of her mouth and throw it into the road. She nodded while Zigic talked about some series he was watching on Netflix. He actually seemed to be enjoying this, as if he'd forgotten they were standing at the edge of a massive break in the case and he kept going for a minute or two after the woman returned to the bar, asking if she'd watched *Jessica Jones* yet. Insisting it was definitely her kind of thing.

'Oh my God, stop,' Ferreira said. 'This case is absolutely, potentially linked to Corinne's murder.'

'You didn't think that a couple of days ago.'

'I do now.'

'Now you want to press on with the search,' he said. 'Look, as yet we've got no solid reason to think the two cases are linked.'

Ferreira pushed her fingers back through her hair in exasperation. 'I don't care. Okay? I don't care if they're linked, I just want to catch this fucker. And Evelyn has gifted us a significant breakthrough. Why can't we take it? I need this.'

'Mel—'

'No. Monday morning I've got to go into Riggott's office and he's going to tell me just how deep this shit I'm in is. Don't you see how much stronger my position will be if I can give him some really good news? Good news about the very case I'm being strung up over.' She took a deep breath, watched him watching her. 'If our positions were reversed I would do this for you in a heartbeat.'

Zigic tipped his head back, eyed the stars for a second before he said, 'Okay. But this was never about not supporting you. I just don't want us to make the situation worse.'

'We won't.' She stood up. 'More wine?'

He drained the last two inches. 'No, I need to get home. Especially since there'll be no trip to the cinema tomorrow now.'

'Hey, think how much trouble I'm going to be in with my choir.'

44

'So, we're not going to talk about this,' Lily said.

Brynn looked to Nina, waiting for her to make the decision, but she kept pushing the food around on her plate, face drawn into a pensive moue. It was the same expression she'd been wearing since Lily was handed over to her in the police station, once her interview was finished.

They'd driven home in a constipated silence, Brynn staring out of the window, Nina concentrating on keeping the car straight on the road and her spine straight in the seat as her hands clutched the steering wheel.

Lily thought they'd want to know what she'd told the police, but the second interrogation never came.

Either they believed she didn't have anything to tell them about Corinne's murder or their own interviews had gone so badly that they were still rerunning them, wondering if they'd been caught out, if they'd implicated each other.

It surprised Lily how little she could remember of the process. Inspector Zigic did most of the talking and she would have rather spoken to Sergeant Ferreira but he explained that she was out of the station on another case. The woman he'd brought in with him radiated a maternal disapproval which made Lily squirm, even though she guessed the whole point of her was to appear non-threatening.

Once the questions started Lily began to get disorientated, the reality of the situation sinking in. It was nothing like she expected and she found that her heart was pounding, her mouth going dry. She felt guilty, even though she'd done nothing wrong, and she wondered how anyone could come into a room like that, with the two-way mirror and the recording equipment, and hold together a coherent string of lies.

She remembered being scared and angry and defending Harry. Something about the woman's steady gaze and Inspector Zigic's gentle but pointed questioning had brought out the familial loyalty in her. The more they suspected Harry the less she wanted to believe it.

The one thing she did remember, very clearly, was the moment that all fell away.

She'd almost said something on the way home but she wanted to be looking at Nina when she brought it up, wanted to see her reaction. And now here they were, sitting opposite each other at the island unit in the kitchen, under the spotlights, eating a dinner nobody could stomach.

'Were you ever going to tell me?' Lily asked.

Nina cast her a weary look. 'Tell you what?'

'That Harry beat Dad up. He put him in hospital.'

Nina's fork clattered onto the plate. 'It was years ago. You were three, for God's sake. Do you want to know everything that happened when you were too young to understand it?'

'Don't pretend this isn't a massive thing,' Lily said. 'You should have told me. And you should have told the police as soon as Mum was murdered. If it wasn't for Jess they'd still be thinking Harry was a normal person instead of a fucking animal.'

'That's enough,' Nina snapped. 'You have no idea what things were like back then. Harry was being bullied at school, he was depressed—'

'Oh, poor Harry. So depressed he had to break Dad's ribs and knock his teeth out.' Lily sneered, because if she didn't stay hard about this she knew she was going to start crying. 'Why didn't you take him to the doctors if he was so fragile? Were you worried they might realise how unhinged he was? Maybe they would have sectioned him. It's what he deserved.'

Nina closed her eyes for a moment, hands flat on the marble countertop. 'Just try, for one minute, to see this from your brother's perspective. Corinne went behind my back and collected Harry from school dressed as a woman. Everyone saw her. Everyone knew who she was. After that they made Harry's life a total misery.'

Lily started to defend Corinne but Nina kept talking.

'Day in, day out. Even some of the teachers. He was getting into fights, being harassed. At one point a group of older boys cornered him in an empty classroom and—' Her jaw hardened and she blinked away the rest of it. 'So, yes, Harry lashed out, and we were all horrified by that. But your father understood where it came from. That's why he forgave Harry, and that's why he did everything he could to protect him afterwards.'

Nina looked tired and weak, the make-up she rarely wore beginning to flake across her cheeks, her carefully styled hair hanging limp. She slipped off the high wooden stool.

'I'd better go and phone Carly,' she said. 'Maybe she's heard something.'

Brynn reached out and took her hand. 'Why don't you see if she wants to bring the boys round? Best we're all together tonight.'

'You're right.'

He stood up and wrapped his arms around her and Lily watched Nina crumple against his chest, saw her shoulders begin to shake and had to look away. Thought bitterly that there had been no tears for Corinne but the threat of charges against Harry was enough to obliterate Nina's composure.

When Nina left the kitchen Brynn started to clear away their plates. He'd spent an hour cooking the meal and they'd barely eaten a single serving between them. Now he was scraping the food into the bin and stacking the dishwasher, keeping up this play of normality.

Even before he moved in he would come here and cook for them and it never seemed strange. He was one of the family, always had

310

been. Sometimes he'd bring women round, but they never stayed with him long enough for them to become part of the family too. Lily barely remembered any of them, only that they all looked the same, dark-haired, petite women, and she remembered the way Nina would talk to them, with exaggerated politeness none of them seemed to see through.

Now she was older she realised Brynn hadn't cared about those girlfriends. He'd been in love with Nina for years, she supposed, and that was why he was always hanging around here, waiting for the marriage to end.

The cynical part of her wondered if he'd been so supportive of Mum's cross-dressing and then her transition because it would clear his path to Nina, but she couldn't dislike him for it.

'Do you think Harry did it?' she asked.

'Of course he didn't.' Brynn came over to the island unit and sat down opposite her. 'I was with him at work, don't forget. Do you really think he could have killed Corinne and turned up like normal?'

'Was he normal?'

'From what I saw, yes.'

'Were you with him that morning?'

'I saw him first thing, Lily. I didn't need to be with him all day to see he was the same old Harry.'

She watched him across the counter, saw his discomfort. This must be what Detective Inspector Zigic saw. Was this why they'd kept Harry in, because they'd seen through Brynn's attempt at covering for him?

'We need to stick together,' he said, as if reading her mind. 'Okay? We need to stay strong for one another.'

Lily didn't answer; she was imagining Harry chasing Mum along that narrow pathway, slamming into her, dragging her into the woods. She could see a figure doing that but somehow Harry's face refused to resolve onto it.

311

Because she didn't want it to be him. She'd lost Mum, she couldn't stand the thought of losing Harry too. Even though she hated him sometimes and he'd been a complete shit about Mum, he was still her brother. She couldn't believe he was a murderer.

She wasn't sure the police believed that either. Maybe they had the last time she talked to Sergeant Ferreira, but this time they didn't just want to talk about the family, they wanted to know about Mum's social life. As they so carefully termed it.

'Did the police ask you about Mum's boyfriends?' she asked.

Brynn cocked his head, smiled. 'Corinne liked women, trust me.'

'Apparently she didn't. Not any more.' Lily picked at the black varnish flaking off her nails. 'They said she was talking to all these men online. They wanted to know if she'd met any of them in real life.'

'Had she?'

'She never mentioned it to me.' A large chip of black varnish flicked onto the counter as she stabbed at it with her thumbnail. She couldn't believe Mum had done that to Sam and she wasn't sure if it mattered that she was cheating with men rather than women but when the police told her she was so shocked she laughed.

But then she thought of the last time they went out together, the lunch they'd had in Cambridge, and how Mum had flirted with the waiter, how pleased she'd seemed when he reciprocated, even though it was obvious he was just doing it for the sake of his tip. Now she knew Mum had gone further than batting her eyelashes and being coyly fascinated by a young man's tattoos.

'Boyfriends' they'd said. More than one. God knows how many, and how serious had she been about them? Were these relationships? Was that even possible?

She wondered if Sam knew yet and how she was coping with the betrayal. Thought she'd be devastated after everything they'd been through together. But maybe not surprised, because even if

312

the marriage was almost over when they started seeing each other Sam had taken Mum away from Nina.

If they'll cheat with you, they'll cheat on you – a mantra her friends had recently picked up and it sounded true.

'The police are wrong,' Brynn said. 'In all the years I knew Colin he never showed any sign of being the other way.'

'But she wasn't Colin any more.'

Brynn dragged his fingers back through his hair. 'No, I know that, love.'

'It'd be dangerous, wouldn't it?' Lily asked. 'If they didn't know she was still transitioning . . .'

'It wouldn't be very sensible.'

'Do you think that's what happened then? Some man got annoyed with her because she was leading him on?'

'It's more likely than Harry being responsible.'

Brynn went back to stacking the dishwasher, rattling the cutlery into the cage, swearing when he dropped a fork into the bottom of the machine.

'You have to be careful how you deal with men, Lily. Remember that. They're not always what you think they are.'

She knew that already. Had learned it years ago, but she liked it when Brynn tried to give her fatherly advice. He was so sweet and serious about it. She only wished he'd told Mum the same thing, but how could you explain it to a eighteen-month-old woman with a fifty-two-year-old brain?

Mum had been a baby when she died, too innocent for the adult games she was playing with those men.

SATURDAY

45

Ferreira was already at Ryan Bhakta's house, sitting on the bonnet of her car, when Zigic arrived. She looked wired and he wondered how much sleep she'd got, guessed it was more than him. Emily had kept them awake all night and the last thing he'd done before he'd left home was warm a bottle so Anna could feed her without getting up.

She wasn't happy about him working this morning but he'd promised it would only be for a couple of hours.

Harry Sawyer's house had been searched yesterday afternoon and Murray had returned with a pair of trainers and several black jumpers which might yield a match with the fibres lifted from Corinne's hoodie. The tests would have to wait until Monday though, so there was no real reason to keep him locked up.

Maybe a weekend of picking over the bones of their interviews would weaken the resolve of one member of the Sawyer family. Jessica had already proved herself willing to speak out, Lily too – although she'd contributed nothing new during her interview – and he suspected any further progress would come from somebody finally finding the confidence to withdraw their support from Harry.

'You know where to look?' Zigic asked, as he hunted in his pockets for the key he'd picked up at the station.

Ferreira nodded. 'Exactly where.'

The door had been fixed after its encounter with the battering ram, a new lock fitted, and the key turned with a hard clunk. He followed Ferreira up to the attic. It wasn't where he'd expected Evelyn Goddard to hide the clothes, seemed far too dangerous. This was clearly a special place to Ryan Bhakta and he doubted that a worn and stained dress, especially one with such horrific memories attached to it, would go unnoticed for a year.

'Why didn't she take the clothes home with her?' he asked, sitting down on the armchair, knowing he was surplus to requirements.

'She said she was worried that taking them out of the house would create legal complications down the line.' Ferreira stood in the centre of the room, looking around.

'I thought you knew where to look.'

She cocked her head, walked over to him. 'It's behind you.'

Zigic got up and dragged the armchair away from the wall, revealing a small white hatch, which she opened to reveal a crawl space under the eaves.

'He must have rearranged the furniture since Evelyn was here last.' Ferreira squatted down and directed her phone's torchlight into the void. 'Gross.'

'So much for avoiding contamination.'

She shifted onto her knees and her head and shoulders disappeared through the door. 'I would have loved this when I was a kid.'

'What about now?'

'Yeah, not so much,' she said, voice muffled as she shuffled further in.

They were wasting their time, he realised. Surely there was no way someone as neat and precise as Evelyn Goddard squeezed through that door, not as far as Ferreira was going.

Zigic went into the adjoining bathroom and walked straight out again. Ryan Bhakta's body was gone but the evidence of his suicide was still there, dried blood on the floor, a pinkish film clinging to the sides of the bathtub. It would fall to the family to clean up and he wondered how long it would be before they could face coming here.

Ferreira had backed out and started to search in the opposite direction, just her boots visible.

318

'Anything?' he asked.

'Got it.'

There was dust on her face and cobwebs all over her hair and clothes when she wriggled back out, clutching the crumpled bundle in a gloved hand.

'You better take this,' she said, looking down at herself.

Zigic pulled on his own gloves and took the package from her. Evelyn had put Ryan's clothes in a Waitrose bag, knotted the top and then slipped it inside a clear plastic sheath from a local dry-cleaner's, wound that round the bag several times. It hadn't been enough to deter spiders and other bugs and as he carefully unwound the sheath dozens of dry husks fell out onto the carpet.

He unpicked the knot and there, inside, was a carefully folded gold dress, its fabric still retaining a faint trace of perfume. Too faint to fully cover the sour tang of stale bodily fluids.

'We've got blood,' Zigic said.

He opened up the bag so she could see inside.

'That's the dress he was wearing the night he was attacked. I've seen the photos.'

'Okay, we're getting somewhere.' He reknotted the bag, feeling a curious sense of anticlimax. They might have the clothes but they didn't have a suspect and there was no guarantee that the DNA samples which forensics should be able to lift from the dress would match anyone already on the system.

Ferreira seemed to be feeling it too, the energy which had propelled her into the crawl space gone. She was standing at the dressing table where Ryan Bhakta had said goodbye to the world. The laptop was still there, his mobile phone next to it.

'We should take these, too.'

Outside, Zigic loaded everything into the boot of his car, already thinking about getting home. He'd swing by the station and drop this lot off, in and out in ten minutes.

Ferreira put her hand up as he drove away and he hoped she wouldn't spend the whole weekend worrying about Monday's meeting.

He managed to get up to forensics and out of the station again without being sidetracked and as he pulled out of the car park the sun broke through the clouds, weak and pale, but sun all the same, and it felt like the first touch of spring.

He drove back down Thorpe Road and into the Waitrose near the train station, which was doing brisker business than he expected, travellers stopping in for coffees and sandwiches, an already rowdy group of men stocking up on beer. A stag do, judging by their outfits; two Batmans, three Power Rangers and the biggest of them done up like Alice in Wonderland. Zigic wondered if he'd lost a bet or if he just liked the dress.

Would they be the types to hassle someone like Corinne or Simone? Would the bearded Alice go along with it to hide his own secret habit? Would he be the one who shouted loudest?

Zigic shook his head. This job.

MONDAY

46

Ferreira spent a long time getting ready. It seemed important to look right today, so Riggott would see that she was taking this seriously.

She chose a trouser suit, black and narrowly tailored, with a cream silk blouse she'd bought online but never worn. As she snapped off the tags she was vaguely surprised at how much she'd paid for it. In the bathroom she scraped her hair back into a ponytail, knowing it made her look hard-faced but wasn't that almost the same thing as being professional?

Adams had left his watch on the shelf above the sink, she noticed. It would have to stay there.

He'd come round on Sunday morning, spent a couple of hours briefing her on the best way to deal with Riggott, as if he'd forgotten that she'd been a DC under him too, knew how he ticked if not always how to play on that. Adams had been through a fair amount of inquiries himself, come out the other side in one piece, reputation somehow intact, so she'd listened, hoping she wouldn't need his advice.

It was a naive hope, though.

The weekend papers had contained several articles on Ryan Bhakta's suicide. Yet more opinion pieces using it as a starting point. Prominent trans rights campaigners had spoken out, twisting the events in Peterborough to fit their own narrative, ignoring the huge unknowns about Ryan which might have undermined their assertions.

Online, things were blowing up. The bloggers didn't need to be so circumspect, no journalists' standards to uphold, no responsibility to fact-check or substantiate. There was speculation about a serial attacker in the city, potentially a serial killer now, as they were mentioning Corinne's murder in the same breath as Ryan's suicide.

And why weren't the police doing more to catch this scum?

Then there were the others. Those angry, poisonous voices re-invigorated over the weekend, proclaiming that Ryan and Corinne deserved what they got. They quoted Bible verses on Twitter and spewed bile over 'unnatural lifestyles', and the only time they broke from the outright hate was to assess Jasmine's fuckability and whether they would have been 'fooled' by her.

Evelyn Goddard hadn't surfaced, not even to give a fresh quote or two, and that surprised Ferreira. She'd been quick to jump on the publicity opportunity of Corinne's murder but over Ryan's death she remained silent.

Guilt, she guessed. Or maybe she'd decided not to pour more fuel on the fire. Evelyn was a pragmatist after all. She must understand that any blow suffered by the Hate Crimes Unit would only make her community more vulnerable, leaving the crimes they suffered to the discretion of CID.

Because it was on the whole unit now. The term 'not fit for purpose' was being bandied about, and seeing it written down, in stark black and white, Ferreira wondered where it had come from. It had the stink of officialdom around it.

She knew the department was on shaky ground, had been since its inception, and with Anti-Terrorism – those serious-eyed, swaggering bastards who worked in absolute isolation across the hall – sucking up budget, propelled by government policy and public fear, it was only a matter of time before the office space and money required by Hate Crimes seemed like a poor return on investment.

Her dressing-up exercise suddenly felt futile. All the profession-alism in the world wouldn't make a difference if the decision had already been taken, months ago maybe, based on balance sheets and political will.

Fuck it.

She'd do her best, whatever.

Riggott's BMW was in his usual spot when she arrived at Thorpe Wood Station and she sat in her car for a couple of minutes, smoking a final cigarette, nerves and anger fighting it out. Anger was the more useful emotion, she thought, so she grabbed that and held on to it as she went in, heading straight up to Riggott's office.

She rapped on his door and he called her in, eyed her top to toe as she closed the door behind her.

'Someone means business.' He waved her into the seat opposite him. 'Alright, what do we do with you, then?'

'I've got a lead on the man who attacked Ryan Bhakta,' Ferreira said. 'We were given a tip-off, we searched his house, and we've found the clothes he was wearing during the assault. They're covered in his attacker's DNA.'

Riggott nodded. 'Interesting timing. Lucky.'

'It was Evelyn Goddard.'

'Gotten yourself in her good graces now, hey?'

'She's feeling guilty,' Ferreira said. 'It turns out she'd been pushing Ryan to come forward and report the true nature of the attack. He was raped, that was why he was so unwilling to disclose further details when I interviewed him. Evelyn had called him the day he killed himself. I believe she feels responsible for his suicide.'

'Meaning you're not?'

Ferreira felt beads of sweat pricking under her arms. 'I'm not responsible. He was a grown man, he made his own decisions.'

'But you feel guilty?' Riggott asked, giving the look she knew from sitting in on interviews with him. 'Don't you?'

'I feel a great deal of sympathy for him,' she said. 'I feel disappointed that his perception of the police led him to believe he wouldn't be well treated if he came forward to report the rape. Maybe, if he had, we'd have caught the man responsible and that would have given him enough of a sense of closure that he wouldn't have felt the need to end his life.'

Riggott nodded, took a drag of his e-cigarette, exhaled vapour. 'Aye, you're more than ready to tackle an investigation. Reckon you'll send the bastards away thinking it's their fault your man topped himself.'

She held herself upright, even though she wanted to crumble.

'There's definitely going to be an investigation?'

'Routine. I read your report.' He flicked at a sheet of paper on his desk. 'Still waiting on Ziggy's. Looks to me like there's bollock-all to it. What d'you do with that recording?'

'Nothing.'

'Delete it, right now.' He moved as if to tap ash off his cigarette, caught himself and smiled at the redundancy of the action. 'Old habits.'

'Why would I delete it? It's fine. I acted properly.'

'Fine if we didn't have a suicide on our hands,' he said. 'I've listened to it, you were cajoling him.'

'I wasn't.'

He raised an eyebrow at her, the wrinkles on that side of his face deeper than on the other. 'Darlin', I listened to it like the bastards who are going to be investigating you are going to listen to it. They want you to've done wrong and you did. You made promises to that lad you knew you couldn't keep.' He pointed at her. 'Delete it.'

She reached into her jacket pocket. 'You know nothing's ever really deleted off a mobile phone?'

'So lose your phone.' He waited. 'You're not leaving this office until that thing's gone. You think I spent four years moulding you into the fine copper you are today to have you fuck yourself up with excessive honesty? Get shot.'

She took a deep breath, found the audio file and deleted it.

'Now what?'

'Now you go back to work and you wait.' He picked up her report and put it in his out tray. 'I want you in CID for a few days.'

'But we're—'

'In the middle of a murder investigation,' Riggott said, mimicking her accent with horrible precision. 'You'll have read the papers, I reckon? Think anyone in the LGBT – what's the other one? Q? – community, think they'll be wanting to cooperate with you right now? Think you'll be getting a warm welcome from Corinne's friends and family? Sure, half of them want you strung up by the toes from what Gilraye tells me.'

'She's aware of it then?' Ferreira snapped. 'Maybe she could actually do something about it today.'

'I'll be making a statement later this morning,' Riggott said, giving her a warning look. 'While you'll be behaving like an angel down here.'

'We're short-handed.'

'Murray can stay up there. She's been tossing her weight around, won't hurt for her to be out of harm's way for a wee while either.' He shook his head. 'What is it with you women? Worse than the lads, so you are.'

'Maybe we just care more.'

'Aye, that or you don't know when to stop.' Riggott swivelled in his chair, turning towards the window, the tops of the trees at Ferry Meadows visible at distance. 'Alright then, off you go.'

The lights were on in Hate Crimes when she got up there, only Zigic in and he was holed up in his office, staring at his computer screen with his hands poised over the keyboard.

She knocked on the window and he beckoned her in.

'Do you want to write this report?' he asked, slumping back in his chair.

'Is it about me?'

He nodded.

'Riggott's made his decision already,' she said, leaning against the closed door. 'Me and Murray are job-swapping until the investigation's over. He thinks it's only going to be a formality.'

'That's good.'

She looked down at the toe of her black leather boot, kept her eyes averted as she told him, 'There's something else. Riggott made me delete the interview with Ryan Bhakta.'

Zigic blew out a long, slow breath, his disapproval clear. 'I suppose he knows better than either of us how to beat an internal investigation.'

The same thing Adams had told her. Listen to Riggott. Take any help he gives you.

'I better not mention it in my report then,' Zigic said, straightening up again, hitting the delete key. 'Makes things simpler, anyway.'

Ferreira curled her fingers around the door handle. 'Can you keep me in the loop on Corinne's murder?'

'You know you can't be involved?'

'Not officially, no, I understand that. But I know the case way better than Murray, I don't want you to miss something because she doesn't appreciate all the connections.'

'Okay.' He smiled, and she guessed it was meant to be reassuring but it didn't feel like that. 'It's only a few days, Mel. You can put up with Adams for that long, surely?'

Her turn to smile. 'As long as he doesn't go thinking he's my boss.'

47

Ferreira had forgotten just how loud CID was. Six times the people making ten times the noise, a constant barrage of voices, phones ringing and keyboard clatter. She didn't want to be disloyal to Hate Crimes but this was a far more energising environment to be in. Even if she did have to go all the way outside when she wanted to smoke.

She'd been given Murray's desk, right at the centre of the room. People moving around her constantly and DC Parr sat opposite, although he was out now, chasing down a suspect in a series of smash-and-grab raids on cash machines in the suburbs.

She wouldn't have minded going out with Parr, stretch her legs, find some distraction from the knowledge that while she was down here Zigic and the team were continuing on a case she'd thought of as her own and now would be denied the pleasure of closing.

Assuming they could close it.

Instead she was examining the files relating to Lee Walton, digging into his past history, which was long, grim and frustrating. The more she read the more she understood why Murray was so hell-bent on pinning Corinne's murder on him. Anything to get this piece of shit off the streets.

His first conviction came at nineteen, after he kidnapped an ex-girlfriend and subjected her to three days of rape and torture, which left her permanently disfigured. He was given six years, served three, came out having learned his lesson.

After that he was reported by several other women, all acquaintances, for a range of sexual offences he kept slipping free of.

Statements withdrawn, intimidation the obvious reason behind the women's sudden reticence, their determination to convince the investigating officers that the sex was consensual, even when it landed them in hospital.

All the evidence was there but without a 'credible victim' the CPS wouldn't prosecute.

The file seemed comprehensive but she knew the true number of victims could be four or five times higher at least.

Ferreira rolled a cigarette and took it outside to smoke on the front steps.

She was supposed to be looking for new angles into Walton. Fresh eyes, Adams said, a psychological perspective. As if there was some deep, underlying malady driving Walton, rather than the usual motivation of serial sex offenders – they did it because they wanted to and because they could.

The main doors opened and Adams came bounding over to her with a big grin on his face. 'Guess whose girlfriend has just landed in A&E?'

'I don't know, but you sure look happy about it.'

'Lee Walton's,' he said, slipping on his suit jacket. 'And don't give me the judgemental eyes – it's her fault he's still walking the streets. If she didn't keep giving him alibis we'd have had him banged up way back.'

'Doesn't look that way from his file.' Ferreira flicked her cigarette butt away. 'It looks like he's still walking the streets because he's got very good at intimidating women into not talking to us.'

'Cumulative effect,' Adams said, starting towards his car. 'We keep talking to her every time it happens, eventually she'll see she's better off helping us. And we're talking murder this time. She gives him up, he's going to be looking at ten years minimum, that's the best chance she'll ever get to run for the hills and start a new life.'

Ferreira followed him, got into the car.

330

'Walton didn't kill Corinne Sawyer,' she said. 'And if we seriously think he did then Zigic should be talking to the girlfriend.'

'First off, she doesn't know that. Second off, I already told him and he's cool with it because I'm actually his superior officer and he has to be.' Adams started the engine. 'You can go back to paperwork if you don't approve.'

'Somebody needs to bring a bit of sensitivity to proceedings,' she said, pulling on her seat belt.

On the drive over he debriefed her about Walton's girlfriend. She didn't really need to hear it, had drawn her own conclusions from reading between the lines of his victims' statements. By the time they were out of the car, crossing towards City Hospital's main doors, Ferreira felt even more convinced that they would get nothing from Dani Shaw.

The nurse who had tipped Adams off said she had a fractured rib, severe bruising and blood in her urine suggesting damage to her kidneys. The nurse had seen Dani Shaw there before, understood what was happening to her, wanted to help.

Most wouldn't, Ferreira thought. Too much trouble to be found when you spoke out against a man as violent as Lee Walton.

They were at Dani's bedside before she noticed them, laid out flat, unable to sit up with her ribs so traumatised. She made no protest as Adams drew the curtain around her bay, only closed her eyes and pressed her lips into a hard line.

She wasn't what Ferreira was expecting. Knowing Walton's type she'd thought Dani would be similar, but she was the exact opposite of the women he'd targeted. Overweight, with long blonde hair streaked platinum in places, tied away from her face, which bore the marks of the kind of cosmetic procedures carried out by disreputable dentists and beauticians with a weekend's training – her mouth over-plumped and uneven, forehead shining smooth under the lights.

'What's he done to you now, Dani?' Adams asked sadly, pulling up the chair next to her bed, making sure he was in her eyeline so she wouldn't miss the concerned expression he was wearing.

'Leave me alone.' Her voice was timid, surprisingly high-pitched.

'We keep finding ourselves here, don't we?'

'I didn't ask you to come.'

'No, you didn't,' Adams conceded. 'But we'll keep coming until you're ready to do something about this. Or, until he kills you.'

Ferreira closed her hands around the bars at the end of the bed, shocked by his bluntness, but the way he delivered it, so regretfully, so damn earnestly, made her realise he knew exactly what he was doing.

A tear ran off Dani's face.

'A bit more force and he'd have punctured your lung,' Adams said.

'He didn't touch me. I fell.'

'And where was young Robbie when this happened?' She didn't answer and Adams sighed. 'Do you really want him growing up seeing this? You think that's healthy for a boy of his age?'

'He's fine.'

'Oh, no. No, he isn't, Dani. He's seeing what Lee's doing to you and one of these days, before too long, he's going to try and protect his mummy, and what do you think Lee will do about that?'

She let out a slight whimper, tried to lift her hand to wipe her face but the movement made her gasp and she laid her palm flat on her stomach. Ferreira noticed the engagement ring, a slim white-gold band bearing a weightier diamond than she'd have thought Walton could afford. She wondered if it had been bought in apology and how much damage a rock that size equated to.

'Have you set a date?' Ferreira gestured towards the ring.

Dani flexed her fingers, straining to see it. 'June. Next year.'

'And do you think you'll survive that long?' she asked.

'He loves me.'

'Is that why he's beating the hell out of you? And is that why he's raping women all over town?'

'He didn't do that,' Dani said fiercely, but in her little girl voice it just sounded naive. 'They're lying.'

A trolley went by on the other side of the curtain, its squeaking wheel loud and close, and Ferreira realised that they didn't have as much privacy here as the drawn curtain had lulled her into believing. The beds on either side of them were silent, their occupants no doubt straining to hear.

Ferreira had spent long enough in hospital last year to know how fascinating other people's dramas became when you were laid up, dying of boredom.

'What about the woman he murdered?' she asked.

Silence.

'You've seen the news, the trans woman on Ferry Meadows.' Ferreira came round the foot of the bed and sat on the edge of the mattress. Dani tried to draw away from her but couldn't. 'Did you know Lee had a thing for cross-dressers?'

'I've told you already.' She turned to Adams. 'Lee was at home when that happened.'

'Like he was at home all the other times some poor woman got attacked?' Ferreira said.

Adams shot her a warning look and she swallowed what she was going to say next, the words a hard lump in her throat. She was angrier than she should have been, sitting here watching Dani Shaw defending the man who'd put her in hospital more than once.

'Dani, we know you're scared,' Adams said. 'We know he's told you to vouch for him – like all the other times he's made you do that in the past.'

'He was at home with me.'

'This is murder now,' Adams went on. 'He'll be out of your life for twenty years. You can take Robbie, get away, move on. You'll be safe once he's locked up.'

The curtain drew back and Ferreira was on her feet instantly, face-to-face with Lee Walton.

It was the first time she'd seen him in the flesh and she struggled, momentarily, to reconcile the ordinariness of his appearance with the crimes she knew he was responsible for. He was short and bland, holding a bunch of white flowers, no different to any other visitor.

Then he turned his attention away from Adams and onto her and the second their eyes met she could see what he was. She took a step forward, forced herself to hold his gaze, wishing violence on him just like the violence she could see him wishing on her.

'Hospital visits, is it?' he asked, smiling slightly. 'Very considerate, but I'm here now, she doesn't need your company.'

'Make the most of it,' Adams said, coming round the bed. 'You won't have chance to talk to her much when you're banged up.'

Walton kept his eyes on Ferreira. 'I'm an innocent man. And this is starting to feel a lot like police harassment.'

She felt her lip twitch at the word and wanted to slap the look of satisfaction it provoked right off his face. Instead she took another step towards him, barely a hand's breadth between them, and she could smell his aftershave, see every pore on his squeaky-clean cheeks. They were breathing each other's air, locked together in a moment of charged silence, until he cocked his head, pivoted on his heel and backed up to let her pass.

'Think on what I told you, Dani,' Adams said.

She only had eyes for Walton though, smiling at him as he laid the flowers on the tray table, then went to kiss her, hands planted on the pillow either side of her head, like he was pinning her down.

Ferreira glanced at Adams and he nodded.

They walked out in silence and Ferreira could feel the anger coming off Adams, was sure she was radiating it too, as she kept replaying those few seconds where Walton seemed to be flaying her skin off her bones.

48

They were working with the minutiae of Corinne's life now, the stuff which often fell between the cracks of an investigation because there were so many other avenues of inquiry to explore. But with no witnesses and minimal forensics they had to start thinking more creatively.

Wahlia had spent the last couple of hours trawling through Corinne's devices – picking up where Ferreira had left off – and the phone records from the Sawyer family. Murray was ploughing through more CCTV, trying to place Harry's or Brynn's vehicles at a place and a time where they shouldn't be, crack their alibis that way.

Zigic had taken the most tedious piece of graft himself, going through every statement and interview again, looking for something they might have missed, some allusion which might be more significant in light of the new information they had about Harry's relationship with Corinne.

It was the kind of task that furred up your eyeballs and made every small muscle in your back throb.

When Jenkins called him about the clothes they'd recovered from Ryan Bhakta's house he gratefully took the excuse to leave the desk and stretch his legs. As he went up to forensics he wondered how much longer it would be such a short run. Most forces had already outsourced their scientific support operations to private contractors and everyone knew it was only a matter of time before this one fell under the cost-cutting axe too. Jenkins had lost her right-hand woman last year, poached by a private lab in Cambridge – something he knew pissed Kate off royally – and she was currently struggling to find a worthy replacement among her rawer recruits.

He found Jenkins in her office, staring at an incomprehensible diagram exploded across the screen. Her pale-skinned face was lightly sunburned across the forehead and cheeks, a white, goggle-shaped stretch over her eyes and nose giving away the skiing trip she'd only returned from this morning.

'Good break?' he asked.

'Wish I was still there,' she said. 'God, I hate the first day back. You'd think I was the only person who worked here judging by the amount they got done last week. Hell of a backlog.'

'But you're onto the Bhakta clothing?'

She smiled. 'Somebody left me a note saying it was urgent.'

'I didn't think you'd take any notice of it.'

The gold dress was laid out on the table, so short and narrow that Zigic could barely believe a grown person would fit in it, even one as slim as Ryan Bhakta. There was dried blood, deep brown, almost black, down the front of it, caught in the folds of the broad neckline. Blood would have poured from his broken nose and split mouth and it would serve to prove he'd been wearing it when he was attacked but it wasn't the evidence they needed.

'He'd got good taste,' Jenkins said, pulling on her gloves. 'Karen Millen, expensive.'

'It's been lying around for over a year. Is that going to be a problem?'

'Do you take on board anything I tell you?' she asked. 'The garment's clean, it's been carefully stored and we've got minimal contamination from the wildlife in her house. Nothing even slightly problematic from a recovery perspective.'

'So you've got samples for us?'

'I have.' She pointed to stains on the front. 'These are probably going to be the victim's, we'll get you a match there. Blood's already a positive for type.'

336

'Anything else?'

'Would I have called you otherwise?' She lifted the dress and carefully turned it over, revealing a mess of different stains, none of them blood to Zigic's untrained eye. 'So, here, we have a water stain. He was attacked outside?'

'The cathedral precincts.'

'That explains the moss, then.' Jenkins sidestepped and pointed to a smear near the hem, flipped it up to show more on the underside. 'And here we have semen.'

Zigic folded his arms, reading how the attack would have unfolded. Ryan slammed to the ground, face damaged, too scared or disorientated to fight back, his attacker holding him down, raping him.

'It's a very small deposit,' he said.

Jenkins raised an eyebrow but nodded. 'It is, yes. I'd guess the primary . . . landing spot, if you like, was elsewhere. Or your attacker used a condom and wasn't quite careful enough when he took it off.'

Zigic wasn't convinced. 'I think, in that situation, you'd be careful. Maybe it's not from the attack. Maybe he had consensual sex before that. It could have been on the dress when he put it on that night and he didn't notice.'

Jenkins gave him one of her withering looks. 'Ziggy, have you ever, in your life, walked out of the house with semen on your clothes?' She put her hand up. 'Actually, don't answer that. This deposit isn't from the victim, anyway. Different blood group. It'll be a day or two but we'll be able to get you a DNA match. Assuming . . .'

'Yeah, I know, assuming I can give you something to match it to.'

Jenkins leaned back against the room's other examination table, nothing on that one, despite the backlog. 'You're the Sawyer case too, I take it?'

He nodded, hearing more than polite interest in her tone. 'Why?'

337

'Look, I'm making no promises but I think I can do a bit better with the material you have to hand on that one.'

'We were told the samples were contaminated.'

'There are degrees of contamination and they directly correlate with degrees of professional expertise.' Jenkins snapped her gloves off, clearly irritated, and brushed a coil of auburn hair behind her pinkly singed ear. 'Knew I'd miss a good case, always the bloody way.'

'I'd have called you back for it if I could have,' Zigic said. 'Nobody's as thorough as you are.'

'Alright, enough with the flattery.' She stamped on the bin, dropped her gloves into it. 'I'm only doing my job. Course, any thank-you gifts will be demurely received.'

'*If* you find something,' Zigic said, heading for the door.

He heard her swear at him as he left the lab and was grateful she was back at work. He was sure she already knew she could give them something useful or she wouldn't have raised the issue. Kate wasn't one for making promises unless she was sure she could deliver.

It didn't mean they could slow down though.

Back at his desk he went to call Ferreira, intending to give her an update, but thought better of it. Riggott didn't want her having anything to do with her previous caseload from Hate Crimes and keeping her informed would only complicate matters. The less she knew, the less likely she was to try and get involved.

He returned to the last interview they'd conducted with Nina Sawyer but couldn't keep his attention on it. He remembered her impeccable make-up and her defiant air, like a woman braced for a final reckoning.

Nina was the person with the most reason to want Corinne dead. She was the one who stood to gain most financially. She was the one Corinne had hurt for the longest, cut the deepest, and even once they'd split up, Corinne couldn't resist putting the knife in for another thrust.

338

Zigic took a mouthful of water from the bottle on the table.

Harry and Brynn would lie to protect Nina. Maybe they'd go so far as to implicate Harry, believing his innocence would keep him from being successfully prosecuted.

Except they only suspected him because of information supplied by Jessica and Lily, who seemed to genuinely fear he might be responsible.

There were too many cross currents muddying the waters of this case. Zigic wondered just how frankly the Sawyer family had discussed Corinne's murder. Did any of the innocent parties know who was responsible, or were they drawing together out of a vague instinct towards mutual preservation without ever daring to ask the vital question?

'Sir,' Murray piped up. 'Harry Sawyer – I've found him.'

Zigic went over to her desk. An unremarkable CCTV street view on-screen but Murray's excitement was palpable.

'What am I looking at?' he asked.

'Sawyer's girlfriend told us he left home just before half past seven, right?' She pointed at the time code with her pen. 'This is Harry stopped at the railway crossing at the edge of Whittlesea. Eight thirty-nine. The Golf. That's barely ten minutes from home, which means we've got almost an hour unaccounted for.'

Zigic watched the barriers lift on-screen, a five-second pause before Harry Sawyer pulled away. Did that signal something? Was he reading too much into it?

Probably.

'There are a dozen reasons why Harry might have lost an hour between leaving the house and getting to where he worked.'

Murray's shoulders rounded. 'There are.'

'Can you track him back to his house?' Zigic asked. 'See what time he left?'

'No, this is the first place I managed to pick him up. He obviously takes the parkways, less chance of getting spotted on them.' She shrugged. 'Maybe it was deliberate. It's not the quickest route. He'd be better going through town.'

'Any sign of Brynn Moran?'

She nodded, consulted the notepad next to her hand. 'He passed the same spot at seven fifty-eight.'

'Meaning they're both in the frame still.'

Murray turned away from the screen. 'Brynn's running late. But Harry . . . that's an hour unaccounted for. It's a major gap in his alibi, sir.'

Zigic played through the options.

'Say Brynn did it then. He kills Corinne around seven fifteen. Goes straight home, washes up, maybe gets rid of the clothes he's wearing—'

'We need to search that house,' Murray said. 'He might be stupid enough to have just dumped them in the washing basket and trusted Nina to clean them.'

Zigic nodded impatiently. 'Right, so he's home and into his vehicle fast enough to only be running ten or fifteen minutes late. There's no reflection time. Wouldn't you expect to see some?'

'Depends. Is he someone who can hold it together?' she asked, reaching for a packet of mints on her desk. 'If he wants everything to look normal – say he's on autopilot at this point and it hasn't hit him yet – then yeah, I suppose he might be able to get on with his day. Not many people manage that though.'

Zigic thought of how Brynn had behaved during the interview. Contained, calm. He didn't seem guilty, wasn't even flustered.

'Harry had time to go to pieces,' Murray said.

'And cover up what he'd done. It's a longer walk home for him, assuming he took a scenic route through Ferry Meadows and up the lynch to avoid any cameras on the way.' Zigic went over to the map on the murder board, traced a line between the locus and Harry's house in Castor. 'That's ten to fifteen minutes. He's already running late. So, he goes home and does the sensible thing – showers, scrubs any traces off himself in case we make him our first port of call.'

'He'll have learned his lesson,' Murray agreed. 'After last time.'

'He knows he needs to get into work or it's going to look suspicious. But maybe he's struggling already, can't quite drag himself together.'

'Or the girlfriend's noticed and she's asking questions.' Murray sucked thoughtfully on her mint. 'If that was my old man coming home when he should've already been at work – covered in muck – I'd be on his case about it.'

'So, she needs to be assuaged.'

'Or convinced to keep her mouth shut,' Murray said.

49

They arrived at the Sawyer house mob-handed. Zigic and Murray in his car, two more patrol cars behind them, ready to execute the search warrant he'd obtained, bring in whoever was there to explain the inconsistencies in Brynn Moran's and Harry Sawyer's alibis.

He hit the button on the intercom for the third time, feeling a rising urge to get out and hammer on the gates, knowing it would do no good.

'They're in there,' Murray said. 'I see three vehicles, one of them's Moran's, right – the twin-cab pickup, sign-written?'

'That's him.'

Plenty of people home to let them in but they were remaining hunkered down behind the gates. He pressed the button once more and this time it prompted a response, no answering voice but the gates began to swing slowly open and he drove onto the driveway, the patrol cars coming in behind him.

The house was lit up against the grey afternoon and, as he headed for the front door, Zigic spotted Nina Sawyer in the room where they'd first spoken to her, standing with her arms folded, body stiff with rage, while Brynn made an entreating gesture at her, Harry a few steps away from him, head in his hands. The group clustered and mute behind the toughened glass, the house taking on the feel of a stage set.

Nina was slow to answer the door and through the glass he saw her composing herself as she approached, smoothing back her hair, setting her face.

'What do you want?' she asked, weariness undercutting the demand.

Murray handed her the search warrant and she glanced at it briefly, her neat, blonde brows furrowing.

'This is ridiculous.'

'It's procedure,' Zigic said.

'What on earth do you expect to find here? We—' She stopped as Murray started away through the house, towards the kitchen, in search of the utility room. 'You have no right to do this. What are your grounds for entering my home?'

'We do have the right, Mrs Sawyer.'

She tapped the warrant against her fingertips, desperate-looking, cornered. It was all unravelling in front of her eyes and she didn't know how to regain control. Behind her Harry and Brynn moved closer together, and Zigic caught the look they shared. Scared, determined, conspiratorial; a matter agreed without words.

'May I at least ask what you're looking for?' Nina said.

'Clothing, primarily.'

Brynn shot another quick glance at Harry, but he'd moved, retreated to the low, uncomfortable sofa, sat with his knees on his elbows, thoroughly defeated.

Nina stared Zigic down. 'I know what you're doing.'

'What's that?'

'You want to put the blame on my family because you can't find who really killed Corinne.'

Zigic held her gaze, saw another brief glimmer of fear in her moss-green eyes. Brynn and Harry were keeping her innocent, he thought, making sure she wouldn't be charged as an accessory. Or trying to. But she knew, on some level, or she wouldn't be afraid.

'I will keep coming back to your family until I get the truth,' he said. 'And so far every single one of you has lied to me and my team.'

He gestured towards PCs Hale and Bright and they moved up the steps into the living room.

'Harry, I'd like you to come with us, please.'

Nina went after them, quickly moving between them and her son.

'You can't arrest him, he hasn't done anything.'

'There are gaps in Harry's alibi, we'd like to discuss that further.'

He stayed rooted to the sofa. 'I didn't kill Corinne.'

'You were an hour late for work,' Zigic said. 'And you lied about that.'

'I was hung-over,' he said, throwing up his hands. 'I'd had too much wine and I overslept.'

'See, there's a perfectly innocent explanation.' Nina spread her arms wide as if to shield her son with her body. 'You don't need to take him anywhere.'

Hale gently moved her aside and Bright took hold of Harry Sawyer under the arm, guiding him to his feet.

'It's okay, Mum. It'll all be alright.'

Nina whirled towards Brynn. 'Do something.'

'Mr Moran is coming with us as well,' Zigic said. 'Since he apparently can't account for his movements at the time of Corinne's murder either.'

'No, he was here,' she said, desperation etched on her face. 'I told that woman, he was here when Corinne was killed.'

'Then you should consider whether you want to stand by the alibi you gave him.' Zigic saw the realisation hit home, her body stiffening. 'Because either you were mistaken or you were lying.'

'Oh my God.' She touched her fingers to her mouth. 'Brynn? What did you do?'

He backed away from her, unsteady on his feet. 'Nina – love – no.'

'You swore to me.' Nina shoved him in the chest, sending him reeling back into the bookshelves. A couple of pictures hit the floor, glass smashing. '"She's talking rubbish," you said. "She just wants to get between us."'

'It *was* rubbish,' Brynn said, his face colouring. Eyes only for Nina now, as if he could force her to believe it if only he could hold

344

her wild gaze. 'You know what she was like. She'd say anything to make you unhappy. Do you really think I'm like that?'

'I don't know what you are any more,' she snarled.

'This is exactly what she wanted. Don't be stupid.'

Nina lashed out, slapped him across the cheek.

Bright was on her instantly, gripping her elbows, trying to draw her away, but she ducked and twisted and Harry was shouting, telling him to take his hands off her, diving towards the pair of them. Hale caught him by the shoulder, losing his footing on the rug. They crashed down in a heap, the cracking sound of bone on marble and Harry Sawyer let out a howl that echoed around the room's high ceiling, rolled onto his back clutching his wrist.

Brynn bolted through the chaos, sweeping his forearm up to knock Zigic off balance as he ran past him, but Zigic was braced for it and threw himself after him. Brynn yanked the front door open and ran full pelt down the driveway.

Zigic swore as he pulled away, amazed at the speed from the older man as he charged into the road, not caring about the traffic, heading for the gateway onto Ferry Meadows.

Metal crunched and horns sounded but they were behind Zigic now and he kept running, trying to find the old speed he knew was in his legs but which had deserted him after months of underuse. He cursed every lie-in he'd had, the dark mornings and the cold weather.

In the distance Brynn's red plaid shirt whipped past dog walkers and idle strollers and Zigic saw them turn to stare in his wake, no idea what was going on here, felt their disapproval as he did the same.

Brynn zigzagged around a woman with a pushchair and she shouted after him, causing him to turn for a split second. He didn't see the dog running across his path or the long lead it was on. The dog let out a piercing yelp and Zigic saw the lead tangled around Brynn's legs and the panic on his face as he tried to free himself.

The little terrier lay crying on the bridge. Its owner crouched over it, swearing at Brynn, and as he tried to stand the man yanked on the lead, unfooting him again but only for a moment.

As he started off once more Zigic launched himself at Brynn, caught him high around the thighs and slammed him down hard, the metal bridge ringing with the impact. He wrenched Brynn's wrists behind his back and cuffed him, aware of the dog owner shouting at him, demanding action. The dog let out another low whine and Zigic dragged Brynn to his feet, seeing blood running down his cheek from a fresh gash.

'I want a solicitor,' he said, unable to meet Zigic's eye.

50

The doctor patched up Brynn Moran's cut face while they waited for his solicitor to arrive. Zigic stood in the treatment room as the young woman worked, watching Brynn carefully, seeing nothing but a numbness in the slack line of his jaw and how he sat on the edge of the bench, slumped over, feet dangling, all the spirit drained out of him.

He didn't even flinch when the needle went into his cheek, shooting it full of anaesthetic before the stitches could be applied. The wound was deep and wide and would leave an ugly scar, but that was the least of his worries right now.

When the doctor was finished Zigic had Moran taken to the cells and begged a couple of ibuprofen for his own injury. A bruise was already blooming on his kneecap from where he took Moran down, a nasty lump on the bone which stung every time he put his weight on his right leg, flexed it or walked or whenever the fabric of his jeans rubbed against it.

Running would be out of the question for a couple of weeks now, he thought grimly, stepping into the lift.

Ferreira was waiting for him in Hate Crimes and she followed him into his office.

'Brynn?' she asked, dropping into the chair opposite Zigic. 'Are you sure?'

'He ran.'

'Where did he think he was going?'

'God knows. I think he just panicked and took off. I don't think there was a big plan behind it. Just flight instinct.' Zigic swallowed the pills with a mouthful of cold coffee. 'Honestly, I'm not convinced he's even responsible yet.'

Ferreira leaned forward, arms on the edge of his desk. 'What did he say?'

'Nothing. I'm waiting for his solicitor. Hopefully he'll come clean now but if not . . . Harry's the one who really knows what went on down there. I'm pretty sure the pair of them were keeping Nina in the dark.'

'So, why not question Harry first? Go see Moran armed.'

'Harry's at City Hospital. He got injured during the arrest.'

Ferreira whistled softly. 'That's going to be a fun report to write up.'

'It was his own fault.'

She tapped his desk with her fingertips. 'I really don't think we should be ruling out Harry, you know. I was wondering – actually – do you think Nina and Brynn were involved before she split with Corinne? Maybe Harry's his kid, he'd take the fall for his own son, wouldn't he?'

Zigic swivelled from side to side in his chair. 'Are you really that bored in CID?'

'I am so bored. Adams has had me going through Walton's files. He's currently throwing a shit-fit of epic magnitude by the way.'

'Because we've caught Corinne's killer?'

'He was banking on using Corinne to leverage Walton's girlfriend into withdrawing her alibis. Which she'll never do.' Ferreira smiled. 'And his ego's a bit bruised, I think.'

The phone on Zigic's desk rang. He picked up, listened for a few moments.

'Brynn's ready to make a statement.'

'Very magnanimous of him,' Ferreira said. 'Does that sound like it'll be a confession to you?'

'If he's got any sense it will be.'

'Can I sit in?' She stood as he did. 'Murray doesn't know the case as well as I do. Be much better this way.'

'You know you can't.' He gestured at his computer. 'Watch the feed though, just in case we miss anything.'

A couple of minutes later he entered Interview Room 1, Murray behind him, trying to conceal annoyance she was carrying on DCI Adams's behalf, no doubt.

Brynn Moran sat in the chair against the wall, sagging under the weight of the suspicion he'd brought on himself. He'd flagged his guilt the moment he bolted out of that house and nothing his solicitor might have said to him in the interim could have improved his options.

She was one of the duty solicitors, Zigic noted, as he sat down opposite her. Mrs Peele. She'd been around forever, was competent and diligent and brought very little ego to proceedings, which was a welcome change from how many of her colleagues conducted themselves. But she wasn't the solicitor Brynn Moran would have if Nina was involved, Zigic suspected. Were the Sawyer family drawing away from him already?

Murray set up the tapes, the time was recorded, the names were stated and before Zigic could say another word Mrs Peele spoke up.

'Mr Moran has instructed me that he is prepared to make full confession regarding the death of Corinne Sawyer. He will not answer any questions and this statement will be his full and final comment on the matter.'

Brynn sat with his arms folded, his hand cupping his jaw, fingertips over the stitches on his cheek. He stared into middle distance, eyes unblinking, mouth slightly open. A doctor could argue it was shock, Zigic thought, but he wasn't going to delay this by questioning the man's current state of mind. Not if he wanted to confess.

He nodded at Mrs Peele. 'Let's hear it then.'

She passed Brynn her notepad and as she did so Zigic saw the extent of the statement. Three lines, printed in large block capitals.

Brynn held the pad against the edge of the table, his chin tucked into his chest. He cleared his throat, a thick, wet noise in the quiet of the room, before he began to speak.

'I am solely responsible for the murder of Corinne Sawyer. At no point were any members of the Sawyer family aware of what I'd done, before or after the event.'

For a few seconds he kept clutching the pad, staring at the words he'd just read out, as if he didn't quite understand what he'd said. Then he put it down, folded his arms once again and inclined his face away from them.

'That is in no way a full confession,' Zigic said. Brynn lifted his shoulder slightly as if trying to shield himself. 'Mrs Peele, this is not acceptable. I think you should impress upon your client the seriousness of the charge he's facing, as well as the penalties for making a false confession.'

'I can assure you, Detective Inspector, that my client is well aware of the gravity of the situation and his confession is valid.' Mrs Peele slipped the notepad away into her satchel. 'I believe that's all we need to say on the matter at present, yes?'

'No, it isn't,' Zigic said, trying to keep the anger and frustration out of his voice but he could hear that he'd failed. 'Why did you kill her, Brynn?'

'Mr Moran is not obliged to answer that,' Mrs Peele said, snapping the catches on her bag.

Zigic ignored her. 'Are you protecting Harry?'

Brynn's chin tucked lower into his chest, jowls rumpling, and he kept staring at the white-painted wall. Zigic wanted to look him dead in the eye, sure that if he could he would see the lie there.

'Why are you prepared to take the fall for him?'

'Really, Inspector—'

'Brynn, you're making a mistake,' he said. 'We have DNA evidence on Corinne's body and if it doesn't match yours then you'll be charged with making a false confession, perverting the course of justice and wasting police time. You're looking at a custodial sentence for that.'

He could hear Brynn's breathing, fast and shallow, a slight whine as he exhaled. He wasn't sure if he'd hit a nerve or if this was just the normal fear of a man confessing to a murder he never believed he'd be caught for.

'You have an alibi,' he said.

No response.

'Or was Nina lying?'

Silence, except for the whistling breath.

Zigic glanced at Murray, saw her studying Moran, eyes narrowed, and he knew she'd seen it too. The tightening of his eyelids in pain or concern.

'No, not that,' Zigic said. 'You're her alibi too, right? You were covering for her.'

Mrs Peele stood up sharply, dropping her satchel onto the table with a crack. 'This interview is over, DI Zigic. Mr Moran has made his statement, he has confessed to the murder of Corinne Sawyer. Any further questions are not yours to pose.'

'Corinne was trying to get between you,' Zigic went on. 'That's what you said back at the house. Is that why she had to die?'

Brynn's body kept contracting, shrinking away from the force of Zigic's voice and the questions he couldn't or wouldn't answer.

'Is Nina worth protecting?' Zigic asked, quietly, conspiratorially. 'You and Colin were like brothers. You were more family to him than you are to Nina.'

Brynn winced, his big upper body folding over like he'd been punched in the heart, face clenching in a pain which looked physical and for a second Zigic wondered if he was having a coronary. But he wasn't.

Mrs Peele shoved her chair back under the table. 'That is *enough*. If you do not end this now I'll be making a formal complaint to your superior officer.'

Zigic nodded to Murray.

'Interview terminated 4.32 p.m.'

51

'He's lying,' Ferreira said, the second Zigic stepped foot in the office. 'I mean, as far as you can lie when you're making such a basic statement. Why didn't he explain himself? He didn't even offer up anything in his defence. Surely his solicitor told him how that would play when it gets to court.'

'Riggott's happy enough with it,' Zigic told her, aiming for the coffee machine. The DCS had forced a glass of whiskey on him in celebration of solving Corinne's murder and he needed to wash the taste of it off his tongue. 'Brynn ran, we can't ignore the significance of that.'

'But he didn't say why he ran.' She threw up her hands. 'Did he think he'd get away? Disappear into Ferry Meadows and live like a wild man in the woods? Was he going to throw himself in the river? What?'

'You saw the feed, Mel. I didn't exactly get chance to press him on it.' Zigic poured the last couple of inches of coffee into a mug. 'Aren't you supposed to be downstairs?'

'This is my case too,' she said, dropping onto the windowsill. 'And I know you. No way are you satisfied with this outcome.'

She was right. He never trusted unforced confessions. They were the preserve of attention-seekers, the unhinged and people bent on sacrificing themselves for others. Brynn was most definitely in the last category and everything they'd heard about his relationship with Colin and then Corinne, his twenty-year affection for Nina and his fatherly attitude towards Harry, made Zigic inclined to doubt him.

Brynn had lingered at the periphery of that family since the beginning, wanting Nina, but too respectful of his friendship with Colin to act on his feelings. Even as he watched him cheat on her with one woman after another, then begin the process of becoming one. He put aside other relationships, presumably, the possibility of his own family, waiting for the Sawyers' inevitable break-up.

He'd already sacrificed his life for them. A false confession to preserve their liberty didn't seem out of character.

'You know what I'm wondering,' Ferreira said, pulling her tobacco out of her pocket. 'What did Corinne do? Brynn reckoned she was trying to get between them, so how did she do that?'

Zigic frowned. 'Maybe Harry knows. My guess is this all comes back to the fight at Christmas.'

'You want me to see if he's any closer to getting out of hospital?' Wahlia asked.

'Yeah, thanks, Bobby.'

Zigic replayed the moment it all erupted, seeing the hurt on Nina's face and the absolute terror on Brynn's.

'We need to talk to Nina, sharpish,' Zigic said. 'Bobby, send a car over to the hospital to fetch her.'

It took almost an hour to retrieve Nina Sawyer and settle her in Interview Room 1. She arrived blanched and shivering in her fine-knit cardigan, looked shell-shocked, sitting there on the hard plastic chair with a takeaway coffee from the hospital cafeteria.

'Did he do it?' she asked, in a faltering voice. 'Did he kill Corinne?'

'Do you think he did?'

'I don't want to believe it.' Nina leaned her elbows on the table, eyes losing focus. 'But I can't think of any other reason for him to run off like that. What was he trying to do?'

Zigic didn't know, not for sure, and he had no intention of letting her direct the flow of this conversation, whether from confusion or design. She was weak right now, distressed and scared, and this was his best chance to lead her into admitting something she'd rather keep secret.

'The morning of Corinne's murder – you told us that Brynn left the house at half past seven. We now know that was impossible.'

'I thought he did,' she said. 'He always left at that time, he was very particular about timekeeping with the men and he was always punctual himself.'

'But not that morning. What time did he really leave?'

Nina bit her lip. 'Maybe he did leave later. I was cleaning the house, I didn't have my watch on. Perhaps it was ten minutes later.'

'Back at the house, you were angry with Brynn.' Zigic watched her face crumple for a moment before she straightened it out with visible effort. 'You assumed right away that he was guilty rather than Harry. Why is that?'

'Because I know my son. He isn't capable of murder.'

'But Brynn is?'

Nina didn't answer, only frowned, evading his gaze. She drew her flimsy grey cardigan tighter around her body. The room was cold, the radiator against the opposite wall not working properly, and some of the late-afternoon chill was seeping in around the thin, high window, bringing the smell of exhaust fumes from the parkway and a hint of rain on the air.

'If Brynn murdered Corinne he must have had a reason,' Zigic said.

No reply.

'You don't seem shocked by the idea. Is Brynn a violent man?'

'No. He's always been very gentle.'

'He's never been violent towards you?'

'Do you think I'd stand for that?'

He didn't, but then you never could tell.

'What about Colin and Brynn, can you recall them ever fighting?'

'Not that I know of.' A sickly smile lifted her mouth. 'They were always very close.'

'Yes, everyone keeps telling us that. Like brothers, right?' Zigic said. 'And yet Brynn has just confessed to murdering Corinne.'

Her eyes widened and was that relief he saw? It certainly wasn't shock, not anger or disgust but something far more complicated. Relief and amusement? Was he reading her wrong? It seemed such a bizarre reaction he couldn't entirely believe it.

'What did Corinne tell you about Brynn?' he asked.

She touched her tongue to her lip and he gave her a moment to consider it, but when he realised an answer wasn't coming, said, 'Corinne was trying to get between you – Brynn's words. So, how did she do that?'

Nina's hand strayed to her throat, fingertips pressed into the hollow there and Zigic thought of Corinne, the life choked out of her.

'She was never going to let me be happy,' she said. 'The girls think I was a terrible wife, they think I pushed Colin away because I was intolerant and selfish, but they have no idea what a nightmare he was to live with. All the demands. The endless accommodations I made so he could live how he wanted to. The moment they saw him as Corinne that was the end of any semblance of normality. He looked ridiculous,' she spat. 'You only saw him after the surgery, but before all of that he was . . . a joke. And he knew it. So, he started trying to rip away my confidence. I was too fat then when I lost weight I was anorexic. When I didn't want to have sex with him as Corinne I was frigid. He actually made me doubt my own sanity for years, because I *knew* there was nothing wrong with me. I *knew* he was just trying to undermine me, but if you hear those things for long enough you start believing them.'

Zigic resisted the urge to ask questions, letting her talk as the first drops of rain pattered against the window.

'He wanted to be a better woman than me,' she said. 'And he thought he could achieve that by destroying me. If I became un-attractive and weak then by comparison he would be strong and beautiful. But he wasn't. He was a neurotic mess. That's why he was such a whore when he was still a man. He didn't want to screw those women, he wanted to be them.' She brushed the back of her fingers across her bottom lip. 'I saw one of them, once. They were together. They didn't see me and I wasn't going to make a scene. She was tall – statuesque, I suppose you'd say – too much make-up, this black hair like a goth. And then, a few weeks later, Colin bought a black wig and started dressing up just like her.'

She smiled without humour, shook her head.

'That's what women were to him. Templates.'

Zigic realised where she was going. He couldn't believe he hadn't seen it sooner, but the photograph on the murder board was old, taken in the summer before her latest round of surgery. 'When Corinne died, she looked like you.'

Nina nodded. 'The hair was new, my colour, my cut. For all I knew she was going to my hairdresser. She changed it just before Christmas. She'd never dressed like that before and there she was – my double.'

'Did anyone else understand what she'd done?'

'Harry saw it right away.'

'But not Brynn?'

'Brynn never notices things like that,' she said, eyes watering. 'That's why I love him. He doesn't care what clothes I wear or if I don't bother with make-up. You have no idea how liberating that is after having every tiny detail of my appearance scrutinised and judged for so many years.'

'Is that why Harry was so angry with Corinne?' Zigic asked. 'Because she was – what – mocking you?'

'She was making a point. She was the new and improved version of me. It wasn't enough that Lily and Jessica considered her their mother.' Nina pressed her hand to her chest. 'Whatever you might think of me I love my children. They are my whole life. But Corinne took them away from me and I couldn't do anything to stop it. It was like she wanted to erase me completely and that was the last part of the process, stealing my appearance.'

It was a calculated and vicious move on Corinne's part, Zigic thought, but Nina mentioning it now felt like a distraction technique, or even another small attack on Corinne designed to excuse Brynn.

'Nina, what did Corinne tell you?'

'She was lying.'

'I don't think you believe that,' Zigic said. 'And I think whatever Corinne told you had a direct bearing on Brynn confessing to her murder. So, you need to tell me.'

Nina blinked a few times, drying her eyes.

'Corinne told me Brynn came on to her.'

'At Christmas?'

'Yes, but she was lying, obviously. Because that's what she did. She was so furious that we were happy, she wanted to destroy us.' Nina's hand curled into a fist in her lap and she shook her head, disbelievingly. 'How the hell she thought I'd actually buy that . . .'

Zigic leaned forward in his chair, knee throbbing as he moved. 'What exactly did she say?'

'That I should throw him out.' A narrow, bitter smile twisted her mouth. 'She said he was in denial about his sexuality and if I stayed with him he'd hurt me. The irony. Can you imagine?'

'Did you ask Brynn about it?'

Nina waved a dismissive hand at him. 'Of course I did and it was complete rubbish. I'd spent long enough with Corinne to know when she was lying.'

52

The side gate was open when Zigic arrived at the Moran home but there was no sign of Brynn's father, the workshop closed up and silent, much to the relief of their neighbours, Zigic imagined. At the foot of the garden he saw a woman moving around in the greenhouse, lugging a stack of hefty black planters.

She must have been in her early seventies, but like her husband she looked younger, dressed in skinny jeans and a Rolling Stones T-shirt, her hair dyed blonde and tied away from her face. The weight of the pots didn't seem to trouble her as she set them down on the ground.

'Mrs Moran?'

She squinted at him. 'Can I help you?'

'DI Zigic.' He held out his hand. 'I came the other day and talked to your husband.'

'He told me.' Her palm was rough and flat, her fingers strong when they gripped his. She had Brynn's hooded and serious eyes, the same fleshy mouth.

'I've got some bad news, Mrs Moran. It might be better if we went inside.'

'Is Brynn alright?' she asked, panic lifting her voice.

'Yes and no.' He gestured back towards the house. 'I really think it would be better if we didn't discuss this out here.'

She led him into the house through a small lean-to, where a dozen seed trays sat on pine shelves, the soil damp, water dripping rhythmically through them onto the lino. Then into a kitchen where their dinner was simmering on the stove, filling the room with a smell of garlic and oregano. She sat down at a round table with two chairs, a forgotten cup of tea scummed over, next to a seed catalogue and notebook with a planting plan sketched out across a double page.

Between the greenhouse and the kitchen she seemed to have aged ten years, the fear dulling her eyes and slackening her skin.

'What is it?' she asked. 'Come on, spit it out.'

'Brynn has confessed to Corinne's murder.'

She gasped, pressing her hand to her chest. 'No, no, he'd never do that. I don't care what's he's told you, it can't be true. He's not got a violent bone in his body and he loved Colin.'

'And Corinne?'

'It was all the same to Brynn. Man or woman. She was still Colin underneath.'

'But they'd fallen out of contact,' Zigic said. 'Was that Nina's doing?'

'She didn't want them seeing each other. She never came right out and said it's her or me but Brynn knew the score.' Maura shook her head sadly. 'He thought she'd get over it eventually. Once she got used to Corinne being how she was. He's like that, always sees the best in people. He told Corinne to be patient, let him talk Nina round gradually.'

'They were still seeing each other then?'

'Round here, yes,' Maura said. 'Corinne used to take me out for lunch, last Friday of the month. We'd been doing that since she left Nina. Brynn and her would have a drink and a natter when she dropped me off.'

Brynn hadn't mentioned it and that bothered Zigic. He had every reason to hide their meetings from Nina but none to keep it from him. Unless he was so paranoid about Nina finding out that he wouldn't even take that risk.

'When was the last time they saw each other?' he asked.

'Just after Christmas. Corinne and me went out as usual and she brought me home afterwards. Brynn was round helping Bob with one of his toys.'

'How were they?'

'Same as always.' Her pale grey brows drew together. 'They never argued, not serious. Why would he kill her?'

'He's refusing to tell us,' Zigic said. 'Maybe he did it for Nina. She's been quite clear about how miserable Corinne made her. Perhaps Brynn was sick of seeing her being treated so badly.'

'Is that what he said?' she asked, beady-eyed now.

'He won't say why he did it.'

Maura nodded triumphantly. 'Then you know he's lying.'

'Not necessarily.' Zigic went to cross his legs, stopped when his bruised knee protested. 'Maybe he's just not prepared to admit what drove him to it.'

'If you believed he'd done it you wouldn't be here talking to me,' Maura said. 'So why are you here, really?'

'I'm not convinced that Brynn killed Corinne. Not yet, anyway.' He shifted in the chair, straightened out his leg to ease the pain. 'But he's refusing to talk to us—'

'I'll talk to him,' Maura said, drawing herself up, ready to apply her maternal weight to the situation. 'I won't let him throw his life away for that woman.'

'That's not possible, I'm afraid.'

Maura walked out of the room, told him to wait there, and he did, listening to the sauce bubbling on the hob and the percussive drip of the water through the seed trays in the lean-to. He thought of what Nina Sawyer had told him about Christmas, still wasn't sure he believed it. There was no good way to verify her account, which was already contradictory, a combination of Harry's eyewitness report and a conversation with Corinne which was purely hearsay at this point.

Assuming it was true it gave Brynn a motive for murder.

But it gave Harry and Nina one as well. A better one.

Until he could force Brynn into giving up further details the confession was unsatisfactory, legally and otherwise.

Maura returned with a photo album, an old one, peach-coloured with gold trim worn away in places from handling. She slapped it down on the table and opened it up.

'Look at this, Brynn and Colin, the first year of school.'

Two boys, the men they would become already discernible in their faces. Brynn round-cheeked and grinning, Colin gaunt, his clothes creased and dirty, but he was smiling too, his arm around Brynn's shoulder.

'They were inseparable.'

She kept turning the pages, taking Zigic through fishing trips and visits to the funfair on the side of the River Nene, the boys growing up, Brynn filling out, Colin staying lean, becoming more poised. He looked for traces of Corinne in him, saw them as they got into their early teens. Colin wearing his hair longer, sometimes in a ponytail, cultivating an androgynous look, part punk, part glam rock.

There were other people in some of the photos, girls in lots but never the same ones for very long. Maura and Bob making the scenes look like regular family snapshots. And in almost every image Zigic saw how Brynn looked to Colin, the camera catching a closeness the naked eye might not.

'Brynn idolised him,' Maura said, lost in their past now, smiling back at the faces smiling out at her. 'You wouldn't believe it now but he was an awkward boy. Cripplingly shy. Couldn't talk to girls. Colin used to do the talking for both of them. He loved women, he listened to them, I reckon that's why he did so well.'

Zigic had to ask her.

'Did it ever go further between the two of them?'

Maura looked up sharply. 'What are you getting at?'

362

'Well, we know Corinne was developing an interest in men, did you ever get a sense that Colin and Brynn—'

Maura snorted. 'Don't be ridiculous.'

'Would you have known if they were . . . experimenting?'

She gave him a pitying look. 'All kids experiment. Are you going to sit there and tell me you never flicked through one of your old man's *Playboys* with your mates? It's what boys do.'

'But Colin wasn't like other boys,' Zigic said. 'Did you know he was cross-dressing?'

She shifted in the chair, closed the photo album. 'He tried to hide it. But I saw the way he looked at my clothes when they were on the washing line. He was always happy to help me with the laundry. He'd fold everything up for me and put it away. I could see from how he touched the blouses. Then one day I just told him, "Try one on if you like."'

'Did he?'

'Yes. He started crying and shaking. He told me he'd put one of his mum's blouses on and she caught him doing it. Nasty bitch beat the hell out of him.' Maura's eyes narrowed at the memory, the anger still festering in her. 'She thought he was gay. She used to call him her little gay boy. Never stopped it, right up till when she died. She had no understanding of what he was going through.'

'But you did?'

'Not right away,' Maura said slowly. 'I knew there were fellas that liked dressing up as women. Not a new thing, is it? I can't say I thought it was normal, but I didn't think it was . . . sick, or anything like that.'

'Did Brynn and Bob know about this?' Zigic asked.

'I told Bob.' She bit her lip, worried at it for a few seconds. 'He weren't happy, tell the truth. Blew his top, didn't want Colin round here any more, didn't want Brynn having anything to do with him.'

'That was an extreme reaction.'

'It was a different time back then,' she said weakly. 'You'll be too young to remember what it was like. I had gay pals before I married Bob so it never bothered me as much as it bothered him. I knew they weren't any different to the rest of us, but he was a country boy, his family were staunch Methodist folk and they reckon anything off the straight and narrow leads you straight into hellfire. That's where Bob was coming from. He thought Colin's behaviour was . . . deviant and he thought he'd "corrupt" Brynn or, I don't know, he believed hanging around with Colin was going to damage him somehow.' Absently she stroked the photo album. 'Bob's not like that any more. He knows better now. Weird, isn't it, everyone thinks you get more conservative as you get older but he's mellowed so much he's like another person.'

Zigic thought of the conversation he'd had with Bob Moran and struggled to believe he'd ever been less than fully accepting of Corinne.

'What happened?' he asked. 'Back then?'

'It was hard.' Maura's weathered fingertips traced along the embossed letters on the album. 'I tried to talk Bob round but he wouldn't have Colin in the house.'

'How did Brynn take that?'

'Badly, of course. Even more so because neither of us told him why. I didn't think it was right to expose Colin's secret and Bob wouldn't do it because he was scared Brynn wouldn't care. In the end Colin made the decision for us. He took himself off a couple of weeks later and we didn't see him for years after that.' She sighed. 'Bob felt terrible. He was convinced Colin had done something stupid. Killed himself or run off down to London and ended up on the streets doing God knows what to survive.'

'And when did Brynn find out the truth?' Zigic asked.

'It was when Nina found out and started kicking up merry hell. I'm not sure Colin would've ever told Brynn to be honest. He was petrified what people would think of him.' Maura smiled regretfully.

'Then he told Brynn and he never batted an eyelid. He made some stupid joke about Colin having the legs for it and that was it. They went on just the same as before.'

She stood up and went over to the hob, adjusted the heat under the big cast-iron pot. 'If Brynn's told you he killed Corinne he'll have said it to protect one of that lot.'

Zigic waited for her to turn back to him, needing to see her first reaction.

'We've been told Brynn made a pass at Corinne.'

'By who? Nina?' Maura held the wooden spoon like a cudgel. 'No, there's no way he'd do that. She's trying to drop him in it so you don't look at her. She's the one who hated Corinne.'

His gut agreed with Maura.

It had felt like a distraction when Nina told him and even she dismissed the idea out of hand. But she was smart. Would know that an accusation quickly undermined would look more damning than one she resolutely pursued. Because she was in the frame for this too and shifting blame was what a guilty person did.

No, Zigic was certain Nina had given Brynn a motive then whipped it away, in the hope that he'd keep toying with it and come to the conclusion that Brynn murdered Corinne because she was trying to break them up and take away the family he'd always wanted.

Strange that she only mentioned it once she knew they doubted his alibi, too.

Did she think it was her or Brynn now?

Nina had always been the person with the strongest motive to kill Corinne. They knew she'd suffered years of emotional trauma as Colin philandered and cross-dressed through their marriage, that she'd suffered depression so deep it became a full-blown breakdown.

Zigic could imagine Brynn confessing to protect her and he wasn't going to allow it to stand.

He thanked Maura for talking to him and she walked him out to his car, a little stooped now under the weight of their conversation and fear for her son.

She grabbed the car door as he moved to close it.

'Please,' she said. 'Talk to Brynn, make him see sense. He can't give his life up for these people.'

53

Zigic called Brynn Moran's solicitor back into the station, then rang down to the custody suite and asked that they bring him up from the cells once again. It would be twenty minutes. Dinner had just been served and he'd be given a chance to eat. Once that was done they could take this as long into the evening as necessary. He was going to throw everything he had at cracking Brynn's confession. Even if he wouldn't come completely clean about Nina's or Harry's potential guilt, Zigic was determined to at least get him to admit to lying about his own.

But before that he wanted to talk to Harry.

He'd arrived in a patrol car while Zigic was out, followed half an hour later by a solicitor. Nina's doing, Zigic assumed, because the woman came from the most well-respected chambers in the city. He knew her from his time in CID but hadn't tangled with her since moving into Hate Crimes. Most of their suspects couldn't afford this standard of legal counsel.

'How's the wrist, Harry?' Zigic asked, as he sat down.

'They gave me painkillers,' he said, lifting the soft cast from the tabletop. 'It still hurts. First time I've ever broken a bone. Miracle really.'

He looked relaxed, a little droopy around the mouth, and if he was on codeine there was no telling how it was affecting him. Or, rather, there was. Zigic had taken them on occasion, recalled how they scrambled his thinking.

He set up the recording, time and date given, names stated in dry voices. This room was stuffy and close, as if all the heat which should have spread into the next one was trapped, pumping out of the radiator behind him.

'Are you happy to answer some questions?' he asked.

Harry nodded. 'No problem.'

'Ms Carter? Your client is on medication – are you happy for him to proceed?'

She cocked her head. 'I will be certain to let you know the moment I am not happy, Detective Inspector Zigic.'

Harry Sawyer opened the half-drunk bottle of mineral water and drained it. Furry tongue Zigic guessed; another side effect of codeine. At least he'd eaten though, judging by the empty sandwich carton still smeared with mayonnaise.

'I was telling you the truth,' Harry said, unprompted. 'Back at the house. I really had had too much to drink that night. I forgot to set my alarm and Carly was as hung-over as me, that's why I was late into work.'

'And why did you and Carly lie about it?'

'I asked her to, you can't blame her. We both knew what you'd think. What with me . . .' He scratched his beard. 'My record. I knew how it would look.'

'It looks bad.'

'Brynn killed Corinne, not me.'

'We have no evidence to support that,' Zigic told him.

'He ran off when you came to arrest him. Obviously he's guilty.'

Zigic rested his chin on his fist. 'What were you and Brynn hiding from Nina?' he asked.

Harry dug the knuckle of his thumb into his eye socket, then blinked away the redness he'd caused. He went to fold his arms but the movement was unwieldy with his wrist in the cast and he stopped, laid it back on the table.

'We know something's been going on,' Zigic said. 'It's best that you tell me now, before it starts to look like deliberate obstruction.'

'It started at Christmas,' Harry said finally. 'She turned up looking like Mum in drag and I knew she was going to make trouble.
She didn't normally look like that. It was deliberate. I thought she'd
done it to upset Mum.'

'And did it upset her?'

'Yeah, but . . .'

He was still reluctant and Zigic realised he was going to have
to tease the truth out of the young man. Too many days lying, he
wasn't ready to give up yet.

'Brynn thought Corinne was trying to get between them,' he
said. 'How was she going about doing that?'

'She was flirting with Brynn. Not even subtly, she kept putting
her hand on his leg, touching his arm, flicking her hair. It was
embarrassing. Tragic.'

'Did Brynn reciprocate?'

Harry shook his head. 'I don't think he even noticed, to tell you
the truth. I could see that was annoying her. She liked to provoke a
reaction and if she couldn't get that . . .' He shrugged. 'I guess that's
why she went for the more direct approach.'

'How direct?'

'She assaulted him. Basically. I don't know what else you'd call
it.' Sweat was sticking Harry's shirt to his armpits, darkening the
fabric at his chest. The room was hot but the sweat had sprung up
suddenly and the sharp tang of his body odour carried fear in it. 'I
went into the kitchen and saw them. Corinne had Brynn backed up
against the cupboards. She'd pretty much pinned him in the corner.
She was cupping his junk.'

'Did he try to push her away?'

'He did when he saw me,' Harry said, and something in his tone
begged to be challenged.

'How was he reacting to Corinne's advances?' Zigic asked.
'Before he saw you?'

Another twist of his face. 'I don't think he was happy about it.'

369

'But you're not sure?'

'There was like a second before he saw me, then he pushed her away.'

'What did you do?'

'I lost it,' Harry said. 'I knew what she was trying to do. She wasn't interested in Brynn, she just wanted something to throw in Mum's face. Mum was so happy with Brynn. As long as I can remember she's been miserable. That's what Dad did to her. I suppose even someone as self-absorbed as Corinne could see that Mum was finally moving on with her life and she wanted to take that away from her.'

'And that's when you threw Corinne out?'

'Yes. I knew if she got anywhere near Mum she'd rub her nose in it. I didn't want everything to blow up.'

'When did Nina find out about this?' Zigic asked.

'Not until afterwards. A week or so. Corinne started ringing Brynn, she was taunting him, telling him she knew he wanted her.' Harry shifted in his seat. 'Mum went through his phone. I don't think she usually did that but, I don't know. She heard a voicemail about it that Corinne left. She phoned her up and told her to stay away from him. It was stupid. She gave her exactly the reaction she wanted.'

Zigic thought of the phone logs they'd pulled. How calmly Brynn Moran sat in this room and volunteered the information about the calls, explaining them away as him trying to make peace between the two women. Now it looked like the final call on that list might not have been made by him at all. Was it Nina confronting Corinne? They'd found no other contact between the women. Had Nina heard the voicemail and reacted immediately? It seemed out of character but something so damning left little room for cool reflection.

'Mum couldn't let it go,' Harry said sadly. 'Corinne knew exactly what buttons to push with her. They weren't the same after that, her and Brynn. They kept playing nice but I could see something had changed. I think she would have thrown him out eventually. She just wasn't strong enough to do it yet.'

Even now, in Harry's eyes, it was all about Nina. Not Brynn as a murderer, but Brynn as someone who had mistreated his beloved mother. He had all the empathy in the world for Nina and not a shred of it spare for Corinne.

'So,' Zigic said, disgusted. 'You knew he had a motive and you didn't tell us. You realise that's obstruction?'

'We didn't know it was even possible he could have done it until you burst into the house this afternoon.' Harry slumped in his seat like a grumpy teenager. 'How were we supposed to know Brynn had something like this in him?'

'You knew.' Zigic jabbed the tabletop. 'You've all been covering this up for days.'

'No, we didn't realise—'

'You didn't *care*. Corinne was dead and none of you cared enough about her to do the right thing and tell us Brynn had a motive.' Zigic threw his hands up. 'She was your mother and she was murdered and you just didn't give a damn.'

54

'Mr Moran has already provided you with a confession,' his solicitor said, once the tapes were running. 'I fail to see any reason for us to be here.'

Mrs Peele wasn't happy to be brought back into the station just when her day should have been ending, Zigic thought. Her suit was crumpled, her hair coming out of its French pleat, and as he walked into the room she'd quickly slipped her feet back into her heels she'd kicked off under the table.

Zigic felt just as wiped out, the painkillers had worn off and his swollen knee was pounding, every heartbeat making the bone thump. Next to him Murray was working on a mug of strong tea but he could see the long day had left its marks on her too. She'd freshened up before they came in and the smell of her body spray was cloying in the overheated interview room.

'We're here', Zigic said, 'because, at present, Mr Moran's confession is regarded as false and we have to decide whether to charge him for that offence or for the murder he claims to have committed.'

He looked to Brynn, who was sitting arms folded and hunched over, but couldn't catch his eye.

A few hours in the cells had taken their toll on him and Zigic wondered if the reality of it was sinking in. That the next ten to fifteen years of his life would be just like this, but worse, because he wouldn't be alone in his next cell, and the basic courtesy accorded to the suspected wasn't always extended to the convicted.

It was a long fall from the Sawyers' sprawling and elegant home to an eight-by-ten box reeking of cleaning fluid and fear.

Zigic hoped he appreciated that.

'Now,' he said, 'I want you to tell me everything that happened on the morning of the murder. Start at the beginning, when you left the house.'

Brynn finally looked up, his eyes were red raw but dry, as if he'd cried himself out in his cell. There were no other signs of emotion on his face, just an obliterated numbness in his slack jaw and heavy lids.

He leaned over and whispered something to his solicitor. She shielded her mouth with her hand when she replied.

'No comment,' he said in a toneless voice.

'Can you tell me what Corinne was wearing when she died?'

Again, 'No comment.'

Zigic took out a map of Ferry Meadows and slid it across the table to Brynn, held out a ballpoint pen.

'Please mark on the map the place where you murdered Corinne Sawyer.'

Brynn kept his arms folded, stared at the recorder bolted to the wall as it absorbed his silence and the buzz and batter of a bluebottle trapped in the strip light.

'Are you refusing to indicate the place where Corinne was murdered?' Zigic asked.

'No comment.'

'Or can you not show us because you don't know?'

'No comment.'

Zigic smiled at him. 'Come on, Brynn, surely you remember where you murdered her.'

He took the map back and replaced it in the folder he'd brought with him. Tucked the pen away in his shirt pocket.

'Okay, I suppose all those paths look the same, we'll come back to the murder scene.' Zigic planted his elbows on the table. 'How did you kill Corinne?'

Brynn closed his eyes for a moment, croaked out, 'No comment.'

'Did she fight back?'

'No comment.' Almost a whisper.

He was cracking but Zigic wasn't entirely sure why. Was it too painful to remember or did he realise that his ridiculous 'confession' was falling apart? His solicitor should have stepped in, advised him to answer the questions – she must have known where this was going – but she didn't. And it occurred to Zigic that she probably didn't believe in his guilt either.

'Why did you kill Corinne?'

'No comment.'

'You must have had a reason,' Zigic said. 'Everyone we've spoken to told us how close the two of you were.'

A violent shudder racked Brynn's body. He clenched his jaw tight, as if the words wanted to come out but he wouldn't let them.

'The way I see it, Harry had a reason to kill Corinne. They've always had an adversarial relationship and Harry doesn't have a alibi for the time of her murder.'

Above them the fly kept striking the plastic housing of the strip light. A high, urgent hum of wings.

'And I can see why Nina would want to murder Corinne.' Zigic tapped the desk with his fingertips. 'So much history there. So much antagonism and pain.'

Brynn shifted his weight in the chair, looked at his solicitor for help.

'These aren't questions, Inspector.'

'You're right. But since Mr Moran has been unable to give us any firm reason to believe his confession, the question facing us now is who is he lying to protect?'

'It's the truth,' Brynn said, in the same flat tone as before.

'No, Brynn. We're disregarding your previous statement. And we're going to charge you for making a false confession and for all of the other offences you've committed, but it's obvious you're trying to cover for Harry or Nina.'

374

'I did it. I killed Corinne.' Brynn unfolded his arms, laid them on the table, exposed his palms as if he was presenting them with the murder weapon. 'It's got nothing to do with either of them.'

'So, tell us how and where and why.'

Brynn cleared his throat. 'I knew she always went running at the same time every morning. I knew her route. I followed her. She didn't know I was behind her because she had her earphones in. I knocked her down and dragged her off the path.' He clasped his right hand around his left, rubbed at the rough skin on his fingers. 'I strangled her. With the cable from her earphones.'

There was no emotion in the words and Zigic couldn't decide what that meant. False confessions were often colourful and dramatic, too much detail given, too much pleasure taken lingering over the moment of death and the feeling of power. But that was the attention-seeker's way and he knew Brynn wasn't here for attention.

A false confession designed to deflect them away from the real culprit wouldn't follow that pattern. It would be like this. Cold and bland.

They'd held back the details of how she died and only the killer would know about her being strangled with that white cable. But it was conceivable that Harry or Nina had told him how they'd done it and now he was just parroting that back.

'No. I still don't believe you. You're covering for Harry or Nina and whichever one of them killed Corinne has told you enough about what happened for you to make a confession.'

'It was me,' Brynn said, through gritted teeth.

'Did one of them encourage you to confess?'

'No.'

'I don't think you'd do it for Harry.' Zigic watched his face for some flicker of acknowledgement, got nothing. 'You'd sacrifice yourself for Nina, though. Wouldn't you?'

'No.'

'She has ample reason to want Corinne dead. Even before we get into what happened at Christmas.'

Brynn swallowed hard, pressed his palms together.

'We've had conflicting versions of events,' Zigic said. 'So, what really happened? Did you come on to Corinne or did she assault you?'

'No comment.'

Zigic sighed, play-acting boredom just as Brynn piqued his interest.

'Back to that, are we?' He eyed the clock, like this would need winding up soon. 'You've told us the where and the how. What about the why?'

'No comment.'

'As I see it, you're the person least likely to want to hurt Corinne,' Zigic said. 'I spoke to your mother this afternoon. She showed me the family photo albums. Colin was very much part of your family, wasn't he?'

Brynn didn't answer.

'Your mum thinks you're innocent.' Zigic smiled, knowing he was unnerving Brynn now. 'She thinks you loved Corinne, just like you loved Colin.'

No movement, no reply. He wasn't even blinking and Zigic realised he was close to something.

'Brynn, if you don't tell us why you did it, how can we judge the validity of your confession?'

'I don't have to tell you,' he said, almost whispering.

'This all escalated at Christmas, right?' Zigic opened his hands up. '*Something* happened between you and Corinne in the kitchen, while you were cooking. We'll come back to who instigated that. Then a couple of days later Corinne calls Nina and tells her to dump you, because you made a pass at her.'

Brynn's breath was speeding up, his face colouring through his beard.

'Isn't that right?'

'No comment,' he mumbled.

'Speak up, please, Mr Moran. For the benefit of the tape.'

Brynn growled, 'No comment.'

'It doesn't really matter who kissed who,' Zigic said. 'What matters is that Nina believed it and she challenged you over it. What did you say?'

'No comment.'

Zigic glanced at the solicitor, saw that she was now completely focused. Even a hardened professional, who'd seen it all, couldn't resist a whiff of sexual scandal, he supposed.

'I don't think that's enough of a motive for you to kill Corinne. But—' Zigic held his finger up. 'For Nina . . . she's finally picked herself up after a very long, very bad marriage. And she has you. New man, new start. Then Corinne comes along and sticks the knife in again. Tells her, "that bloke you think's so great, well, guess what, he wants me".'

Brynn's eyelids fluttered, a twitch not a blink.

'Corinne came to that lunch for you,' Zigic said. 'She'd changed her appearance, made herself look just like Nina because she thought it's how you'd want her to be. So, I think Harry's right. Corinne sexually assaulted you.'

'No.'

'No, what?'

Brynn hesitated, face flushing a deeper red. 'No comment.'

'Nina was furious. After everything Colin put her through, everything Corinne did to her – the lies and bullying, turning her daughters against her – this was the last straw. You were the one good thing she had in her life and Corinne wanted to take you away.'

Brynn shook his head.

'Nina killed Corinne,' Zigic said, voice rising. 'She did it and you're trying to cover for her. Aren't you?'

'No.'

'Nina has no alibi. She has years of motive.'

'No.'

'And now she's got you so besotted that you're going to throw away your life for her after she murdered a person you've loved since you were a boy.'

'No!'

'Yes!' Zigic shouted back at him. 'You didn't murder Corinne. She was too important to you. This was a vicious, hateful murder. I know you loved Corinne too much to kill her.'

Brynn let out a keening whine and slumped over the table, his head in his hands. His solicitor touched his shoulder, leaned in to whisper something in his ear. He shook her off, straightened up, looking like it took every ounce of strength he had.

'I did love her,' he said quietly. 'I've always loved her.'

Overhead the fly kept batting against the light fitting and it was the only noise in the room for a couple of minutes, as Brynn retreated into his memory. It looked painful in there, Zigic thought, seeing how his brow furrowed, his mouth drawing into a grimace.

He wondered if the memories had always hurt or if murdering Corinne had tainted them so thoroughly that Brynn wouldn't even be able to escape back into them during the long years he would serve in prison.

'At first I didn't realise what was going on,' he said. 'I thought it was just because of how close me and Colin were. Everyone said we were like brothers but it wasn't like that. It was more. And he felt the same about me. I know he did. But he was scared of showing it so he joked about it, but I know what we did and I know that doesn't mean nothing.'

Brynn wiped his nose on the back of his hand.

'I wanted to tell him how I felt for so long. I'd decided to do it when we were both sixteen and no one could stop us being together. Then he disappeared and I moved on.' A tear ran down Brynn's reddened cheek and he scrubbed it away angrily. 'By the time Colin came home it was too late to say anything and then he met Nina and I convinced myself I'd imagined it all. But I didn't.'

He fixed Zigic with an intense stare, willing him to share that certainty. Zigic was sure Brynn believed it, but that didn't make any of it true.

'We both went on like normal. I went out with women. Lots of women. But none of them were right, then Corinne appeared and it was like I was being given another chance. Because she was a woman and that would make it easier for both of us. I had no idea Colin was that way but I was so happy when I found out. I nearly told him how I felt right then, but I stopped myself, because everything was so mad with him and Nina and I didn't want to put any more pressure on him.' Brynn looked up at the ceiling. 'God, why did I wait? None of this needed to happen.'

Zigic felt himself sink back in his seat as Brynn talked, knowing the fight was over, hearing the truth coming out. This level of emotion, this deep and complete, there was no faking it. He felt it in his own throat, the force of Brynn's despair and longing.

'Corinne was the one who wanted me to move in with Nina,' he said. 'I did love her – I've always loved Nina. That was real.' His lower lip trembled. 'I thought I was over Corinne. I hardly saw her. I was happy with Nina and the kids. Then Corinne turned up at Christmas . . .'

'And she looked like Nina,' Zigic said softly.

Brynn nodded. 'I couldn't even look at her. It was like the only two people I've ever properly loved had been . . . merged. And there she was. Perfect.'

For a long moment he went silent, eyes losing focus, back in the kitchen, Zigic guessed, remembering the point at which this all began to spiral out of control.

'Corinne came in to see if I needed a hand and we started talking.' He closed his eyes. 'I don't know what I was thinking. I just kissed her.'

'How did she react?'

His face darkened and he held his palms to his burning cheeks. 'She laughed and told me not to be so silly. I wanted to explain but then Harry was in the kitchen and he was hauling Corinne away.'

'Did you tell him what happened?'

'He made his own mind up and I decided not to put him straight,' Brynn said. 'I realised I'd made a total bloody fool of myself and I didn't want Nina to find out. I told him she'd lose it if she knew what Corinne did.' Brynn pressed his knuckles against his mouth. 'I never thought Corinne would tell her.'

It was one long excuse and as Brynn talked Zigic found himself hardening against the man. He was the instigator but it was Corinne who ended up suffering.

'So you murdered Corinne because she told Nina you kissed her?' Zigic asked, letting his incredulity show.

Brynn squirmed. 'It wasn't that.'

'Because she rejected you?'

'She didn't want me but she didn't want Nina and me to be happy either. Not after that.'

As if Corinne was the unreasonable one, Zigic thought. He held back what he wanted to say, nodded slightly for Brynn to continue.

'She called Nina and we had a blazing row. I thought I'd convinced her it was all rubbish but Corinne wouldn't back off. She kept ringing and I told her to leave us alone.'

The phone calls he'd so smoothly written off as him peacekeeping between the two women, Zigic thought. Brynn was a better liar than he'd given him credit for, but he'd been living a lie for almost as long as Corinne had, performing his role more convincingly than she had too.

'I thought it was over and done with.' He sighed. 'But then Nina went cold on me. She hated Corinne but she still believed her.'

'And killing Corinne was the only way to prove to Nina that she was the most important woman in your life?'

'No, she didn't know about this. None of them did.' He chopped the table with the side of his hand. 'I just wanted Corinne to stay out of our relationship. She had no right to interfere. I tried to reason with her but she wouldn't listen. I was just trying to protect my family.' His head dropped. 'I didn't want to do it, believe me. She drove me to it.'

Zigic stood up to charge him, heard the contempt in his voice as he watched Brynn crumple again, more sorry for himself than he was for Corinne and all the other people he'd hurt.

As Murray moved to guide him out of the interview room and back down to the custody suite Zigic stopped her.

'Why did you run?' he asked.

Brynn looked around the room. 'This. I wanted to spare them all.'

Murray nodded at Zigic, letting him know that she'd tell the custody sergeant that Moran needed to be put on suicide watch. Zigic wondered how high the risk really was. Brynn could have stopped in the road outside the Sawyer house and let a car plough into him. Maybe part of him wanted to end it but not enough and he doubted he'd have the fortitude to do it now either. He was a coward at heart. Too weak to face up to his own sexuality, too weak to accept Corinne rejecting him or the loss of a family which was never his. Part of Zigic hoped he tried it though. Used his clothing as a noose and discovered just how painful and terrifying it was to be choked to death. He wanted Brynn Moran to know how Corinne felt as her death came rushing up on her.

Ferreira was waiting for him in Hate Crimes.

'Happy with that?' she asked.

'As happy as you can be when some arsehole tells you they've killed someone for a really shitty reason.' Zigic went over to the murder board, seeing how low they'd prioritised Brynn among the suspects. 'I'm sure he's telling the truth now, anyway.'

Ferreira came over to him. 'He is. Jenkins emailed about half an hour ago. She's got a type match on saliva from Corinne's hoodie.

Negative for Harry and Nina, positive for Brynn. DNA will be tomorrow but it looks right.'

'You could have told me that earlier.' He eyed the clock. 'I could be home now.'

She smiled. 'DNA doesn't tell you why though, does it? And you know you always need the why.'

TUESDAY

55

Ferreira wanted to take him down inside but Adams vetoed the idea. She didn't push it, not after he made it clear she shouldn't even be there.

The fact that she'd done all the legwork on the attacks counted for nothing while she was under investigation and forbidden from any active involvement in the case. It stung, more than she'd admit, but she wanted to be here for this at least. Witness Lee Walton's arrest, have him know she was the one who'd brought him down.

'Don't say anything, don't do anything,' Adams told her, as they approached the hospital's main entrance, the four uniforms with them peeling off to take up discreet positions which would keep them out of direct sight as Lee Walton came through the doors.

'What about if he gets you in a headlock?' she asked.

'Not even then.'

She shrugged. 'Your funeral.'

Morning visiting hours were in progress. Friends and family coming and going, bringing food and magazines and faces plastered with worry as they passed the inevitable gaggle of smokers. Ferreira wanted a cigarette but didn't know if she had time. It was the nerves as much as a nicotine craving; she could feel the adrenalin coursing through her veins and knew she wouldn't get to use it.

This would be quick and clean, Adams insisted.

His phone bleated and he checked the display, whistled to put the waiting uniforms on guard. The nurse on Dani Shaw's ward had confirmed he was there, arriving to take her home, had promised them a heads-up when he left.

A minute passed and Adams was getting antsy, watching the door.

Then they emerged, Dani Shaw painfully rising from the wheelchair and thanking the porter who'd brought her down, struggling to stand, her hand going to her bruised ribs. Walton took hold of her upper arm, appearing to steady her but Ferreira saw how tight his grip was as they walked out into the morning sun, his fingers squeezing harder still when Adams stepped into his path.

'Alright, Lee, you know the drill.'

'Are you fucking kidding me?' he said. 'I'm taking my girl-friend home. She's had an accident. Don't you people have any decency?'

'We'll see she gets home safely,' Adams told him. 'Which is more than you can do for her.'

The uniforms moved in, bristling at the promise of a ruckus. Walton looked at them, sneered.

'Five of you?' Flicked his eyes towards Ferreira. 'Six, sorry. Didn't see you there.'

Next to him Dani Shaw was visibly shrinking, waiting for some sign how to react, so completely ruled by the man that she couldn't even decide for herself how she felt about what was happening.

'Come along easy, or don't,' Adams said. 'You know what I'd prefer.'

'Are you arresting me?'

'Lee Walton, I'm arresting you for the rape of Ryan Bhakta—'

Dani gasped, and at that the uniforms moved in, turned him and cuffed him as Adams finished his speech, spitting out the final words.

'This is bollocks!' Walton craned his neck towards Dani. 'This is rubbish, babe.'

PC Jackson held his shoulder, the other hand on the cuffs, started walking him away. Walton was stumbling over his feet, trying to turn to Dani again.

386

'Don't listen to them.' They marched him to a patrol car. 'Don't believe a fucking word that bitch says to you.'

She was crying, fat tears rolling down her cheeks, and she looked helpless, clutching a small pink wash bag with 'Princess' punched along its front in diamanté points, a plaster on the back of her hand where a cannula had been removed.

'Dani, Sergeant Ferreira is going to take you home now, okay?'

She glared at Adams, eyes small and wet. 'Why are you doing this to us?'

Adams sighed regretfully, frowned at her. 'You know what he is, Dani, and you know what he's capable of. This is what we do to men like him. We stop them.'

'He didn't rape a *man*. Whoever said that's lying.'

'DNA doesn't lie.'

'You made a mistake then.' She looked to Ferreira, who showed Dani the most sympathetic face she could muster. 'Lee isn't like that. He wouldn't. He just wouldn't do that.'

'It isn't a mistake,' she said, going over to her. 'Come on, let me take you home. You don't want to wait around here for a taxi, do you?'

Dani let herself be walked across the road, moving tentatively, holding her side. Ferreira opened the passenger door of her car and helped Dani in, seeing how she winced as she sat down.

Adams looked at her across the top of her car, waiting before he got into his own, said, quietly, 'You're the good cop, remember.'

Dani Shaw said very little on the drive through the city centre and Ferreira was glad the traffic was slow, Bourges Boulevard heavily congested, as usual, because she needed time to think, work out how she was going to get this woman to open up after she'd spent years covering for her boyfriend.

'I broke a couple of my ribs once,' she said. 'There's no pain like it, is there? Every time you breathe, you move. It's like being stabbed.'

Dani didn't answer but Ferreira kept going.

'Did they give you a prescription for painkillers?'

'Yes.'

'We should stop and get it filled. The ones they gave you at the hospital will be wearing off soon.'

'I don't need to stop anywhere,' Dani said, her high-pitched voice clogged with the tears she was swallowing down, trying to do what she thought Lee would want her to. 'I've got plenty at home.'

'Ibuprofen isn't going to be up to the job, believe me. You need codeine at least.'

'I've got codeine.'

From the last time he did this to her, Ferreira thought. But she didn't say it. She was being the good cop and that meant biting her tongue until she could taste blood.

They passed the Crown court and the cathedral, Ferreira slowing again at another set of red lights.

'That's where he did it,' she said, pointing to the entrance of the cathedral precincts. 'Down there. He followed this man out of a club, knocked him down, smashed in his face, and raped him.'

Dani refused to look, staring down into her lap. 'Lee isn't gay.'

'The man he attacked was dressed as a woman at the time.' Ferreira pulled off again, over the crossing, towards the next one, but the lights changed, another stop. 'Lee knew it was a man though. Underneath.'

'I don't believe you.'

'We recovered Lee's DNA from the man's clothing. It was all over the dress the victim was wearing.'

'You're fitting him up,' Dani said. 'I know how you people work.'

Dani kept her eyes fixed dead ahead, but Ferreira could see her reserve wobbling, the dimples in her chin. She'd seen it at the hospital. There was more than just shock on Dani's face. She'd been disgusted and Ferreira knew that somewhere, deep down, she knew it was true.

388

'Did you know Lee was attracted to cross-dressers?'

'He isn't,' she snapped.

'Do you check his computer?' Ferreira asked, flicking her indicator as she turned off the roundabout, going past the gasworks, the tower sitting low today. 'You go through his search history?'

'No.'

'Never? You're not curious what he looks at?'

'No.'

'You should be,' Ferreira said. 'It'd tell you everything about him.'

'I know Lee.'

'Yeah, you do, don't you?' Up onto the parkway, out towards Werrington, and she eased off the accelerator, buying more time.

Dani wasn't reacting.

She was used to staying silent, Ferreira realised. Lee Walton had ground her down across the years, through a combination of threats and rewards. He'd broken her but hardened her too and getting through wasn't going to be easy.

'You're worth more than this, Dani,' she said softly. 'How many times has he put you in the hospital?'

'I fell.'

'We're not on record here,' Ferreira said, tucking the car in behind a slow-moving lorry. 'It doesn't matter what you say to me. This is just us. But aren't you scared he's going to kill you one day? Or your son?'

'He loves us.'

'He's using you. Your relationship makes him look respectable. You normalise him, Dani. And when he attacks someone you vouch for him.' She brought her voice back down. 'And how does he repay you for this? He beats you up.'

'I told you, I fell.'

'We both know that's a lie. Why did he hit you this time?'

Dani's fingers curled around the armrest on the door and she pressed her mouth shut. Ferreira could hear her breathing, slow and shallow, knew she was trying to minimise the swell of her lungs against her ribcage, but it was getting harder to do because she was agitated now.

'You don't need to keep defending him.' They were at the edge of the estate. 'He's going to prison. He won't be able to touch you any more.'

'No.'

'We can help you,' Ferreira said, hearing the edge of desperation in her own voice. 'There are charities, refuges, we can get you and Robbie far away from him. Don't you want Robbie to have the very best chance he can in life?'

'Lee's his dad.'

'And do you want him to grow up like that, too?'

'We're getting married,' Dani said, fist striking her thigh.

'No, you're not. Lee's going to be locked up. I promise you that. We've got him this time. No excuses, no doubts, he can't bully this victim into backing down. He's being questioned right now and charged and he's going to go straight into prison and he will not get out.' Ferreira pulled off the road, into a lay-by, turned to face Dani. 'You don't need to be scared of him any more.'

'He said you'd do this. You're trying to get inside my head.'

'He doesn't love you,' Ferreira said. 'If he loved you he wouldn't want anyone else. He wouldn't be roaming the streets raping people, would he?'

'I want to go home.'

Ferreira took out her phone, found the photograph of Ryan Bhakta done up as Jasmine, smiling at the camera, all glitter and fake lashes and cheekbones.

'This is what Lee wants.' Dani recoiled from the image. 'Do you see this dress he's wearing? We've recovered Lee's semen from it.'

Dani slammed her hand into the dashboard. 'Shut up! Shut up, you lying fucking bitch!'

'It's the truth, Dani. Lee isn't the man you think he is.'

390

Tears were running freely down Dani's cheeks and she wiped them away angrily, her neck flushing, face burning.

'Think about how he's treated you. Is that love? Do you see that in films? Nobody ever made a romantic comedy about a man who breaks his girlfriend's ribs.'

Dani buried her face in her hands, huge racking sobs shaking her shoulders and among them moans of pain as the tissue around her ribs screamed. How could she live like this? Ferreira thought despairingly. How could anyone exist in this bubble of physical pain and emotional desolation and still be convinced it was love?

'You can move on, Dani. Find someone who deserves you. A good man, someone who'll be the kind of father Robbie needs.'

'I can't.'

She shook her head but the fight was draining out of her.

'Dani, listen to me. I want you to think of every time he raised a fist to you, every slap, every hair pull, every time he made you have sex when you didn't want to. Think about every insult and threat and lie he told you.' She was almost whispering, using the firm but quiet cajoling voice which cut through tears and anger. 'I want you to think about the times he came home reeking of another woman, with blood on his clothes, and how wrong you knew that was. Remember how that felt? Not being able to question him, not daring to say anything. Think about everything you've taken from him and how strong you are, deep down, because a weak woman couldn't have survived it. Think about all of that and tell me you don't deserve better.'

56

In front of the interview-room door Adams prowled like a fighter waiting for his ring walk. That's how Zigic imagined he saw this delay, as they waited for Lee Walton's solicitor to finish her discussion with him. He'd be playing the innocent, incredulous and annoyed.

Zigic leaned against the wall and tried to tune Adams out. This had been a long time coming for him and Zigic understood his impatience but it didn't stop him feeling irritated by the spiky energy and the smug expression Adams wore, like this had all been his own doing rather than tenacity on Ferreira's part.

She should be the one interviewing Walton, taking the collar and the kudos which would come with it.

'Fuck this.' Adams stopped dead. 'They've had enough time.'

He shoved open the door and Zigic followed, taking in the scene they'd interrupted, Walton in his solicitor's face, finger stabbing the air in front of her chest. She was a petite woman, so young she must be newly qualified, and she looked relieved at their entrance. Not a good sign for Walton but he should have thought of that before he started giving her attitude. He was too rattled to keep his true nature in check, Zigic realised. Knew they had him now and all the bravado of their previous encounter was gone.

'You want to watch that temper, Lee,' Adams said, already grinning. 'Ms Dyer is here to look out for your best interests, remember.'

The woman straightened up in her seat, smoothed a hand back over her hair and tucked a few stray strands into the bun knotted at the nape of her neck. She gave a near-imperceptible nod to Adams but Zigic saw her client had noticed it.

They took their seats at the table, Zigic directly opposite Walton, as they'd already decided. Adams would sit back, let him lead. Or at least that was the theory. Zigic doubted Adams would be able to contain himself any more than Lee Walton could, too many trial runs behind them for this to be anything except a headbutting contest.

Adams set up the tapes while Walton composed himself, hands on the table, one fist tucked into his palm. Next to him Ms Dyer turned a fresh page on a yellow legal pad and made a quick note across the top. She was playing the part now, Zigic thought, wouldn't give them any trouble.

He put his own paperwork down: a blue folder, well stuffed.

Walton eyed it warily, cleared his throat, ready to deny any knowledge of whatever came out of it.

'So, here we are again,' Adams said. 'Anything you want to get off your chest before we start, Lee?'

'No.'

'Nothing about Ryan Bhakta?'

'I don't know what you're talking about.'

Adams leaned back in his chair, giving Zigic his cue. He opened the file and took out the photograph of Ryan Bhakta they'd lifted from his driver's licence. It showed him handsome and unsmiling, his fine-boned face smoothed by the light. No scars on his skin, his nose perfect, the picture taken before the attack.

'Do you recognise this man?' Zigic asked.

Walton gave it a cursory glance. 'No.'

Another photograph came out; Jasmine, in her gold dress and long brown wig, face painted, smiling into the lens.

'How about now?'

He swallowed. 'No.'

'Lee never saw her face,' Adams said, a vicious thrill in his voice. 'He took her down from behind. Didn't you?'

'I don't know what you're talking about.' Walton turned to his solicitor. 'I'm being victimised here. I want that on record.'

'Noted,' Zigic said. He lined the photographs up and pushed them both across the table. 'Do you see the resemblance, Lee?'

'It's the same person, yeah. I get it. But I don't know him. Her.' Walton dragged his feet under his chair, the sound of his rigger boots scraping across the lino floor. 'Whatever you want to call it.'

'"It"? Adams asked. 'No, Lee, not "it". His name was Ryan, but when you raped him he was dressed as Jasmine. So you can say you raped him or you raped her but not "it".'

'I never touched this . . . person. I don't know them. I've never seen them before in my life.'

Zigic tapped the photo of Jasmine. 'Take another look, Lee. A good look this time. We want you to be absolutely sure of what you're saying.'

Walton leaned forward slightly, shoulders rounding as he made a show of studying the image. Adams reached across the table suddenly and lifted it into his face.

'There you go. Up close and personal. What do you think? Look familiar?'

'No.' Walton moved away, the back of his chair cracking as he threw his weight into it. 'Is that it? You came and dragged me away from my sick girlfriend to show me pictures of someone I never even met?'

'Dani's not sick,' Adams said. 'Damaged, traumatised, yes. But we all know the only thing that's wrong with her was done by you.'

Ms Dyer looked up from the notes she was making. 'That doesn't sound relevant to the case in hand, Detective Inspector.'

'Chief Inspector.' Adams gave her a slight smile. 'Lee's a bit of a star around here. He gets the big guns.'

Zigic didn't even roll his eyes.

'On the 17th of December 2014 you followed Ryan Bhakta into the cathedral precincts,' Adams said. 'You knocked him down and repeatedly smashed his face into the ground.'

Walton snorted.

'You then proceeded to rape him.'

'This is rubbish.' He threw his hands up but the display was less convincing than the one he made when they questioned him over Corinne Sawyer's murder. The reflexes of a liar rather than genuine incredulity. There was no confidence in his movements, none of that teasing sting he'd thrown at them before. 'I'm straight. And I'm not a rapist.'

There was a knock on the interview-room door and Adams called the person in with an irritated bark.

Walton's gaze locked on Ferreira instantly, jaw hardening.

'Hey.' Adams slapped the table. 'Eyes on me, Lee.'

Zigic got up, heard Adams announcing his departure as he closed the door, backing Ferreira into the hallway. She was buzzing, face lit, almost bouncing on her toes.

'What are you doing?' he asked. 'What is it?'

'I thought you should know. I've got Dani Shaw to turn. She's in with Murray now, she's giving a full statement about Lee, the previous attacks, how he forced her to furnish him with alibis and used violence to coerce her.' She smiled. 'We've fucking nailed him.'

Zigic clapped her on the shoulder. 'That is brilliant, Mel.'

'It was Ryan Bhakta that did it. She looked the other way on every woman he attacked but the idea that Lee might be gay just tipped her over the edge.' Ferreira shook her head. 'She's going on about wanting an HIV test now. I thought it might be useful. Knock his confidence, you know.'

Adams voice boomed through the door and they both looked over.

'Like that, is it?'

'He's getting off on this,' Zigic said.

'He's waited a long time to nail Walton. Maybe let him enjoy it?'

Zigic grabbed the door handle, paused. 'I'm going to make sure you get the credit for this. We wouldn't have him if it wasn't for you.'

'Just doing my job.' She shrugged. 'You better get in there before Adams goes off.'

Ferreira walked away and he returned to the interview room.

Walton was staring down at the tabletop, Adams standing, leaning against the wall with his arms folded, looking as cocky as it was possible to look without actually puffing his chest out.

'Detective Inspector Zigic enters the interview room,' he said, for the benefit of the tape. 'In your absence Lee has been reiterating his sexual orientation. Apparently he "loves women". Which is rather hard to believe given his long history of violence towards them.'

'Not relevant,' Ms Dyer said, sounding almost bored.

'Okay, let's talk about something very relevant.' Zigic sat down again, removed another photograph from the file; the gold dress laid out under forensic lights, areas marked up, the deposits labelled. 'This is the dress Ryan Bhakta was wearing the night he was raped.'

All the colour drained from Walton's face as he stared at the image, giving it a degree of attention none of the others had warranted, as if he could sear away the evidence with the force of his gaze.

'Ah, there we go, Lee.' Adams was almost laughing. 'This is new, isn't it? You've always been so careful about not leaving your DNA splashed about. But not this time.'

Zigic watched him, saw his eyes darting from side to side, heard how his breath hitched in his chest. Behind him Adams was tapping his foot against the floor but remaining mercifully quiet otherwise. Even he knew sometimes it took silence to break a person.

'It was consensual,' Walton said, voice scratchy and weak.

'Bullshit,' Adams snapped. 'You smashed his face in. You raped him.'

'I don't know what happened to him after I left, but the sex was consensual.'

'He tells it very differently,' Zigic said, already thinking of the interview they no longer had, thanks to Riggott insisting that Ferreira delete it.

'Nah, this is Lee's usual routine.' Adams slid into his seat, leaned across the table, finger pointing at Walton. 'But it won't work this time. We've got blood and semen and a horrific catalogue of injuries. You're not going to play "he said, she said" on this one.'

Walton kept his eyes on Zigic. Something had changed behind them, a hardening, a sense of calculations made, a lie committed to.

'She – Jasmine, did you say she called herself? – she was on the game. I was walking back to my car through the precincts, she said it'd be fifty quid for anal. I thought "why not?" She was way better-looking than most of the manky old pieces round this way.' He rubbed the back of his neck, dragged up an expression of faint embarrassment as if he really had been caught out. 'I did wonder why she was so cheap but I figured maybe she was new and didn't know the going rates. I didn't know she was a fella. She was clever, kept it well tucked up. And, in fairness, I'd had a couple of drinks.'

Adams let out a full-throated laugh. 'Is that your defence, Lee? Seriously?'

'It's what happened,' he said, attention still fixed on Zigic. 'She was fine when I left her. I don't know what she did afterwards. Must've been her next client, because I sure as hell didn't beat her up.'

'His medical records tell a very different story,' Zigic said. 'You raped him and you violently assaulted him.'

'No, I had sex with him. That's all.'

'Forget it,' Adams said. 'If Lee's happy to walk into court and spin this rubbish out as his defence that's his business.'

Walton did look happy to do that, sitting straight up in his chair, his confidence returned. Zigic guessed it was because he'd used a similar line in the past and walked free. Or maybe he thought he'd get to Ryan Bhakta between now and the trial, convince him to retract his statement just like he had all those women in before him. But Ryan was beyond his threats.

'Anything else you want to add?' Adams asked.

'I've told you everything I can.'

'Alright.' Adams stood up, buttoned his suit jacket and officially charged Walton with the rape and assault of Ryan Bhakta, 'Also known as Jasmine.'

Zigic watched Walton take it in, nod when Adams had finished. He was going to pursue this lie for as far as he needed to and Zigic only hoped a jury would be smart enough to see through it.

They called a uniform to take him down into custody and returned to a round of applause in CID. Murray was leading it, standing near the doorway beaming at Adams as he went over to her and gave her a fist bump, then a bear hug. She was almost in tears, half relieved, half shattered, and Zigic realised just how much pursuing Walton had taken out of her.

This was Murray's collar and Ferreira's and yet they'd been in here waiting for the result rather than taking him to task like they deserved to. He wished they'd had the chance to finish him off, knew it would have stung Walton far more having to make his false statement to them rather than two men.

Mel was sitting on the edge of a desk, watching it all play out, an unlit rollie between her fingers.

'You get a confession?' she asked.

'No, but his version of events isn't going to stand up in court.'

'He's going to be looking at more charges now Dani's turned on him,' she said. 'Colleen's already been on the phone to one of his victims, she's coming in to make a statement later.'

The door to Riggott's office opened. 'Get in here, you two.'

Ferreira flicked an eyebrow up at Zigic. 'Daddy's happy with you now.'

She slipped past him, heading out to smoke, and he followed Adams into Riggott's office, where the bottle was already on the table, three glasses lined up ready to toast their success.

57

It was dark when Ferreira got to Simon Trent's house. Half the front windows along the street were lit up with their curtains still open, the bare walls and big televisions exposed.

The blinds were closed at Simon's house though, only the thinnest hint of light bleeding between the wooden slats, but his car was at the kerb outside and upstairs a figure moved behind a frosted window.

She knocked on the front door, hearing music playing inside, and when Donna answered the smell of food cooking wafted out at her.

'What do you want?' Donna asked, the same hard demeanour as at their first encounter, even if she'd worked at softening her appearance.

'I need to speak to Simon.'

'He doesn't want to talk to you.'

'This is important, Donna,' she said. 'And I am going to talk to Simon. I can do it here or I can find him at work tomorrow. Which do you think he'd prefer?'

She considered it for a second. 'I'll fetch him.'

The door closed in her face and Ferreira swore softly. She shuffled where she stood and punched her hands into her pockets, skin stinging from the frost in the air and the wind tearing up the narrow street, rattling a gate left improperly tethered and the metal chimes on their neighbour's porch.

Simon opened the door, damp-haired and flushed, in a white dressing gown he clutched close over his hairless chest; Simone surfacing.

'I told you, I don't have anything else to say.'

'It's okay, Simon, that's not why I'm here.' She stepped towards him but he didn't move and she realised he wouldn't let her in either. 'I just wanted you to know we caught the man who attacked you. He's been charged, he's in custody right now, and we think we've got a strong case against him. He's going to be locked up for a very long time.'

She'd expected relief but he only pulled the door up tighter against the side of his body and tucked his chin into the collar of his robe.

'Simon, this is good news.' She tried to smile but he didn't respond. 'You don't have to be scared of him any more.'

He let out a gulping sob. 'Do you seriously think he's the only person I need to worry about?'

Simon slammed the door before she could answer and Ferreira raised her fist to knock again, but stopped. He was still suppressing Simone, still hiding to keep his wife happy, and nothing she could say would change any of that. He would survive and find an accommodation between the two parts of his life or he wouldn't.

A numbing dissatisfaction came over her as she climbed into her car. She hadn't expected him to break into song or even be particularly grateful, but she thought she'd see some glimmer of relief once he knew his attacker was off the street.

It had never been about the assault, she thought, as she drove away from his house. It was his relationship with Donna making him small and timid, the need to be a man for her, all of the time, without compromise.

At the junction with London Road she turned right, away from the city centre, only dimly aware of what she was doing. She followed a route she'd driven every night for six months, down the rat run of narrow streets, Victorian terraces and short strips of shops, more flats now then there had been when she and Liam moved in. Old factory units had been pulled down and the sites redeveloped, the area improved.

She didn't know if he still lived there. Could have easily checked but once it was over she packed up every memory and feeling and stowed them away and whenever he threatened to push himself forward again she'd find someone else to fill his place. For a few nights or a few hours or sometimes not even that long.

He was easier to replace than she expected and she wondered if that was a failing on his part or hers. If she'd told herself he was 'the one' because she wanted out of her parents' place, a new man to go along with the new route her career was taking as she progressed into CID.

There was a space outside the house and she stopped for a moment, idling in the middle of the road, looking up at the curtained window which had been their bedroom. She remembered waking up with her face buried in his chest, the tangle of sheets and the smell of him she wouldn't wash off before she went to work, wanting to be marked by his scent.

She remembered tracing the lines of his face while he slept, imagining how he'd age, how good they would always look together, and yet now, she realised, she couldn't even recall what colour his eyes were.

A van pulled up behind her and the driver leaned on the horn.

The empty parking space was beckoning her but what good would it do to sit here in the dark reminiscing about someone who had long since stopped moving her? Who had maybe never been the man she told herself she was in love with. Six months; it was meaningless.

She pulled away and the van tucked into the space she'd left behind her.

Was that him?

His boyfriend?

Liam had always liked them rough.

She could turn round and know for certain; instead she kept driving. It didn't matter and hadn't mattered for years. That stupid song had brought it back but it had been nothing but a phantom pain sharpened by alcohol and the febrile atmosphere of the cases she'd been working.

She was not Donna Trent or Nina Sawyer or Sam Hyde, even if she felt she understood what their men had put them through, forcing them to live half-lives, constantly negotiating and acquiescing because they loved them too much to leave them and too much to risk letting them be who they really were.

Could she have lived like that? Tiptoeing around Liam's true self, always fearing what he was doing? Becoming suspicious then paranoid then finally, years down the line, when it was too late, realising her life had been wasted on containing someone else's within safe parameters.

You had a lucky escape, she told herself.

And this time she believed it.

At the top of the road she stopped to buy tobacco. In the corner shop a fresh bundle of newspapers sat on the counter.

Zigic had made a statement earlier this afternoon. He'd named Brynn Moran and a small photo of him sat at the bottom-right corner of the front page, the rest of it dominated by the image of Corinne which Sam Hyde had given them. It showed a woman smiling, content, face turned up into the sunshine, looking forward to her new life.

News of Walton's arrest wouldn't hit until tomorrow and she wasn't sure how that would be received. It would expose Ryan Bhakta's secret life and she expected his family would find themselves hounded to give their side of events. It would go national, as the press used this new development to reinvigorate the flagging story. She tried not to consider how that was going to affect the investigation into her role in his suicide but the fear was still there.

She called Adams as she pulled into the car park under her building. There was music and a drunken buzz in the background when he answered. Half of CID had decamped to the pub at the end of the shift to celebrate bringing down Walton, patting each other on the backs for work they hadn't actually done.

'Where are you?' he asked.

'Home.'

'Come down for a few drinks. We're in the 'Spoons.'

It was a minute's walk away but she couldn't face the noise and the enforced bonhomie, or the route which would take her past the place where Simon Trent was attacked.

'I've got drink already.'

A door opened, a bell sounding and then it was quiet his end. 'Ah, you need company. Admit it.'

She smiled in response to the one she could hear in his voice. 'I was just going to ask if you've eaten yet.'

'I've had a couple of chips.'

'So, you're good then?'

'That depends . . .'

'On?'

'Are you going to cook?'

'I was thinking about it, yeah.'

He made a mulling sound. 'I am so curious to see whether you can actually cook.'

'You know where I am.'

Ferreira ended the call and headed across Cathedral Square towards the M&S in the shopping centre. There were a few stragglers just like her walking the aisles, appraising one another as they stocked up on ready meals and wine. Coming back, juggling the carrier bags between her hands, she looked at the cathedral lit up against the early-evening sky, thinking about Ryan Bhakta and wondering why he had gone down there, a question she would never get an answer to now.

Was it possible Lee Walton was telling the truth? Had Ryan been selling himself? She couldn't believe it but she knew it was a depressingly common occupation for trans women, although it was usually for economic reasons and Ryan didn't seem to be short of money. The notion of him doing it for pleasure didn't ring true either, but there was always the danger it might for a jury arriving with prejudices and preconceptions she didn't share.

Footsteps came up fast behind her. 'Hey, Mary Berry's hot granddaughter.'

'Mary Berry?' She handed Adams the carrier bags.

'You never know, she might have copped off with a swarthy Portuguese fisherman in her youth.'

'We do have the fittest ones.'

They walked through the cut alongside Barclays bank, onto Priestgate, Adams telling her about Murray doing shots off some poor young PC's back, that she was threatening them all with karaoke back at her place and you wouldn't believe the pipes on her.

In the lift he leaned in and kissed her, tasting of beer and whisky and cigarettes. 'You two owned Walton.'

'Yeah, I've had the managerial approval from Zigic, already.'

The doors slid apart.

'What and my good opinion doesn't matter?' he asked. 'I'm the senior officer.'

'You're not the boss of me.'

'I am while you're in CID.'

'We're not in CID now.' She opened the door and shoved him through it. 'My turn to be boss.'

TWO WEEKS LATER

Epilogue

For the first time in months Zigic was woken by the alarm on his phone and the sound drove him to his feet in a panic, heart thumping. Why wasn't Emily crying? What was wrong with her? Was she still breathing?

He stumbled across the room, eyes adjusting to the thin light creeping in around the blinds and through the slim gap under the door, went to the side of her cot and put a tentative hand on her chest, felt it rising and falling and finally his own calmed to a sensible rhythm.

The mattress called to him but he resisted it, put on his warmest running gear, found his trainers at the back of the cupboard under the stairs, the soles crusted with dried mud he scattered across the hall floor as he stretched; Anna was going to give him hell for that. Maybe breakfast in bed when he got back would buy him some good grace though. Maybe.

Earphones in, he headed into the dawn chill, following Station Road as it gave way to a dirt track which took him down to the river and onto Orton Mere, a route he hadn't run since last summer; his legs reminding him of the fact with each step. By the time he reached Ferry Meadows he'd found his rhythm, the twinges and aches all shaken off, a flush of endorphins kicking in hard enough that he decided to tackle the long loop around Gunwale Lake.

There were a few other runners out, all togged up the same as him. More lone women than he expected but barely three weeks after Corinne Sawyer's murder the immediate danger was forgotten, or maybe the lighter mornings had lulled them into a false sense of security.

Her body had been released to the family last week. Not Sam Hyde, though; legally she didn't count as family, not while Corinne was still married. So Nina Sawyer had taken possession of her and the manner of her send-off.

Sam had phoned him in tears the day Corinne was removed from the morgue, unable or unwilling to understand how the law dictated the process, that a marriage took precedence over their relationship even if it was being terminated. A few hours later Jessica rang, asking if they could petition a court to wrestle Corinne's remains from her mother, who had decided that she would be cremated as Colin, hair cut, suited and returned to the state he was born in. A final act of revenge which even Zigic thought was beneath her.

He advised Jessica to speak to a solicitor, knowing it would be pointless, but he had nothing else to give her.

Nina had waited a long time to take control of her husband and Zigic doubted whether anything could stop her erasing Corinne once and for all.

There was going to be a wake for Corinne, at least, organised by Evelyn Goddard and held at the Meadham. She'd sent an invitation, which surprised Zigic, and he knew he'd go although he didn't expect a warm welcome. They had found Corinne's killer and Ryan Bhakta's rapist but how much that counted for remained to be seen.

He wasn't sure if Ferreira would attend. The wake was on Thursday, the results of the investigation into her behaviour during the case were due today. He imagined her decision would depend on how this morning's meeting went.

A lot of her decisions were going to be hanging on that conversation.

Zigic ran on, cutting through the trees, liking the feeling of uneven ground under his feet and the concentration it demanded of him for a few minutes, how it excluded every other thought in his head until he came out the other side and hit the track back towards the village.

The kitchen was lit up when he got home and he let himself in the front door to find a dustpan and brush waiting for him on the welcome mat. He quickly cleaned up the clods of earth he'd left behind him, then went into the kitchen where Anna was feeding Emily, a cup of green tea on the table in front of her and the radio playing.

He kissed both of them, went for a bottle of water from the fridge.

'Good run?' Anna asked.

'Punishing.'

'Go and get showered, I'll make you breakfast.'

The boys made it down before he did and the kitchen was full of their excited voices when he returned. He stood at the door for a moment, watching them squabble over their cereals, Stefan losing because he refused to let go of his new Batman figure. Anna was going to have fun getting it off him before he went to school. Yesterday he'd put the caped crusader's head in his mouth and bitten down so hard Anna didn't dare to try and remove it in case she pulled out his front teeth. Instead she waited for his jaw to tire and got them to class ten minutes late with an apology about 'her silly husband' going to work with her keys.

Zigic ate breakfast with one eye on the time, wanting to be in early and have a talk with Ferreira before she went to meet Riggott. The DCS had given no indication of what was coming and Zigic suspected that meant bad news, even though everything about the incident suggested a slap on the wrists at worst. He wondered if Riggott was doing it to teach her a lesson, prolong the agony so it made an impact her light punishment wouldn't.

It was certainly his style, but as Zigic drove into the station, he couldn't quite convince himself it was a likely outcome.

411

Ferreira was in already, an open window in Hate Crimes giving her away, but he couldn't see her car. Upstairs he found her sitting on the sill, staring at the floor as she smoked, lost in her thoughts.

He sat down next her. 'This is a bit excessive, isn't it? You're not waiting to face a firing squad.'

She smiled, but it didn't reach her eyes. 'That is actually how it feels, though.'

'Riggott's winding you up. He doesn't want you to forget this in a hurry. That's all.'

'I don't think so.' She tossed her cigarette butt out of the window and immediately started rolling another. 'Something's going on here. Someone would have heard, you know what this station's like.'

'Riggott's office never leaks,' Zigic said.

She didn't seem in the mood for conversation so he just sat in silence with her, traffic noise at their backs, cars coming and going as the shifts changed over, wired voices and tired voices calling to each other as they passed on the station steps. Until Ferreira turned suddenly, recognising the expensive purr of Riggott's BMW.

She stood sharply, smoothed her hair and went to put on another coat of lipstick, using her phone as a mirror.

'You need to wait until he calls you,' Zigic said.

'I'm done waiting. I've been waiting for two fucking weeks. I need to know.'

Zigic got between her and the door, spread his hands. 'Just give him a minute to get into his office. You don't want to steam straight in there.'

'Yeah, I do.'

His desk phone rang and he rushed to answer it, telling her to wait, but he saw her leave the office as he lifted the receiver.

'Ziggy, you and Mel, in my office, please.'

He caught up with her in the stairwell.

'What are you doing?' she asked. 'I don't need a chaperone.'

'He wants to see both of us.'

412

She stopped, dropped back against the wall. 'I'm fucked, aren't I? If he wants you in there as well, it's going to be bad.'

'It's probably something else,' he said, but the statement didn't even sound convincing to him and she moved through CID towards Riggott's office like she was heading for inevitable doom. There were only a couple of other officers in there to witness their arrival but Zigic was sure they would be certain to update the rest of their shift when they turned up, sparing no detail, embellishing where they could.

The door was open and they went straight in.

Zigic started to speak but the expression on Riggott's face stopped him.

'Sit down, the pair of you.' He shrugged off his coat, hung it up on the hook behind the door and took his time getting back behind his desk.

Ferreira shot a questioning look at Zigic, eyes wide.

'Judging by the look on your faces and the fact that I trained the both of you, I reckon you'll have figured out this isn't good news.'

'Sir, this isn't fair,' Ferreira said, sliding forward on her chair, like she was preparing to launch herself at him. 'Whatever I did, it was with the best intentions. And it led to us catching a serial rapist with a long history of violence against women.'

'This isn't about you, Mel.'

'I'm not stupid, I know it's not really about what I did. It's all PR-related rubbish.'

Riggott took out his e-cigarette. 'No, it isn't about you *at all*. You're in the clear. I'm to give you a severe talking-to but we'll schedule that for a later date.'

Ferreira eased herself back, relieved, but not enough to unpeel her hands from the arm of the chair. Zigic felt it too, the tension coming off Riggott, permeating the whole room. As he watched him straightening out the things on his desk, getting them just so, Zigic realised only one thing could be motivating this reticence. Not a serious crime occurring overnight, not a need to scramble into action or the revelation of some cock-up they'd made.

There was only one explanation.

'We're being closed down, aren't we?' he said.

Riggott nodded. 'End of the month. Anti-Terrorism will be expanding into your office.'

'And where will we be going?' Zigic asked.

'You'll be returning to CID.'

Ferreira looked at Zigic as if she expected him to do something about the news, as if she believed he actually could.

'We don't need a dedicated office to run the department,' he said. 'Christ, we never needed all that space, anyway. Surely you can find us another room.'

'Sorry, son, it's out of my hands.'

'This is bullshit,' Ferreira spat. 'You know as well as we do that hate crimes are rising year on year, and they're getting more serious. This isn't just graffiti and pamphlets any more, we're talking violent assaults, rape, murder. People were just starting to see how important this is and we're being shut down.'

'This has been on the cards for a long time,' Riggott said, voice even and reasonable in a way it very rarely was, and Zigic knew he didn't like the decision either. The only time he acted like this was when he was working hard on suppressing his temper. 'People are scared of what's happening in Europe, they think it's only a matter of time before we get another major terror attack on British soil. This decision was taken very high up the ladder.'

Zigic knew it was going to hit him soon, the anger, but for now all he felt was numbness and a vague kind of satisfaction that he'd read the developing situation correctly. Mel wasn't giving up without a fight, though, and he half listened as she mounted a fruitless defence of Hate Crimes.

'Do you know how many people have died as a result of terrorism in this country during the last twelve months?' she asked. 'None.'

Riggott was letting her get it out of her system too, leaning forward like he was engaging with her, but Zigic knew that expression from watching Anna deal with Stefan in full flight. He was waiting for Ferreira to wear herself out.

'Zero people,' she said. 'We've dealt with six murders during the same period, dozens of serious assaults, rape, God knows how many instances of harassment and criminal damage. How are we bad value for money here?'

Riggott rubbed his temple, started to speak but she cut him off.

'This fucking government,' Ferreira said. 'You know what the real issue is? People who suffer from hate-based prejudice don't vote for *them*. This is fear-mongering and vote-buying.'

'Do you hear me saying ignore the crimes?' Riggott asked. 'You'll still investigate, you'll still be the first-choice officers to deal with these cases. You'll simply be doing it from within CID.'

'But it's symbolic,' she said. 'If you get rid of the dedicated unit people see that they don't matter to us any more.'

Riggott crashed back in his leather chair, took a long drag on his e-cig. 'You walked in here shitting yourself about losing your job, so think on, missy.'

'That's irrelevant.'

'You reckon I can stop this?' he said, voice rising in pitch and volume. 'You reckon I like being told how to run my officers by some Oxbridge tube down in London? No, I fucking don't, but that's how it is and none of us can do a damn thing about it. So, suck it up, be happy you'll not be off working for Serco looking up drug mules' fannies with a wee flashlight, and get back to the fucking fray.'

Zigic stood, tapped Ferreira on the shoulder.

'Come on, Mel.'

The CID floor was busier than when they went in and all eyes turned as they walked out. Maybe Riggott's office did leak. Or maybe they weren't used to hearing two voices shouting behind that particular door.

Upstairs Ferreira yanked off her jacket and threw it onto her desk, sending pens and an empty coffee cup flying, along with a string of curses in English and Portuguese, then kicked the back of her chair so hard it toppled the computer monitor.

'Are you done?' Zigic asked.

'How can you be so fucking calm about this?' she demanded. 'We're being screwed over here. Everyone we should be helping is being screwed over.'

'And do you think throwing a tantrum is going to change that?'

'It's making me feel better.' She pushed her hands back through her hair. 'God, you can be so . . . Serbian sometimes.'

He smiled. 'Racist.'

'I can be as racist as I like,' she said, dropping into her chair. 'There's no Hate Crimes Unit to stop me.'

'There is for another month.' Zigic sat down on the edge of her desk, hands tucked between his thighs. 'And no matter what happens when we move into CID, we'll keep pushing for this stuff to be taken seriously. We're still a team, Mel. Nothing changes that.'

Acknowledgements

Huge, gushing thanks first, and always, to my fabulous editor Alison Hennessey, who has been integral in shaping the finished book you hold in your hands now. Without her wisdom and guidance it would be much the lesser story and I count myself incredibly lucky to have her on my side.

It's been my pleasure and privilege to work with an energetic, warm and endlessly enthusiastic team at Harvill Secker and Vintage. Heartfelt thanks to Maria, Vicki, Bethan, Anna and Áine, along with everyone else behind the scenes who helped turn those sheets of loose paper into a finished book. And then took such wonderful care bringing it onto the shelves and out to readers.

The crime scene is notorious for its supportive nature – as well as its hard drinking, filthy humour and general all round magnificence – and like most authors, I find myself drawing on the hive mind for practical advice and moral support throughout the writing year. In a solitary profession knowing friends are just a click away makes all the difference. I couldn't begin to name everyone but you know who you are and big thanks to you all.

Special honours to Nick Quantrill, Jay Stringer and Luca Veste, who have kept me sane, laughing and fully appraised of developments in lower league football. They say it's rare to make proper, lasting friendships as adults but only because they haven't met you boys.

Thanks as well to all those in the blogging and reviewing community who have generously given their time and expertise to read early copies of this and all the previous books. Your support is so

417

important to writers and, as a reader, you've led me to many brilliant authors too. There are just too many to name but please know I am deeply grateful to you for helping Zigic and Ferreira find their audience.

The highlight of the bookish year has to be festival season and I owe massive thanks to the teams at Bloody Scotland, Book Week Scotland, Edinburgh Book Festival, ChipLitFest, Essex Book Festival and Noirwich for allowing me on their stages and giving me the very best excuse to slip away from work. If you've been thinking about attending any of these marvellous events, think no longer – book those tickets and go enjoy!

Finally, to my family, thank you for the shopping trips and lazy lunches and the occasional bolts of crazy inspiration. Love you guys.